Virginia Woolf

THE VOYAGE OUT

Introduction by Michael Cunningham

Notes by Deborah Lutz

GRADUATE CENTER OF
THE CITY UNIVERSITY OF NEW YORK

THE MODERN LIBRARY

NEW YORK

2001 Modern Library Paperback Edition

Biographical note copyright © 2000 by Random House, Inc.
Introduction copyright © 2000 by Michael Cunningham
Notes and Reading Group Guide copyright © 2001 by Random House, Inc.

Grateful acknowledgment is made to Harcourt, Inc. for permission to reprint excerpts from "Mr. Bennett and Mrs. Brown" from *The Captain's Death Bed and Other Essays* by Virginia Woolf. Copyright © 1950 and copyright renewed 1978 by Harcourt, Inc. Excerpts from "Am I a Snob?" from *Moments of Being* by Virginia Woolf. Copyright © 1976 by Quentin Bell and Angelica Garnett. Excerpts from "Modern Fiction" in *The Common Reader* by Virginia Woolf. Copyright © 1925 by Harcourt, Inc. and renewed 1953 by Leonard Woolf. Reprinted by permission of Harcourt, Inc.

LIBRARY OF CONGRESS CATALOGING-IN-PUBLICATION DATA
Woolf, Virginia, 1882–1941.
The voyage out/Virginia Woolf; introduction by
Michael Cunningham; notes by Deborah Lutz.
p.   cm.
ISBN 0-375-75727-9
1. British—South America—Fiction.   2. Man-woman relationships—Fiction.
3. Ocean travel—Fiction.   4. Young women—Fiction.   I. Title.
PR6045.O72   V68   2001
823'.912—dc21   00-52724

Modern Library website address: www.modernlibrary.com

Printed in the United States of America

2 4 6 8 9 7 5 3 1

VIRGINIA WOOLF

Virginia Woolf (née Stephen)—the novelist, critic, and essayist whose feminist and modernist concerns changed the course of twentieth-century literature—was born in London on January 25, 1882. Her father, Sir Leslie Stephen, was an eminent Victorian historian and biographer who oversaw his daughter's education. "To read what one liked because one liked it, never to pretend to admire what one did not—that was his only lesson in the art of reading," she recalled. "To write in the fewest possible words, as clearly as possible, exactly what one meant—that was his only lesson in the art of writing. All the rest must be learnt for oneself." She experienced a traumatic adolescence following the deaths of her mother and stepsister, and suffered mental breakdowns the rest of her life. After Sir Leslie's death in 1904 she settled in the Bloomsbury district of London with her siblings—Vanessa, Thoby, and Adrian—and soon became a central figure in the Bloomsbury group, an intellectual circle that included writers and artists such as Lytton Strachey, Clive Bell, and John Maynard Keynes. In 1912 she married Leonard Woolf, another member of the group, and in 1917 the couple founded the Hogarth Press, which published the early works of Katherine Mansfield, T. S. Eliot, E. M. Forster, and Sigmund Freud. Over the next quarter century Woolf's sensibilities all but dominated the world of English letters. Fearing another onset of mental illness, Virginia Woolf drowned herself in the River Ouse, near her country home in Sussex, on March 28, 1941. "With the death of Virginia Woolf, a whole pattern of culture is broken," reflected T. S. Eliot at the time. "She was the centre, not merely of an esoteric group, but of the literary life of London. Her position was due to a concurrence of qualities and circumstances which never happened before, and which I do not think will ever happen again."

Woolf devoted much of her creative energy to forging new forms in fiction. She made a remarkable debut as a novelist with *The Voyage Out* (1915). Her second novel, *Night and Day* (1919), was a conventional love story that disappointed critics, but *Jacob's Room* (1922), an impressionistic elegy to the lost heroes of World War I, marked a turning point in her career. ("A new type of fiction has swum into view," noted E. M. Forster.) Woolf scored another triumph with *Mrs. Dalloway* (1925), a stream-of-consciousness novel often compared with James Joyce's *Ulysses*, and secured her reputation as a major writer with *To the Lighthouse* (1927), which Eudora Welty deemed "a vision of reality ... an instantaneous burst of coherence over chaos and the dark." Her subsequent fiction includes *Orlando* (1928), the historical fantasy written for Vita Sackville-West; *The Waves* (1931), an extended prose poem generally considered to be her masterpiece; *The Years* (1937), a brilliant fantasia on the Proustian theme of Time; and *Between the Acts* (1941), a powerful evocation of English life in the months leading up to World War II. "The novel, of course, was never to be the same after the day she started work on it," reflected Welty. " 'Breaking the mold' she called the task she set herself. As novel succeeded novel she proceeded to break, in turn, each mold of her own."

Though best remembered for her novels, Woolf also wrote nearly fifty short stories, many of which served as a testing ground for her longer fiction. The new kind of narrative forms she created in experimental sketches such as "Kew Gardens" (1919) and "The Mark on the Wall" (1919) paved the way for *Jacob's Room* and other innovative novels. Woolf's first collection of short fiction, *Monday or Tuesday*, was published by the Hogarth Press in 1921. Her other compilations include *A Haunted House and Other Short Stories* (1944) and *Mrs. Dalloway's Party* (1975). "[Her stories] seem as perfect, and as functional for all their beauty, as spider webs," observed Welty. "The extreme beauty of her writing is due greatly to one fact, that the imprisonment of life in the word was as much a matter of the senses with Virginia Woolf as it was a concern of the intellect."

A discerning and influential literary critic as well as a novelist, Woolf began contributing book reviews to the *Times Literary Supplement* in 1905. "Whether you are writing a review or a love letter, the great thing is to be confronted with a very vivid idea of your subject," she once remarked. Woolf published but three volumes of criticism during her lifetime: *Mr. Bennett and Mrs. Brown* (1924), *The Common Reader* (1925), and *The Second Common Reader* (1932). Following his wife's death Leonard Woolf brought out several compilations of her essays and reviews, including *The Death of the Moth and Other Essays* (1942), *The Moment and Other Essays* (1947), *The Captain's Death Bed and Other Essays* (1950), *Granite and Rainbow* (1958), and *Collected Essays* (four volumes, 1967). In assessing Woolf's critical acumen, Welty wrote: "That beautiful mind! That was the thing. Lucid, passionate, independent, acute, proudly and incessantly nourished, eccentric for honorable reasons, sensitive for every reason, it has marked us forever."

The Woolf canon comprises several other notable works of nonfiction. Perhaps the most famous are her two feminist polemics, *A Room of One's Own* (1930) and *Three Guineas* (1938). In addition she wrote two biographies: *Flush* (1933), a whimsical account of the life of Elizabeth Barrett Browning's spaniel, and *Roger Fry* (1940), a tribute to the painter, art critic, and curator who became a kind of father figure to the Bloomsbury group. *A Writer's Diary*, a volume culled by Leonard Woolf from his wife's personal papers, was published posthumously in 1953. "I have never read any book that conveyed more truthfully what a writer's life is like," said W. H. Auden. The memoir *Moments of Being* (1976) contains her only autobiogaphical writing. Woolf's voluminous correspondence was compiled in *The Letters of Virginia Woolf* (six volumes, 1975–1980), and her extensive journals were amassed in *The Diary of Virginia Woolf* (four volumes, 1977–1982).

"Virginia Woolf was a great artist, one of the glories of our time, and she never published a line that was not worth reading," judged Katherine Anne Porter. "The least of her novels would have made the reputation of a lesser writer, the least of her critical writings compare more than favorably with the best criticism of the past half-century.... She lived in the naturalness of her vocation. The world of the arts was her native territory; she ranged freely under her own sky, speaking her mother tongue fearlessly. She was at home in that place as much as anyone ever was." Forster concurred: "Virginia Woolf got through an immense amount of work, she gave acute pleasure in new ways, and pushed the light of the English language a little further against darkness."

CONTENTS

INTRODUCTION

Michael Cunningham

The Voyage Out, Virginia Woolf's first novel, is, like every novel, a chronicle of its author's attempts to learn how to write a novel. That may be more apparent in a first novel than it is in a fifth; but all novels, if they're good, are by definition experiments, even if their structures and themes are traditional, just as novelists, if they're good, spend their lives learning how to write novels, and die still trying.

Woolf spent nine years writing *The Voyage Out*, beginning when she was twenty-four years old. No subsequent book would take her half as long or go through so many drafts. After *The Voyage Out* she produced the more conventional *Night and Day*, which she wrote, in part, to demonstrate to herself and others that she could in fact write a conventional novel. Then she embarked upon a twenty-five-year roil of troubled fertility during which she produced *Jacob's Room, Mrs. Dalloway, To the Lighthouse, Orlando, The Waves,* and *Between the Acts,* among other books. To a greater extent than any novelist except Joyce, she invented the Modernist novel, a drastic departure from the traditional form, with its heroics and high emotions; its morality; its unwavering point of view; and its unambiguous beginning, middle, and end. The novel, in Woolf's hands, became prismatic, ambiguous, at least slightly chaotic, amoral, poetic, and concerned itself primarily with outwardly unremarkable people. It strove less to tell an uplifting tale and more to render life as lived, in its endless overlaps of the quotidian and the profound. Since Woolf's time, novels in the traditional mode have continued to be written by the boxcar load, but the novel as an art form has never been the same.

Published in 1915, when Woolf had just turned thirty-three, *The Voyage Out* contains most of the elements of conventional narrative. It involves a love affair, an engagement, and a death; and it progresses, in orderly fashion, from its beginning through its middle to its end. But because it is a relatively familiar romance written by a great writer it defies convention to at least the same degree that it honors convention. Woolf believed (these are my words, not hers) that the meticulously structured, often inspirational novels of her time had about as much to do with the world and those who live in it as did a boat full of colonials and missionaries venturing into a jungle determined to subdue it. It was one of Woolf's contributions to insist, in her fiction, that the world is too huge and mysterious, too impenetrably itself, for fiction as fiction is so often written; that any writer's attempt to clear the field of its vines and creepers, to frighten off the hostile animals so as to set up a table for tea and begin to demonstrate a proper sense of right and wrong, is unlikely to come to a good or useful end. In her fiction Woolf bore witness to the world, saw and recorded some of its patterns, but did not attempt to enforce upon it any particular order or demand that it produce an order of its own. For this innovation she has often been accused of writing about nothing at all.

The Voyage Out employs the oldest and most venerable of narrative devices, the journey. It specifically concerns the fate of Rachel Vinrace, whose vivacious and compelling mother died when she was eleven, leaving her to be raised by her chilly father and two spinster aunts. Rachel is, at twenty-four, almost pathologically unformed. She knows nothing whatever about sex, has had only a smattering of education, and is hard put to hold up her end in an ordinary conversation. She is, however, a relatively accomplished pianist, and playing the piano is her one true passion. In her way she is the idealized Artist with a capital A—incompetent at and largely indifferent to everything except her art.

The novel begins with an ocean voyage on board a modest passenger steamer, the *Euphrosyne* (so named by Woolf as a private joke—it was the title of a collection of solemn poetry she considered ridiculous, published by her husband and some of her friends). The ship is sailing from England to South America, and then sailing up the Amazon. On board, Rachel is befriended—"adopted" might be more accurate—by her aunt, Helen Ambrose, a forceful, unsentimental woman in her early forties who is at least as central to the novel as Rachel. They disembark at Santa Marina, a village on the South American coast, take up residence in a haphazard villa with a neglected garden, and become involved with the denizens of the village's only hotel, among them two young men: St. John Hirst, who bears a strong resemblance to Lytton Strachey and who falls in love with Helen, and Terence Hewet, an aspiring novelist, who argues many of Woolf's own positions about writing and who falls in love with Rachel.

Ultimately, certain members of the group undertake a second voyage, up a river and into the jungle, and that is what changes everything.

The Voyage Out tells the tale of its doomed lovers amid a chorus of other stories, other points of view. Rachel Vinrace and Terence Hewet are, variously, the central, galvanizing figures and peripheral characters who play, at best, a supporting role in the stories of Helen Ambrose, St. John Hirst, Susan Warrington, Miss Allan, and others. An essential element of Woolf's genius, visible from the beginning of her career, is her insistence on a fictive world too large and complex to focus its exclusive attention on any individual life. Try to enter the consciousness of a person, any person, and you are led immediately to dozens of other people, each of whom is integral, each in a different way. Woolf understood that every character about whom she wrote, even the most marginal, was visiting her novel from a novel of his or her own, and that that other, unwritten novel had as its main concerns the passions and fate of this character—this dowager or child or septuagenarian, this young woman who appears in the novel at hand only long enough to walk through a park. Although *The Voyage Out* is more orderly than most of the books Woolf went on to write, it is nevertheless bent out of traditional shape by these other, phantom novels (the one about the Ambrose family, the ones about St. John Hirst and Mrs. Thornbury and Evelyn Murgatroyd, not to mention Richard and Clarissa Dalloway, who appear briefly in *The Voyage Out* and will, of course, figure later in a book very much their own). They intrude on the story of Rachel and Terence out of necessity, not only because they are part of it but because they and Rachel and Terence are all part of a much larger story, a story too vast to tell.

Although the facts of Woolf's life and death have tended to overshadow the appreciation of her work—she is too often thought of as a personality first and a writer second—her work and her life do in fact converge, particularly in this, her first novel. She insisted on writing only about people and states of feeling she knew well. She despised the Victorian penchant for elaborate invention, and so based most of her characters and situations, at least to some extent, on the people she knew and the things that had happened to her.

She was born Virginia Stephen in 1882, the third of four children. Her older sister, Vanessa, a complex and formidable person, a gifted painter, was arguably one of the three or four great loves of Virginia's life and was certainly one of the models for Helen Ambrose. Virginia would always be drawn to charming, capable women—she especially admired social ease, which she felt she lacked entirely—and Helen Ambrose is the first in a long line of Woolf women, including Clarissa Dalloway in *Mrs. Dalloway*, Mrs. Ramsay in *To the Lighthouse*, Susan in *The Waves*, and Maggie Pargiter in *The Years*, whom she would base on various aspects of various living women. She would use Vanessa and their mother, Julia; she would draw on her friendships with London society women like Kitty Maxse and Violet Dickinson, and, later, on her more volatile relationships with Vita Sackville-West and Ethel Smyth.

Like Helen Ambrose and Rachel Vinrace, like most of the characters Woolf would create throughout her career, the Stephen children grew up among the lower ranks of the upper classes. That meant, in late Victorian England, that the Stephens inhabited a large house, had servants, and took holidays, but kept a close eye on accounts. They sent their sons to college but not their daughters; and while college for women was unusual at the time, it was not unknown. The decision to send only the boys to college was, finally, an economic one, made in spite of the fact that of the Stephen children Virginia was clearly the most gifted and the most intellectually curious. By way of compensation Virginia's father, Leslie, insisted that he could give her a perfectly adequate education at home.

Leslie Stephen was nothing so simple as a villain, but by all known accounts the word "difficult" would be a generous description of him as husband and father. A prominent historian and biographer (he would probably be both proud and horrified to learn that, almost a century after his death, he is primarily known as Virginia's father), he believed himself to be a genius, worried that he was not a genius, and laid claim to all the privileges to which genius at its most romantic may consider itself entitled. He suffered noisy, melodramatic agonies (over his work, over household finances); he threw tantrums; he required extravagant amounts of attention, sympathy, and reassurance and, receiving them, often demanded more. His determination not to suffer fools gladly, or at all, could terminate a dinner party; and his idea of an ideal evening's entertainment often involved all present sitting silent as he read aloud.

At the same time he did in fact attend carefully to young Virginia's education, gave her excellent books to read, took genuine pleasure in her precocity. She recognized his failings but loved him, and she and Vanessa argued the subject of his selfishness versus his goodness all their lives.

He was first married to one of Thackeray's daughters, with whom he had a "backward" (possibly autistic) daughter named Laura, and after his first wife died he married Julia Duckworth, a widow with three children of her own, one of them a son named

Gerald, who would sexually molest Virginia when she was six and would, over two decades later, publish *The Voyage Out* under the imprimatur of his publishing company, Duckworth & Co.

Julia, Virginia's mother, was a woman of great beauty and magnetism, the willing handmaiden to Leslie's tyrannical fragility, and while Julia and Leslie Stephen are most directly portrayed as Mr. and Mrs. Ramsay in *To the Lighthouse,* traces of one or both of them appear throughout Woolf's fiction. Helen Ambrose's husband, Ridley, is a version of Leslie, similarly self-absorbed but far less demanding; and some aspects of Virginia's complicated feelings about Julia—rage and romance prominent among them—may have informed the invention of Clarissa Dalloway, that shimmering vision of aloof sophistication who appears, enchants, and vanishes.

When Virginia was thirteen Julia died of rheumatic fever and, more ambiguously, of the incessant strain that accrued from having been married to Leslie. She was just forty-nine. The day after Julia's death, when Virginia was taken in to see the body, she believed she saw a man sitting on the edge of her deceased mother's bed. Although she recorded no details about the hallucination (she was half convinced she'd simply pretended to hallucinate, to draw attention to herself) one thinks of Rachel's dream in *The Voyage Out,* in which she finds herself "... alone with a little deformed man who squatted on the floor gibbering, with long nails. His face was pitted and like the face of an animal."

After her mother's death Virginia suffered the first of the breakdowns that would plague her the rest of her life. She became so anxious that for months she was not allowed to read or study, and was kept to the simplest possible regimen of rest, regular meals, and short walks. She often became hysterical and paranoid; as she would write years later in the notes for her essay "A Sketch of the Past," "I was terrified of people—used to turn red if spoken to."[1]

After Julia Stephen died her place was taken by Stella, Julia's daughter from her previous marriage. Stella consoled Leslie in his transports of grief and guilt. She managed the Stephen household.

---

1. Monk's House Papers, A5C, University of Sussex.

When she married, Leslie proposed that she and her new husband live in the Stephen house; the young couple managed to mollify him by moving into a house several doors down. Within two years of Julia's death, Stella died herself.

Leslie then turned to eighteen-year-old Vanessa to be his new helpmate, and while Vanessa ran the household as best she could she, unlike Julia or Stella, refused to subjugate herself. She treated Leslie as her sworn enemy. She offered him only rudimentary sympathy, sat in grim silence as he raged and wept over her monthly presentations of the household finances. Virginia's loyalties were divided, though in the end she always, inevitably, sided with Vanessa. In creating Helen and Ridley Ambrose, Virginia to some extent reimagined her parents' marriage as if Leslie had been married to a woman more like Vanessa—a woman who refused to be crushed. Even in writing the Ambroses, though, she could only liberate Helen by rendering Ridley less and less physically present, until by the middle of the book he is virtually invisible. He essentially goes to his room to work, and never comes out again.

When Leslie Stephen died of bowel cancer in 1904, after a long and dreadful struggle exacerbated by less-than-competent doctors, the Stephen children were set free. Although Virginia had loved Leslie to the best of her ability, she later wrote in her diary that, had he lived much longer, "His life would have entirely ended mine."[2] Virginia and Vanessa, along with their brothers, Thoby and Adrian, left their father's gloomy house at Hyde Park Gate, took their modest inheritance, and rented an inexpensive house in the then-disreputable neighborhood of Bloomsbury. Thoby, the older of the Stephen sons, began bringing around some of the people he'd met at Cambridge: Clive Bell, Saxon Sydney-Turner, Desmond MacCarthy, Lytton Strachey, and Leonard Woolf. The Bloomsbury group was launched.

Not long after the move to Bloomsbury, however, the four Stephen children took a trip to Greece and Turkey, where first Vanessa and then Thoby fell ill. Upon returning to England

2. *Diary of Virginia Woolf, Vol. III* (New York: Harcourt Brace Jovanovich, 1977), entry for November 1928, p. 208.

Vanessa recovered but Thoby, whom Virginia adored, died, at least in part because his doctor spent ten days treating him for malaria before realizing that he in fact had typhoid fever.

It was about that time that Virginia began writing *The Voyage Out* (which she called, in its early stages, *Melymbrosia*), a novel in which a young woman whose mother has died goes on a journey to a strange place, begins her worldly education, worries about the perils of marriage but becomes engaged, catches a mysterious fever, is treated by a useless doctor, and dies before she can marry. During the years Woolf spent writing the book she rejected several proposals of marriage, including one from Lytton Strachey. She finally married Leonard, and suffered another breakdown—a terrible one—soon after her wedding. At Leonard's urging the new couple set up house in Richmond, then a quiet suburb of London, where he hoped Virginia would be better able to remain calm and lucid.

Writing *The Voyage Out* was a struggle for her—she not only doubted her gifts but felt she was already rather old to be working on a first novel—and from its initial conception to its finished state the book went through eight or nine drafts. Early in the effort she wrote to her friend Madge Vaughan:

My only defense is that I write of things as I see them; & I am quite conscious all the time that it is a very narrow, & rather bloodless point of view. I think—if I were Mr. Gosse writing to Mrs. Green!—I could explain a little why this is so from external reasons, such as education, way of life, &c. And so perhaps I may get something better as I grow older. George Eliot was near 40 I think, when she wrote her first novel, the Scenes [of Clerical Life].

But my present feeling is that this vague & dream like world, without love, or heart, or passion, or sex, is the world I really care about, & find interesting. For, though they are dreams to you, & I can't express them at all adequately, these things are perfectly real to me.

But please don't think for a moment that I am satisfied, or think that my view takes in any whole. Only it seems to me, better to write of the things I do feel, than to dabble in things I frankly don't understand in the least. That is the kind of blunder—in literature—which seems to me ghastly & unpardonable: people, I mean, who wallow in emotions without understanding them.[3]

On publication, *The Voyage Out* was well received. A critic at the *Observer* wrote that it was "done with something startlingly like genius . . . among ordinary novels it is a wild swan among good grey geese."[4] E. M. Forster wrote, "Here at last is a book which attains unity as surely as *Wuthering Heights*, though by a different path, a book which, while written by a woman and presumably from a woman's point of view, soars straight out of local questionings into the intellectual day."[5] Still, Woolf was never fully satisfied with *The Voyage Out*. For the American edition, published by George H. Duran in 1920, she not only corrected typographical errors in the Duckworth edition but excised a number of sections, most of which she subsequently reinstated when *The Voyage Out* was included in the 1929 Uniform Edition of her novels, published by the Hogarth Press. That version is the one presented here.

Shortly after *The Voyage Out* first appeared in 1915, she and Leonard bought the printing press that would eventually lead to the forming of the Hogarth Press. Following the appearance of her second novel, *Night and Day*, which was also published by Duckworth & Co., Woolf would for the rest of her writing life publish herself, and it is not coincidence that she then began producing her truly experimental work, the stories "The Mark on the Wall" and "Kew Gardens," among others, and the novel *Jacob's Room*. That is when she discovered, "all in a flash, as if flying," a free-form, organic approach to fiction that, she wrote, " . . . showed me how I could embody all my deposit of experience in a shape that fitted it. . . ."[6] She had become, she said, "the only woman in England free to write what I like."[7]

3. Monk's House Papers, VW to Madge Vaughan, June 1906.
4. Unsigned review, *Observer,* April 4, 1915.
5. E. M. Forster, *Daily News and Leader,* April 8, 1915.
6. *The Letters of Virginia Woolf, Vol. IV* (New York: Harcourt Brace Jovanovich, 1979), VW to Ethel Smyth, October 16, 1930.
7. *Diary, Vol. III,* entry for September 22, 1925.

If she felt her freedom restricted when she wrote *The Voyage Out*, she managed nevertheless to abundantly demonstrate early versions of the gifts she took to transcendent extremes in her later work. Woolf was then and remains today unparalleled in her ability to convey the sensations and complexities of the experience known as being alive. Any number of writers manage the big moments beautifully; few do as much with what it feels like to live through an ordinary hour on a usual day. As she said when speaking to a reading group, "In the course of your daily life this week . . . you have overheard scraps of talk that filled you with amazement. You have gone to bed at night bewildered by the complexity of your feelings. In one day thousands of ideas have coursed through your brains; thousands of emotions have met, collided, and disappeared in astonishing disorder."[8] She was revolutionary in her shunning of the outwardly dramatic (most famously when she dispatched Mrs. Ramsay in a single sentence in *To the Lighthouse*), and her insistence on the inwardly dramatic—her implied conviction that what's important in a life, what remains at its end, is less likely to be its supposed climaxes than its unexpected moments of awareness, often arising out of unremarkable experience, so deeply personal they can rarely be explained.

If this belief seems only slightly unusual today it was almost scandalous early in the century, when serious writers were expected to write about large and "serious" subjects. The generation of writers that immediately preceded Woolf—prominent Edwardians like Arnold Bennett, John Galsworthy, and H. G. Wells—tended to scorn the younger Georgians—like Woolf, Joyce, and T. S. Eliot—for what they considered inadequate attention to the histories and circumstances of their characters and for a more general lack of mythic scope and scale; a lack of "greatness," if you will. Woolf countered by insisting that everything one needed to know about human life was contained in every human action. It was contained, for instance, in two old women gossiping over their tea or in a sad young man wandering through London, more or less the

---

8. Virginia Woolf, "Mr. Bennett and Mrs. Brown," in *The Captain's Death Bed and Other Essays* (New York: Harcourt Brace & Co., 1950), p. 118.

way the blueprint for an entire organism is contained in each of its cells. The trick was to see those two women or that young man completely, and then to see the invisible lines that connected them to other people, and then others, until you had at least in theory the whole of existence laid out before you.

So Woolf was drawn, throughout her career, to unexceptional lives (barring *Orlando,* which she wrote for the exceptional Vita Sackville-West), the better to see the enormity contained in them without the distractions of battle, quest, or heroic romance. Her artists are never successful; her scholars and politicians have never gone as far as they'd hoped. She said in her 1924 lecture "Mr. Bennett and Mrs. Brown," about the experience of sharing a railway carriage with an elderly stranger:

The elderly lady ... whom I will call Mrs. Brown ... was one of those clean, threadbare old ladies whose extreme tidiness—everything buttoned, fastened, tied together, mended and brushed up—suggests more extreme poverty than rags and dirt. There was something pinched about her—a look of suffering, of apprehension, and, in addition, she was extremely small. Her feet, in their clean little boots, scarcely touched the floor. I felt that she had nobody to support her; that she had to make up her mind for herself; that, having been deserted, or left a widow, years ago, she had led an anxious, harried life, bringing up an only son, perhaps, who, as likely as not, was by this time beginning to go to the bad....

Myriads of irrelevant and incongruous ideas crowd into one's head on such occasions; one sees the person, one sees Mrs. Brown, in the centre of all sorts of different scenes. I thought of her in a seaside house, among queer ornaments; sea-urchins, models of ships in glass cases. Her husband's medals were on the mantelpiece. She popped in and out of the room, perching on the edges of chairs, picking meals out of saucers, indulging in long, silent stares.... There she sits in the corner of the carriage—that carriage which is travelling, not from Richmond to Waterloo, but from one age of English literature to the next, for Mrs. Brown is eternal, Mrs. Brown is human nature, Mrs. Brown changes only on the surface, it is the novelists who get in and out—there she sits and not one of the Edwardian writers has so much as looked at her. They have looked very powerfully, searchingly, and sympathetically out of the window; at factories, at Utopias, even at the decoration and upholstery of the carriage; but never at her, never at life, never at human nature. . . .

I asked (the Edwardians)—they are my elders and betters—How shall I begin to describe this woman's character? And they said: "Begin by saying that her father kept a shop in Harrogate. Ascertain the rent. Ascertain the wages of shop assistants in the year 1878. Discover what her mother died of. Describe cancer. Describe calico. Describe—" But I cried: "Stop! Stop!" And I regret to say that I threw that ugly, that clumsy, that incongruous tool out of the window, for I knew that if I began describing the cancer and the calico, my Mrs. Brown, that vision to which I cling though I know no way of imparting it to you, would have been dulled and tarnished and vanished forever.[9]

It is pure Woolf, then—it could be Woolf herself speaking—when Rachel says of her elderly aunts, who are still living their uneventful lives in England as she sails to South America:

"And there's a sort of beauty in it—there they are at Richmond at this very moment building things up. They're all wrong, perhaps, but there's a sort of beauty in it. . . . It's so unconscious, so modest. And yet they feel things. They do mind if people die. Old spinsters are always doing things. I don't quite know what they do. Only that was what I felt when I lived with them. It was very real."

Rachel appreciates the commonplace. She is intelligent (but not spectacularly so), perceptive (but not incisive). She is so naïve as to be practically blank. In part because she is so guileless, Rachel is open to the forces of revelation that lay dormant almost everywhere. As she wanders along a river the day after a party—the first truly exciting party to which she's ever been—she passes flowering trees "which Helen had said were worth the voyage out merely to see. April had burst their buds, and they bore large blossoms among their glossy leaves with petals of a thick wax-like substance

9. "Mr. Bennett and Mrs. Brown," pp. 98–112.

coloured an exquisite cream or pink or deep crimson." Most writers would be content with this: a girl walks among beautiful trees and thinks about her first real party, which has offered the possibility of love. Woolf, however, takes it considerably further:

> So she might have walked until she had lost all knowledge of her way, had it not been for the interruption of a tree, which, although it did not grow across her path, stopped her as effectively as if the branches had struck her in the face. It was an ordinary tree, but to her it appeared so strange that it might have been the only tree in the world. Dark was the trunk in the middle, and the branches sprang here and there, leaving jagged intervals of light between them as distinctly as if it had but that second risen from the ground. Having seen a sight that would last her for a lifetime, and for a lifetime would preserve that second, the tree once more sank into the ordinary ranks of trees, and she was able to seat herself in its shade and to pick the red flowers with the thin green leaves which were growing beneath it.

Parties pale—love itself pales—beside a glimpse of the ineffable, what Flannery O'Connor would call "the very heart of mystery,"[10] and which O'Connor found, variously, in grandmothers, murderers, a stain on a ceiling, and a sty full of pigs.

If O'Connor was a Catholic visionary, Woolf was a secular one. She searched for the quintessential; she strove to know (or invent) the world's secret names for itself. And so Rachel, her first heroine, is not so much a woman of actions or qualities as she is an engine of perception. At a picnic, early in the book, when Terence asks Rachel what she is looking at so intently, she answers, "Human beings." She is simple enough, strange enough, to say something like that; something so direct and wise yet so insufficient. It is part of the novel's business to keep showing her these human beings, and these singular and eternal trees, until she begins not only to see them but to take them in. The effort will ultimately kill her.

As Rachel moves through the book she has Helen as confidante

10. Flannery O'Connor, "Revelation," in *Flannery O'Connor: Collected Works* (The Library of America, 1988), p. 65.

and counterpoint: Helen who is worldly where Rachel is ignorant, weary where Rachel is untried. It could be argued that they are the truly central couple in the book. Helen is, to me, the book's most interesting character by far, and is one of the strongest women Woolf ever created. If, during the course of the narrative, Rachel progresses from innocence to the beginnings of experience, Helen progresses from the comic to the tragic. She enters as a clown, and exists a deity.

The book opens with her, making her way with her husband to the dock where the ship is waiting. When we are introduced to her she could easily be one of the silly, colorful minor figures out of Fielding, Austen, or Dickens:

> As the streets that lead from the Strand to the Embankment are very narrow, it is better not to walk down them arm-in-arm. If you persist, lawyers' clerks will have to make flying leaps into the mud; young lady typists will have to fidget behind you. In the streets of London where beauty goes unregarded, eccentricity must pay the penalty, and it is better not to be very tall, to wear a long blue cloak, or to beat the air with your left hand.

The captivating, rather dreadful Clarissa Dalloway, who with her husband, Richard, boards late in the voyage and disembarks early, and who could not more clearly embody the life-quenching, anti-intellectual propriety of Victorian England, says of Helen and her husband:

> "It's what I've always said about literary people—they're far the hardest of any to get on with.... These people ... might have been, one feels, just like everybody else, if they hadn't got swallowed up by Oxford or Cambridge or some such place, and been made cranks of. The man's really delightful (if he'd cut his nails), and the woman has quite a fine face, only she dresses, of course, in a potato sack, and wears her hair like a Liberty shopgirl's. They talk about art, and think us such poops for dressing in the evening. However, I can't help that; I'd rather die than come in to dinner without changing—wouldn't you? It matters ever so much more than the soup."

As the book goes on Helen moves steadily toward its center of gravity, just as the book moves deeper and deeper into a realm of women and young, womanly men. The husbands and fathers—the forces of putative authority—are discarded, one by one. First Richard Dalloway gathers up his wife and leaves the ship when it reaches the coast of North Africa, then Helen and Ridley take Rachel with them while Rachel's father continues up the Amazon, and finally Ridley disappears into his bottomless, vaguely delineated work. They are replaced by a cadre of women, some of whom are at least as forceful as the men. Among them are Miss Allan, who is about to complete a *Primer of English Literature,* from Beowulf to Swinburne; the beautiful Evelyn Murgatroyd, a malcontent and thwarted revolutionary; and Mrs. Flushing, vital and vulgar, a voracious art collector who proclaims loudly, "Nothin' that's more than twenty years old interests me."

They are replaced, also, by two men of a sort very different from the Ridleys and Richards: the fey and brittle St. John Hirst, and the fey and almost painfully sincere Terence Hewet.

In Santa Marina Helen becomes Rachel's mentor and she also becomes, by degrees, the book's moral core, a voice of straightforward, profound unknowing on the subjects of love, art, vision, and how life might be most fully lived—all subjects the vanished men have, at one time or another, picked up from some dusty corner, looked at idly, and pronounced too trivial to contemplate. She becomes the advocate for and protector of life; she comes to resemble, in spirit at least, the nurse Woolf would invent some ten years later, knitting on a bench in Regent's Park beside the sleeping Peter Walsh in *Mrs. Dalloway:*

In her grey dress, moving her hands indefatigably yet quietly, she seemed like the champion of the rights of sleepers, like one of those spectral presences which rise in twilight in woods made of sky and branches. The solitary traveller, haunter of lanes, disturber of ferns, and devastator of great hemlock plants, looking up, suddenly sees the giant figure at the end of the ride.[11]

11. Virginia Woolf, *Mrs. Dalloway* (New York: Harcourt Brace Jovanovich, 1998), p. 73.

Woolf wrote, to some extent, about life in a parallel dimension, one ruled by female spirits. Things were not necessarily better there—she was nothing so simple as a Utopian—but it held in highest esteem virtues very different from those embraced by the world in which masculine gods ruled.

Helen's acme, her great scene, takes place late in the book, in the jungle, where Terence and Rachel finally declare their love for each other. When the party arrives in the rain forest Helen seats herself on a fallen tree, opens her parasol, and looks out over the river. Exhorted by the others to explore, she says, "Oh, no, one's only got to use one's eye. There's everything here—everything. What will you gain by walking?" And so she sits, with St. John at her side (literally in her shade), as Rachel and Terence wander off together.

It is by way of Helen and the jungle that the book reaches its most strange and archetypal interlude, the moment that might be called its climax. Terence and Rachel are strolling in the long grass, talking about their love (their love is made up almost entirely of talk), when Helen pounces on them.

> A hand dropped abrupt as iron on Rachel's shoulder; it might have been a bolt from heaven. She fell beneath it, and the grass whipped across her eyes and filled her mouth and ears. Through the waving stems she saw a figure, large and shapeless against the sky. Helen was upon her. Rolled this way and that, now seeing only forests of green, and now the high blue heaven, she was speechless and almost without sense. At last she lay still, all the grasses shaken round her and before her by her panting. Over her loomed two great heads, the heads of a man and woman, of Terence and Helen.

It is not only the book's strangest moment; it is also the book's only scene of (implied) sexual congress, and it involves three people. For whatever it's worth—I'm truly not sure how much it is or isn't worth—Woolf spent most of her life bound up in threesomes, most prominently herself, Vanessa, and Vanessa's husband, Clive Bell, and, some years later, herself, Leonard, and Vita Sackville-West.

Although in her work Woolf ignored sex to the greatest possible degree, and was skeptical of mysticism, she believed in an immense connectedness. As a writer she was deeply concerned not only with the kinship of people (she became friendly with E. M. Forster, who gave us the phrase "only connect"), but with simultaneity; with the fact that the world is made up of beings, human and animal, all living at once; that all are both related and utterly strange to one another; and that what connects them, most importantly, is the medium of time—the plain fact of finding themselves alive at the same moment; and then, somewhat altered, at the next moment; and the next and the next. She stringently rejected religion but flirted all her life with the notion of the soul or, if not the soul, a certain *beingness* that emanated from living and inanimate things; even from the earth itself. She made it her business to try to account not only for the movements of her characters' flesh but the existence and interactions of their spirits in a world that also possessed a life of its own.

Here is Clarissa Dalloway one night on the *Euphrosyne:*

She then fell into a sleep, which was as usual extremely sound and refreshing, but visited by fantastic dreams of great Greek letters talking round the room, when she woke and laughed to herself, remembering where she was and that the Greek letters were real people, lying asleep not many yards away. Then, thinking of the black sea outside tossing beneath the moon, she shuddered, and thought of her husband and the others as companions on the voyage. The dreams were not confined to her indeed, but went from one brain to another. They all dreamt of each other that night, as was natural, considering how thin the partitions were between them, and how strangely they had been lifted off the earth to sit next each other in mid-ocean, and see every detail of each others' faces, and hear whatever they chanced to say.

If *The Voyage Out* is filled with early evidence of Woolf's style and vision it is also full of the conflicts that would mark her life and work until the year both ended. Always, there is the question of whether women can survive, as intellectual and emotional beings, in society generally and in marriage in particular. If relatively few of Woolf's women are unambiguously destroyed by marriage not one of them clearly benefits from it, and while she was too conscientious to simply present her women as the victims of tyrannical men they are often subject to a kind of erosion as their mates refuse, year after year, to take them quite fully seriously. In *The Voyage Out* Susan Warrington—not exactly young and less than beautiful, consecrated to the care of her ancient aunt—is rescued by Arthur Venning's marriage proposal, and while the fate she's escaped is clearly a grim one there's no strong sense that the fate she's headed for—a respectable little house outside London, a child or two—is a significant improvement.

Even the gentle, idealistic Terence, who is *The Voyage Out*'s most outspoken defender of women's rights, is suspect. On one hand he says to Rachel, while he is courting her:

> "Just consider: It's the beginning of the twentieth century, and until a few years ago no woman had ever come out by herself and said things at all. There it was going on in the background, for all those thousands of years, this curious silent unrepresented life. Of course we're always writing about women—abusing them, or jeering at them, or worshiping them; but it's never come from women themselves. I believe we still don't know in the least how they live, or what they feel, or what they do precisely.... If I were a woman I'd blow some one's brains out. Don't you laugh at us a great deal? Don't you think it's all a great humbug?"

On the other hand, after he and Rachel are engaged, he begins to tease her, tellingly, about her piano-playing, and to urge her to get busy answering the congratulatory notes they've received. When she complains about the blandness of the notes, he lectures her on the virtues of the various women they know:

> "… and Mrs. Thornbury too; she's got too many children I grant you, but if half-a-dozen of them had gone to the bad instead of rising infallibly to the tops of their trees—hasn't she a kind of beauty—of elemental simplicity as Flushing would say? Isn't she rather like a large old tree murmuring in the moonlight, or a river going on and on and on?"

And he adds,

"By the way, Ralph's been made governor of the Carroway Islands—the youngest governor in the service; very good, isn't it?"

Men, it seems, even the most conscientious of them, are still prone to praise women as trees or rivers, and to report only on the careers of other men.

The Voyage Out is saturated with the tension between Woolf's own desire to record the pure sensation of living, her desire to tell a story, and her desire to use her fiction to make potent arguments about serious questions. It is hard to find twenty consecutive pages in *The Voyage Out* that don't contain some discussion between two or more characters on an issue of great import. She would in her later books more seamlessly manage the combination of art and argument. *Jacob's Room,* her elegy for her brother Thoby, is by implication an antiwar novel, as is *Mrs. Dalloway. Mrs. Dalloway,* the first of her great books, began in Woolf's mind not only as the story of a society woman who would die, either by accident or her own hand, and as a novel about the aftermath of World War I, but as a general indictment of medical science and of the English social and political systems. The Prime Minister was to be a prominent (and, we assume, less than attractive) character, and the ham-fisted doctors were to play significantly larger parts. It is a testament to Woolf as an artist that her interest in humanness, and her respect for the ambiguity of human existence, always won out, and the finished books are about complex people who consider themselves the heroes of their own stories. Still, it is rare to find in her work any instance of an intelligent, humane politician, a competent doctor, or an adherent of religion who is not at least slightly deranged. Woolf lived, after all, through the devastation of World War I, which she called "a preposterous masculine fiction."[12] She lived at a time when doctors treated mental disorders by extracting teeth (she her-

12. *Letters, Vol. II,* VW to Margaret Llewlyn Davies, January 23, 1916.

self had several pulled), in the belief that an infection of the teeth could somehow poison the brain.

If, in Woolf's fictive world, everyone is directly threatened by politics, religion, and medicine, and women additionally threatened by men who want them to be charming idiots, there exists as well, and perhaps most threateningly for all, the real possibility of a misspent life. When she was young Woolf lived at a time of almost frantic productivity (most members of the Bloomsbury group report working every day of the week), in a world clearly in need of urgent attention. *Ennui* and a sense of futility, though they can't have been unknown, were not much acknowledged; not at a time when women were fighting for the vote, the class system was drastically changing, and the Great War was about to begin. The question was not *whether* to do but *what* to do. Woolf was, by her own estimation, almost as much concerned with politics as she was with art. She determined to do whatever she could to curtail suffering, especially that of women. Leonard was himself a ferociously political animal, and their accords and arguments—their respect for each other's adamant, deeply considered views—were essential parts of their companionable, asexual marriage.

Woolf worried, especially early on, over the question of a life spent creating versus one spent organizing. The minds of artists and philosophers were the minds she most respected, but good fiction often deals in ambiguities that are not much use in accomplishing social change. If it is the activist's responsibility to depose the tyrant it is the novelist's responsibility to understand and record what it's like to *be* the tyrant. What, then, of an artist's desire to change the world not only over time, by accretion, but now, as soon as possible, for living people who are in pain?

In *The Voyage Out* Woolf stacks the deck, perhaps unconsciously, by putting the arguments in favor of direct political action into the mouths of the least sympathetic figures, be they men or women. Richard Dalloway, a politician who is not only a prig but a mediocre and duplicitous prig, says to Helen of a book she's reading:

"May I ask how you've spent your time? Reading—philosophy?" (He saw the black book.) "Metaphysics and fishing!" he exclaimed. "If I had to live again I believe I should devote myself to one or the other." He began turning the pages.

" 'Good, then, is indefinable,' " he read out. "How jolly to think that's going on still! 'So far as I know there is only one ethical writer, Professor Henry Sidgwick, who has clearly recognized and stated this fact.' That's the kind of thing we used to talk about when we were boys."

A life of action is posed most vehemently, however, by the flirtatious, hysterical Evelyn Murgatroyd, who says to Rachel:

"I belong to a club in London. It meets every Saturday, so it's called the Saturday Club. We're supposed to talk about art, but I'm sick of talking about art—what's the good of it? With all kinds of real things going on round one? It isn't as if they'd got anything to say about art, either. So what I'm going to tell 'em is that we've talked enough about art, and we'd better talk about life for a change. Questions that really matter to people's lives, the White Slave Traffic, Women Suffrage, the Insurance Bill, and so on."

The Saturday Club bears a striking resemblance to the Friday Club, a London discussion group that put on occasional exhibitions and met to talk about art and politics. Woolf went sometimes but felt, as she so often did where any group or committee was concerned, that the fundamental aims were admirable but the results more bemusing than profound. She wrote, "One half of the Committee shriek Whistler and French Impressionists, and the other are stalwart British."[13] She had, ineluctably, the soul and temperament of a writer, and always saw human frailty above anything else.

Midway through the writing of *The Voyage Out* Woolf tried teaching literature to working men and women at an evening institute set up by a local college, but it was not particularly successful and she lasted at it less than two years. While her intentions were

13. Letter from VW to Violet Dickinson, July 10, 1905, Berg Collection, New York Public Library.

good her tendency toward social and intellectual snobbery interfered. She complained her students were incompetent or illiterate
or both; she became exasperated by the stumbling efforts of foreigners who spoke only rudimentary English and what she called
"anemic shop girls" who could manage very little writing during
their one hour off for dinner. Woolf wrote in despair to her friend
Violet Dickinson that her efforts were all but useless, given the material she had to work with. "I have an old Socialist of 50," she
wrote, "who thinks he must bring the Parasite (the Aristocrat) . . .
into an Essay upon Autumn; and a Dutchman who thinks . . . I have
been teaching him Arithmetic."[14]

As she matured Woolf would essentially separate the two activi-
ties, and along with her fiction write uncompromising and widely
influential essays, among them "A Room of One's Own" and
"Three Guineas." Her essays, of course, reflect her fiction, just as
her fiction reflects her essays, but she dealt with the problem of art
versus politics in the simplest and most direct possible manner, by
dividing her efforts: by being alternately a writer of fiction and a
writer of polemics. Her essays, as she would surely have wished,
have proven to be as durable as her novels (especially "A Room of
One's Own"), though they have also proven, ironically, to be the
less controversial of her two main bodies of work.

The right of Woolf's novels to occupy the literary pantheon is
undisputed. Still, there are to this day few major writers whose
merits provoke so much argument. She is probably most widely
criticized for being class-bound—for writing convincingly, and at
length, only about members of the upper classes, the people she
not only knew best but liked best. This is simply true—it would be
foolish to try and deny it—though for those of us who admire her
work what she did accomplish so far outstrips what she failed to accomplish that the failing sheds some of its weight. When the world
produces a novelist able to write fully about everything and everyone, we will have no need of further novels.

Still, it seems pertinent to at least briefly discuss Woolf and class,

14. Letter from VW to Violet Dickinson, October 1907, Berg Collection, New York
Public Library.

particularly in regard to her first novel, where her strengths do not yet so entirely overwhelm her weaknesses. In *The Voyage Out,* the only novel in which she would attempt to set the action in a place she had never been, the South Americans are not characters at all, and the only one with any role to speak of is a murderously incompetent local doctor. If she was much concerned with questions of empire and subjugation while she wrote the book, she didn't noticeably address herself to the reactions of those most affected. There is, at least to this North American reader, a surprisingly unquestioned torpor to the lives and acts of the complacently fortunate English people in the book. What, after all, are they all *doing* there, not for days or weeks but months, sitting on verandahs and complaining about one thing or another, arguing about the issues of the day over meals prepared and served by invisible servers? What are they resting from, or preparing for, that justifies such an enormous span of leisure?

Woolf's nephew Quentin Bell wrote, in his biography of her, that:

> There was much in Good Society that she found hateful and frightening; but there was always something in it that she loved. To be at the centre of things, to know people who disposed of enormous power, who could take certain graces and prerogatives for granted, to mingle with the decorative and decorated world, to hear the butler announce a name that was old when Shakespeare was alive, these were things to which she could never be wholly indifferent. She was in fact a romantic snob.[15]

Woolf, however, was nothing if not self-aware, painfully and sometimes even debilitatingly so. She could be hard on others, but she worried over almost everything it was possible to worry over in her own character. She knew she was a snob; she admitted she was a snob. She did not consider it one of her worst or most interesting failings.

15. Quentin Bell, *Virginia Woolf: A Biography,* Volume I (New York: Harcourt Brace Jovanovich, 1972), pp. 79–80.

Late in her life she did, in fact, deliver a humorous lecture on the subject, "Am I a Snob?," to the Memoir Club, in which she said:

> Witness this letter. Why is it always on top of all my letters? Because it has a coronet—if I get a letter stamped with a coronet that letter miraculously floats on top. I often ask—why? I know perfectly well that none of my friends will ever be, or ever has been impressed by anything I do to impress them. Yet I do it—here is the letter—on top. This shows, like a rash or a spot, that I have the disease.... I want coronets; but they must be old coronets; coronets that carry land with them and country houses; coronets that breed simplicity, eccentricity, ease; ...[16]

And so, there she stands.

Woolf's work is also criticized for a certain tea-table delicacy, for veering away from all matters concerning the flesh, even though it was written during a period when sex was considered, for the first time in centuries, a permissible subject. While Woolf was fully aware of the power of sexuality she had little interest in going into its particulars. *The Voyage Out* does contain an implied rape, in the form of a kiss forced on Rachel by Richard Dalloway, but Woolf would never again venture even that far into the physically violent possibilities between women and men. She would later depict a kiss, one with very different consequences, in *Mrs. Dalloway,* when Sally Seton surprises the young Clarissa by kissing her, suddenly and unexpectedly, only once, while they are briefly separated from the incessant company of men. These are the two major sexual episodes in Woolf's entire body of work, and each involves one of the Dalloways, those emblems of all that Woolf found terrible and compelling in English society. Richard assaults Rachel, and Clarissa, in the later book, is assaulted, more kindly, by Sally. Interestingly, it is Clarissa who is more undone by the experience of being kissed.

Woolf did appreciate the complexity of sex—its risks and marvels, its capacity to transform lives. Her characters' sexuality is al-

16. Virginia Woolf, "Am I a Snob?" in *Moments of Being* (New York: Harcourt Brace, 1985), p. 96.

ways highly idiosyncratic and deeply personal; she understood, more fully than many authors who were far more explicit on the subject, that everyone possesses a sexual geography as particular to him or her as a fingerprint. Richard Dalloway's kiss excites Rachel even as it humiliates and terrifies her, and Sally Seton's kiss implies for Clarissa in *Mrs. Dalloway* a fleeting promise, lost almost as soon as found, that runs to depths far greater than those implied by questions of hetero- versus homosexuality.

What there is of sexuality in *The Voyage Out* feels somewhat more rudimentary than the submerged sexuality in Woolf's later work. St. John worships Helen without a trace of lust, and when Rachel falls in love with Terence their courtship consists almost entirely of ardent, romantic talk. While they wander through the jungle—the kind of symbol often favored by first novelists—it is difficult to determine what if anything occurs between them bodily, and of course Woolf kills Rachel before any of the messier acts can be practiced upon her.

Rachel and Terence are physically unprepossessing. Rachel is not beautiful, "except in some dresses, in some lights," and Terence is "inclined to be stout." It feels, simultaneously, like part of Woolf's sexual reticence to insist so on the homeliness of her romantic protagonists and like part of her heroism, to insist that it is not only the outwardly beautiful who are transformed by love.

Again, there she stands.

Since *The Voyage Out* appeared, eighty-five years prior to this writing, Woolf's reputation has risen and fallen and risen again. While she lived she became a best-selling author. The money she earned from the surprising success of her 1937 novel, *The Years*, enabled her to buy the fur coat into the pocket of which she would, four years later, put a stone and drown herself. Her picture appeared in *Vogue* in 1926, and her likeness can still be seen in a mosaic on the floor of the foyer of the National Gallery in London, holding a pen and wearing a toga amid a gathering of gods, goddesses, and muses.

After her death in 1941 she fell out of fashion, until her work was taken up by feminist scholars in the 1960s. She quickly became, in the popular imagination, at least as much a personality as she was an artist. Edward Albee's 1962 play, *Who's Afraid of Virginia Woolf?*, and the 1966 movie starring Richard Burton and Elizabeth Taylor, made her name familiar to many people who had not only never read a word of hers but weren't entirely sure whether or not she was a real person and, if so, what she had done to become famous enough to have a play and a movie named after her. For those who *had* read her, a cottage industry of sorts grew up, composed mainly of essays and books that claimed that her work, her character, her genius, and her suicide could only be understood in light of her lesbianism, her enslavement to Leonard, her mental disorder, her oppression as a woman, and/or the fact that she had survived incest. Few figures have inspired such possessiveness, such rampant subjectivity. Those of us who care for her have always tended to do so ferociously. Monk's House, her country house, which is open to the public six months of the year, is usually full of people, many of them as hushed and attentive as if visiting a shrine. If one walks from Monk's House to the River Ouse, where Woolf drowned herself, one usually passes others either coming or going.

Woolf's reputation as an artist is somewhat difficult to parse from the popular romance that has grown up out of her life and death. In addition to the aforementioned quarrels about her focus on the upper classes and her reticence in matters of sex, she is widely known as a "difficult" writer; and while that may be true, the word "difficult" is often applied in a dismissive tone that differs noticeably from the tone the same word takes on when applied to a writer like Joyce. There is often a sense, even among serious readers, that Joyce is bracingly difficult and Woolf merely irritatingly difficult. As someone who has written about Woolf I find myself hearing from a number of people, generally in tones of pride or annoyance, that they simply can't read her. We are all, of course, entitled to our disinclinations, but I can't help wondering if these people would proclaim with the same righteous indignation their inability to read authors like Joyce, Kafka, or Faulkner. I tend to feel that an inability to read Woolf should be presented as a problem with the reader, not the writer, though that opinion is by no means universal.

Some of the barriers set up against Woolf's full standing as a major artist arise not from her innovation or her difficulty, it seems, but from the fact that she was innovative, difficult, and a woman; a woman whose narratives tended to arise out of domestic situations; who insisted that domestic situations were at least as important to those who inhabited them as foreign wars and the deaths of kings. Clearly the battle Woolf took up has not yet been won, at least not at the beginning of the twenty-first century. Although she detested criticism I suspect she would not mind knowing that she remains a figure of controversy—better that than hallowed and forgotten. Unlike many venerated authors, she is still read and discussed.

Great art contains not only its own questions but its own answers, and one of its more satisfying aspects is its way of outliving its detractors; of marching into time with all its beauties, excesses, subtleties, insights, and deficiencies in full view. Battles lost or battles won, Woolf's work, from *The Voyage Out* which launched her, to *Between the Acts* which helped to kill her, is very much alive. Generations of readers come and go, fashions change, but we have Woolf's books, and will always have them. We have a passage like this, from *The Voyage Out:*

The preliminary discomforts and harshnesses, which generally make the first days of a sea voyage so cheerless and trying to the temper, being somehow lived through, the succeeding days passed pleasantly enough. October was well advanced, but steadily burning with a warmth that made the early months of the summer appear very young and capricious. Great tracts of the earth lay now beneath the autumn sun, and the whole of England, from the bald moors to the Cornish rocks, was lit up from dawn to sunset, and showed in stretches of yellow, green, and purple. Under that illumination even the roofs of the great towns glittered. In thousands of small gardens, millions of dark-red flowers were blooming, until the old ladies who had tended them so carefully came down the paths with their scissors, snipped through their juicy stalks, and laid them upon cold stone ledges in the village church. Innumerable parties of picnickers coming home at sunset cried, "Was there ever such a day as this?" "It's you," the young men whispered; "Oh, it's you," the young women replied. All old people and many sick people were drawn, were it only for a foot or two, into the open air, and prognosticated pleasant things about the course of the world. As for the confidences and expressions of love that were heard not only in cornfields but in lamplit rooms, where the windows opened on the garden, and men with cigars kissed women with gray hairs, they were not to be counted. Some said that the sky was an emblem of the life they had had; others that it was the promise of the life to come. Long-tailed birds clattered and screamed, and crossed from wood to wood, with golden eyes in their plumage.

ACKNOWLEDGMENTS: I relied for information about Virginia Woolf's life and work on two biographies: *Virginia Woolf: A Biography*, by Quentin Bell (New York: Harcourt Brace Jovanovich, 1972); and *Virginia Woolf*, by Hermione Lee (New York: Knopf, 1997).

MICHAEL CUNNINGHAM'S novel *The Hours*, inspired by Virginia Woolf's *Mrs. Dalloway*, won the PEN/Faulkner Award and Pulitzer Prize in 1999. His other novels include *A Home at the End of the World* and *Flesh and Blood*. He teaches at Columbia University, and lives in New York City.

TO
L. W.

THE VOYAGE OUT

Chapter I

As the streets that lead from the Strand to the Embankment are very narrow, it is better not to walk down them arm-in-arm. If you persist, lawyers' clerks will have to make flying leaps into the mud; young lady typists will have to fidget behind you. In the streets of London where beauty goes unregarded, eccentricity must pay the penalty, and it is better not to be very tall, to wear a long blue cloak, or to beat the air with your left hand.

One afternoon in the beginning of October when the traffic was becoming brisk a tall man strode along the edge of the pavement with a lady on his arm. Angry glances struck upon their backs. The small, agitated figures—for in comparison with this couple most people looked small—decorated with fountain pens, and burdened with despatch-boxes, had appointments to keep, and drew a weekly salary, so that there was some reason for the unfriendly stare which was bestowed upon Mr. Ambrose's height and upon Mrs. Ambrose's cloak. But some enchantment had put both man and woman beyond the reach of malice. In his case one might guess from the moving lips that it was thought; and in hers from the eyes fixed stonily straight in front of her at a level above the eyes of most that it was sorrow. It was only by scorning all she met that she kept herself from tears, and the friction of people brushing past her was evidently painful. After watching the traffic on the Embankment for a minute or two with a stoical gaze she twitched her husband's sleeve, and they crossed between the swift discharge of motor cars. When they were safe on the further side, she gently withdrew her arm from his, allowing her mouth at the same time to relax, to tremble; then tears rolled down, and, leaning her elbows on the balustrade, she shielded her face from the curious. Mr. Ambrose attempted consolation; he patted her shoulder; but she showed no signs of admitting him, and feeling it awkward to stand beside a grief that was greater than his, he crossed his arms behind him, and took a turn along the pavement.

The embankment juts out in angles here and there, like pulpits; instead of preachers, however, small boys occupy them, dangling string, dropping pebbles, or launching wads of paper for a cruise. With their sharp eye for eccentricity, they were inclined to think Mr. Ambrose awful; but the quickest witted cried "Bluebeard!"[1] as he passed. In case they should proceed to tease his wife, Mr. Ambrose flourished his stick at them, upon which they decided that he was grotesque merely, and four instead of one cried "Bluebeard!" in chorus.

Although Mrs. Ambrose stood quite still, much longer than is natural, the little boys let her be. Some one is always looking into the river near Waterloo Bridge; a couple will stand there talking for half an hour on a fine afternoon; most people, walking for pleasure, contemplate for three minutes; when, having compared the occasion with other occasions, or made some sentence, they pass on. Sometimes the flats and churches and hotels of Westminster are like the outlines of Constantinople in a mist; sometimes the river is an opulent purple, sometimes mud-colored, sometimes sparkling blue like the sea. It is always worth while to look down and see what is happening. But this lady looked neither up nor down; the only thing she had seen, since she stood there, was a circular iridescent patch slowly floating past with a straw in the middle of it. The straw and the patch swam again and again behind the tremulous medium of a great welling tear, and the tear rose and fell and dropped into the river. Then there struck close upon her ears—

> Lars Porsena of Clusium
> By the nine Gods he swore—

and then more faintly, as if the speaker had passed her on his walk—

> That the Great House of Tarquin
> Should suffer wrong no more.[2]

Yes, she knew she must go back to all that, but at present she must weep. Screening her face she sobbed more steadily than she had yet done, her shoulders rising and falling with great regularity. It was this figure that her husband saw when, having reached the polished Sphinx, having entangled himself with a man selling picture postcards, he turned; the stanza instantly stopped. He came up to her, laid his hand on her shoulder, and said, "Dearest." His voice was supplicating. But she shut her face away from him, as much as to say, "You can't possibly understand."

As he did not leave her, however, she had to wipe her eyes, and to raise them to the level of the factory chimneys on the other bank. She saw also the arches of Waterloo Bridge and the carts moving across them, like the line of animals in a shooting gallery. They were seen blankly, but to see anything was of course to end her weeping and begin to walk.

"I would rather walk," she said, her husband having hailed a cab already occupied by two city men.

The fixity of her mood was broken by the action of walking. The shooting motor cars, more like spiders in the moon than terrestrial objects, the thundering drays, the jingling hansoms, and little black broughams, made her think of the world she lived in. Somewhere up there above the pinnacles where the smoke rose in a pointed hill, her children were now asking for her, and getting a soothing reply. As for the mass of streets, squares, and public buildings which parted them, she only felt at this moment how little London had done to make her love it, although thirty of her forty years had been spent in a street. She knew how to read the people who were passing her; there were the rich who were running to and from each others' houses at this hour; there were the bigoted workers driving in a straight line to their offices; there were the poor who were unhappy and rightly malignant. Already, though there was sunlight in the haze, tattered old men and women were nodding off to sleep upon the seats. When one gave up seeing the beauty that clothed things, this was the skeleton beneath.

A fine rain now made her still more dismal; vans with the odd names of those engaged in odd industries—Sprules, Manufacturer of Saw-dust; Grabb, to whom no piece of waste paper comes amiss—fell flat as a bad joke; bold lovers, sheltered behind one cloak, seemed to her sordid, past their passion; the flower women, a contented company, whose talk is always worth hearing, were sodden hags; the red, yellow, and blue flowers, whose heads were pressed together, would not blaze. Moreover, her husband, walking with a quick rhythmic stride, jerking his free hand occasionally, was either a Viking or a stricken Nelson;[3] the sea-gulls had changed his note.

"Ridley, shall we drive? Shall we drive, Ridley?"

Mrs. Ambrose had to speak sharply; by this time he was far away.

The cab, by trotting steadily along the same road soon withdrew them from the West End, and plunged them into London. It appeared that this was a great manufacturing place, where the people were engaged in making things, as though the West End, with its electric lamps, its vast plate-glass windows all shining yellow, its carefully-finished houses, and tiny live figures trotting on the pavement, or bowled along on wheels in the road, was the finished work. It appeared to her a very small bit of work for such an enormous factory to have made. For some reason it appeared to her as a small golden tassel on the edge of a vast black cloak.

Observing that they passed no other hansom cab, but only vans and waggons, and that not one of the thousand men and women she saw was either a gentleman or a lady, Mrs. Ambrose understood that after all it is the ordinary thing to be poor, and that London is the city of innumerable poor people. Startled by this discovery and seeing herself pacing a circle all the days of her life round Piccadilly Circus she was greatly relieved to pass a building put up by the London County Council for Night Schools.

"Lord, how gloomy it is!" her husband groaned. "Poor creatures!"

What with misery for her children, the poor, and the rain, her mind was like a wound exposed to dry in the air.

At this point the cab stopped, for it was in danger of being crushed like an egg-shell. The wide Embankment which had had room for cannon-balls and squadrons, had now shrunk to a cobbled lane steaming with smells of malt and oil and blocked by waggons. While her husband read the placards pasted on the brick announcing the hours at which certain ships would sail for Scotland, Mrs. Ambrose did her best to find information. From a world exclusively occupied in feeding waggons with sacks, half obliterated too in a fine yellow fog, they got neither help nor attention. It seemed a miracle when an old man approached, guessed their condition, and proposed to row them out to their ship in the little boat which he kept moored at the bottom of a flight of steps. With some hesitation they trusted themselves to his care, took their places, and were soon waving up and down upon the water, London having shrunk to two lines of buildings on either side of them, square buildings and oblong buildings placed in rows like a child's avenue of bricks.

The river, which had a certain amount of troubled yellow light in it, ran with great force; bulky barges floated down swiftly escorted by tugs; police boats shot past everything; the wind went with the current. The open rowing-boat in which they sat bobbed and curtseyed across the line of traffic. In mid-stream the old man stayed his hands upon the oars, and as the water rushed past them, remarked that once he had taken many passengers across, where now he took scarcely any. He seemed to recall an age when his boat, moored among rushes, carried delicate feet across to lawns at Rotherhithe.[4]

"They want bridges now," he said, indicating the monstrous out-line of the Tower Bridge. Mournfully Helen regarded him, who was putting water between her and her children. Mournfully she gazed at the ship they were approaching; anchored in the middle of the stream they could dimly read her name—*Euphrosyne.*[5]

Very dimly in the falling dusk they could see the lines of the rig-ging, the masts and the dark flag which the breeze blew out squarely behind.

As the little boat sidled up to the steamer, and the old man shipped his oars, he remarked once more pointing above, that ships all the world over flew that flag the day they sailed. In the minds of both the passengers the blue flag appeared a sinister token, and this the moment for presentiments, but nevertheless they rose, gathered their things together, and climbed on deck.

Down in the saloon on her father's ship, Miss Rachel Vinrace, aged twenty-four, stood waiting for her uncle and aunt nervously. To begin with, though nearly related, she scarcely remembered them; to go on with, they were elderly people, and finally, as her fa-ther's daughter she must be in some sort prepared to entertain them. She looked forward to seeing them as civilised people generally look forward to the first sight of civilised people, as though they were of the nature of an approaching physical discomfort,—a tight shoe or a draughty window. She was already unnaturally braced to receive them. As she occupied herself in laying forks severely straight by the side of knives, she heard a man's voice saying gloomily:

"On a dark night one would fall down these stairs head fore-most," to which a woman's voice added, "And be killed."

As she spoke the last words the woman stood in the doorway. Tall, large-eyed, draped in purple shawls, Mrs. Ambrose was ro-mantic and beautiful; not perhaps sympathetic, for her eyes looked straight and considered what they saw. Her face was much warmer than a Greek face; on the other hand it was much bolder than the face of the usual pretty Englishwoman.

"Oh, Rachel, how d'you do," she said, shaking hands.

"How are you, dear," said Mr. Ambrose, inclining his forehead to be kissed. His niece instinctively liked his thin angular body, and the big head with its sweeping features, and the acute, innocent eyes.

"Tell Mr. Pepper," Rachel bade the servant. Husband and wife then sat down on one side of the table, with their niece opposite to them.

"My father told me to begin," she explained. "He is very busy with the men.... You know Mr. Pepper?"

A little man who was bent as some trees are by a gale on one side of them had slipped in. Nodding to Mr. Ambrose, he shook hands with Helen.

"Draughts," he said, erecting the collar of his coat.

"You are still rheumatic?" asked Helen. Her voice was low and seductive, though she spoke absently enough, the sight of town and river being still present to her mind.

"Once rheumatic, always rheumatic, I fear," he replied. "To some extent it depends on the weather, though not so much as people are apt to think."

"One does not die of it, at any rate," said Helen.

"As a general rule—no," said Mr. Pepper.

"Soup, Uncle Ridley?" asked Rachel.

"Thank you, dear," he said, and, as he held his plate out, sighed audibly, "Ah! she's not like her mother." Helen was just too late in thumping her tumbler on the table to prevent Rachel from hearing, and from blushing scarlet with embarrassment.

"The way servants treat flowers," she said hastily. She drew a green vase with a crinkled lip towards her, and began pulling out the tight little chrysanthemums, which she laid on the table-cloth, arranging them fastidiously side by side.

There was a pause.

"You knew Jenkinson, didn't you, Ambrose?" asked Mr. Pepper across the table.

"Jenkinson of Peterhouse?"[6]

"He's dead," said Mr. Pepper.

"Ah, dear!—I knew him—ages ago," said Ridley. "He was the

hero of the punt accident, you remember? A queer card. Married a young woman out of a tobacconist's, and lived in the Fens—never heard what became of him."

"Drink—drugs," said Mr. Pepper with sinister conciseness. "He left a commentary. Hopeless muddle, I'm told."

"The man had really great abilities," said Ridley.

"His introduction to Jellaby holds its own still," went on Mr. Pepper, "which is surprising, seeing how text-books change."

"There was a theory about the planets, wasn't there?" asked Ridley.

"A screw loose somewhere, no doubt of it," said Mr. Pepper, shaking his head.

Now a tremor ran through the table, and a light outside swerved. At the same time an electric bell rang sharply again and again.

"We're off," said Ridley.

A slight but perceptible wave seemed to roll beneath the floor; then it sank; then another came, more perceptible. Lights slid right across the uncurtained window. The ship gave a loud melancholy moan.

"We're off!" said Mr. Pepper. Other ships, as sad as she, answered her outside on the river. The chuckling and hissing of water could be plainly heard, and the ship heaved so that the steward bringing plates had to balance himself as he drew the curtain. There was a pause.

"Jenkinson of Cats—d'you still keep up with him?" asked Ambrose.

"As much as one ever does," said Mr. Pepper. "We meet annually. This year he has had the misfortune to lose his wife, which made it painful, of course."

"Very painful," Ridley agreed.

"There's an unmarried daughter who keeps house for him, I believe, but it's never the same, not at his age."

Both gentlemen nodded sagely as they carved their apples.

"There was a book, wasn't there?" Ridley enquired.

"There *was* a book, but there never *will* be a book," said Mr. Pepper with such fierceness that both ladies looked up at him.

"There never will be a book, because some one else has written it for him," said Mr. Pepper with considerable acidity. "That's what comes of putting things off, and collecting fossils, and sticking Norman arches on one's pigsties."

"I confess I sympathise," said Ridley with a melancholy sigh. "I have a weakness for people who can't begin."

"... The accumulations of a lifetime wasted," continued Mr. Pepper. "He had accumulations enough to fill a barn."

"It's a vice that some of us escape," said Ridley. "Our friend Miles has another work out to-day."

Mr. Pepper gave an acid little laugh. "According to my calculations," he said, "he has produced two volumes and a half annually, which, allowing for time spent in the cradle and so forth, shows a commendable industry."

"Yes, the old Master's saying of him has been pretty well realised," said Ridley.

"A way they had," said Mr. Pepper. "You know the Bruce collection?—not for publication, of course."

"I should suppose not," said Ridley significantly. "For a Divine he was—remarkably free."

"The Pump in Neville's Row,[7] for example?" enquired Mr. Pepper.

"Precisely," said Ambrose.

Each of the ladies, being after the fashion of their sex, highly trained in promoting men's talk without listening to it, could think—about the education of children, about the use of fog sirens in an opera—without betraying herself. Only it struck Helen that Rachel was perhaps too still for a hostess, and that she might have done something with her hands.

"Perhaps——?" she said at length, upon which they rose and left, vaguely to the surprise of the gentlemen, who had either thought them attentive or had forgotten their presence.

"Ah, one could tell strange stories of the old days," they heard Ridley say, as he sank into his chair again. Glancing back, at the doorway, they saw Mr. Pepper as though he had suddenly loosened his clothes, and had become a vivacious and malicious old ape.

Winding veils round their heads, the women walked on deck. They were now moving steadily down the river, passing the dark shapes of ships at anchor, and London was a swarm of lights with a pale yellow canopy drooping above it. There were the lights of the great theatres, the lights of the long streets, lights that indicated huge squares of domestic comfort, lights that hung high in air. No darkness would ever settle upon those lamps, as no darkness had settled upon them for hundreds of years. It seemed dreadful that the town should blaze for ever in the same spot; dreadful at least to people going away to adventure upon the sea, and beholding it as a circumscribed mound, eternally burnt, eternally scarred. From the deck of the ship the great city appeared a crouched and cowardly figure, a sedentary miser.

Leaning over the rail, side by side, Helen said, "Won't you be cold?" Rachel replied, "No.... How beautiful!" she added a moment later. Very little was visible—a few masts, a shadow of land here, a line of brilliant windows there. They tried to make head against the wind.

"It blows—it blows!" gasped Rachel, the words rammed down her throat. Struggling by her side, Helen was suddenly overcome by the spirit of movement, and pushed along with her skirts wrapping themselves round her knees, and both arms to her hair. But slowly the intoxication of movement died down, and the wind became rough and chilly. They looked through a chink in the blind and saw that long cigars were being smoked in the dining-room; they saw Mr. Ambrose throw himself violently against the back of his chair, while Mr. Pepper crinkled his cheeks as though they had been cut in wood. The ghost of a roar of laughter came out to them, and was drowned at once in the wind. In the dry yellow-lighted room Mr. Pepper and Mr. Ambrose were oblivious of all tumult; they were in Cambridge, and it was probably about the year 1875.

"They're old friends," said Helen, smiling at the sight. "Now, is there a room for us to sit in?"

Rachel opened a door.

"It's more like a landing than a room," she said. Indeed it had nothing of the shut stationary character of a room on shore. A table was rooted in the middle, and seats were stuck to the sides. Happily the tropical suns had bleached the tapestries to a faded blue-green colour, and the mirror with its frame of shells, the work of the steward's love, when the time hung heavy in the southern seas, was quaint rather than ugly. Twisted shells with red lips like unicorn's horns ornamented the mantelpiece, which was draped by a pall of purple plush from which depended a certain number of balls. Two windows opened on to the deck, and the light beating through them when the ship was roasted on the Amazons had turned the prints on the opposite wall to a faint yellow colour, so that "The Coliseum" was scarcely to be distinguished from Queen Alexandra[8] playing with her Spaniels. A pair of wicker armchairs by the fireside invited one to warm one's hands at a grate full of gilt shavings; a great lamp swung above the table—the kind of lamp which makes the light of civilisation across dark fields to one walking in the country.

"It's odd that every one should be an old friend of Mr. Pepper's," Rachel started nervously, for the situation was difficult, the room cold, and Helen curiously silent.

"I suppose you take him for granted?" said her aunt.

"He's like this," said Rachel, lighting on a fossilised fish in a basin, and displaying it.

"I expect you're too severe," Helen remarked.

Rachel immediately tried to qualify what she had said against her belief.

"I don't really know him," she said, and took refuge in facts, believing that elderly people really like them better than feelings. She produced what she knew of William Pepper. She told Helen that he always called on Sundays when they were at home; he knew about a great many things—about mathematics, history, Greek, zoology, economics, and the Icelandic Sagas. He had turned Persian poetry into English prose, and English prose into Greek iambics; he was an authority upon coins, and—one other thing—oh yes, she thought it was vehicular traffic.

He was here either to get things out of the sea, or to write upon the probable course of Odysseus, for Greek after all was his hobby.

"I've got all his pamphlets," she said. "Little pamphlets. Little yellow books." It did not appear that she had read them.

"Has he ever been in love?" asked Helen, who had chosen a seat. This was unexpectedly to the point.

"His heart's a piece of old shoe leather," Rachel declared, dropping the fish. But when questioned she had to own that she had never asked him.

"I shall ask him," said Helen.

"The last time I saw you, you were buying a piano," she continued. "Do you remember—the piano, the room in the attic, and the great plants with the prickles?"

"Yes, and my aunts said the piano would come through the floor, but at their age one wouldn't mind being killed in the night?" she enquired.

"I heard from Aunt Bessie not long ago," Helen stated. "She is afraid that you will spoil your arms if you insist upon so much practising."

"The muscles of the forearm—and then one won't marry?"

"She didn't put it quite like that," replied Mrs. Ambrose.

"Oh, no—of course she wouldn't," said Rachel with a sigh.

Helen looked at her. Her face was weak rather than decided, saved from insipidity by the large enquiring eyes; denied beauty, now that she was sheltered indoors, by the lack of colour and definite outline. Moreover, a hesitation in speaking, or rather a tendency to use the wrong words, made her seem more than normally incompetent for her years. Mrs. Ambrose, who had been speaking much at random, now reflected that she certainly did not look forward to the intimacy of three or four weeks on board ship which was threatened. Women of her own age usually boring her, she supposed that girls would be worse. She glanced at Rachel again. Yes! how clear it was that she would be vacillating, emotional, and when you said something to her it would make no more lasting impression than the stroke of a stick upon water. There was nothing to take hold of in girls—nothing hard, permanent, satisfactory. Did Willoughby say three weeks, or did he say four? She tried to remember.

At this point, however, the door opened and a tall burly man entered the room, came forward and shook Helen's hand with an emotional kind of heartiness, Willoughby himself, Rachel's father, Helen's brother-in-law. As a great deal of flesh would have been needed to make a fat man of him, his frame being so large, he was not fat; his face was a large framework too, looking, by the smallness of the features and the glow in the hollow of the cheek, more fitted to withstand assaults of the weather than to express sentiments and emotions, or to respond to them in others.

"It is a great pleasure that you have come," he said, "for both of us."

Rachel murmured in obedience to her father's glance.

"We'll do our best to make you comfortable. And Ridley. We think it an honour to have charge of him. Pepper'll have some one to contradict him—which I daren't do. You find this child grown, don't you? A young woman, eh?"

Still holding Helen's hand he drew his arm round Rachel's shoulder, thus making them come uncomfortably close, but Helen forbore to look.

"You think she does us credit?" he asked.

"Oh, yes," said Helen.

"Because we expect great things of her," he continued, squeezing his daughter's arm and releasing her. "But about you now." They sat down side by side on the little sofa. "Did you leave the children well? They'll be ready for school, I suppose. Do they take after you or Ambrose? They've got good heads on their shoulders, I'll be bound?"

At this Helen immediately brightened more than she had yet done, and explained that her son was six and her daughter ten. Everybody said that her boy was like her and her girl like Ridley. As for brains, they were quick brats, she thought, and modestly she ventured on a little story about her son,—how left alone for a minute he had taken the pat of butter in his fingers, run across the room with it, and put it on the fire—merely for the fun of the thing, a feeling which she could understand.

"And you had to show the young rascal that these tricks wouldn't do, eh?"

"A child of six? I don't think they matter."

"I'm an old-fashioned father."

"Nonsense, Willoughby; Rachel knows better."

Much as Willoughby would doubtless have liked his daughter to praise him she did not; her eyes were unreflecting as water, her fingers still toying with the fossilised fish, her mind absent. The elder people went on to speak of arrangements that could be made for Ridley's comfort—a table placed where he couldn't help looking at the sea, far from boilers, at the same time sheltered from the view of people passing. Unless he made this a holiday, when his books were all packed, he would have no holiday whatever; for out at Santa Marina Helen knew, by experience, that he would work all day; his boxes, she said, were packed with books.

"Leave it to me—leave it to me!" said Willoughby, obviously intending to do much more than she asked of him. But Ridley and Mr. Pepper were heard fumbling at the door.

"How are you, Vinrace?" said Ridley, extending a limp hand as he came in, as though the meeting were melancholy to both, but on the whole more so to him.

Willoughby preserved his heartiness, tempered by respect. For the moment nothing was said.

"We looked in and saw you laughing," Helen remarked. "Mr. Pepper had just told a very good story."

"Pish. None of the stories were good," said her husband peevishly.

"Still a severe judge, Ridley?" enquired Mr. Vinrace.

"We bored you so that you left," said Ridley, speaking directly to his wife.

As this was quite true Helen did not attempt to deny it, and her next remark, "But didn't they improve after we'd gone?" was unfortunate, for her husband answered with a droop of his shoulders, "If possible they got worse."

The situation was now one of considerable discomfort for every one concerned, as was proved by a long interval of constraint and silence. Mr. Pepper, indeed, created a diversion of a kind by leaping on to his seat, both feet tucked under him, with the action of a spinster who detects a mouse, as the draught struck at his ankles. Drawn up there, sucking at his cigar, with his arms encircling his knees, he looked like the image of Buddha, and from this elevation began a discourse, addressed to nobody, for nobody had called for it, upon the unplumbed depths of ocean. He professed himself surprised to learn that although Mr. Vinrace possessed ten ships, regularly plying between London and Buenos Aires, not one of them was bidden to investigate the great white monsters of the lower waters.

"No, no," laughed Willoughby, "the monsters of the earth are too many for me!"

Rachel was heard to sigh, "Poor little goats!"

"If it weren't for the goats there'd be no music, my dear; music depends upon goats," said her father rather sharply, and Mr. Pepper went on to describe the white, hairless, blind monsters lying curled on the ridges of sand at the bottom of the sea, which would explode if you brought them to the surface, their sides bursting asunder and scattering entrails to the winds when released from pressure, with considerable detail and with such show of knowledge, that Ridley was disgusted, and begged him to stop.

From all this Helen drew her own conclusions, which were gloomy enough. Pepper was a bore; Rachel was an unlicked girl, no doubt prolific of confidences, the very first of which would be: "You see, I don't get on with my father." Willoughby, as usual, loved his business and built his Empire, and between them all she would be considerably bored. Being a woman of action, however, she rose, and said that for her part she was going to bed. At the door she glanced back instinctively at Rachel expecting that as two of the same sex they would leave the room together. Rachel rose, looked vaguely into Helen's face and remarked with her slight stammer, "I'm going out to t-t-triumph in the wind."

Mrs. Ambrose's worst suspicions were confirmed; she went down the passage lurching from side to side, and fending off the wall now with her right arm, now with her left; at each lurch she exclaimed emphatically, "Damn!"

CHAPTER II

Uncomfortable as the night, with its rocking movement, and salt smells, may have been, and in one case undoubtedly was, for Mr. Pepper had insufficient clothes upon his bed, the breakfast next morning wore a kind of beauty. The voyage had begun, and had begun happily with a soft blue sky, and a calm sea. The sense of untapped resources, things to say as yet unsaid, made the hour significant, so that in future years the entire journey perhaps would be represented by this one scene, with the sound of sirens hooting in the river the night before, somehow mixing in.

The table was cheerful with apples and bread and eggs. Helen handed Willoughby the butter, and as she did so cast her eye on him and reflected, "And she married you, and she was happy, I suppose."

She went off on a familiar train of thought, leading on to all kinds of well-known reflections, from the old wonder, why Theresa had married Willoughby?

"Of course, one sees all that," she thought, meaning that one sees that he is big and burly, and has a great booming voice, and a fist and a will of his own; "but——" here she slipped into a fine analysis of him which is best represented by one word, "sentimental," by which she meant that he was never simple and honest about his feelings. For example, he seldom spoke of the dead, but kept anniversaries with singular pomp. She suspected him of nameless atrocities with regard to his daughter, as indeed she had always suspected him of bullying his wife. Naturally she fell to comparing her own fortunes with the fortunes of her friend, for Willoughby's wife had been perhaps the one woman Helen called friend, and this comparison often made the staple of their talk. Ridley was a scholar, and Willoughby was a man of business. Ridley was bringing out the third volume of Pindar[1] when Willoughby was launching his first ship. They built a new factory the very year the commentary on Aristotle—was it?—appeared at the University Press. "And Rachel," she looked at her, meaning, no doubt, to decide the argument, which was otherwise too evenly balanced, by declaring that Rachel was not comparable to her own children. "She really might be six years old," was all she said, however, this judgment referring to the smooth unmarked outline of the girl's face, and not condemning her otherwise, for if Rachel were ever to think, feel, laugh, or express herself, instead of dropping milk from a height as though to see what kind of drops it made, she might be interesting though never exactly pretty. She was like her mother, as the image in a pool on a still summer's day is like the vivid flushed face that hangs over it.

Meanwhile Helen herself was under examination, though not from either of her victims. Mr. Pepper considered her; and his meditations, carried on while he cut his toast into bars and neatly buttered them, took him through a considerable stretch of autobiography. One of his penetrating glances assured him that he was right last night in judging that Helen was beautiful. Blandly he passed her the jam. She was talking nonsense, but not worse nonsense than people usually do talk at breakfast, the cerebral circulation, as he knew to his cost, being apt to give trouble at that hour. He went on saying "No" to her, on principle, for he never yielded to a woman on account of her sex. And here, dropping his eyes to his plate, he became autobiographical. He had not married himself for the sufficient reason that he had never met a woman who commanded his respect. Condemned to pass the susceptible years of youth in a railway station in Bombay, he had seen only coloured women, military women, official women; and his ideal was a woman who could read Greek, if not Persian, was irreproachably fair in the face, and able to understand the small things he let fall while undressing. As it was he had contracted habits of which he was not in the least ashamed. Certain odd minutes every day went to learning things by heart; he never took a ticket without noting the number; he devoted January to Petronius, February to Catullus, March to the Etruscan vases[2] perhaps; anyhow he had done good work in India, and there was nothing to regret in his life except the fundamental defects which no wise man regrets, when the present is still his. So concluding he looked up suddenly and smiled. Rachel caught his eye.

"And now you've chewed something thirty-seven times, I suppose?" she thought, but said politely aloud, "Are your legs troubling you to-day, Mr. Pepper?"

"My shoulder blades?" he asked, shifting them painfully. "Beauty has no effect upon uric acid that I'm aware of," he sighed, contemplating the round pane opposite, through which the sky and sea showed blue. At the same time he took a little parchment volume from his pocket and laid it on the table. As it was clear that he invited comment, Helen asked him the name of it. She got the name; but she got also a disquisition upon the proper method of making roads. Beginning with the Greeks, who had, he said, many difficulties to contend with, he continued with the Romans, passed to England and the right method, which speedily became the wrong method, and wound up with such a fury of denunciation directed against the road-makers of the present day in general, and the road-makers of Richmond Park in particular, where Mr. Pepper had the habit of cycling every morning before breakfast, that the spoons fairly jingled against the coffee cups, and the insides of at least four rolls mounted in a heap beside Mr. Pepper's plate.

"Pebbles!" he concluded, viciously dropping another bread pellet upon the heap. "The roads of England are mended with pebbles! 'With the first heavy rainfall,' I've told 'em, 'your road will be a swamp.' Again and again my words have proved true. But d'you suppose they listen to me when I tell 'em so, when I point out the consequences, the consequences to the public purse, when I recommend 'em to read Coryphæus?[3] Not a bit of it; they've other interests to attend to. No, Mrs. Ambrose, you will form no just opinion of the stupidity of mankind until you have sat upon a Borough Council!" The little man fixed her with a glance of ferocious energy.

"I have had servants," said Mrs. Ambrose, concentrating her gaze. "At this moment I have a nurse. She's a good woman as they go, but she's determined to make my children pray. So far, owing to great care on my part, they think of God as a kind of walrus; but now that my back's turned——Ridley," she demanded, swinging round upon her husband, "what shall we do if we find them saying the Lord's Prayer when we get home again?"

Ridley made the sound which is represented by "Tush."

But Willoughby, whose discomfort as he listened was manifested by a slight movement rocking of his body, said awkwardly, "Oh, surely, Helen, a little religion hurts nobody."

"I would rather my children told lies," she replied, and while Willoughby was reflecting that his sister-in-law was even more eccentric than he remembered, pushed her chair back and swept upstairs. In a second they heard her calling back, "Oh, look! We're out at sea!"

They followed her on to the deck. All the smoke and the houses had disappeared, and the ship was out in a wide space of sea very fresh and clear though pale in the early light. They had left London sitting on its mud. A very thin line of shadow tapered on the horizon, scarcely thick enough to stand the burden of Paris, which nevertheless rested upon it. They were free of roads, free of mankind, and the same exhilaration at their freedom ran through them all. The ship was making her way steadily through small waves which slapped her and then fizzled like effervescing water, leaving a little border of bubbles and foam on either side. The colourless October sky above was thinly clouded as if by the trail of woodfire smoke, and the air was wonderfully salt and brisk. Indeed it was too cold to stand still. Mrs. Ambrose drew her arm within her husband's, and as they moved off it could be seen from the way in which her sloping cheek turned up to his that she had something private to communicate. They went a few paces and Rachel saw them kiss.

Down she looked into the depth of the sea. While it was slightly disturbed on the surface by the passage of the *Euphrosyne*, beneath it was green and dim, and it grew dimmer and dimmer until the sand at the bottom was only a pale blur. One could scarcely see the black ribs of wrecked ships, or the spiral towers made by the burrowings of great eels, or the smooth green-sided monsters who came by flickering this way and that.

———"And, Rachel, if any one wants me, I'm busy till one," said her father, enforcing his words as he often did, when he spoke to his daughter, by a smart blow upon the shoulder.

"Until one," he repeated. "And you'll find yourself some employment, eh? Scales, French, a little German, eh? There's Mr. Pepper who knows more about separable verbs than any man in Europe, eh?" and he went off laughing. Rachel laughed, too, as indeed she had laughed ever since she could remember, without thinking it funny, but because she admired her father.

But just as she was turning with a view perhaps to finding some employment, she was intercepted by a woman who was so broad and so thick that to be intercepted by her was inevitable. The discreet tentative way in which she moved, together with her sober black dress, showed that she belonged to the lower orders; nevertheless she took up a rock-like position, looking about her to see that no gentry were near before she delivered her message, which had reference to the state of the sheets, and was of the utmost gravity.

"How ever we're to get through this voyage, Miss Rachel, I really can't tell," she began with a shake of her head. "There's only just sheets enough to go round, and the master's has a rotten place you could put your fingers through. And the counterpanes. Did you notice the counterpanes? I thought to myself a poor person would have been ashamed of them. The one I gave Mr. Pepper was hardly fit to cover a dog.... No, Miss Rachel, they could *not* be mended;

they're only fit for dust sheets. Why, if one sewed one's finger to the bone, one would have one's work undone the next time they went to the laundry."

Her voice in its indignation wavered as if tears were near.

There was nothing for it but to descend and inspect a large pile of linen heaped upon a table. Mrs. Chailey handled the sheets as if she knew each by name, character, and constitution. Some had yellow stains, others had places where the threads made long ladders; but to the ordinary eye they looked much as sheets usually do look, very chill, white, cold, and irreproachably clean.

Suddenly Mrs. Chailey, turning from the subject of sheets, dismissing them entirely, clenched her fists on the top of them, and proclaimed, "And you couldn't ask a living creature to sit where I sit!"

Mrs. Chailey was expected to sit in a cabin which was large enough, but too near the boilers, so that after five minutes she could hear her heart "go," she complained, putting her hand above it, which was a state of things that Mrs. Vinrace, Rachel's mother, would never have dreamt of inflicting—Mrs. Vinrace who knew every sheet in her house, and expected of every one the best they could do, but no more.

It was the easiest thing in the world to grant another room, and the problem of sheets simultaneously and miraculously solved itself, the spots and ladders not being past cure after all, but——

"Lies! Lies! Lies!" exclaimed the mistress indignantly, as she ran up on to the deck. "What's the use of telling me lies?"

In her anger that a woman of fifty should behave like a child and come cringing to a girl because she wanted to sit where she had not leave to sit, she did not think of the particular case, and, unpacking her music, soon forgot all about the old woman and her sheets.

Mrs. Chailey folded her sheets, but her expression testified to flatness within. The world no longer cared about her, and a ship was not a home. When the lamps were lit yesterday, and the sailors went tumbling above her head, she had cried; she would cry this evening; she would cry to-morrow. It was not home. Meanwhile she arranged her ornaments in the room which she had won too easily. They were strange ornaments to bring on a sea voyage—china pugs, tea-sets in miniature, cups stamped floridly with the arms of the city of Bristol, hair-pin boxes crusted with shamrock, antelopes' heads in coloured plaster, together with a multitude of tiny photographs, representing downright workmen in their Sunday best, and women holding white babies. But there was one portrait in a gilt frame, for which a nail was needed, and before she sought it Mrs. Chailey put on her spectacles and read what was written on a slip of paper at the back:

"This picture of her mistress is given to Emma Chailey by Willoughby Vinrace in gratitude for thirty years of devoted service."

Tears obliterated the words and the head of the nail.

"So long as I can do something for your family," she was saying, as she hammered at it, when a voice called melodiously in the passage.

"Mrs. Chailey! Mrs. Chailey!"

Chailey instantly tidied her dress, composed her face, and opened the door.

"I'm in a fix," said Mrs. Ambrose, who was flushed and out of breath. "You know what gentlemen are. The chairs too high—the tables too low—there's six inches between the floor and the door. What I want's a hammer, an old quilt, and have you such a thing as a kitchen table? Anyhow, between us"——she now flung open the door of her husband's sitting-room, and revealed Ridley pacing up and down, his forehead all wrinkled, and the collar of his coat turned up.

"It's as though they'd taken pains to torment me!" he cried, stopping dead. "Did I come on this voyage in order to catch rheumatism and pneumonia? Really one might have credited Vinrace with more sense. My dear," Helen was on her knees under a table, "you are only making yourself untidy, and we had much better recognise the fact that we are condemned to six weeks of unspeakable misery. To come at all was the height of folly, but now that we are here I suppose that I can face it like a man. My diseases of course will be increased—I feel already worse than I did yesterday, but we've only ourselves to thank, and the children happily——"

"Move! Move! Move!" cried Helen, chasing him from corner to corner with a chair as though he were an errant hen. "Out of the way, Ridley, and in half an hour you'll find it ready."

She turned him out of the room, and they could hear him groaning and swearing as he went along the passage.

"I daresay he isn't very strong," said Mrs. Chailey, looking at Mrs. Ambrose compassionately, as she helped to shift and carry.

"It's books," sighed Helen, lifting an armful of sad volumes from the floor to the shelf. "Greek from morning to night. If ever Miss Rachel marries, Chailey, pray that she may marry a man who doesn't know his ABC."

The preliminary discomforts and harshnesses, which generally make the first days of a sea voyage so cheerless and trying to the temper, being somehow lived through, the succeeding days passed pleasantly enough. October was well advanced, but steadily burning with a warmth that made the early months of the summer appear very young and capricious. Great tracts of the earth lay now beneath the autumn sun, and the whole of England, from the bald moors to the Cornish rocks, was lit up from dawn to sunset, and showed in stretches of yellow, green, and purple. Under that illumination even the roofs of the great towns glittered. In thousands of small gardens, millions of dark-red flowers were blooming, until the old ladies who had tended them so carefully came down the paths with their scissors, snipped through their juicy stalks, and laid them upon cold stone ledges in the village church. Innumerable parties of picnickers coming home at sunset cried, "Was there ever such a day as this?" "It's you," the young men whispered; "Oh, it's you," the young women replied. All old people and many sick people were drawn, were it only for a foot or two, into the open air, and prognosticated pleasant things about the course of the world. As for the confidences and expressions of love that were heard not only in cornfields but in lamplit rooms, where the windows opened on the garden, and men with cigars kissed women with grey hairs, they were not to be counted. Some said that the sky was an emblem of the life they had had; others that it was the promise of the life to come. Long-tailed birds clattered and screamed, and crossed from wood to wood, with golden eyes in their plumage.

But while all this went on by land, very few people thought about the sea. They took it for granted that the sea was calm; and there was no need, as there is in many houses when the creeper taps on the bedroom windows, for the couples to murmur before they kiss, "Think of the ships to-night," or "Thank Heaven, I'm not the man in the lighthouse!" For all they imagined, the ships when they vanished on the sky-line dissolved, like snow in water. The grown-up view, indeed, was not much clearer than the view of the little creatures in bathing drawers who were trotting in to the foam all along the coasts of England, and scooping up buckets full of water. They saw white sails or tufts of smoke pass across the horizon, and if you had said that these were waterspouts, or the petals of white sea flowers, they would have agreed.

The people in ships, however, took an equally singular view of England. Not only did it appear to them to be an island, and a very small island, but it was a shrinking island in which people were imprisoned. One figured them first swarming about like aimless ants, and almost pressing each other over the edge; and then, as the ship withdrew, one figured them making a vain clamour, which, being unheard, either ceased, or rose into a brawl. Finally, when the ship was out of sight of land, it became plain that the people of England were completely mute. The disease attacked other parts of the earth; Europe shrank, Asia shrank, Africa and America shrank, until it seemed doubtful whether the ship would ever run against any of those wrinkled little rocks again. But, on the other hand, an immense dignity had descended upon her; she was an inhabitant of the great world, which has so few inhabitants, travelling all day across an empty universe, with veils drawn before her and behind. She was more lonely than the caravan crossing the desert; she was infinitely more mysterious, moving by her own power and sustained by her own resources. The sea might give her death or some unexampled joy, and none would know of it. She was a bride going forth to her husband, a virgin unknown of men; in her vigour and purity she might be likened to all beautiful things, worshipped and felt as a symbol.

Indeed if they had not been blessed in their weather, one blue day being bowled up after another, smooth, round, and flawless. Mrs. Ambrose would have found it very dull. As it was, she had her embroidery frame set up on deck, with a little table by her side on which lay open a black volume of philosophy. She chose a thread from the vari-coloured tangle that lay in her lap, and sewed red into the bark of a tree, or yellow into the river torrent. She was working at a great design of a tropical river running through a tropical forest, where spotted deer would eventually browse upon masses of fruit, bananas, oranges, and giant pomegranates, while a troop of naked natives whirled darts into the air. Between the stitches she looked to one side and read a sentence about the Reality of Matter, or the Nature of Good. Round her men in blue jerseys knelt and scrubbed the boards, or leant over the rails and whistled, and not far off Mr. Pepper sat cutting up roots with a penknife. The rest were occupied in other parts of the ship: Ridley at his Greek—he had never found quarters more to his liking; Willoughby at his documents, for he used a voyage to work off arrears of business; and Rachel—Helen, between her sentences of philosophy, wondered sometimes what Rachel *did* do with herself? She meant vaguely to go and see. They had scarcely spoken two words to each other since that first evening; they were polite when they met, but there had been no confidence of any kind. Rachel seemed to get on very well with her father—much better, Helen thought, than she ought to—and was as ready to let Helen alone as Helen was to let her alone.

At that moment Rachel was sitting in her room doing absolutely nothing. When the ship was full this apartment bore some magnificent title and was the resort of elderly sea-sick ladies who left the deck to their youngers. By virtue of the piano, and a mess of books on the floor, Rachel considered it her room, and there she would sit for hours playing very difficult music, reading a little German, or a little English when the mood took her, and doing—as at this moment—absolutely nothing.

The way she had been educated, joined to a fine natural in-
dolence, was of course partly the reason of it, for she had been educated as the majority of well-to-do girls in the last part of the
nineteenth century were educated. Kindly doctors and gentle
old professors had taught her the rudiments of about ten different
branches of knowledge, but they would as soon have forced her to
go through one piece of drudgery thoroughly as they would have
told her that her hands were dirty. The one hour or the two hours
weekly passed very pleasantly, partly owing to the fact that the
window looked upon the back of a shop, where figures appeared
against the red windows in winter, partly to the accidents that are
bound to happen when more than two people are in the same room
together. But there was no subject in the world which she knew accurately. Her mind was in the state of an intelligent man's in the beginning of the reign of Queen Elizabeth; she would believe
practically anything she was told, invent reasons for anything she
said. The shape of the earth, the history of the world, how trains
worked, or money was invested, what laws were in force, which
people wanted what, and why they wanted it, the most elementary
idea of a system in modern life—none of this had been imparted to
her by any of her professors or mistresses. But this system of education had one great advantage. It did not teach anything, but it put
no obstacle in the way of any real talent that the pupil might
chance to have. Rachel, being musical, was allowed to learn nothing
but music; she became a fanatic about music. All the energies that
might have gone into languages, science, or literature, that might
have made her friends, or shown her the world, poured straight into
music. Finding her teachers inadequate, she had practically taught
herself. At the age of twenty-four she knew as much about music as
most people do when they are thirty; and could play as well as nature intended her to, which, as became daily more obvious, was a
really generous allowance. If this one definite gift was surrounded
by dreams and ideas of the most extravagant and foolish description, no one was any the wiser.

Her education being thus ordinary, her circumstances were no
more out of the common. She was an only child and had never been

bullied and laughed at by brothers and sisters. Her mother having died when she was eleven, two aunts, the sisters of her father, brought her up, and they lived for the sake of the air in a comfortable house in Richmond. She was of course brought up with excessive care, which as a child was for her health; as a girl and a young woman for what it seems almost crude to call her morals. Until quite lately she had been completely ignorant that for women such things existed. She groped for knowledge in old books, and found it in repulsive chunks, but she did not naturally care for books and thus never troubled her head about the censorship which was exercised first by her aunts, later by her father. Friends might have told her things, but she had few of her own age,—Richmond being an awkward place to reach,—and, as it happened, the only girl she knew well was a religious zealot, who in the fervour of intimacy talked about God, and the best ways of taking up one's cross, a topic only fitfully interesting to one whose mind reached other stages at other times.

But lying in her chair, with one hand behind her head, the other grasping the knob on the arm, she was clearly following her thoughts intently. Her education left her abundant time for thinking. Her eyes were fixed so steadily upon a ball on the rail of the ship that she would have been startled and annoyed if anything had chanced to obscure it for a second. She had begun her meditations with a shout of laughter, caused by the following translation from *Tristan:*[4]

> In shrinking trepidation
> His shame he seems to hide
> While to the king his relation
> He brings the corpse-like Bride.
> Seems it so senseless what I say?

She cried that it did, and threw down the book. Next she had picked up *Cowper's Letters,*[5] the classic prescribed by her father which had bored her, so that one sentence chancing to say something about the smell of broom in his garden, she had thereupon seen the little hall at Richmond laden with flowers on the day of her mother's funeral, smelling so strong that now any flower-scent brought back the sickly horrible sensation; and so from one scene she passed, half-hearing, half-seeing, to another. She saw her Aunt Lucy arranging flowers in the drawing-room.

"Aunt Lucy," she volunteered, "I don't like the smell of broom; it reminds me of funerals."

"Nonsense, Rachel," Aunt Lucy replied; "don't say such foolish things, dear. I always think it a particularly cheerful plant."

Lying in the hot sun her mind was fixed upon the characters of her aunts, their views, and the way they lived. Indeed this was a subject that lasted her hundreds of morning walks round Richmond Park, and blotted out the trees and the people and the deer. Why did they do the things they did, and what did they feel, and what was it all about? Again she heard Aunt Lucy talking to Aunt Eleanor. She had been that morning to take up the character of a servant, "And, of course, at half-past ten in the morning one expects to find the housemaid brushing the stairs." How odd! How unspeakably odd! But she could not explain to herself why suddenly as her aunt spoke the whole system in which they lived had appeared before her eyes as something quite unfamiliar and inexplicable, and themselves as chairs or umbrellas dropped about here and there without any reason. She could only say with her slight stammer, "Are you f-f-fond of Aunt Eleanor, Aunt Lucy?" to which her aunt replied, with her nervous hen-like twitter of a laugh, "My dear child, what questions you do ask!"

"How fond? Very fond?" Rachel pursued.

"I can't say I've ever thought 'how,'" said Miss Vinrace. "If one cares one doesn't think 'how,' Rachel," which was aimed at the niece who had never yet "come" to her aunts as cordially as they wished.

"But you know I care for you, don't you, dear, because you're your mother's daughter, if for no other reason, and there *are* plenty of other reasons"—and she leant over and kissed her with some emotion, and the argument was spilt irretrievably about the place like the proverbial bucket of milk.

By these means Rachel reached that stage in thinking, if thinking it can be called, when the eyes are intent upon a ball or a knob and the lips cease to move. Her efforts to come to an understanding had only hurt her aunt's feelings, and the conclusion must be that it is better not to try. To feel anything strongly was to create an abyss between oneself and others who feel strongly perhaps but differently. It was far better to play the piano and forget all the rest. The conclusion was very welcome. Let these odd men and women— her aunts, the Hunts, Ridley, Helen, Mr. Pepper, and the rest—be symbols,—featureless but dignified, symbols of age, of youth, of motherhood, of learning, and beautiful often as people upon the stage are beautiful. It appeared that nobody ever said a thing they meant, or ever talked of a feeling they felt, but that was what music was for. Reality dwelling in what one saw and felt, but did not talk about, one could accept a system in which things went round and round quite satisfactorily to other people, without often troubling to think about it, except as something superficially strange. Absorbed by her music she accepted her lot very complacently, blazing into indignation perhaps once a fortnight, and subsiding as she subsided now. Inextricably mixed in dreamy confusion, her mind seemed to enter into communion, to be delightfully expanded and combined, with the spirit of the whitish boards on deck, with the spirit of the sea, with the spirit of Beethoven Op.111, even with the spirit of poor William Cowper there at Olney. Like a ball of thistledown it kissed the sea, rose, kissed it again, and thus rising and kissing passed finally out of sight. The rising and falling of the ball of thistledown was represented by the sudden droop forward of her own head, and when it passed out of sight she was asleep.

Ten minutes later Mrs. Ambrose opened the door and looked at her. It did not surprise her to find that this was the way in which Rachel passed her mornings. She glanced round the room at the piano, at the books, at the general mess. In the first place she considered Rachel aesthetically; lying unprotected she looked somehow like a victim dropped from the claws of a bird of prey, but considered as a woman, a young woman of twenty-four, the sight gave rise to reflections. Mrs. Ambrose stood thinking for at least two minutes. She then smiled, turned noiselessly and went, lest the sleeper should waken, and there should be the awkwardness of speech between them.

CHAPTER III

Early next morning there was a sound as of chains being drawn roughly overhead; the steady heart of the *Euphrosyne* slowly ceased to beat; and Helen, poking her nose above deck, saw a stationary castle upon a stationary hill. They had dropped anchor in the mouth of the Tagus, and instead of cleaving new waves perpetually, the same waves kept returning and washing against the sides of the ship.

As soon as breakfast was done, Willoughby disappeared over the vessel's side, carrying a brown leather case, shouting over his shoulder that every one was to mind and behave themselves, for he would be kept in Lisbon doing business until five o'clock that afternoon.

At about that hour he reappeared, carrying his case, professing himself tired, bothered, hungry, thirsty, cold, and in immediate need of his tea. Rubbing his hands, he told them the adventures of the day: how he had come upon poor old Jackson combing his moustache before the glass in the office, little expecting his descent, had put him through such a morning's work as seldom came his way; then treated him to a lunch of champagne and ortolans; paid a call upon Mrs. Jackson, who was fatter than ever, poor woman, but

asked kindly after Rachel—and O Lord, little Jackson had confessed to a confounded piece of weakness—well, well, no harm was
done, he supposed, but what was the use of his giving orders if they
were promptly disobeyed? He had said distinctly that he would
take no passengers on this trip. Here he began searching in his
pockets and eventually discovered a card, which he planked down
on the table before Rachel. On it she read, "Mr. and Mrs. Richard
Dalloway, 23 Browne Street, Mayfair."

"Mr. Richard Dalloway," continued Vinrace, "seems to be a gentleman who thinks that because he was once a member of Parliament,
and his wife's the daughter of a peer, they can have what they like
for the asking. They got round poor little Jackson anyhow. Said they
must have passages—produced a letter from Lord Glenaway, asking me as a personal favour—overruled any objections Jackson
made (I don't believe they came to much), and so there's nothing
for it but to submit, I suppose."

But it was evident that for some reason or other Willoughby was
quite pleased to submit, although he made a show of growling.

The truth was that Mr. and Mrs. Dalloway had found themselves
stranded in Lisbon. They had been travelling on the Continent for
some weeks, chiefly with a view to broadening Mr. Dalloway's
mind. Unable for a season, by one of the accidents of political life,
to serve his country in Parliament, Mr. Dalloway was doing the best
he could to serve it out of Parliament. For that purpose the Latin
countries did very well, although the East, of course, would have
done better.

"Expect to hear of me next in Petersburg or Teheran," he had
said, turning to wave farewell from the steps of the Travellers'. But
a disease had broken out in the East, there was cholera in Russia,
and he was heard of, not so romantically, in Lisbon. They had been
through France; he had stopped at manufacturing centres where,
producing letters of introduction, he had been shown over works,
and noted facts in a pocket-book. In Spain he and Mrs. Dalloway
had mounted mules, for they wished to understand how the peasants live. Are they, for example, ripe for rebellion? Mrs. Dalloway
had then insisted upon a day or two at Madrid with the pictures. Fi-

nally they arrived in Lisbon and spent six days which, in a jour-
nal privately issued afterwards, they described as of "unique interest." Richard had audiences with ministers, and foretold a crisis at
no distant date, "the foundations of government being incurably
corrupt. Yet how blame, etc."; while Clarissa inspected the royal
stables, and took several snapshots showing men now exiled and
windows now broken. Among other things she photographed
Fielding's grave,[1] and let loose a small bird which some ruffian had
trapped, "because one hates to think of anything in a cage where
English people lie buried," the diary stated. Their tour was thoroughly unconventional, and followed no meditated plan. The foreign correspondents of the *Times* decided their route as much as
anything else. Mr. Dalloway wished to look at certain guns, and was
of opinion that the African coast is far more unsettled than people
at home were inclined to believe. For these reasons they wanted a
slow inquisitive kind of ship, comfortable, for they were bad sailors,
but not extravagant, which would stop for a day or two at this port
and at that, taking in coal while the Dalloways saw things for themselves. Meanwhile they found themselves stranded in Lisbon, unable for the moment to lay hands upon the precise vessel they
wanted. They heard of the *Euphrosyne*, but heard also that she was
primarily a cargo boat, and only took passengers by special arrangement, her business being to carry dry goods to the Amazons,
and rubber home again. "By special arrangement," however, were
words of high encouragement in their ears, for they came of a class
where almost everything was specially arranged, or could be if necessary. On this occasion all that Richard did was to write a note to
Lord Glenaway, the head of the line which bears his title; to call on
poor old Jackson; to represent to him how Mrs. Dalloway was so-
and-so, and he had been something or other else, and what they
wanted was such and such a thing. It was done. They parted with
compliments and pleasure on both sides, and here, a week later,
came the boat rowing up to the ship in the dusk with the Dalloways
on board of it; in three minutes they were standing together on the
deck of the *Euphrosyne*. Their arrival, of course, created some stir,
and it was seen by several pairs of eyes that Mrs. Dalloway was a tall

slight woman, her body wrapped in furs, her head in veils, while Mr. Dalloway appeared to be a middle-sized man of sturdy build, dressed like a sportsman on an autumnal moor. Many solid leather bags of a rich brown hue soon surrounded them, in addition to which Mr. Dalloway carried a despatch box, and his wife a dressing-case suggestive of diamond necklaces and bottles with silver tops.

"It's so like Whistler!"[2] she exclaimed, with a wave towards the shore, as she shook Rachel by the hand, and Rachel had only time to look at the grey hills on one side of her before Willoughby introduced Mrs. Chailey, who took the lady to her cabin.

Momentary though it seemed, nevertheless the interruption was upsetting; every one was more or less put out by it, from Mr. Grice, the steward, to Ridley himself. A few minutes later Rachel passed the smoking-room, and found Helen moving arm-chairs. She was absorbed in her rearrangements, and on seeing Rachel remarked confidentially:

"If one can give men a room to themselves where they will sit, it's all to the good. Arm-chairs are *the* important things——" She began wheeling them about. "Now, does it still look like a bar at a railway station?"

She whipped a plush cover off a table. The appearance of the place was marvellously improved.

Again, the arrival of the strangers made it obvious to Rachel, as the hour of dinner approached, that she must change her dress; and the ringing of the great bell found her sitting on the edge of her berth in such a position that the little glass above the washstand reflected her head and shoulders. In the glass she wore an expression of tense melancholy, for she had come to the depressing conclusion, since the arrival of the Dalloways, that her face was not the face she wanted, and in all probability never would be.

However, punctuality had been impressed on her, and whatever face she had, she must go in to dinner with it.

These few minutes had been used by Willoughby in sketching to the Dalloways the people they were to meet, and checking them upon his fingers.

"There's my brother-in-law, Ambrose, the scholar (I daresay

you've heard his name), his wife, my old friend Pepper, a very quiet fellow, but knows everything, I'm told. And that's all. We're a very small party. I'm dropping them on the coast."

Mrs. Dalloway, with her head a little on one side, did her best to recollect Ambrose—was it a surname?—but failed. She was made slightly uneasy by what she had heard. She knew that scholars married any one—girls they met in farms on reading parties; or little suburban women who said disagreeably, "Of course I know it's my husband you want; not *me*."

But Helen came in at that point, and Mrs. Dalloway saw with relief that though slightly eccentric in appearance, she was not untidy, held herself well, and her voice had restraint in it, which she held to be the sign of a lady. Mr. Pepper had not troubled to change his neat ugly suit.

"But after all," Clarissa thought to herself as she followed Vinrace in to dinner, "*every one's* interesting really."

When seated at the table she had some need of that assurance, chiefly because of Ridley, who came in late, looked decidedly unkempt, and took to his soup in profound gloom.

An imperceptible signal passed between husband and wife, meaning that they grasped the situation and would stand by each other loyally. With scarcely a pause Mrs. Dalloway turned to Willoughby and began:

"What I find so tiresome about the sea is that there are no flowers in it. Imagine fields of hollyhocks and violets in mid-ocean! How divine!"

"But somewhat dangerous to navigation," boomed Richard, in the bass, like the bassoon to the flourish of his wife's violin. "Why, weeds can be bad enough, can't they, Vinrace? I remember crossing in the *Mauretania* once, and saying to the Captain—Richards—did you know him?—'Now tell me what perils you really dread most for your ship, Captain Richards?' expecting him to say icebergs, or derelicts, or fog, or something of that sort. Not a bit of it. I've always remembered his answer. *'Sedgius aquatici,'* he said, which I take to be a kind of duck-weed."

Mr. Pepper looked up sharply, and was about to put a question when Willoughby continued:

"They've an awful time of it—those captains! Three thousand souls on board!"

"Yes, indeed," said Clarissa. She turned to Helen with an air of profundity. "I'm convinced people are wrong when they say it's work that wears one; it's responsibility. That's why one pays one's cook more than one's housemaid, I suppose."

"According to that, one ought to pay one's nurse double; but one doesn't," said Helen.

"No; but think what a joy to have to do with babies, instead of saucepans!" said Mrs. Dalloway, looking with more interest at Helen, a probable mother.

"I'd much rather be a cook than a nurse," said Helen. "Nothing would induce me to take charge of children."

"Mothers always exaggerate," said Ridley. "A well-bred child is no responsibility. I've travelled all over Europe with mine. You just wrap 'em up warm and put 'em in the rack."

Helen laughed at that. Mrs. Dalloway exclaimed, looking at Ridley:

"How like a father! My husband's just the same. And then one talks of the equality of the sexes!"

"Does one?" said Mr. Pepper.

"Oh, some do!" cried Clarissa. "My husband had to pass an irate lady every afternoon last session who said nothing else, I imagine."

"She sat outside the house; it was very awkward," said Dalloway. "At last I plucked up courage and said to her, 'My good creature, you're only in the way where you are. You're hindering me, and you're doing no good to yourself.'"

"And then she caught him by the coat, and would have scratched his eyes out——" Mrs. Dalloway put in.

"Pooh—that's been exaggerated," said Richard. "No, I pity them, I confess. The discomfort of sitting on those steps must be awful."

"Serve them right," said Willoughby curtly.

"Oh, I'm entirely with you there," said Dalloway. "Nobody can condemn the utter folly and futility of such behaviour more than I do; and as for the whole agitation, well! may I be in my grave before a woman has the right to vote in England! That's all I say."

The solemnity of her husband's assertion made Clarissa grave.

"It's unthinkable," she said. "Don't tell me you're a suffragist?" she turned to Ridley.

"I don't care a fig one way or t'other," said Ambrose. "If any creature is so deluded as to think that a vote does him or her any good, let him have it. He'll soon learn better."

"You're not a politician, I see," she smiled.

"Goodness, no," said Ridley.

"I'm afraid your husband won't approve of me," said Dalloway aside, to Mrs. Ambrose. She suddenly recollected that he had been in Parliament.

"Don't you ever find it rather dull?" she asked, not knowing exactly what to say.

Richard spread his hands before him, as if inscriptions bearing on what she asked him were to be read in the palms of them.

"If you ask me whether I ever find it rather dull," he said, "I am bound to say yes; on the other hand, if you ask me what career do you consider on the whole, taking the good with the bad, the most enjoyable and enviable, not to speak of its more serious side, of all careers, for a man, I am bound to say, 'The Politician's.'"

"The Bar or politics, I agree," said Willoughby. "You get more run for your money."

"All one's faculties have their play," said Richard. "I may be treading on dangerous ground; but what I feel about poets and artists in general is this: on your own lines, you can't be beaten—granted; but off your own lines—puff—one has to make allowances. Now, I shouldn't like to think that any one had to make allowances for me."

"I don't quite agree, Richard," said Mrs. Dalloway. "Think of Shelley. I feel that there's almost everything one wants in 'Adonais.'"[3]

"Read 'Adonais' by all means," Richard conceded. "But whenever I hear of Shelley I repeat to myself the words of Matthew Arnold, 'What a set! What a set!' "[4]

This roused Ridley's attention. "Matthew Arnold? A detestable prig!" he snapped.

"A prig—granted," said Richard; "but, I think, a man of the world. That's where my point comes in. We politicians doubtless seem to you" (he had grasped somehow that Helen was the representative of the arts) "a gross commonplace set of people; but we see both sides; we may be clumsy, but we do our best to get a grasp of things. Now your artists *find* things in a mess, shrug their shoulders, turn aside to their visions—which I grant may be very beautiful—and *leave* things in a mess. Now that seems to me evading one's responsibilities. Besides, we aren't all born with the artistic faculty."

"It's dreadful," said Mrs. Dalloway, who, while her husband spoke, had been thinking. "When I'm with artists I feel so intensely the delights of shutting oneself up in a little world of one's own, with pictures and music and everything beautiful, and then I go out into the streets and the first child I meet with its poor, hungry, dirty little face makes me turn round and say, 'No, I *can't* shut myself up—I *won't* live in a world of my own. I should like to stop all the painting and writing and music until this kind of thing exists no longer.' Don't you feel," she wound up, addressing Helen, "that life's a perpetual conflict?"

Helen considered for a moment. "No," she said. "I don't think I do."

There was a pause, which was decidedly uncomfortable. Mrs. Dalloway then gave a little shiver, and asked whether she might have her fur cloak brought to her. As she adjusted the soft brown fur about her neck a fresh topic struck her.

"I own," she said, "that I shall never forget the *Antigone*.[5] I saw it at Cambridge years ago, and it's haunted me ever since. Don't you think it's quite the most modern thing you ever saw?" she asked Ridley. "It seemed to me I'd known twenty Clytemnestras.[6] Old Lady Ditchling for one. I don't know a word of Greek, but I could listen to it for ever—"

Here Mr. Pepper struck up:

πολλὰ τὰ δεινὰ, κοὐδὲν ἀν-
θρώπον δεινότερον πέλει.
τοῦτο καὶ πολοῦ πέραν
πόντου χειμερίῳ νότῳ
χωρεῖ, περβρυχίοισι
περῶν ὑπ᾿ οἴδμασι.

Mrs. Dalloway looked at him with compressed lips.

"I'd give ten years of my life to know Greek," she said, when he had done.

"I could teach you the alphabet in half an hour," said Ridley, "and you'd read Homer in a month. I should think it an honour to instruct you."

Helen, engaged with Mr. Dalloway and the habit, now fallen into decline, of quoting Greek in the House of Commons, noted, in the great commonplace book that lies open beside us as we talk, the fact that all men, even men like Ridley, really prefer women to be fashionable.

Clarissa exclaimed that she could think of nothing more delightful. For an instant she saw herself in her drawing-room in Browne Street with a Plato open on her knees—Plato in the original Greek. She could not help believing that a real scholar, if specially interested, could slip Greek into her head with scarcely any trouble.

Ridley engaged her to come to-morrow.

"If only your ship is going to treat us kindly!" she exclaimed, drawing Willoughby into play. For the sake of guests, and these were distinguished, Willoughby was ready with a bow of his head to vouch for the good behaviour even of the waves.

"I'm dreadfully bad; and my husband's not very good," sighed Clarissa.

"I am never sick," Richard explained, "At least, I have only been actually sick once," he corrected himself. "That was crossing the Channel. But a choppy sea, I confess, or still worse, a swell, makes me distinctly uncomfortable. The great thing is never to miss a meal. You look at the food, and you say, 'I can't'; you take a mouthful, and Lord knows how you're going to swallow it; but persevere, and you often settle the attack for good. My wife's a coward."

They were pushing back their chairs. The ladies were hesitating at the doorway.

"I'd better show the way," said Helen, advancing.

Rachel followed. She had taken no part in the talk; no one had spoken to her; but she had listened to every word that was said. She had looked from Mrs. Dalloway to Mr. Dalloway, and from Mr. Dalloway back again. Clarissa, indeed, was a fascinating spectacle. She wore a white dress and a long glittering necklace. What with her clothes, and her arch delicate face, which showed exquisitely pink beneath hair turning grey, she was astonishingly like an eighteenth-century masterpiece—a Reynolds or a Romney.[7] She made Helen and the others look coarse and slovenly beside her. Sitting lightly upright she seemed to be dealing with the world as she chose; the enormous solid globe spun round this way and that beneath her fingers. And her husband! Mr. Dalloway rolling that rich deliberate voice was even more impressive. He seemed to come from the humming oily centre of the machine where the polished rods are sliding, and the pistons thumping; he grasped things so firmly but so loosely; he made the others appear like old maids cheapening remnants. Rachel followed in the wake of the matrons, as if in a trance; a curious scent of violets came back from Mrs. Dalloway, mingling with the soft rustling of her skirts, and the tinkling of her chains. As she followed, Rachel thought with supreme self-abasement, taking in the whole course of her life and the lives of all her friends, "She said we lived in a world of our own. It's true. We're perfectly absurd."

"We sit in here," said Helen, opening the door of the saloon.

"You play?" said Mrs. Dalloway to Mrs. Ambrose, taking up the score of *Tristan* which lay on the table.

"My niece does," said Helen, laying her hand on Rachel's shoulder.

"Oh, how I envy you!" Clarissa addressed Rachel for the first time. "D'you remember this? Isn't it divine?" She played a bar or two with ringed fingers upon the page.

"And then Tristan goes like this, and Isolde! Have you been to Bayreuth?"[8]

"No, I haven't," said Rachel.

"Then that's still to come. I shall never forget my first *Parsifal*[9]—a grilling August day, and those fat old German women, come in their stuffy high frocks, and then the dark theatre, and the music beginning, and one couldn't help sobbing. A kind man went and fetched me water, I remember; and I could only cry on his shoulder! It caught me here" (she touched her throat). "It's like nothing else in the world! But where's your piano?"

"It's in another room," Rachel explained.

"But you will play to us?" Clarissa entreated. "I can't imagine anything nicer than to sit out in the moonlight and listen to music—only that sounds too like a schoolgirl! You know," she said, turning to Helen a little mysteriously, "I don't think music's altogether good for people—I'm afraid not."

"Too great a strain?" asked Helen.

"Too emotional," said Clarissa. "One notices it at once when a boy or girl takes up music as a profession. Sir William Broadley told me just the same thing. Don't you hate the kind of attitudes people go into over Wagner—like this—" She cast her eyes to the ceiling, clasped her hands, and assumed a look of intensity. "It really doesn't mean that they appreciate him; in fact, I always think it's the other way round. The people who really care about an art are always the least affected. D'you know Henry Philips, the painter?" she asked.

"I have seen him," said Helen.

"To look at, one might think he was a successful stockbroker, and not one of the greatest painters of the age. That's what I like."

"There are a great many successful stockbrokers, if you like looking at them," said Helen.

Rachel wished vehemently that her aunt would not be so perverse.

"When you see a musician with long hair, don't you know instinctively that he's bad?" Clarissa asked, turning to Rachel. "Watts and Joachim[10]—they looked just like you and me."

"And how much nicer they'd have looked with curls!" said Helen. "The question is, are you going to aim at beauty or are you not?"

"Cleanliness!" said Clarissa, "I do want a man to look clean!"

"By cleanliness you mean well-cut clothes," said Helen.

"There's something one knows a gentleman by," said Clarissa, "but one can't say what it is."

"Take my husband now, does he look like a gentleman?"

The question seemed to Clarissa in extraordinarily bad taste. "One of the things that can't be said," she would have put it. She could find no answer, but a laugh.

"Well, anyhow," she said, turning to Rachel, "I shall insist upon your playing to me to-morrow."

There was that in her manner that made Rachel love her.

Mrs. Dalloway hid a tiny yawn, a mere dilation of the nostrils.

"D'you know," she said, "I'm extraordinarily sleepy. It's the sea air. I think I shall escape."

A man's voice, which she took to be that of Mr. Pepper, strident in discussion, and advancing upon the saloon, gave her the alarm.

"Good-night—good-night!" she said. "Oh, I know my way—do pray for calm! Good-night!"

Her yawn must have been the image of a yawn. Instead of letting her mouth droop, dropping all her clothes in a bunch as though they depended on one string, and stretching her limbs to the utmost end of her berth, she merely changed her dress for a dressing-gown, with innumerable frills, and wrapping her feet in a rug, sat down with a writing-pad on her knee. Already this cramped little cabin was the dressing-room of a lady of quality. There were bottles containing liquids; there were trays, boxes, brushes, pins. Evidently not an inch of her person lacked its proper instrument. The scent which had intoxicated Rachel pervaded the air. Thus established, Mrs. Dalloway began to write. A pen in her hands became a thing one caressed paper with, and she might have been stroking and tickling a kitten as she wrote:

Picture us, my dear, afloat in the very oddest ship you can imagine. It's not the ship, so much as the people. One does come across queer sorts as one travels. I must say I find it hugely amusing. There's the manager of the line—called Vinrace—a nice big Englishman, doesn't say much—you know the sort. As for the rest—they might have come trailing out of an old number of *Punch*. They're like people playing croquet in the 'sixties. How long they've all been shut up in this ship I don't know—years and years I should say—but one feels as though one had boarded a little separate world, and they'd never been on shore, or done ordinary things in their lives. It's what I've always said about literary people—they're far the hardest of any to get on with. The worst of it is, these people—a man and his wife and a niece—might have been, one feels, just like everybody else, if they hadn't got swallowed up by Oxford or Cambridge or some such place, and been made cranks of. The man's really delightful (if he'd cut his nails), and the woman has quite a fine face, only she dresses, of course, in a potato sack, and wears her hair like a Liberty shopgirl's. They talk about art, and think us such poops for dressing in the evening. However, I can't help that; I'd rather die than come in to dinner without changing—wouldn't you? It matters ever so much more than the soup. (It's odd how things like that *do* matter so much more than what's generally supposed to matter. I'd rather have my head cut off than wear flannel next the skin.) Then there's a nice shy girl—poor thing—I wish one could rake her out before it's too late. She has quite nice eyes and hair, only, of course, she'll get funny too. We ought to start a society for broadening the minds of the young—much more useful than missionaries, Hester! Oh, I'd forgotten, there's a dreadful little thing called Pepper. He's just like his name. He's indescribably insignificant, and rather queer in his temper, poor dear. It's like sitting down to dinner with an ill-conditioned fox-terrier, only one can't comb him out, and sprinkle him with powder, as one would one's dog. It's a pity, sometimes, one can't treat people like dogs! The great comfort is that we're away from newspapers, so that Richard will have a real holiday this time. Spain wasn't a holiday . . .

"You coward!" said Richard, almost filling the room with his sturdy figure.

"I did my duty at dinner!" cried Clarissa.

"You've let yourself in for the Greek alphabet, anyhow."

"Oh, my dear! Who *is* Ambrose?"

"I gather that he was a Cambridge don; lives in London now, and edits classics."

"Did you ever see such a set of cranks? The woman asked me if I thought her husband looked like a gentleman!"

"It was hard to keep the ball rolling at dinner, certainly," said Richard. "Why is it that the women, in that class, are so much queerer than the men?"

"They're not half bad-looking, really—only—they're so odd!"

They both laughed, thinking of the same things, so that there was no need to compare their impressions.

"I see I shall have quite a lot to say to Vinrace," said Richard. "He knows Sutton and all that set. He can tell me a good deal about the conditions of shipbuilding in the North."

"Oh, I'm glad. The men always *are* so much better than the women."

"One always has something to say to a man certainly," said Richard. "But I've no doubt you'll chatter away fast enough about the babies, Clarice."

"Has she got children? She doesn't look like it somehow."

"Two. A boy and girl."

A pang of envy shot through Mrs. Dalloway's heart.

"We *must* have a son, Dick," she said.

"Good Lord, what opportunities there are now for young men!" said Dalloway, for his talk had set him thinking. "I don't suppose there's been so good an opening since the days of Pitt."[11]

"And it's yours!" said Clarissa.

"To be a leader of men," Richard soliloquised. "It's a fine career. My God—what a career!"

The chest slowly curved beneath his waistcoat.

"D'you know, Dick, I can't help thinking of England," said his wife meditatively, leaning her head against his chest. "Being on this ship seems to make it so much more vivid—what it means to be English. One thinks of all we've done, and our navies, and the people in India and Africa, and how we've gone on century after century, sending out boys from little country villages—and of men like you, Dick, and it makes one feel as if one couldn't bear *not* to be English! Think of the light burning over the House, Dick! When I stood on deck just now I seemed to see it. It's what one means by London."

"It's the continuity," said Richard sententiously. A vision of English history, King following King, Prime Minister Prime Minister, and Law Law had come over him while his wife spoke. He ran his mind along the line of conservative policy, which went steadily from Lord Salisbury to Alfred, and gradually enclosed, as though it were a lasso that opened and caught things, enormous chunks of the habitable globe.

"It's taken a long time, but we've pretty nearly done it," he said; "it remains to consolidate."

"And these people don't see it!" Clarissa exclaimed.

"It takes all sorts to make a world," said her husband. "There would never be a government if there weren't an opposition."

"Dick, you're better than I am," said Clarissa. "You see round, where I only see *there*." She pressed a point on the back of his hand.

"That's my business, as I tried to explain at dinner."

"What I like about you, Dick," she continued, "is that you're always the same, and I'm a creature of moods."

"You're a pretty creature, anyhow," he said, gazing at her with deeper eyes.

"You think so, do you? Then kiss me."

He kissed her passionately, so that her half-written letter slid to the ground. Picking it up, he read it without asking leave.

"Where's your pen?" he said; and added in his little masculine hand:

R. D. *loquitur:* Clarice has omitted to tell you that she looked exceedingly pretty at dinner, and made a conquest by which she has bound herself to learn the Greek alphabet. I will take this occasion of adding that we are both enjoying ourselves in these outlandish parts, and only wish for the presence of our friends (yourself and John, to wit) to make the trip perfectly enjoyable as it promises to be instructive....

Voices were heard at the end of the corridor. Mrs. Ambrose was speaking low; William Pepper was remarking in his definite and rather acid voice, "That is the type of lady with whom I find myself distinctly out of sympathy. She——"

But neither Richard nor Clarissa profited by the verdict, for directly it seemed likely that they would overhear, Richard crackled a sheet of paper.

"I often wonder," Clarissa mused in bed, over the little white volume of Pascal[12] which went with her everywhere, "whether it is really good for a woman to live with a man who is morally her superior, as Richard is mine. It makes one so dependent. I suppose I feel for him what my mother and women of her generation felt for Christ. It just shows that one can't do without *something*." She then fell into a sleep, which was as usual extremely sound and refreshing; but, visited by fantastic dreams of great Greek letters stalking round the room, she woke up and laughed to herself, remembering where she was and that the Greek letters were real people, lying asleep not many yards away. Then, thinking of the black sea outside tossing beneath the moon, she shuddered, and thought of her husband and the others as companions on the voyage. The dreams were not confined to her indeed, but went from one brain to another. They all dreamt of each other that night, as was natural, considering how thin the partitions were between them, and how strangely they had been lifted off the earth to sit next each other in mid-ocean, and see every detail of each other's faces, and hear whatever chance prompted them to say.

CHAPTER IV

Next morning Clarissa was up before any one else. She dressed, and was out on deck, breathing the fresh air of a calm morning, and, making the circuit of the ship for the second time, ran straight into the lean person of Mr. Grice, the steward. She apologised, and at the same time asked him to enlighten her: what were those shiny brass stands for, half glass on the top? She had been wondering, and could not guess. When he had done explaining, she cried enthusiastically:

"I do think that to be a sailor must be the finest thing in the world!"

"And what d'you know about it?" said Mr. Grice, kindling in a strange manner. "Pardon me. What does any man or woman brought up in England know about the sea? They profess to know; but they don't."

The bitterness with which he spoke was ominous of what was to come. He led her off to his own quarters, and, sitting on the edge of a brass-bound table, looking uncommonly like a sea-gull, with her white tapering body and thin alert face, Mrs. Dalloway had to listen to the tirade of a fanatical man. Did she realise, to begin with, what a very small part of the world the land was? How peaceful, how beautiful, how benignant in comparison with the sea? The deep waters could sustain Europe unaided if every earthly animal died of the plague tomorrow. Mr. Grice recalled dreadful sights which he had seen in the richest city of the world—men and women standing in line hour after hour to receive a mug of greasy soup. "And I thought of the good flesh down here waiting and asking to be caught. I'm not exactly a Protestant, and I'm not a Catholic, but I could almost pray for the days of popery to come again—because of the fasts."

As he talked he kept opening drawers and moving little glass jars. Here were the treasures which the great ocean had bestowed upon him—pale fish in greenish liquids, blobs of jelly with streaming tresses, fish with lights in their heads, they lived so deep.

"They have swum about among bones," Clarissa sighed.

"You're thinking of Shakespeare," said Mr. Grice, and taking down a copy from a shelf well lined with books, recited in an emphatic nasal voice:

Full fathom five thy father lies,[1]

"A grand fellow, Shakespeare," he said, replacing the volume.

Clarissa was so glad to hear him say so.

"Which is your favourite play? I wonder if it's the same as mine?"

"Henry the Fifth," said Mr. Grice.

"Joy!" cried Clarissa. "It is!"

Hamlet was what you might call too introspective for Mr. Grice, the sonnets too passionate; Henry the Fifth was to him the model of an English gentleman. But his favourite reading was Huxley, Herbert Spencer, and Henry George; while Emerson and Thomas Hardy[2] he read for relaxation. He was giving Mrs. Dalloway his views upon the present state of England when the breakfast bell rung so imperiously that she had to tear herself away, promising to come back and be shown his sea-weeds.

The party, which had seemed so odd to her the night before, was already gathered round the table, still under the influence of sleep, and therefore uncommunicative, but her entrance sent a little flutter like a breath of air through them all.

"I've had the most interesting talk of my life!" she exclaimed, taking her seat beside Willoughby. "D'you realise that one of your men is a philosopher and a poet?"

"A very interesting fellow—that's what I always say," said Willoughby, distinguishing Mr. Grice. "Though Rachel finds him a bore."

"He's a bore when he talks about currents," said Rachel. Her eyes were full of sleep, but Mrs. Dalloway still seemed to her wonderful.

"I've never met a bore yet!" said Clarissa.

"And I should say the world was full of them!" exclaimed Helen. But her beauty, which was radiant in the morning light, took the contrariness from her words.

"I agree that it's the worst one can possibly say of any one," said Clarissa. "How much rather one would be a murderer than a bore!" she added, with her usual air of saying something profound. "One can fancy liking a murderer. It's the same with dogs. Some dogs are awful bores, poor dears."

It happened that Richard was sitting next to Rachel. She was curiously conscious of his presence and appearance—his well-cut clothes, his crackling shirt-front, his cuffs with blue rings round them, and the square-tipped, very clean fingers, with the red stone on the little finger of the left hand.

"We had a dog who was a bore and knew it," he said, addressing her in cool, easy tones. "He was a Skye terrier, one of those long chaps, with little feet poking out from their hair like—like caterpillars—no, like sofas I should say. Well, we had another dog at the same time, a black brisk animal—a Schipperke, I think, you call them. You can't imagine a greater contrast. The Skye so slow and deliberate, looking up at you like some old gentleman in the club, as much as to say, 'You don't really mean it, do you?' and the Schipperke as quick as a knife. I liked the Skye best, I must confess. There was something pathetic about him."

The story seemed to have no climax.

"What happened to him?" Rachel asked.

"That's a very sad story," said Richard, lowering his voice and peeling an apple. "He followed my wife in the car one day and got run over by a brute of a cyclist."

"Was he killed?" asked Rachel.

But Clarissa at her end of the table had overheard.

"Don't talk of it!" she cried. "It's a thing I can't bear to think of to this day."

Surely the tears stood in her eyes?

"That's the painful thing about pets," said Mr. Dalloway; "they die. The first sorrow I can remember was for the death of a dormouse. I regret to say that I sat upon it. Still, that didn't make one any the less sorry. Here lies the duck that Samuel Johnson[3] sat on, eh? I was big for my age."

"Then we had canaries," he continued, "a pair of ringdoves, a lemur, and at one time a martin."

"Did you live in the country?" Rachel asked him.

"We lived in the country for six months of the year. When I say 'we' I mean four sisters, a brother, and myself. There's nothing like coming of a large family. Sisters particularly are delightful."

"Dick, you were horribly spoilt!" cried Clarissa across the table.

"No, no. Appreciated," said Richard.

Rachel had other questions on the tip of her tongue; or rather one enormous question, which she did not in the least know how to put into words. The talk appeared too airy to admit of it.

"Please tell me—everything." That was what she wanted to say. He had drawn apart one little chink and showed astonishing treasures. It seemed to her incredible that a man like that should be willing to talk to her. He had sisters and pets, and once lived in the country. She stirred her tea round and round; the bubbles which swam and clustered in the cup seemed to her like the union of their minds.

The talk meanwhile raced past her, and when Richard suddenly started in a jocular tone of voice, "I'm sure Miss Vinrace, now, has secret leanings toward Catholicism," she had no idea what to answer, and Helen could not help laughing at the start she gave.

However, breakfast was over and Mrs. Dalloway was rising. "I always think religion's like collecting beetles," she said, summing up the discussion as she went up the stairs with Helen. "One person has a passion for black beetles; another hasn't; it's no good arguing about it. What's *your* black beetle now?"

"I suppose it's my children," said Helen.

"Ah—that's different," Clarissa breathed. "Do tell me. You have a boy, haven't you? Isn't it detestable, leaving them?"

It was as though a blue shadow had fallen across a pool. Their eyes became deeper, and their voices more cordial.

Instead of joining them as they began to pace the deck, Rachel was indignant with the prosperous matrons, who made her feel outside their world and motherless, and turning back, she left them abruptly. She slammed the door of her room, and pulled out her music. It was all old music—Bach and Beethoven, Mozart and Purcell—the pages yellow, the engraving rough to the finger. In three minutes she was deep in a very difficult, very classical fugue in A, and over her face came a queer remote impersonal expression of complete absorption and anxious satisfaction. Now she stumbled; now she faltered and had to play the same bar twice over; but an invisible line seemed to string the notes together, from which rose a shape, a building. She was so far absorbed in this work, for it was really difficult to find how all these sounds should stand together, and drew upon the whole of her faculties, that she never heard a knock at the door. It was burst impulsively open, and Mrs. Dalloway stood in the room, leaving the door open, so that a strip of the white deck and of the blue sea appeared through the opening. The shape of the Bach fugue crashed to the ground.

"Don't let me interrupt," Clarissa implored. "I heard you playing, and I couldn't resist. I adore Bach!"

Rachel flushed and fumbled her fingers in her lap. She stood up awkwardly.

"It's too difficult," she said.

"But you were playing quite splendidly! I ought to have stayed outside."

"No," said Rachel.

She slid *Cowper's Letters* and *Wuthering Heights*[4] out of the arm-chair, so that Clarissa was invited to sit there.

"What a dear little room!" she said, looking round. "Oh, *Cowper's Letters*! I've never read them. Are they nice?"

"Rather dull," said Rachel.

"He wrote awfully well, didn't he?" said Clarissa; "—if one likes that kind of thing—finished his sentences and all that. *Wuthering Heights!* Ah—that's more in my line. I really couldn't exist without the Brontës! Don't you love them? Still, on the whole, I'd rather live without them than without Jane Austen."

Lightly and at random though she spoke, her manner conveyed an extraordinary degree of sympathy and desire to befriend.

"Jane Austen? I don't like Jane Austen," said Rachel.

"You monster!" Clarissa exclaimed. "I can only just forgive you. Tell me why?"

"She's so—so—well, so like a tight plait," Rachel floundered.

"Ah—I see what you mean. But I don't agree. And you won't when you're older. At your age I only liked Shelley. I can remember sobbing over him in the garden.

> He has outsoared the shadow of our night,
> Envy and calumny and hate and pain—

you remember?

> Can touch him not and torture not again
> From the contagion of the world's slow stain.[5]

How divine!—and yet what nonsense!" She looked lightly round the room. "I always think it's *living*, not dying, that counts. I really respect some snuffy old stockbroker who's gone on adding up column after column all his days, and trotting back to his villa at Brixton with some old pug dog he worships, and a dreary little wife sitting at the end of the table, and going off to Margate for a fortnight—I assure you I know heaps like that—well, they seem to me *really* nobler than poets whom every one worships, just because they're geniuses and die young. But I don't expect *you* to agree with me!"

She pressed Rachel's shoulder.

"Um-m-m—" she went on quoting—

Unrest which men miscall delight—

"when you're my age you'll see that the world is *crammed* with delightful things. I think young people make such a mistake about that—not letting themselves be happy. I sometimes think that happiness is the only thing that counts. I don't know you well enough to say, but I should guess you might be a little inclined to—when one's young and attractive—I'm going to say it!—*every*thing's at one's feet." She glanced round as much as to say, "not only a few stuffy books and Bach."

"I long to ask questions," she continued. "You interest me so much. If I'm impertinent, you must just box my ears."

"And I—I want to ask questions," said Rachel with such earnestness that Mrs. Dalloway had to check her smile.

"D'you mind if we walk?" she said. "The air's so delicious."

She snuffed it like a racehorse as they shut the door and stood on deck.

"Isn't it good to be alive?" she exclaimed, and drew Rachel's arm within hers.

"Look, look! How exquisite!"

The shores of Portugal were beginning to lose their substance; but the land was still the land, though at a great distance. They could distinguish the little towns that were sprinkled in the folds of the hills, and the smoke rising faintly. The towns appeared to be very small in comparison with the great purple mountains behind them.

"Honestly, though," said Clarissa, having looked, "I don't like views. They're too inhuman." They walked on.

"How odd it is!" she continued impulsively. "This time yesterday we'd never met. I was packing in a stuffy little room in the hotel. We know absolutely nothing about each other—and yet—I feel as if I *did* know you!"

"You have children—your husband was in Parliament?"

"You've never been to school, and you live——?"

"With my aunts at Richmond."

"Richmond?"

"You see, my aunts like the Park."

"And you don't! I understand!" Clarissa laughed.

"I like walking in the Park alone; but not—with the dogs," she finished.

"No; and some people *are* dogs; aren't they?" said Clarissa, as if she had guessed a secret. "But not every one—oh no, not every one."

"Not every one," said Rachel, and stopped.

"I can quite imagine you walking alone," said Clarissa; "and thinking—in a little world of your own. But how you will enjoy it—some day!"

"I shall enjoy walking with a man—is that what you mean?" said Rachel, regarding Mrs. Dalloway with her large enquiring eyes.

"I wasn't thinking of a man particularly," said Clarissa. "But you will."

"No. I shall never marry," Rachel determined.

"I shouldn't be so sure of that," said Clarissa. Her sidelong glance told Rachel that she found her attractive although she was inexplicably amused.

"Why do people marry?" Rachel asked.

"That's what you're going to find out," Clarissa laughed.

Rachel followed her eyes and found that they rested, for a second, on the robust figure of Richard Dalloway, who was engaged in striking a match on the sole of his boot; while Willoughby expounded something, which seemed to be of great interest to them both.

"There's nothing like it," she concluded. "Do tell me about the Ambroses. Or am I asking too many questions?"

"I find you easy to talk to," said Rachel.

The short sketch of the Ambroses was, however, somewhat perfunctory, and contained little but the fact that Mr. Ambrose was her uncle.

"Your mother's brother?"

When a name has dropped out of use, the lightest touch upon it tells. Mrs. Dalloway went on:

"Are you like your mother?"

"No; she was different," said Rachel.

She was overcome by an intense desire to tell Mrs. Dalloway things she had never told any one—things she had not realised herself until this moment.

"I am lonely," she began. "I want—" She did not know what she wanted, so that she could not finish the sentence; but her lip quivered.

But it seemed that Mrs. Dalloway was able to understand without words.

"I know," she said, actually putting one arm round Rachel's shoulder. "When I was your age I wanted too. No one understood until I met Richard. He gave me all I wanted. He's man and woman as well." Her eyes rested upon Mr. Dalloway, leaning upon the rail, still talking. "Don't think I say that because I'm his wife—I see his faults more clearly than I see any one else's. What one wants in the person one lives with is that they should keep one at one's best. I often wonder what I've done to be so happy!" she exclaimed, and a tear slid down her cheek. She wiped it away, squeezed Rachel's hand, and exclaimed:

"How good life is!" At that moment, standing out in the fresh breeze, with the sun upon the waves, and Mrs. Dalloway's hand upon her arm, it seemed indeed as if life which had been unnamed before was infinitely wonderful, and too good to be true.

Here Helen passed them, and seeing Rachel arm-in-arm with a comparative stranger, looking excited, was amused, but at the same time slightly irritated. But they were immediately joined by Richard, who had enjoyed a very interesting talk with Willoughby and was in a sociable mood.

"Observe my Panama," he said, touching the brim of his hat.

"Are you aware, Miss Vinrace, how much can be done to induce fine weather by appropriate headdress? I have determined that it is a hot summer day; I warn you that nothing you can say will shake me. Therefore I am going to sit down. I advise you to follow my example." Three chairs in a row invited them to be seated.

Leaning back, Richard surveyed the waves.

"That's a very pretty blue," he said. "But there's a little too much of it. Variety is essential to a view. Thus, if you have hills you ought to have a river; if a river, hills. The best view in the world in my opinion is that from Boars Hill on a fine day—it must be a fine day, mark you—A rug?—Oh, thank you, my dear.... In that case you have also the advantage of associations—the Past."

"D'you want to talk, Dick, or shall I read aloud?"

Clarissa had fetched a book with the rugs.

"*Persuasion,*" announced Richard, examining the volume.

"That's for Miss Vinrace," said Clarissa. "She can't bear our beloved Jane."

"That—if I may say so—is because you have not read her," said Richard. "She is incomparably the greatest female writer we possess."

"She is the greatest," he continued, "and for this reason: she does not attempt to write like a man. Every other woman does; on that account, I don't read 'em."

"Produce your instances, Miss Vinrace," he went on, joining his finger-tips. "I'm ready to be converted."

He waited, while Rachel vainly tried to vindicate her sex from the slight he put upon it.

"I'm afraid he's right," said Clarissa. "He generally is—the wretch!"

"I brought *Persuasion,*" she went on, "because I thought it was a little less threadbare than the others—though, Dick, it's no good *your* pretending to know Jane by heart, considering that she always sends you to sleep!"

"After the labours of legislation, I deserve sleep," said Richard.

"You're not to think about those guns," said Clarissa, seeing that his eye, passing over the waves, still sought the land meditatively, "or about navies, or empires, or anything." So saying she opened the book and began to read:

" 'Sir Walter Elliott, of Kellynch Hall, in Somersetshire, was a man who, for his own amusement, never took up any book but the *Baronetage*'—don't you know Sir Walter?—'There he found occupation for an idle hour, and consolation in a distressed one.' She does write well, doesn't she? 'There—' " She read on in a light humorous voice. She was determined that Sir Walter should take her husband's mind off the guns of Britain, and divert him in an exquisite, quaint, sprightly, and slightly ridiculous world. After a time it appeared that the sun was sinking in that world, and the points becoming softer. Rachel looked up to see what caused the change. Richard's eyelids were closing and opening; opening and closing. A loud nasal breath announced that he no longer considered appearances, that he was sound asleep.

"Triumph!" Clarissa whispered at the end of a sentence. Suddenly she raised her hand in protest. A sailor hesitated; she gave the book to Rachel, and stepped lightly to take the message— "Mr. Grice wished to know if it was convenient," etc. She followed him. Ridley, who had prowled unheeded, started forward, stopped, and, with a gesture of disgust, strode off to his study. The sleeping politician was left in Rachel's charge. She read a sentence, and took a look at him. In sleep he looked like a coat hanging at the end of a bed; there were all the wrinkles, and the sleeves and trousers kept their shape though no longer filled out by legs and arms. You can then best judge the age and state of the coat. She looked him all over until it seemed to her that he must protest.

He was a man of forty perhaps; and here there were lines round his eyes, and there curious clefts in his cheeks. Slightly battered he appeared, but dogged and in the prime of life.

"Sisters and a dormouse and some canaries," Rachel murmured, never taking her eyes off him. "I wonder, I wonder." She ceased, her chin upon her hand, still looking at him. A bell chimed behind them, and Richard raised his head. Then he opened his eyes which wore for a second the queer look of a short-sighted person's whose spectacles are lost. It took him a moment to recover from the impropriety of having snored, and possibly grunted, before a young lady. To wake and find oneself left alone with one was also slightly disconcerting.

"I suppose I've been dozing," he said. "What's happened to every one? Clarissa?"

"Mrs. Dalloway has gone to look at Mr. Grice's fish," Rachel replied.

"I might have guessed," said Richard. "It's a common occurrence. And how have you improved the shining hour? Have you become a convert?"

"I don't think I've read a line," said Rachel.

"That's what I always find. There are too many things to look at. I find nature very stimulating myself. My best ideas have come to me out of doors."

"When you were walking?"

"Walking—riding—yachting—I suppose the most momentous conversations of my life took place while perambulating the great court at Trinity. I was at both universities. It was a fad of my father's. He thought it broadening to the mind. I think I agree with him. I can remember—what an age ago it seems!—settling the basis of a future state with the present Secretary for India. We thought ourselves very wise. I'm not sure we weren't. We were happy, Miss Vinrace, and we were young—gifts which make for wisdom."

"Have you done what you said you'd do?" she asked.

"A searching question! I answer—Yes and No. If on the one hand I have not accomplished what I set out to accomplish—which of us does?—on the other I can fairly say this: I have not lowered my ideal."

He looked resolutely at a sea-gull, as though his ideal flew on the wings of the bird.

"But," said Rachel, "what *is* your ideal?"

"There you ask too much, Miss Vinrace," said Richard playfully.

She could only say that she wanted to know, and Richard was sufficiently amused to answer.

"Well, how shall I reply? In one word—Unity. Unity of aim, of dominion, of progress. The dispersion of the best ideas over the greatest area."

"The English?"

"I grant that the English seem, on the whole, whiter than most men, their records cleaner. But, good Lord, don't run away with the idea that I don't see the drawbacks—horrors—unmentionable things done in our very midst! I'm under no illusions. Few people, I suppose, have fewer illusions than I have. Have you ever been in a factory, Miss Vinrace?—No, I suppose not—I may say I hope not."

As for Rachel, she had scarcely walked through a poor street, and always under the escort of father, maid, or aunts.

"I was going to say that if you'd ever seen the kind of thing that's going on round you, you'd understand what it is that makes me and men like me politicians. You asked me a moment ago whether I'd done what I set out to do. Well, when I consider my life, there is one fact I admit that I'm proud of; owing to me some thousands of girls in Lancashire—and many thousands to come after them—can spend an hour every day in the open air which their mothers had to spend over their looms. I'm prouder of that, I own, than I should be of writing Keats and Shelley into the bargain!"

It became painful to Rachel to be one of those who write Keats and Shelley into the bargain. She liked Richard Dalloway, and warmed as he warmed. He seemed to mean what he said.

"I know nothing!" she exclaimed.

"It's far better that you should know nothing," he said paternally, "and you wrong yourself, I'm sure. You play very nicely, I'm told, and I've no doubt you've read heaps of learned books."

Elderly banter would no longer check her.

"You talk of unity," she said. "You ought to make me understand."

"I never allow my wife to talk politics," he said seriously. "For this reason. It is impossible for human beings, constituted as they are, both to fight and to have ideals. If I have preserved mine, as I am thankful to say that in great measure I have, it is due to the fact that I have been able to come home to my wife in the evening and to find that she has spent her day in calling, music, play with the children, domestic duties—what you will; her illusions have not been destroyed. She gives me courage to go on. The strain of public life is very great," he added.

This made him appear a battered martyr, parting every day with some of the finest gold, in the service of mankind.

"I can't think," Rachel exclaimed, "how any one does it!"

"Explain, Miss Vinrace," said Richard. "This is a matter I want to clear up."

His kindness was genuine, and she determined to take the chance he gave her, although to talk to a man of such worth and authority made her heart beat.

"It seems to me like this," she began, doing her best first to recollect and then to expose her shivering private visions.

"There's an old widow in her room, somewhere, let us suppose in the suburbs of Leeds."

Richard bent his head to show that he accepted the widow.

"In London you're spending your life, talking, writing things, getting bills through, missing what seems natural. The result of it all is that she goes to her cupboard and finds a little more tea, a few lumps of sugar, or a little less tea and a newspaper. Widows all over the country I admit do this. Still, there's the mind of the widow— the affections; those you leave untouched. But you waste your own."

"If the widow goes to her cupboard and finds it bare," Richard answered, "her spiritual outlook we may admit will be affected. If I may pick holes in your philosophy, Miss Vinrace, which has its merits, I would point out that a human being is not a set of compartments, but an organism. Imagination, Miss Vinrace; use your imagination; that's where you young Liberals fail. Conceive the world as a whole. Now for your second point; when you assert that in trying to set the house in order for the benefit of the young generation I am wasting my higher capabilities, I totally disagree with you. I can conceive no more exalted aim—to be the citizen of the Empire. Look at it in this way, Miss Vinrace; conceive the state as a complicated machine; we citizens are parts of that machine; some fulfil more important duties; others (perhaps I am one of them) serve only to connect some obscure parts of the mechanism, concealed from the public eye. Yet if the meanest screw fails in its task, the proper working of the whole is imperilled."

It was impossible to combine the image of a lean black widow, gazing out of her window, and longing for some one to talk to, with the image of a vast machine, such as one sees at South Kensington, thumping, thumping, thumping. The attempt at communication had been a failure.

"We don't seem to understand each other," she said.

"Shall I say something that will make you very angry?" he replied.

"It won't," said Rachel.

"Well, then; no woman has what I may call the political instinct. You have very great virtues; I am the first, I hope, to admit that; but I have never met a woman who even saw what is meant by statesmanship. I am going to make you still more angry. I hope that I never shall meet such a woman. Now, Miss Vinrace, are we enemies for life?"

Vanity, irritation, and a thrusting desire to be understood, urged her to make another attempt.

"Under the streets, in the sewers, in the wires, in the telephones, there is something alive; is that what you mean? In things like dust-carts, and men mending roads? You feel that all the time when you walk about London, and when you turn on a tap and the water comes?"

"Certainly," said Richard. "I understand you to mean that the whole of modern society is based upon cooperative effort. If only more people would realise that, Miss Vinrace, there would be fewer of your old widows in solitary lodgings!"

Rachel considered.

"Are you a Liberal or are you a Conservative?" she asked.

"I call myself a Conservative for convenience sake," said Richard, smiling. "But there is more in common between the two parties than people generally allow."

There was a pause, which did not come on Rachel's side from

any lack of things to say; as usual she could not say them, and was further confused by the fact that the time for talking probably ran short. She was haunted by absurd jumbled ideas—how, if one went back far enough, everything perhaps was intelligible; everything was in common; for the mammoths who pastured in the fields of Richmond High Street had turned into paving stones and boxes full of ribbon, and her aunts.

"Did you say you lived in the country when you were a child?" she asked.

Crude as her manners seemed to him, Richard was flattered. There could be no doubt that her interest was genuine.

"I did," he smiled.

"And what happened?" she asked. "Or do I ask too many questions?"

"I'm flattered, I assure you. But—let me see—what happened? Well, riding, lessons, sisters. There was an enchanted rubbish heap, I remember, where all kinds of queer things happened. Odd, what things impress children! I can remember the look of the place to this day. It's a fallacy to think that children are happy. They're not; they're unhappy. I've never suffered so much as I did when I was a child."

"Why?" she asked.

"I didn't get on well with my father," said Richard shortly. "He was a very able man, but hard. Well—it makes one determined not to sin in that way oneself. Children never forget injustice. They forgive heaps of things grown-up people mind; but that sin is the unpardonable sin. Mind you—I daresay I was a difficult child to manage; but when I think what I was ready to give! No, I was more sinned against than sinning. And then I went to school, where I did very fairly well; and then, as I say, my father sent me to both universities.... D'you know, Miss Vinrace, you've made me think? How little, after all, one can tell anybody about one's life! Here I sit; there you sit; both, I doubt not, chock-full of the most interesting experiences, ideas, emotions; yet how communicate? I've told you what every second person you meet might tell you."

"I don't think so," she said. "It's the way of saying things, isn't it, not the things?"

"True," said Richard. "Perfectly true." He paused. "When I look back over my life—I'm forty-two—what are the great facts that stand out? What were the revelations, if I may call them so? The misery of the poor and—(he hesitated and pitched over) 'love'!"

Upon that word he lowered his voice; it was a word that seemed to unveil the skies for Rachel.

"It's an odd thing to say to a young lady," he continued. "But have you any idea what—what I mean by that? No; of course not. I don't use the word in a conventional sense. I use it as young men use it. Girls are kept very ignorant, aren't they. Perhaps it's wise— perhaps—You *don't* know?"

He spoke as if he had lost consciousness of what he was saying.

"No; I don't," she said, scarcely speaking above her breath.

"Warships, Dick! Over there! Look!"

Clarissa, released from Mr. Grice, appreciative of all his sea- weeds, skimmed towards them, gesticulating.

She had sighted two sinister grey vessels, low in the water, and bald as bone, one closely following the other with the look of eye- less beasts seeking their prey. Consciousness returned to Richard instantly.

"By George!" he exclaimed, and stood shielding his eyes.

"Ours, Dick?" said Clarissa.

"The Mediterranean Fleet," he answered.

The *Euphrosyne* was slowly dipping her flag. Richard raised his hat. Convulsively Clarissa squeezed Rachel's hand.

"Aren't you glad to be English!" she said.

The warships drew past, casting a curious effect of discipline and sadness upon the waters, and it was not until they were again invisible that people spoke to each other naturally. At lunch the talk was all of valour and death, and the magnificent qualities of British admirals. Clarissa quoted one poet, Willoughby quoted another. Life on board a man-of-war was splendid, so they agreed, and sailors, whenever one met them, were more than usually admirable.

This being so, no one liked it when Helen remarked that it

seemed to her as wrong to keep sailors as to keep a Zoo, and that as for dying on a battle-field, surely it was time we ceased to praise courage—"or to write bad poetry about it," snarled Pepper.

But Helen was really wondering why Rachel, sitting silent, looked so queer and flushed.

CHAPTER V

She was not able to follow up her observations, however, or to come to any conclusion, for by one of those accidents which are liable to happen at sea, the whole course of their lives was now put out of order.

Even at tea the floor rose beneath their feet and pitched too low again, and at dinner the ship seemed to groan and strain as though a lash were descending. She who had been a broad-backed dray-horse, upon whose hind-quarters pierrots might waltz, became a colt in a field. The plates slanted away from the knives, and Mrs. Dalloway's face blanched for a second as she helped herself and saw the potatoes roll this way and that. Willoughby, of course, extolled the virtues of his ship, and quoted what had been said of her by experts and distinguished passengers, for he loved his own possessions. Still, dinner was uneasy, and directly the ladies were alone Clarissa owned that she would be better off in bed, and went, smiling bravely.

Next morning the storm was on them, and no politeness could ignore it. Mrs. Dalloway stayed in her room. Richard faced three meals, eating valiantly at each; but at the third, certain glazed asparagus swimming in oil finally conquered him.

"That beats me," he said, and withdrew.

"Now we are alone once more," remarked William Pepper, looking round the table; but no one was ready to engage him in talk, and the meal ended in silence.

On the following day they met—but as flying leaves meet in the air. Sick they were not; but the wind propelled them hastily into rooms, violently downstairs. They passed each other gasping on deck; they shouted across tables. They wore fur coats; and Helen was never seen without a bandanna on her head. For comfort they retreated to their cabins, where with tightly wedged feet they let the ship bounce and tumble. Their sensations were the sensations of potatoes in a sack on a galloping horse. The world outside was merely a violent grey tumult. For two days they had a perfect rest from their old emotions. Rachel had just enough consciousness to suppose herself a donkey on the summit of a moor in a hailstorm, with its coat blown into furrows; then she became a wizened tree, perpetually driven back by the salt Atlantic gale.

Helen, on the other hand, staggered to Mrs. Dalloway's door, knocked, could not be heard for the slamming of doors and the battering of wind, and entered.

There were basins, of course. Mrs. Dalloway lay half-raised on a pillow, and did not open her eyes. Then she murmured, "Oh, Dick, is that you?"

Helen shouted—for she was thrown against the wash stand—"How are you?"

Clarissa opened one eye. It gave her an incredibly dissipated appearance. "Awful!" she gasped. Her lips were white inside.

Planting her feet wide, Helen contrived to pour champagne into a tumbler with a tooth-brush in it.

"Champagne," she said.

"There's a tooth-brush in it," murmured Clarissa and smiled; it might have been the contortion of one weeping. She drank.

"Disgusting," she whispered, indicating the basins. Relics of humour still played over her face like moonshine.

"Want more?" Helen shouted. Speech was again beyond Clarissa's reach. The wind laid the ship shivering on her side. Pale agonies crossed Mrs. Dalloway in waves. When the curtains flapped, grey lights puffed across her. Between the spasms of the storm, Helen made the curtain fast, shook the pillows, stretched the bed-clothes, and smoothed the hot nostrils and forehead with cold scent.

"You *are* good!" Clarissa gasped. "Horrid mess!"

She was trying to apologise for white underclothes fallen and scattered on the floor. For one second she opened a single eye, and saw that the room was tidy. "That's nice," she gasped.

Helen left her; far, far away she knew that she felt a kind of lik-ing for Mrs. Dalloway. She could not help respecting her spirit and her desire, even in the throes of sickness, for a tidy bedroom. Her petticoats, however, rose above her knees.

Quite suddenly the storm relaxed its grasp. It happened at tea; the expected paroxysm of the blast gave out just as it reached its climax and dwindled away, and the ship instead of taking the usual plunge went steadily. The monotonous order of plunging and ris-ing, roaring and relaxing, was interfered with, and every one at table looked up and felt something loosen within them. The strain was slackened and human feelings began to peep again, as they do when daylight shows at the end of a tunnel.

"Try a turn with me," Ridley called across to Rachel.

"Foolish!" cried Helen, but they went stumbling up the ladder. Choked by the wind their spirits rose with a rush, for on the skirts of all the grey tumult was a misty spot of gold. Instantly the world dropped into shape; they were no longer atoms flying in the void, but people riding a triumphant ship on the back of the sea. Wind and space were banished; the world floated like an apple in a tub, and the mind of men, which had been unmoored also, once more attached itself to the old beliefs.

Having scrambled twice round the ship and received many sound cuffs from the wind, they saw a sailor's face positively shine golden. They looked, and beheld a complete yellow circle of sun; next minute it was traversed by sailing strands of cloud, and then completely hidden. By breakfast the next morning, however, the sky was swept clean, the waves, although steep, were blue, and after their view of the strange under-world, inhabited by phantoms, people began to live among tea-pots and loaves of bread with greater zest than ever.

Richard and Clarissa, however, still remained on the borderland. She did not attempt to sit up; her husband stood on his feet, contemplated his waistcoat and trousers, shook his head, and then lay down again. The inside of his brain was still rising and falling like the sea on the stage. At four o'clock he woke from sleep and saw the sunlight make a vivid angle across the red plush curtains and the grey tweed trousers. The ordinary world outside slid into his mind, and by the time he was dressed he was an English gentleman again.

He stood beside his wife. She pulled him down to her by the lapel of his coat, kissed him, and held him fast for a minute.

"Go and get a breath of air, Dick," she said. "You look quite washed out.... How nice you smell!... And be polite to that woman. She was so kind to me."

Thereupon Mrs. Dalloway turned to the cool side of her pillow, terribly flattened but still invincible.

Richard found Helen talking to her brother-in-law, over two dishes of yellow cake and smooth bread and butter.

"You look very ill!" she exclaimed on seeing him. "Come and have some tea."

He remarked that the hands that moved about the cups were beautiful.

"I hear you've been very good to my wife," he said. "She's had an awful time of it. You came in and fed her with champagne. Were you among the saved yourself?"

"I? Oh, I haven't been sick for twenty years—sea-sick, I mean."

"There are three stages of convalescence, I always say," broke in the hearty voice of Willoughby, "The milk stage, the bread-and-butter stage, and the roast-beef stage. I should say you were at the bread-and-butter stage." He handed him the plate.

"Now, I should advise a hearty tea, then a brisk walk on deck; and by dinner-time you'll be clamouring for beef, eh?" He went off laughing, excusing himself on the score of business.

"What a splendid fellow he is!" said Richard. "Always keen on something."

"Yes," said Helen, "he's always been like that."

"This is a great undertaking of his," Richard continued. "It's a business that won't stop with ships, I should say. We shall see him in Parliament, or I'm much mistaken. He's the kind of man we want in Parliament—the man who has done things."

But Helen was not much interested in her brother-in-law.

"I expect your head's aching, isn't it?" she asked, pouring a fresh cup.

"Well, it is," said Richard. "It's humiliating to find what a slave one is to one's body in this world. D'you know, I can never work without a kettle on the hob. As often as not I don't drink tea, but I must feel that I can if I want to."

"That's very bad for you," said Helen.

"It shortens one's life; but I'm afraid, Mrs. Ambrose, we politicians must make up our minds to that at the outset. We've got to burn the candle at both ends, or——"

"You've cooked your goose!" said Helen brightly.

"We can't make you take us seriously, Mrs. Ambrose," he protested. "May I ask how you've spent your time? Reading—philosophy?" (He saw the black book.) "Metaphysics and fishing!" he exclaimed. "If I had to live again I believe I should devote myself to one or the other." He began turning the pages.

" 'Good, then, is indefinable,' " he read out. "How jolly to think that's going on still! 'So far as I know there is only one ethical writer, Professor Henry Sidgwick,[1] who has clearly recognised and stated this fact.' That's just the kind of thing we used to talk about when we were boys. I can remember arguing until five in the morning with Duffy—now Secretary for India—pacing round and round those cloisters until we decided it was too late to go to bed, and we went for a ride instead. Whether we ever came to any conclusion—that's another matter. Still, it's the arguing that counts. It's things like that that stand out in life. Nothing's been quite so vivid since. It's the philosophers, it's the scholars," he continued, "they're the people who pass the torch, who keep the light burning by which we live. Being a politician doesn't necessarily blind one to that, Mrs. Ambrose."

"No. Why should it?" said Helen. "But can you remember if your wife takes sugar?"

She lifted the tray and went off with it to Mrs. Dalloway.

Richard twisted a muffler twice round his throat and struggled up on deck. His body, which had grown white and tender in a dark room, tingled all over in the fresh air. He felt himself a man undoubtedly in the prime of life. Pride glowed in his eye as he let the wind buffet him and stood firm. With his head slightly lowered he sheered round corners, strode uphill, and met the blast. There was a collision. For a second he could not see what the body was he had run into. "Sorry." "Sorry." It was Rachel who apologised. They both laughed, too much blown about to speak. She drove open the door of her room and stepped into its calm. In order to speak to her, it was necessary that Richard should follow. They stood in a whirlpool of wind; papers began flying round in circles, the door crashed to, and they tumbled, laughing, into chairs. Richard sat upon Bach.

"My word! What a tempest!" he exclaimed.

"Fine, isn't it?" said Rachel. Certainly the struggle and wind had given her a decision she lacked; red was in her cheeks, and her hair was down.

"Oh, what fun!" he cried. "What am I sitting on? Is this your room? How jolly!"

"There—sit there," she commanded. Cowper slid once more.

"How jolly to meet again," said Richard. "It seems an age. *Cowper's Letters?*... *Bach?*... *Wuthering Heights?*... Is this where you meditate on the world, and then come out and pose poor politicians with questions? In the intervals of sea-sickness I've thought a lot of our talk. I assure you, you made me think."

"I made you think! But why?"

"What solitary icebergs we are, Miss Vinrace! How little we can communicate! There are lots of things I should like to tell you about—to hear your opinion of. Have you ever read Burke?"

"Burke?" she repeated. "Who was Burke?"

"No? Well, then, I shall make a point of sending you a copy. *The Speech on the French Revolution—The American Rebellion?*[22] Which shall it be, I wonder?" He noted something in his pocket-book. "And then you must write and tell me what you think of it. This reticence— this isolation—that's what's the matter with modern life! Now, tell me about yourself. What are your interests and occupations? I should imagine that you were a person with very strong interests. Of course you are! Good God! When I think of the age we live in, with its opportunities and possibilities, the mass of things to be done and enjoyed—why haven't we ten lives instead of one? But about yourself?"

"You see, I'm a woman," said Rachel.

"I know—I know," said Richard, throwing his head back, and drawing his fingers across his eyes.

"How strange to be a woman! A young and beautiful woman," he continued sententiously, "has the whole world at her feet. That's true, Miss Vinrace. You have an inestimable power—for good or for evil. What couldn't you do——" he broke off.

"What?" asked Rachel.

"You have beauty," he said. The ship lurched. Rachel fell slightly forward. Richard took her in his arms and kissed her. Holding her tight, he kissed her passionately, so that she felt the hardness of his body and the roughness of his cheek printed upon hers. She fell back in her chair, with tremendous beats of the heart, each of which sent black waves across her eyes. He clasped his forehead in his hands.

"You tempt me," he said. The tone of his voice was terrifying. He seemed choked in fight. They were both trembling. Rachel stood up and went. Her head was cold, her knees shaking, and the physical pain of the emotion was so great that she could only keep herself moving above the great leaps of her heart. She leant upon the rail of the ship, and gradually ceased to feel, for a chill of body and mind crept over her. Far out between the waves little black and white sea-birds were riding. Rising and falling with smooth and graceful movements in the hollows of the waves they seemed singularly detached and unconcerned.

"You're peaceful," she said. She became peaceful too, at the same time possessed with a strange exultation. Life seemed to hold infinite possibilities she had never guessed at. She leant upon the rail and looked over the troubled grey waters, where the sunlight was fitfully scattered upon the crests of the waves, until she was cold and absolutely calm again. Nevertheless something wonderful had happened.

At dinner, however, she did not feel exalted, but merely uncomfortable, as if she and Richard had seen something together which is hidden in ordinary life, so that they did not like to look at each other. Richard slid his eyes over her uneasily once, and never looked at her again. Formal platitudes were manufactured with effort, but Willoughby was kindled.

"Beef for Mr. Dalloway!" he shouted. "Come now—after that walk you're at the beef stage, Dalloway!"

Wonderful masculine stories followed about Bright and Disraeli[3] and coalition governments, wonderful stories which made the people at the dinner-table seem featureless and small. After dinner, sitting alone with Rachel under the great swinging lamp, Helen was struck by her pallor. It once more occurred to her that there was something strange in the girl's behaviour.

"You look tired. Are you tired?" she asked.

"Not tired," said Rachel. "Oh yes, I suppose I am tired."

Helen advised bed, and she went, not seeing Richard again. She must have been very tired for she fell asleep at once, but after an hour or two of dreamless sleep, she dreamt. She dreamt that she was walking down a long tunnel, which grew so narrow by degrees that she could touch the damp bricks on either side. At length the tunnel opened and became a vault; she found herself trapped in it, bricks meeting her wherever she turned, alone with a little deformed man who squatted on the floor gibbering, with long nails. His face was pitted and like the face of an animal. The wall behind him oozed with damp, which collected into drops and slid down. Still and cold as death she lay, not daring to move, until she broke the agony by tossing herself across the bed, and woke crying "Oh!"

Light showed her the familiar things: her clothes, fallen off the chair; the water jug gleaming white; but the horror did not go at once. She felt herself pursued, so that she got up and actually locked her door. A voice moaned for her; eyes desired her. All night long barbarian men harassed the ship; they came scuffling down the passages, and stopped to snuffle at her door. She could not sleep again.

CHAPTER VI

"That's the tragedy of life—as I always say!" said Mrs. Dalloway. "Beginning things and having to end them. Still, I'm not going to let *this* end, if you're willing." It was the morning, the sea was calm, and the ship once again was anchored not far from another shore.

She was dressed in her long fur cloak, with the veils wound round her head, and once more the rich boxes stood on top of each other so that the scene of a few days back seemed to be repeated.

"D'you suppose we shall ever meet in London?" said Ridley ironically. "You'll have forgotten all about me by the time you step out there."

He pointed to the shore of the little bay, where they could now see the separate trees with moving branches.

"How horrid you are!" she laughed. "Rachel's coming to see me anyhow—the instant you get back," she said, pressing Rachel's arm. "Now—you've no excuse!"

With a silver pencil she wrote her name and address on the fly-leaf of *Persuasion,* and gave the book to Rachel. Sailors were shouldering the luggage, and people were beginning to congregate. There were Captain Cobbold, Mr. Grice, Willoughby, Helen, and an obscure grateful man in a blue jersey.

"Oh, it's time," said Clarissa. "Well, good-bye. I *do* like you," she murmured as she kissed Rachel. People in the way made it unnecessary for Richard to shake Rachel by the hand; he managed to look at her very stiffly for a second before he followed his wife down the ship's side.

The boat separating from the vessel made off towards the land, and for some minutes Helen, Ridley, and Rachel leant over the rail, watching. Once Mrs. Dalloway turned and waved; but the boat steadily grew smaller and smaller until it ceased to rise and fall, and nothing could be seen save two resolute backs.

"Well, that's over," said Ridley after a long silence. "We shall never see *them* again," he added, turning to go to his books. A feeling of emptiness and melancholy came over them; they knew in their hearts that it was over; that they had parted for ever; and the knowledge filled them with far greater depression than the length of their acquaintance seemed to justify. Even as the boat pulled away they could feel other sights and sounds beginning to take the place of the Dalloways, and the feeling was so unpleasant that they tried to resist it. For so, too, would they be forgotten.

In much the same way that Mrs. Chailey downstairs was sweeping the withered rose-leaves off the dressing-table, so Helen was anxious to make things straight again after the visitors had gone. Rachel's obvious languor and listlessness made her an easy prey, and indeed Helen had devised a kind of trap. That something had happened she now felt pretty certain; moreover, she had come to think that they had been strangers long enough; she wished to know what the girl was like, partly of course because Rachel showed no disposition to be known. So, as they turned from the rail, she said:

"Come and talk to me instead of practising," and led the way to the sheltered side where the deck-chairs were stretched in the sun. Rachel followed her indifferently. Her mind was absorbed by Richard; by the extreme strangeness of what had happened, and by a thousand feelings of which she had not been conscious before. She made scarcely any attempt to listen to what Helen was saying, as Helen indulged in commonplaces to begin with. While Mrs.

Ambrose arranged her embroidery, sucked her silk, and threaded her needle, she lay back gazing at the horizon.

"Did you like those people?" Helen asked her casually.

"Yes," she replied blankly.

"You talked to him, didn't you?"

She said nothing for a minute.

"He kissed me," she said without any change of tone.

Helen started, looked at her, but could not make out what she felt.

"M-m-m'yes," she said, after a pause. "I thought he was that kind of man."

"What kind of man?" said Rachel.

"Pompous and sentimental."

"I liked him," said Rachel.

"So you didn't mind?"

For the first time since Helen had known her Rachel's eyes lit up brightly.

"I did mind," she said vehemently. "I dreamt. I couldn't sleep."

"Tell me what happened," said Helen. She had to keep her lips from twitching as she listened to Rachel's story. It was poured out abruptly with great seriousness and no sense of humour.

"We talked about politics. He told me what he had done for the poor somewhere. I asked him all sorts of questions. He told me about his own life. The day before yesterday, after the storm, he came in to see me. It happened then, quite suddenly. He kissed me. I don't know why." As she spoke she grew flushed. "I was a good deal excited," she continued. "But I didn't mind till afterwards; when—" she paused, and saw the figure of the bloated little man again—"I became terrified."

From the look in her eyes it was evident she was again terrified. Helen was really at a loss what to say. From the little she knew of Rachel's upbringing she supposed that she had been kept entirely ignorant as to the relations of men with women. With a shyness which she felt with women and not with men she did not like to explain simply what these are. Therefore she took the other course and belittled the whole affair.

"Oh, well," she said, "he was a silly creature, and if I were you, I'd think no more about it."

"No," said Rachel, sitting bolt upright, "I shan't do that. I shall think about it all day and all night until I find out exactly what it does mean."

"Don't you ever read?" Helen asked tentatively.

"*Cowper's Letters*—that kind of thing. Father gets them for me or my Aunts."

Helen could hardly restrain herself from saying out loud what she thought of a man who brought up his daughter so that at the age of twenty-four she scarcely knew that men desired women and was terrified by a kiss. She had good reason to fear that Rachel had made herself incredibly ridiculous.

"You don't know many men?" she asked.

"Mr. Pepper," said Rachel ironically.

"So no one's ever wanted to marry you?"

"No," she answered ingenuously.

Helen reflected that as, from what she had said, Rachel certainly would think these things out, it might be as well to help her.

"You oughtn't to be frightened," she said. "It's the most natural thing in the world. Men will want to kiss you, just as they'll want to marry you. The pity is to get things out of proportion. It's like noticing the noises people make when they eat, or men spitting; or, in short, any small thing that gets on one's nerves."

Rachel seemed to be inattentive to these remarks. "Tell me," she said suddenly, "what are those women in Piccadilly?"

"In Piccadilly? They are prostitutes," said Helen.

"It *is* terrifying—it *is* disgusting," Rachel asserted, as if she included Helen in her hatred.

"It is," said Helen. "But——"

"I did like him," Rachel mused, as if speaking to herself. "I wanted to talk to him; I wanted to know what he'd done. The women in Lancashire——"

It seemed to her as she recalled their talk that there was something lovable about Richard, good in their attempted friendship, and strangely piteous in the way they had parted.

The softening of her mood was apparent to Helen.

"You see," she said, "you must take things as they are; and if you want friendship with men you must run risks. Personally," she continued, breaking into a smile, "I think it's worth it; I don't mind being kissed; I'm rather jealous, I believe, that Mr. Dalloway kissed you and didn't kiss me. Though," she added, "he bored me considerably."

But Rachel did not return the smile or dismiss the whole affair, as Helen meant her to. Her mind was working very quickly, inconsistently and painfully. Helen's words hewed down great blocks which had stood there always, and the light which came in was cold. After sitting for a time with fixed eyes, she burst out:

"So that's why I can't walk alone!"

By this new light she saw her life for the first time a creeping hedged-in thing, driven cautiously between high walls, here turned aside, there plunged in darkness, made dull and crippled for ever— her life that was the only chance she had—the short season between two silences.

"Because men are brutes! I hate men!" she exclaimed.

"I thought you said you liked him?" said Helen.

"I liked him, and I liked being kissed," she answered, as if that only added more difficulties to her problem.

Helen was surprised to see how genuine both shock and problem were, but she could think of no way of easing the difficulty except by going on talking. She wanted to make her niece talk, and so to understand why this rather dull, kindly, plausible politician had made so deep an impression on her, for surely at the age of twenty-four this was not natural.

"And did you like Mrs. Dalloway too?" she asked.

As she spoke she saw Rachel redden; for she remembered silly things she had said, and also, it occurred to her that she treated this exquisite woman rather badly, for Mrs. Dalloway had said that she loved her husband.

"She was quite nice, but a thimble-pated creature," Helen continued. "I never heard such nonsense! Chitter-chatter-chitter-chatter—fish and the Greek alphabet—never listened to a word any one said—chock-full of idiotic theories about the way to bring up children—I'd far rather talk to him any day. He was pompous, but he did at least understand what was said to him."

The glamour insensibly faded a little both from Richard and Clarissa. They had not been so wonderful after all, then, in the eyes of a mature person.

"It's very difficult to know what people are like," Rachel remarked, and Helen saw with pleasure that she spoke more naturally. "I suppose I was taken in."

There was little doubt about that according to Helen, but she restrained herself and said aloud:

"One has to make experiments."

"And they *were* nice," said Rachel. "They were extraordinarily interesting." She tried to recall the image of the world as a live thing that Richard had given her, with drains like nerves, and bad houses like patches of diseased skin. She recalled his watchwords—Unity—Imagination, and saw again the bubbles meeting in her teacup as he spoke of sisters and canaries, boyhood and his father, her small world becoming wonderfully enlarged.

"But all people don't seem to you equally interesting, do they?" asked Mrs. Ambrose.

Rachel explained that most people had hitherto been symbols; but that when they talked to one they ceased to be symbols, and became——"I could listen to them for ever!" she exclaimed, and became absorbed in her thoughts. She then jumped up, disappeared downstairs for a minute, and came back with a fat red book.

"*Who's Who*," she said, laying it upon Helen's knee and turning the pages. "It gives short lives of people—for instance: 'Sir Roland Beal; born 1852; parents from Moffatt; educated at Rugby; passed first into R.E.; married 1878 the daughter of T. Fishwick; served in the Bechuanaland Expedition 1884–85 (honourably mentioned). Clubs: United Service, Naval and Military. Recreations: an enthusiastic curler.'"

Sitting on the deck at Helen's feet she went on turning the pages and reading biographies of bankers, writers, clergymen, sailors, surgeons, judges, professors, statesmen, editors, philanthropists, merchants, and actresses; what clubs they belonged to, where they lived, what games they played, and how many acres they owned.

She became absorbed in the book.

Helen meanwhile stitched at her embroidery and thought over the things they had said. Her conclusion was that she would very much like to show her niece, if it were possible, how to live, or as she put it, how to be a reasonable person. She thought that there must be something wrong in this confusion between politics and kissing politicians, and that an elder person ought to be able to help.

"I quite agree," she said, "that people are very interesting; only—" Rachel looked up enquiringly.

"Only I think you ought to discriminate," she ended. "It's a pity to be intimate with people who are—well, rather second-rate, like the Dalloways, and to find it out later."

"But how does one know?" Rachel asked.

"I really can't tell you," replied Helen candidly, after a moment's thought. "You'll have to find out for yourself. But try and — Why don't you call me Helen?" she added. "'Aunt's' a horrid name. I never liked my Aunts."

"I should like to call you Helen," Rachel answered.

"D'you think me very unsympathetic?"

Rachel reviewed the points which Helen had certainly failed to understand; they arose chiefly from the difference of nearly twenty years in age between them, which made Mrs. Ambrose appear too humorous and cool in a matter of such moment.

"No," she said. "Some things you don't understand, of course."

"Of course," Helen agreed. "So now you can go ahead and be a person on your own account," she added.

The vision of her own personality, of herself as a real ever-lasting thing, different from anything else, unmergeable, like the sea or the wind, flashed into Rachel's mind, and she became profoundly excited at the thought of living.

"I can be m-m-myself," she stammered, "in spite of you, in spite of the Dalloways, and Mr. Pepper, and Father, and my Aunts, in spite of these?"

"In spite of every one," said Helen gravely. She then put down her needle, and explained a plan which had come into her head as they talked. Instead of wandering on down the Amazons until she reached some sulphurous tropical port, where one had to lie within doors all day beating off insects with a fan, the sensible thing to do surely was to spend the season with them in their villa by the seaside, where among other advantages Mrs. Ambrose herself would be at hand to——

"After all, Rachel," she broke off, "it's silly to pretend that because there's twenty years' difference between us we therefore can't talk to each other like human beings."

"No; because we like each other," said Rachel.

"Yes," Mrs. Ambrose agreed.

That fact, together with other facts, had been made clear by their twenty minutes' talk, although how they had come to these conclusions they could not have said.

However they were come by, they were sufficiently serious to send Mrs. Ambrose a day or two later in search of her brother-in-law. She found him sitting in his room working, applying a stout blue pencil authoritatively to bundles of filmy paper. Papers lay to left and to right of him, there were great envelopes so gorged with papers that they spilt papers on to the table. Above him hung a photograph of a woman's head. The need of sitting absolutely still before a Cockney photographer had given her lips a queer little pucker, and her eyes for the same reason looked as though she thought the whole situation ridiculous. Nevertheless it was the head of an individual and interesting woman, who would no doubt have turned and laughed at Willoughby if she could have caught his eye; but when he looked up at her he sighed profoundly. In his mind this work of his, the great factories at Hull which showed like mountains at night, the ships that crossed the ocean punctually, the schemes for combining this and that and building up a solid mass of industry, was all an offering to her; he laid his success at her feet; and was always thinking how to educate his daughter so that Theresa might be glad. He was a very ambitious man; and although he had not been particularly kind to her while she lived, as Helen thought, he now believed that she watched him from Heaven, and inspired what was good in him.

Mrs. Ambrose apologised for the interruption, and asked whether she might speak to him about a plan of hers. Would he consent to leave his daughter with them when they landed, instead of taking her on up the Amazons?

"We would take great care of her," she added, "and we should really like it."

Willoughby looked very grave and carefully laid aside his papers.

"She's a good girl," he said at length. "There is a likeness?"—he nodded his head at the photograph of Theresa and sighed. Helen looked at Theresa pursing up her lips before the Cockney photographer. It suggested her in an absurd human way, and she felt an intense desire to share some joke.

"She's the only thing that's left to me," sighed Willoughby. "We go on year after year without talking about these things——" He broke off. "But it's better so. Only, life's very hard."

Helen was sorry for him, and patted him on the shoulder, but she felt uncomfortable when her brother-in-law expressed his feelings, and took refuge in praising Rachel, and explaining why she thought her plan might be a good one.

"True," said Willoughby when she had done. "The social conditions are bound to be primitive. I should be out a good deal. I agreed because she wished it. And of course I have complete confidence in you.... You see, Helen," he continued, becoming confidential, "I want to bring her up as her mother would have wished. I don't hold with these modern views—any more than you do, eh? She's a nice quiet girl, devoted to her music—a little less of *that* would do no harm. Still, it's kept her happy, and we lead a very quiet life at Richmond. I should like her to begin to see more people. I want to take her about with me when I get home. I've half a mind to rent a house in London, leaving my sisters at Richmond, and take her to see one or two people who'd be kind to her for my sake. I'm beginning to realise," he continued, stretching himself out, "that all this is tending to Parliament, Helen. It's the only way to get things done as one wants them done. I talked to Dalloway about it. In that case, of course, I should want Rachel to be able to take more part in things. A certain amount of entertaining would be necessary—dinners, an occasional evening party. One's constituents like to be fed, I believe. In all these ways Rachel could be of great help to me. So," he wound up, "I should be very glad, if we arrange this visit (which must be upon a business footing, mind), if you could see your way to helping my girl, bringing her out,—she's a little shy now,—making a woman of her, the kind of woman her mother would have liked her to be," he ended, jerking his head at the photograph.

Willoughby's selfishness, though consistent as Helen saw with real affection for his daughter, made her determined to have the girl to stay with her, even if she had to promise a complete course of instruction in the feminine graces. She could not help laughing at the notion of it—Rachel a Tory hostess!—and marvelling as she left him at the astonishing ignorance of a father.

Rachel, when consulted, showed less enthusiasm than Helen could have wished. One moment she was eager, the next doubtful. Visions of a great river, now blue, now yellow in the tropical sun and crossed by bright birds, now white in the moon, now deep in shade with moving trees and canoes sliding out from the tangled banks, beset her. Helen promised a river. Then she did not want to leave her father. That feeling seemed genuine too, but in the end Helen prevailed, although when she had won her case she was beset by doubts, and more than once regretted the impulse which had entangled her with the fortunes of another human being.

CHAPTER VII

From a distance the *Euphrosyne* looked very small. Glasses were turned upon her from the decks of great liners, and she was pronounced a tramp, a cargo-boat, or one of those wretched little passenger steamers where people rolled about among the cattle on deck. The insect-like figures of Dalloways, Ambroses, and Vinraces were also derided, both from the extreme smallness of their persons and the doubt, which only strong glasses could dispel, as to whether they were really live creatures or only lumps on the rigging. Mr. Pepper with all his learning had been mistaken for a cormorant, and then, as unjustly, transformed into a cow. At night, indeed, when the waltzes were swinging in the saloon, and gifted passengers reciting, the little ship—shrunk to a few beads of light out among the dark waves, and one high in air upon the mast-head—seemed something mysterious and impressive to heated partners resting from the dance. She became a ship passing in the night—an emblem of the loneliness of human life, an occasion for queer confidences and sudden appeals for sympathy.

On and on she went, by day and by night, following her path, until one morning broke and showed the land. Losing its shadow-like appearance it became first cleft and mountainous, next coloured grey and purple, next scattered with white blocks which gradually separated themselves, and then, as the progress of the ship acted upon the view like a field-glass of increasing power, became streets of houses. By nine o'clock the *Euphrosyne* had taken up her position in the middle of a great bay; she dropped her anchor; immediately, as if she were a recumbent giant requiring examination, small boats came swarming about her. She rang with cries; men jumped on to her; her deck was thumped by feet. The lonely little island was invaded from all quarters at once, and after four weeks of silence it was bewildering to hear human speech. Mrs. Ambrose alone heeded none of this stir. She was pale with suspense while the boat with mail bags was making towards them. Absorbed in her letters she did not notice that she had left the *Euphrosyne*, and felt no sadness when the ship lifted up her voice and bellowed thrice like a cow separated from its calf.

"The children are well!" she exclaimed. Mr. Pepper, who sat opposite with a great mound of bag and rug upon his knees, said "Gratifying." Rachel, to whom the end of the voyage meant a complete change of perspective, was too much bewildered by the approach of the shore to realise what children were well of why it was gratifying. Helen went on reading.

Moving very slowly, and rearing absurdly high over each wave, the little boat was now approaching a white crescent of sand. Behind this was a deep green valley, with distinct hills on either side. On the slope of the right-hand hill white houses with brown roofs were settled, like nesting sea-birds, and at intervals cypresses striped the hill with black bars. Mountains whose sides were flushed with red, but whose crowns were bald, rose as a pinnacle, half-concealing another pinnacle behind it. The hour being still early, the whole view was exquisitely light and airy; the blues and greens of sky and tree were intense but not sultry. As they drew nearer and could distinguish details, the effect of the earth with its minute objects and colours and different forms of life was overwhelming after four weeks of the sea, and kept them silent.

"Three hundred years old," said Mr. Pepper meditatively at length.

As nobody said "What?" he merely extracted a bottle and swallowed a pill. The piece of information that died within him was to the effect that three hundred years ago five Elizabethan barques had anchored where the *Euphrosyne* now floated. Half-drawn up upon the beach lay an equal number of Spanish galleons, unmanned, for the country was still a virgin land behind a veil. Slipping across the water, the English sailors bore away bars of silver, bales of linen, timbers of cedar wood, golden crucifixes knobbed with emeralds. When the Spaniards came down from their drinking, a fight ensued, the two parties churning up the sand, and driving each other into the surf. The Spaniards, bloated with fine living upon the fruits of the miraculous land, fell in heaps; but the hardy Englishmen, tawny with sea-voyaging, hairy for lack of razors, with muscles like wire, fangs greedy for flesh, and fingers itching for gold, despatched the wounded, drove the dying into the sea, and soon reduced the natives to a state of superstitious wonderment. Here a settlement was made; women were imported; children grew. All seemed to favour the expansion of the British Empire, and had there been men like Richard Dalloway in the time of Charles the First, the map would undoubtedly be red where it is now an odious green. But it must be supposed that the political mind of that age lacked imagination, and, merely for want of a few thousand pounds and a few thousand men, the spark died that should have been a conflagration. From the interior came Indians with subtle poisons, naked bodies, and painted idols; from the sea came vengeful Spaniards and rapacious Portuguese; exposed to all these enemies (though the climate proved wonderfully kind and the earth abundant) the English dwindled away and all but disappeared. Somewhere about the middle of the seventeenth century a single sloop watched its season and slipped out by night, bearing within it all that was left of the great British colony, a few men, a few women, and perhaps a dozen dusky children. English history then denies all knowledge of the place. Owing to one cause and another civilisation shifted its centre to a spot some four or five hundred miles to the south, and to-day Santa Marina is not much larger than it was three hundred years ago. In population it is a happy compromise, for Portuguese fathers wed Indian mothers, and their children intermarry with the Spanish. Although they got their ploughs from Manchester, they make their coats from their own sheep, their silk from their own worms, and their furniture from their own cedar trees, so that in arts and industries the place is still much where it was in Elizabethan days.

The reasons which had drawn the English across the sea to found a small colony within the last ten years are not so easily described, and will never perhaps be recorded in history books. Granted facility of travel, peace, good trade, and so on, there was besides a kind of dissatisfaction among the English with the older countries and the enormous accumulations of carved stone, stained glass, and rich brown painting which they offered to the tourist. The movement in search of something new was of course infinitely small, affecting only a handful of well-to-do people. It began by a few schoolmasters serving their passage out to South America as the pursers of tramp steamers. They returned in time for the summer term, when their stories of the splendours and hardships of life at sea, the humours of sea-captains, the wonders of night and dawn, and the marvels of the place delighted outsiders, and sometimes found their way into print. The country itself taxed all their powers of description, for they said it was much bigger than Italy, and really nobler than Greece. Again, they declared that the natives were strangely beautiful, very big in stature, dark, passionate, and quick to seize the knife. The place seemed new and full of new forms of beauty, in proof of which they showed handkerchiefs which the women had worn round their heads, and primitive carvings coloured bright greens and blues. Somehow or other, as fashions do, the fashion spread; an old monastery was quickly turned into a hotel, while a famous line of steamships altered its route for the convenience of passengers.

Oddly enough it happened that the least satisfactory of Helen Ambrose's brothers had been sent out years before to make his fortune, at any rate to keep clear of racehorses, in the very spot which had now become so popular. Often, leaning upon the column in the verandah, he had watched the English ships with English schoolmasters for pursers steaming into the bay. Having at length earned enough to take a holiday, and being sick of the place, he proposed to put his villa, on the slope of the mountain, at his sister's disposal. She, too, had been a little stirred by the talk of a new world which went on round her, and the chance, when they were planning to spend the winter out of England, seemed too good to be missed. For these reasons she determined to accept Willoughby's offer of free passages on his ship, to place the children with their grand-parents, and to do the thing thoroughly while she was about it.

Taking seats in a carriage drawn by long-tailed horses while pheasants' feathers erect between their ears, the Ambroses, Mr. Pepper, and Rachel rattled out of the harbour. The day increased in heat as they drove up the hill. The road passed through the town, where men seemed to be beating brass and crying "Water," where the passage was blocked by mules and cleared by whips and curses, where the women walked barefoot, their heads balancing baskets, and cripples hastily displayed mutilated members; it issued among steep green fields, not so green but that the earth showed through. Great trees now shaded all but the centre of the road, and a mountain stream, so shallow and so swift that it plaited itself into strands as it ran, raced along the edge. Higher they went, until Ridley and Rachel walked behind; next they turned along a lane scattered with stones, where Mr. Pepper raised his stick and silently indicated a shrub, bearing among sparse leaves a voluminous purple blossom; and at a rickety canter the last stage of the way was accomplished.

The villa was a roomy white house, which, as is the case with most continental houses, looked to an English eye frail, ramshackle, and absurdly frivolous, more like a pagoda in a tea-garden than a place where one slept. The garden called urgently for the services of gardener. Bushes waved their branches across the paths, and the blades of grass, with spaces of earth between them, could be counted. In the circular piece of ground in front of the verandah were two cracked vases, from which red flowers dropped, with a stone fountain between them, now parched in the sun. The circular garden led to a long garden, where the gardener's shears had scarcely been, unless now and then, when he cut a bough of blossom for his beloved. A few tall trees shaded it, and round bushes with wax-like flowers mobbed their heads together in a row. A garden smoothly laid with turf, divided by thick hedges, with raised beds of bright flowers, such as we keep within walls in England, would have been out of place upon the side of this bare hill. There was no ugliness to shut out, and the villa looked straight across the shoulder of a slope, ribbed with olive trees, to the sea.

The indecency of the whole place struck Mrs. Chailey forcibly. There were no blinds to shut out the sun, nor was there any furniture to speak of for the sun to spoil. Standing in the bare stone hall, and surveying a staircase of superb breadth, but cracked and carpetless, she further ventured the opinion that there were rats, as large as terriers at home, and that if one put one's foot down with any force one would come through the floor. As for hot water—at this point her investigations left her speechless.

"Poor creature!" she murmured to the sallow Spanish servant-girl who came out with the pigs and hens to receive them, "no wonder you hardly look like a human being!" Maria accepted the compliment with an exquisite Spanish grace. In Chailey's opinion they would have done well to stay on board an English ship, but none knew better than she that her duty commanded her to stay.

When they were settled in, and in train to find daily occupation, there was some speculation as to the reasons which induced Mr. Pepper to stay, taking up his lodging in the Ambrose's house. Efforts had been made for some days before landing to impress upon him the advantages of the Amazons.

"That great stream!" Helen would begin, gazing as if she saw a visionary cascade, "I've a good mind to go with you myself, Willoughby—only I can't. Think of the sunsets and the moonrises— I believe the colours are unimaginable."

"There are wild peacocks," Rachel hazarded.

"And marvellous creatures in the water," Helen asserted.

"One might discover a new reptile," Rachel continued.

"There's certain to be a revolution, I'm told," Helen urged.

The effect of these subterfuges was a little dashed by Ridley, who, after regarding Pepper for some moments, sighed aloud, "Poor fellow!" and inwardly speculated upon the unkindness of women.

Mr. Pepper stayed, however, in apparent contentment for six days, playing with a microscope and a notebook in one of the many sparsely furnished sitting-rooms, but on the evening of the seventh day, as they sat at dinner, he appeared more restless than usual. The dinner-table was set between two long windows which were left uncurtained by Helen's orders. Darkness fell as sharply as a knife in this climate, and the town then sprang out in circles and lines of bright dots beneath them. Buildings which never showed by day showed by night, and the sea flowed right over the land judging by the moving lights of the steamers. The sight fulfilled the same purpose as an orchestra in a London restaurant, and silence had its setting. William Pepper observed it for some time; he put on his spectacles to contemplate the scene.

"I've identified the big block to the left," he observed, and pointed with his fork at a square formed by several rows of lights.

"One should infer that they can cook vegetables," he added.

"An hotel?" said Helen.

"Once a monastery," said Mr. Pepper.

Nothing more was said then, but, the day after, Mr. Pepper returned from a midday walk, and stood silently before Helen who was reading in the verandah.

"I've taken a room over there," he said.

"You're not going?" she exclaimed.

"On the whole—yes," he remarked. "No private cook can cook vegetables."

Knowing his dislike of questions, which she to some extent shared, Helen asked no more. Still, an uneasy suspicion lurked in her mind that William was hiding a would. She flushed to think that her words, or her husband's, or Rachel's had penetrated and stung. She was half-moved to cry, "Stop, William; explain!" and would have returned to the subject at luncheon if William had not shown himself inscrutable and chill, lifting fragments of salad on the point of his fork, with the gesture of a man pronging seaweed, detecting gravel, suspecting germs.

"If you all die of typhoid I won't be responsible!" he snapped.

"If you die of dulness, neither will I," Helen echoed in her heart. She reflected that she had never yet asked him whether he had been in love. They had got further and further from that subject instead of drawing nearer to it, and she could not help feeling it a relief when William Pepper, with all his knowledge, his microscope, his note-books, his genuine kindliness and good sense, but a certain dryness of soul, took his departure. Also she could not help feeling it sad that friendships should end thus, although in this case to have the room empty was something of a comfort, and she tried to console herself with the reflection that one never knows how far other people feel the things one would certainly feel in their place.

CHAPTER VIII

The next few months passed away, as many years can pass away, without definite events, and yet, if suddenly disturbed, it would be seen that such months or years had a character unlike others. The three months which had passed had brought them to the beginning of March. The climate had kept its promise, and the change of season from winter to spring had made very little difference, so that Helen, who was sitting in the drawing-room with a pen in her hand, could keep the windows open though a great fire of logs burnt on one side of her. Below the sea was still blue and the roofs still brown and white, though the day was fading rapidly. It was dusk in the room, which, large and empty at all times, now appeared larger and emptier than usual. Her own figure, as she sat writing with a pad on her knee, shaded the general effect of size and lack of detail, for the flames which ran along the branches, suddenly devouring little green tufts, burnt intermittently and sent irregular illuminations across her face and the plaster walls. There were no pictures on the walls but here and there boughs laden with heavy-petalled flowers spread widely against them. Of the books fallen on the bare floor and heaped upon the large table, it was only possible in this light to trace the outline.

Mrs. Ambrose was writing a very long letter. Beginning "Dear Bernard," it went on to describe what had been happening in the Villa San Gervasio during the past three months, as, for instance, that they had had the British Consul to dinner, and had been taken over a Spanish man-of-war, and had seen a great many processions and religious festivals, which were so beautiful that Mrs. Ambrose couldn't conceive why, if people must have a religion, they didn't all become Roman Catholics. They had made several expeditions though none of any length. It was worth coming if only for the sake of the flowering trees which grew wild quite near the house, and the amazing colours of sea and earth. The earth, instead of being brown, was red, purple, green. "You won't believe me," she added, "there is no colour like it in England." She adopted, indeed, a con-descending tone towards that poor island, which was now advanc-ing chilly crocuses and nipped violets in nooks, in copses, in cosy corners, tended by rosy old gardeners in mufflers, who were always touching their hats and bobbing obsequiously. She went on to de-ride the islanders themselves. Rumours of London all in a ferment over a General Election had reached them even out here. "It seems incredible," she went on, "that people should care whether Asquith is in or Austen Chamberlain[1] out, and while you scream yourselves hoarse about politics you let the only people who are trying for something good starve or simply laugh at them. When have you ever encouraged a living artist? Or bought his best work? Why are you all so ugly and so servile? Here the servants are human beings. They talk to one as if they were equals. As far as I can tell there are no aristocrats."

Perhaps it was the mention of aristocrats that reminded her of Richard Dalloway and Rachel, for she ran on with the same penful to describe her niece.

"It's an odd fate that has put me in charge of a girl," she wrote, "considering that I have never got on well with women, or had much to do with them. However, I must retract some of the things that I have said against them. If they were properly educated I don't see why they shouldn't be much the same as men—as satisfactory I mean; though, of course, very different. The question is, how should one educate them? The present method seems to me abominable. This girl, though twenty-four, had never heard that men desire women, and, until I explained it, did not know how children were born. Her ignorance upon other matters as important" (here Mrs. Ambrose's letter may not be quoted)… "was complete. It seems to me not merely foolish but criminal to bring people up like that. Let alone the suffering to them, it explains why women are what they are—the wonder is they're no worse. I have taken it upon myself to enlighten her, and now, though still a good deal prejudiced and liable to exaggerate, she is more or less a reasonable human being. Keeping them ignorant, of course, defeats its own object, and when they begin to understand they take it all much too seriously. My brother-in-law really deserved a catastrophe—which he won't get. I now pray for a young man to come to my help; some one, I mean, who would talk to her openly, and prove how absurd most of her ideas about life are. Unluckily such men seem almost as rare as the women. The English colony certainly doesn't provide one; artists, merchants, cultivated people— they are stupid, conventional, and flirtatious…." She ceased, and with her pen in her hand sat looking into the fire, making the logs into caves and mountains, for it had grown too dark to go on writing. Moreover, the house began to stir as the hour of dinner approached; she could hear the plates being chinked in the dining-room next door, and Chailey instructing the Spanish girl where to put things down in vigorous English. The bell rang; she rose, met Ridley and Rachel outside, and they all went in to dinner.

Three months had made but little difference in the appearance either of Ridley or Rachel; yet a keen observer might have thought that the girl was more definite and self-confident in her manner than before. Her skin was brown, her eyes certainly brighter, and she attended to what was said as though she might be going to contradict it. The meal began with the comfortable silence of people who are quite at their ease together. Then Ridley, leaning on his elbow and looking out of the window, observed that it was a lovely night.

"Yes," said Helen. She added, "The season's begun," looking at the lights beneath them. She asked Maria in Spanish whether the hotel was not filling up with visitors. Maria informed her with pride that there would come a time when it was positively difficult to buy eggs—the shopkeepers would not mind what prices they asked, for they would get them, at any rate, from the English.

"That's an English steamer in the bay," said Rachel, looking at a triangle of lights below. "She came in early this morning."

"Then we may hope for some letters and send ours back," said Helen.

For some reason the mention of letters always made Ridley groan, and the rest of the meal passed in a brisk argument between husband and wife as to whether he was or was not wholly ignored by the entire civilised world.

"Considering the last batch," said Helen, "you deserve beating. You were asked to lecture, you were offered a degree, and some silly woman praised not only your books but your beauty—she said he was what Shelley would have been if Shelley had lived to fifty-five and grown a beard. Really, Ridley, I think you're the vainest man I know," she ended, rising from the table, "which I my tell you is saying a good deal."

Finding her letter lying before the fire she added a few lines to it, and then announced that she was going to take the letters now—Ridley must bring his—and Rachel?

"I hope you've written to your Aunts? It's high time."

The women put on cloaks and hats, and after inviting Ridley to come with them, which he emphatically refused to do, exclaiming that Rachel he expected to be a fool, but Helen surely knew better, they turned to go. He stood over the fire gazing into the depths of the looking-glass, and compressing his face into the likeness of a commander surveying a field of battle, or a martyr watching the flames lick his toes, rather than of a secluded Professor.

Helen laid hold of his beard.

"Am I a fool?" she said.

"Let me go, Helen."

"Am I a fool?" she repeated.

"Vile woman!" he exclaimed, and kissed her.

"We'll leave you to your vanities," she called back as they went out of the door.

It was a beautiful evening, still light enough to see a long way down the road, though the stars were coming out. The pillar-box was let into a high yellow wall where the lane met the road, and having dropped the letters into it, Helen was for turning back.

"No, no," said Rachel, taking her by the wrist. "We're going to see life. You promised."

"Seeing life" was the phrase they used for their habit of strolling through the town after dark. The social life of Santa Marina was carried on almost entirely by lamplight, which the warmth of the nights and the scents culled from flowers made pleasant enough. The young women, with their hair magnificently swept in coils, a red flower behind the ear, sat on the doorsteps, or issued out on to balconies, while the young men ranged up and down beneath, shouting up a greeting from time to time and stopping here and there to enter into amorous talk. At the open windows merchants could be seen making up the day's account, and the older women lifting jars from shelf to shelf. The streets were full of people, men for the most part, who interchanged their views of the world as they walked, or gathered round the wine-tables at the street corner, where an old cripple was twanging his guitar strings, while a poor girl cried her passionate song in the gutter. The two Englishwomen excited some friendly curiosity, but no one molested them.

Helen sauntered on, observing the different people in their shabby clothes, who seemed so careless and so natural, with satisfaction.

"Just think of the Mall to-night!" she exclaimed at length. "It's the fifteenth of March. Perhaps there's a Court." She thought of the crowd waiting in the cold spring air to see the grand carriages go by. "It's very cold, if it's not raining," she said. "First there are men selling picture postcards; then there are wretched little shop-girls with round bandboxes; then there are bank clerks in tail coats; and then—any number of dressmakers. People from South Kensington drive up in a hired fly; officials have a pair of bays; earls, on the other hand, are allowed one footman to stand up behind; dukes have two, royal dukes—so I was told—have three; the king, I suppose, can have as many as he likes. And the people believe in it!"

Out here it seemed as though the people of England must be shaped in the body like the kings and queens, knights and pawns of the chessboard, so strange were their differences, so marked and so implicitly believed in.

They had to part in order to circumvent a crowd.

"They believe in God," said Rachel as they regained each other. She meant that the people in the crowd believed in Him; for she remembered the crosses with bleeding plaster figures that stood where foot-paths joined, and the inexplicable mystery of a service in a Roman Catholic church.

"We shall never understand!" she sighed.

They had walked some way and it was now night, but they could see a large iron gate a little way farther down the road on their left.

"Do you mean to go right up to the hotel?" Helen asked.

Rachel gave the gate a push; it swung open, and, seeing no one about and judging that nothing was private in this country, they walked straight on. An avenue of trees ran along the road, which was completely straight. The trees suddenly came to an end; the road turned a corner, and they found themselves confronted by a large square building. They had come out upon the broad terrace which ran round the hotel and were only a few feet distant from the windows. A row of long windows opened almost to the ground. They were all of them uncurtained, and all brilliantly lighted, so that they could see everything inside. Each window revealed a different section of the life of the hotel. They drew into one of the broad columns of shadow which separated the windows and gazed in. They found themselves just outside the dining-room. It was being swept; a waiter was eating a bunch of grapes with his leg across the corner of a table. Next door was the kitchen, where they were washing up; white cooks were dipping their arms into cauldrons, while the waiters made their meal voraciously off broken meats, sopping up the gravy with bits of crumb. Moving on, they became lost in a plantation of bushes, and then suddenly found themselves outside the drawing-room, where the ladies and gentlemen, having dined well, lay back in deep armchairs, occasionally speaking or turning over the pages of magazines. A thin woman was flourishing up and down the piano.

"What is a dahabeeyah, Charles?" the distinct voice of a widow, seated in an arm-chair by the window, asked her son.

It was the end of the piece, and his answer was lost in the general clearing of throats and tapping of knees.

"They're all old in this room," Rachel whispered.

Creeping on, they found that the next window revealed two men in shirt-sleeves playing billiards with two young ladies.

"He pinched my arm!" the plump young woman cried, as she missed her stroke.

"Now you two—no ragging," the young man with the red face reproved them, who was marking.

"Take care or we shall be seen," whispered Helen, plucking Rachel by the arm. Incautiously her head had risen to the middle of the window.

Turning the corner they came to the largest room in the hotel, which was supplied with four windows, and was called the Lounge, although it was really a hall. Hung with armour and native embroideries, furnished with divans and screens, with shut off convenient corners, the room was less formal than the others, and was evidently the haunt of youth. Signor Rodriguez, whom they knew to be the manager of the hotel, stood quite near them in the doorway surveying the scene—the gentlemen lounging in chairs, the couples leaning over coffee-cups, the game of cards in the centre under profuse clusters of electric light. He was congratulating himself upon the enterprise which had turned the refectory, a cold stone room with pots on trestles, into the most comfortable room in the house. The hotel was very full, and proved his wisdom in decreeing that no hotel can flourish without a lounge.

The people were scattered about in couples or parties of four, and either they were actually better acquainted, or the informal room made their manners easier. Through the open window came an uneven humming sound like that which rises from a flock of sheep pent within hurdles at dusk. The card-party occupied the centre of the foreground.

Helen and Rachel watched them play for some minutes without being able to distinguish a word. Helen was observing one of the men intently. He was a lean, somewhat cadaverous man of about her own age, whose profile was turned to them, and he was the partner of a highly-coloured girl, obviously English by birth.

Suddenly, in the strange way in which some words detach themselves from the rest, they heard him say quite distinctly:—

"All you want is practice, Miss Warrington; courage and practice—one's no good without the other."

"Hughling Elliot! Of course!" Helen exclaimed. She ducked her head immediately, for at the sound of his name he looked up. The game went on for a few minutes, and was then broken up by the approach of a wheeled chair, containing a voluminous old lady who paused by the table and said:—

"Better luck to-night, Susan?"

"All the luck's on our side," said a young man who until now had kept his back turned to the window. He appeared to be rather stout, and had a thick crop of hair.

"Luck, Mr. Hewet?" said his partner, a middle-aged lady with spectacles. "I assure you, Mrs. Paley, our success is due solely to our brilliant play."

"Unless I go to bed early I get practically no sleep at all," Mrs. Paley was heard to explain, as if to justify her seizure of Susan, who got up and proceeded to wheel the chair to the door.

"They'll get some one else to take my place," she said cheerfully. But she was wrong. No attempt was made to find another player, and after the young man had built three stories of a card-house, which fell down, the players strolled off in different directions.

Mr. Hewet turned his full face towards the window. They could see that he had large eyes obscured by glasses; his complexion was rosy; his lips clean-shaven; and, seen among ordinary people, it appeared to be an interesting face. He came straight towards them, but his eyes were fixed not upon the eavesdroppers but upon a spot where the curtain hung in folds.

"Asleep?" he said.

Helen and Rachel started to think that some one had been sitting near to them unobserved all the time. There were legs in the shadow. A melancholy voice issued from above them.

"Two women," it said.

A scuffling was heard on the gravel. The women had fled. They did not stop running until they felt certain that no eye could penetrate the darkness, and the hotel was only a square shadow in the distance, with red holes regularly cut in its blackness.

CHAPTER IX

An hour passed, and the downstairs rooms at the hotel grew dim and were almost deserted, while the little box-like squares above them were brilliantly irradiated. Some forty or fifty people were going to bed. The thump of jugs set down on the floor above could be heard and the chink of china, for there was not as thick a partition between the rooms as one might wish, so Miss Allan, the elderly lady who had been playing bridge, determined, giving the wall a smart rap with her knuckles. It was only matchboard, she decided, run up to make many little rooms of one large one. Her grey petticoats slipped to the ground, and, stooping, she folded her clothes with neat, if not loving fingers, screwed her hair into a plait, wound her father's great gold watch, and opened the complete works of Wordsworth. She was reading the "Prelude,"[1] partly because she always read the "Prelude" abroad, and partly because she was engaged in writing a short *Primer of English Literature*—Beowulf to Swinburne[2]—which would have a paragraph on Wordsworth. She was deep in the fifth book, stopping indeed to pencil a note, when a pair of boots dropped, one after another, on the floor above her. She looked up and speculated. Whose boots were they, she wondered. She then became aware of a swishing sound next door—

a woman, clearly, putting away her dress. It was succeeded by a gentle tapping sound, such as that which accompanies hair-dressing. It was very difficult to keep her attention fixed upon the "Prelude." Was it Susan Warrington tapping? She forced herself, however, to read to the end of the book, when she placed a mark between the pages, sighed contentedly, and then turned out the light.

Very different was the room through the wall, though as like in shape as one egg-box is like another. As Miss Allan read her book, Susan Warrington was brushing her hair. Ages have consecrated this hour, and the most majestic of all domestic actions, to talk of love between women; but Miss Warrington being alone could not talk; she could only look with extreme solicitude at her own face in the glass. She turned her head from side to side, tossing heavy locks now this way now that; and then withdrew a pace or two, and considered herself seriously.

"I'm nice-looking," she determined. "Not pretty—possibly," she drew herself up a little. "Yes—most people would say I was handsome."

She was really wondering what Arthur Venning would say. Her feeling about him was decidedly queer. She would not admit to herself that she was in love with him or that she wanted to marry him, yet she spent every minute when she was alone in wondering what he thought of her, and in comparing what they had done today with what they had done the day before.

"He didn't ask me to play, but he certainly followed me into the hall," she meditated, summing up the evening. She was thirty years of age, and owing to the number of her sisters and the seclusion of life in a country parsonage had as yet had no proposal of marriage. The hour of confidences was often a sad one, and she had been known to jump into bed, treating her hair unkindly, feeling herself overlooked by life in comparison with others. She was a big, well-made woman, the red lying upon her cheeks in patches that were too well defined, but her serious anxiety gave her a kind of beauty.

She was just about to pull back the bed-clothes when she exclaimed, "Oh, but I'm forgetting," and went to her writing-table. A brown volume lay there stamped with the figure of the year. She proceeded to write in the square ugly hand of a mature child, as she wrote daily year after year, keeping the diaries, though she seldom looked at them.

"A.M.—Talked to Mrs. H. Elliot about country neighbours. She knows the Manns; also the Selby-Carroways. How small the world is! Like her. Read a chapter of *Miss Appleby's Adventure* to Aunt E. P.M.—Played lawn-tennis with Mr. Perrott and Evelyn M. Don't *like* Mr. P. Have a feeling that he is not 'quite,' though clever certainly. Beat them. Day splendid, view wonderful. One gets used to no trees, though much too bare at first. Cards after dinner. Aunt E. cheerful, though twingy, she says. Mem.: *ask about damp sheets.*"

She knelt in prayer, and then lay down in bed, tucking the blankets comfortably about her, and in a few minutes her breathing showed that she was asleep. With its profoundly peaceful sighs and hesitations it resembled that of a cow standing up to its knees all night through in the long grass.

A glance into the next room revealed little more than a nose, prominent above the sheets. Growing accustomed to the darkness, for the windows were open and showed grey squares with splinters of starlight, one could distinguish a lean form, terribly like the body of a dead person, the body indeed of William Pepper, asleep too. Thirty-six, thirty-seven, thirty-eight—here were three Portuguese men of business, asleep presumably, since a snore came with the regularity of a great ticking clock. Thirty-nine was a corner room, at the end of the passage, but late though it was—"one" struck gently downstairs—a line of light under the door showed that some one was still awake.

"How late you are, Hugh!" a woman, lying in bed, said in a peevish but solicitous voice. Her husband was brushing his teeth, and for some moments did not answer.

"You should have gone to sleep," he replied. "I was talking to Thornbury."

"But you know that I never can sleep when I'm waiting for you," she said.

To that he made no answer, but only remarked. "Well then, we'll turn out the light." They were silent.

The faint but penetrating pulse of an electric bell could now be heard in the corridor. Old Mrs. Paley, having woken hungry but without her spectacles, was summoning her maid to find the biscuit-box. The maid having answered the bell, drearily respectful even at this hour though muffled in a mackintosh, the passage was left in silence. Downstairs all was empty and dark; but on the upper floor a light still burnt in the room where the boots had dropped so heavily above Miss Allan's head. Here was the gentleman who, a few hours previously, in the shade of the curtain, had seemed to consist entirely of legs. Deep in an armchair he was reading the third volume of Gibbon's *History of the Decline and Fall of Rome* by candle light. As he reached he knocked the ash automatically, now and again, from his cigarette and turned the page, while a whole procession of splendid sentences entered his capacious brow and went marching through his brain in order. It seemed likely that this process might continue for an hour or more, until the entire regiment had shifted its quarters, had not the door opened, and the young man, who was inclined to be stout, come in with large naked feet.

"Oh, Hirst, what I forgot to say was—"

"Two minutes," said Hirst, raising his finger.

He safely stowed away the last words of the paragraph.

"What was it you forgot to say?" he asked.

"D'you think you *do* make enough allowance for feelings?" asked Mr. Hewet. He had again forgotten what he had meant to say.

After intense contemplation of the immaculate Gibbon Mr. Hirst smiled at the question of his friend. He laid aside his book and considered.

"I should call yours a singularly untidy mind," he observed. "Feelings? Aren't they just what we do allow for? We put love up there, and all the rest somewhere down below." With his left hand he indicated the top of a pyramid, and with his right the base.

"But you didn't get out of bed to tell me that," he added severely.

"I got out of bed," said Hewet vaguely, "merely to talk I suppose."

"Meanwhile I shall undress," said Hirst. When naked of all but his shirt, and bent over the basin, Mr. Hirst no longer impressed one with the majesty of his intellect, but with the pathos of his young yet ugly body, for he stooped, and he was so thin that there were dark lines between the different bones of his neck and shoulders.

"Women interest me," said Hewet, who, sitting on the bed with his chin resting on his knees, paid no attention to the undressing of Mr. Hirst.

"They're so stupid," said Hirst. "You're sitting on my pyjamas."

"I suppose they *are* stupid?" Hewet wondered.

"There can't be two opinions about that, I imagine," said Hirst, hopping briskly across the room, "unless you're in love—that fat woman Warrington?" he enquired.

"Not one fat woman—all fat women," Hewet sighed.

"The women I saw to-night were not fat," said Hirst, who was taking advantage of Hewet's company to cut his toe-nails.

"Describe them," said Hewet.

"You know I can't describe things!" said Hirst. "They were much like other women, I should think. They always are."

"No; that's where we differ," said Hewet. "I say everything's different. No two people are in the least the same. Take you and me now."

"So I used to think once," said Hirst. "But now they're all types. Don't take us,—take this hotel. You could draw circles round the whole lot of them, and they'd never stray outside."

("You can kill a hen by doing that"), Hewet murmured.

"Mr. Hughling Elliot, Mrs. Hughling Elliot, Miss Allan, Mr. and Mrs. Thornbury—one circle," Hirst continued. "Miss Warrington, Mr. Arthur Venning, Mr. Perrott, Evelyn M. another circle; then there are a whole lot of natives; finally ourselves."

"Are we all alone in our circle?" asked Hewet.

"Quite alone," said Hirst. "You try to get out, but you can't. You only make a mess of things by trying."

"I'm not a hen in a circle," said Hewet. "I'm a dove on a tree-top."

"I wonder if this is what they call an ingrowing toe-nail?" said Hirst, examining the big toe on his left foot.

"I flit from branch to branch," continued Hewet. "The world is profoundly pleasant." He lay back on the bed, upon his arms.

"I wonder if it's really nice to be as vague as you are?" asked Hirst, looking at him. "It's the lack of continuity—that's what's so odd about you," he went on. "At the age of twenty-seven, which is nearly thirty, you seem to have drawn no conclusions. A party of old women excites you still as though you were three."

Hewet contemplated the angular young man who was neatly brushing the rims of his toe-nails into the fireplace in silence for a moment.

"I respect you, Hirst," he remarked.

"I envy you—some things," said Hirst. "One: your capacity for not thinking; two: people like you better than they like me. Women like you, I suppose."

"I wonder whether that isn't really what matters most?" said Hewet. Lying now flat on the bed he waved his hand in vague circles above him.

"Of course it is," said Hirst. "But that's not the difficulty. The difficulty is, isn't it, to find an appropriate object?"

"There are no female hens in your circle?" asked Hewet.

"Not the ghost of one," said Hirst.

Although they had known each other for three years Hirst had never yet heard the true story of Hewet's loves. In general conversation it was taken for granted that they were many, but in private the subject was allowed to lapse. The fact that he had money enough to do no work, and that he had left Cambridge after two terms owing to a difference with the authorities, and had then travelled and drifted, made his life strange at many points where his friends' lives were much of a piece.

"I don't see your circles—I don't see them," Hewet continued. "I see a thing like a teetotum spinning in and out—knocking into things—dashing from side to side—collecting numbers—more and more and more, till the whole place is thick with them. Round and round they go—out there, over the rim—out of sight."

His fingers showed that the waltzing teetotums had spun over the edge of the counterpane and fallen off the bed into infinity.

"Could you contemplate three weeks alone in this hotel?" asked Hirst, after a moment's pause.

Hewet proceeded to think.

"The truth of it is that one never is alone, and one never is in company," he concluded.

"Meaning?" said Hirst.

"Meaning? Oh, something about bubbles—auras—what d'you call 'em? You can't see my bubble; I can't see yours; all we see of each other is a speck, like the wick in the middle of that flame. The flame goes about with us everywhere; it's not ourselves exactly, but what we feel; the world in short, or people mainly; all kinds of people."

"A nice streaky bubble yours must be!" said Hirst.

"And supposing my bubble could run into some one else's bubble——"

"And they both burst?" put in Hirst.

"Then—then—then—" pondered Hewet, as if to himself, "it would be an e—nor—mous world," he said, stretching his arms to their full width, as though even so they could hardly clasp the billowy universe, for when he was with Hirst he always felt unusually sanguine and vague.

"I don't think you altogether as foolish as I used to, Hewet," said Hirst. "You don't know what you mean but you try to say it."

"But aren't you enjoying yourself here?" said Hewet.

"On the whole—yes," said Hirst. "I like observing people. I like looking at things. This country is amazingly beautiful. Did you notice how the top of the mountain turned yellow tonight? Really we must take our lunch and spend the day out. You're getting disgustingly fat." He pointed at the calf of Hewet's bare leg.

"We'll get up an expedition," said Hewet energetically. "We'll ask the entire hotel. We'll hire donkeys and———"

"Oh, Lord!" said Hirst, "do shut it! I can see Miss Warrington and Miss Allan and Mrs. Elliot and the rest squatting on the stones and quacking, 'How jolly!'"

"We'll ask Venning and Perrott and Miss Murgatroyd—every one we can lay hands on," went on Hewet. "What's the name of the little old grasshopper with the eyeglasses? Pepper?—Pepper shall lead us."

"Thank God, you'll never get the donkeys," said Hirst.

"I must make a note of that," said Hewet, slowly dropping his feet to the floor. "Hirst escorts Miss Warrington; Pepper advances alone on a white ass; provisions equally distributed—or shall we hire a mule? The matrons—there's Mrs. Paley, by Jove!—share a carriage."

"That's where you'll go wrong," said Hirst. "Putting virgins among matrons."

"How long should you think that an expedition like that would take, Hirst?" asked Hewet.

"From twelve to sixteen hours I should say," said Hirst. "The time usually occupied by a first confinement."

"It will need considerable organisation," said Hewet. He was now padding softly round the room, and stopped to stir the books on the table. They lay heaped one upon another.

"We shall want some poets too," he remarked. "Not Gibbon; no; d'you happen to have *Modern Love* or *John Donne*?[23] You see, I contemplate pauses when people get tired of looking at the view, and then it would be nice to read something rather difficult aloud."

"Mrs. Paley *will* enjoy herself," said Hirst.

"Mrs. Paley will enjoy it certainly," said Hewet. "It's one of the saddest things I know—the way elderly ladies cease to read poetry. And yet how appropriate this is:

> I speak as one who plumbs
> Life's dim profound,
> One who at length can sound
> Clear views and certain.

> But—after love what comes?
> A scene that lours,
> A few sad vacant hours,
> And then, the Curtain.[4]

I daresay Mrs. Paley is the only one of us who can really understand that."

"We'll ask her," said Hirst. "Please, Hewet, if you must go to bed, draw my curtain. Few things distress me more than the moonlight."

Hewet retreated, pressing the poems of Thomas Hardy beneath his arm, and in their beds next door to each other both the young men were soon asleep.

Between the extinction of Hewet's candle and the rising of a dusky Spanish boy who was the first to survey the desolation of the hotel in the early morning, a few hours of silence intervened. One could almost hear a hundred people breathing deeply, and however wakeful and restless it would have been hard to escape sleep in the middle of so much sleep. Looking out of the windows, there was only darkness to be seen. All over the shadowed half of the world people lay prone, and a few flickering lights in empty streets marked the places where their cities were built. Red and yellow omnibuses were crowding each other in Piccadilly; sumptuous women were rocking at a standstill; but here in the darkness an owl flitted from tree to tree, and when the breeze lifted the branches the moon flashed as if it were a torch. Until all people should awake again the houseless animals were abroad, the tigers and the stags, and the elephants coming down in the darkness to drink at pools. The wind at night blowing over the hills and woods was purer and fresher than the wind by day, and the earth, robbed of detail, more mysterious than the earth coloured and divided by roads and fields. For six hours this profound beauty existed, and then as the east grew whiter and whiter the ground swam to the surface, the roads were revealed, the smoke rose and the people stirred, and the sun shone upon the windows of the hotel at Santa Marina until they were uncurtained, and the gong blaring all through the house gave notice of breakfast.

Directly breakfast was over, the ladies as usual circled vaguely, picking up papers and putting them down again, about the hall.

"And what are you going to do to-day?" asked Mrs. Elliot, drifting up against Miss Warrington.

Mrs. Elliot, the wife of Hughling the Oxford Don, was a short woman, whose expression was habitually plaintive. Her eyes moved from thing to thing as though they never found anything sufficiently pleasant to rest upon for any length of time.

"I'm going to try to get Aunt Emma out into the town," said Susan. "She's not seen a thing yet."

"I call it so spirited of her at her age," said Mrs. Elliot, "coming all this way from her own fireside."

"Yes, we always tell her she'll die on board ship," Susan replied. "She was born on one," she added.

"In the old days," said Mrs. Elliot, "a great many people were. I always pity the poor woman so! We've got a lot to complain of!" She shook her head. Her eyes wandered about the table, and she remarked irrelevantly, "The poor little Queen of Holland! Newspaper reporters practically, one may say, at her bedroom door!"

"Were you talking of the Queen of Holland?" said the pleasant voice of Miss Allan, who was searching for the thick pages of *The Times* among a litter of thin foreign sheets.

"I always envy any one who lives in such an excessively flat country," she remarked.

"How very strange!" said Mrs. Elliot. "I find a flat country so depressing."

"I'm afraid you can't be very happy here then, Miss Allan," said Susan.

"On the contrary," said Miss Allan, "I am exceedingly fond of mountains." Perceiving *The Times* at some distance, she moved off to secure it.

"Well, I must find my husband," said Mrs. Elliot, fidgeting away.

"And I must go to my aunt," said Miss Warrington, and taking up the duties of the day they moved away.

Whether the flimsiness of foreign sheets and the coarseness of their type is any proof of frivolity and ignorance, there is no doubt that English people scarcely consider news read there as news, any more than a programme bought from a man in the street on the occasion of a public ceremony inspires confidence in what it says. A very respectable elderly pair, having inspected the long tables of newspapers, did not think it worth their while to read more than the headlines.

"The debate on the fifteenth should have reached us by now," Mrs. Thornbury murmured. Mr. Thornbury, who was beautifully clean and had red rubbed into his handsome worn face like traces of paint on a weather-beaten wooden figure, looked over his glasses and saw that Miss Allan had *The Times*.

The couple therefore sat themselves down in armchairs and waited.

"Ah, there's Mr. Hewet," said Mrs. Thornbury. "Mr. Hewet," she continued, "do come and sit by us. I was telling my husband how much you reminded me of a dear old friend of mine—Mary Umpleby. She was a most delightful woman, I assure you. She grew roses. We used to stay with her in the old days."

"No young man likes to have it said that he resembles an elderly spinster," said Mr. Thornbury.

"On the contrary," said Mr. Hewet, "I always think it a compliment to remind people of some one else. But Miss Umpleby—why did she grow roses?"

"Ah, poor thing," said Mrs. Thornbury, "that's a long story. She had gone through dreadful sorrows. At one time I think she would have lost her senses if it hadn't been for her garden. The soil was very much against her—a blessing in disguise; she had to be up at dawn—out in all weathers. And then there are creatures that eat roses. But she triumphed. She always did. She was a brave soul." She sighed deeply but at the same time with resignation.

"I did not realise that I was monopolising the paper," said Miss Allan, coming up to them.

"We were so anxious to read about the debate," said Mrs. Thornbury, accepting it on behalf of her husband.

"One doesn't realise how interesting a debate can be until one has sons in the navy. My interests are equally balanced, though; I have sons in the army too; and one son who makes speeches at the Union—my baby!"

"Hirst would know him, I expect," said Hewet.

"Mr. Hirst has such an interesting face," said Mrs. Thornbury. "But I feel one ought to be very clever to talk to him. Well, William?" she enquired, for Mr. Thornbury grunted.

"They're making a mess of it," said Mr. Thornbury. He had reached the second column of the report, a spasmodic column, for the Irish members had been brawling three weeks ago at Westminster over a question of naval efficiency. After a disturbed paragraph or two, the column of print once more ran smoothly.

"You have read it?" Mrs. Thornbury asked Miss Allan.

"No, I am ashamed to say I have only read about the discoveries in Crete," said Miss Allan.

"Oh, but I would give so much to realise the ancient world!" cried Mrs. Thornbury. "Now that we old people are alone,—we're on our second honeymoon,—I am really going to put myself to school again. After all we are *founded* on the past, aren't we, Mr. Hewet? My soldier son says that there is still a great deal to be learnt from Hannibal. One ought to know so much more than one does. Somehow when I read the paper, I begin with the debates first, and, before I've done, the door always opens—we're a very large party at home—and so one never does think enough about the ancients and all they've done for us. But *you* begin at the beginning, Miss Allan."

"When I think of the Greeks I think of them as naked black men," said Miss Allan, "which is quite incorrect, I'm sure."

"And you, Mr. Hirst?" said Mrs. Thornbury, perceiving that the gaunt young man was near. "I'm sure you read everything."

"I confine myself to cricket and crime," said Hirst. "The worst of coming from the upper classes," he continued, "is that one's friends are never killed in railway accidents."

Mr. Thornbury threw down the paper, and emphatically dropped his eyeglasses. The sheets fell in the middle of the group, and were eyed by them all.

"It's not gone well?" asked his wife solicitously.

Hewet picked up one sheet and read, "A lady was walking yesterday in the street of Westminster when she perceived a cat in the window of a deserted house. The famished animal——"

"I shall be out of it anyway," Mr. Thornbury interrupted peevishly.

"Cats are often forgotten," Miss Allan remarked.

"Remember, William, the Prime Minister has reserved his answer," said Mrs. Thornbury.

"At the age of eighty, Mr. Joshua Harris of Eeles Park, Brondesbury, has had a son," said Hirst.

". . . The famished animal, which had been noticed by workmen for some days, was rescued, but—by Jove! it bit the man's hand to pieces!"

"Wild with hunger, I suppose," commented Miss Allan.

"You're all neglecting the chief advantage of being abroad," said Mr. Hughling Elliot, who had joined the group. "You might read your news in French, which is equivalent to reading no news at all."

Mr. Elliot had a profound knowledge of Coptic,[5] which he concealed as far as possible, and quoted French phrases so exquisitely that it was hard to believe that he could also speak the ordinary tongue. He had an immense respect for the French.

"Coming?" he asked the two young men. "We ought to start before it's really hot."

"I beg of you not to walk in the heat, Hugh," his wife pleaded, giving him an angular parcel enclosing half a chicken and some raisins.

"Hewet will be our barometer," said Mr. Elliot. "He will melt before I shall."

Indeed, if so much as a drop had melted off his spare ribs, the bones would have lain bare. The ladies were left alone now surrounding *The Times* which lay upon the floor. Miss Allan looked at her father's watch.

"Ten minutes to eleven," she observed.

"Work?" asked Mrs. Thornbury.

"Work," replied Miss Allan.

"What a fine creature she is!" murmured Mrs. Thornbury, as the square figure in its manly coat withdrew.

"And I'm sure she has a hard life," sighed Mrs. Elliot.

"Oh, it *is* a hard life," said Mrs. Thornbury. "Unmarried women—earning their livings—it's the hardest life of all."

"Yet she seems pretty cheerful," said Mrs. Elliot.

"It must be very interesting," said Mrs. Thornbury. "I envy her her knowledge."

"But that isn't what women want," said Mrs. Elliot.

"I'm afraid it's all a great many can hope to have," sighed Mrs. Thornbury. "I believe that there are more of us than ever now. Sir Harley Lethbridge was telling me only the other day how difficult it is to find boys for the navy   partly because of their teeth, it is true. And I have heard young women talk quite openly of———"

"Dreadful, dreadful!" exclaimed Mrs. Elliot. "The crown, as one may call it, of a woman's life. I, who know what it is to be childless———" she sighed and ceased.

"But we must not be hard," said Mrs. Thornbury. "The conditions are so much changed since I was a young woman."

"Surely *maternity* does not change," said Mrs. Elliot.

"In some ways we can learn a great deal from the young," said Mrs. Thornbury. "I learn so much from my own daughters."

"I believe that Hughling really doesn't mind," said Mrs. Elliot. "But then he has his work."

"Women without children can do so much for the children of others," observed Mrs. Thornbury gently.

"I sketch a great deal," said Mrs. Elliot, "but that isn't really an occupation. It's so disconcerting to find girls just beginning doing better than one does oneself? And nature's difficult—very difficult!"

"Are there not institutions—clubs—that you could help?" asked Mrs. Thornbury.

"They are so exhausting," said Mrs. Elliot. "I look strong, because of my colour; but I'm not; the youngest of eleven never is."

"If the mother is careful before," said Mrs. Thornbury judicially, "there is no reason why the size of the family should make any difference. And there is no training like the training that brothers and sisters give each other. I am sure of that. I have seen it with my own children. My eldest boy, Ralph, for instance——"

But Mrs. Elliot was inattentive to the elder lady's experience, and her eyes wandered about the hall.

"My mother had two miscarriages, I know," she said suddenly. "The first because she met one of those great dancing bears—they shouldn't be allowed; the other—it was a horrid story—our cook had a child and there was a dinner party. So I put my dyspepsia down to that."

"And a miscarriage is so much worse than a confinement," Mrs. Thornbury murmured absent-mindedly, adjusting her spectacles and picking up *The Times*. Mrs. Elliot rose and fluttered away.

When she had heard what one of the million voices speaking in the paper had to say, and noticed that a cousin of hers had married a clergyman at Minehead—ignoring the drunken women, the golden animals of Crete, the movements of battalions, the dinners, the re- forms, the fires, the indignant, the learned and benevolent, Mrs. Thornbury went upstairs to write a letter for the mail.

The paper lay directly beneath the clock; the two together seem- ing to represent stability in a changing world. Mr. Perrott passed through; Mr. Venning poised for a second on the edge of a table. Mrs. Paley was wheeled past. Susan followed. Mr. Venning strolled after her. Portuguese military families, their clothes suggesting late rising in untidy bedrooms, trailed across, attended by confidential nurses carrying noisy children. As midday drew on, and the sun beat straight upon the roof, an eddy of great flies droned in a circle; iced drinks were served under the palms; the long blinds were pulled down with a shriek, turning all the light yellow. The clock now had a silent hall to tick in, and an audience of four or five som- nolent merchants. By degrees white figures with shady hats came in at the door, admitting a wedge of the hot summer day, and shutting it out again. After resting in the dimness for a minute, they went upstairs. Simultaneously, the clock wheezed one, and the gong sounded, beginning softly, working itself into a frenzy, and ceasing. There was a pause. Then all those who had gone upstairs came down; cripples came, planting both feet on the same step lest they should slip; prim little girls came, holding the nurse's finger; fat old men came still buttoning waistcoats. The gong had been sounded in the garden, and by degrees recumbent figures rose and strolled in to eat, since the time had come for them to feed again. There were pools and bars of shade in the garden even at midday, where two or three visitors could lie working or talking at their ease.

Owing to the heat of the day, luncheon was generally a silent meal, when people observed their neighbors and took stock of any new faces there might be, hazarding guesses as to who they were and what they did. Mrs. Paley, although well over seventy and crippled in the legs, enjoyed her food and the peculiarities of her fellow-beings. She was seated at a small table with Susan.

"I shouldn't like to say what *she* is!" she chuckled, surveying a tall woman dressed conspicuously in white, with paint in the hollows of her cheeks, who was always late, and always attended by a shabby female follower, at which remark Susan blushed, and wondered why her aunt said such things.

Lunch went on methodically, until each of the seven courses was left in fragments and the fruit was merely a toy, to be peeled and sliced as a child destroys a daisy, petal by petal. The food served as an extinguisher upon any faint flame of the human spirit that might survive the midday heat, but Susan sat in her room afterwards, turning over and over the delightful fact that Mr. Venning had come to her in the garden, and had sat there quite half an hour while she read aloud to her aunt. Men and women sought different corners where they could lie unobserved, and from two to four it might be said without exaggeration that the hotel was inhabited by bodies without souls. Disastrous would have been the result if a fire or a death had suddenly demanded something heroic of human nature, but by a merciful dispensation, tragedies come in the hungry hours. Towards four o'clock the human spirit again began to lick the body, as a flame licks a black promontory of coal. Mrs. Paley felt it unseemly to open her toothless jaw so widely, though there was no one near, and Mrs. Elliot surveyed her round flushed face anxiously in the looking-glass.

Half an hour later, having removed the traces of sleep, they met each other in the hall, and Mrs. Paley observed that she was going to have her tea.

"You like your tea too, don't you?" she said, and invited Mrs. Elliot, whose husband was still out, to join her at a special table which she had placed for her under a tree.

"A little silver goes a long way in this country," she chuckled.

She sent Susan back to fetch another cup.

"They have such excellent biscuits here," she said, contemplating a plateful. "Not sweet biscuits, which I don't like—dry biscuits.... Have you been sketching?"

"Oh, I've done two or three little daubs," said Mrs. Elliot, speaking rather louder than usual. "But it's so difficult after Oxfordshire, where there are so many trees. The light's so strong here. Some people admire it, I know, but I find it very fatiguing."

"I really don't need cooking, Susan," said Mrs. Paley, when her niece returned. "I must trouble you to move me."

Everything had to be moved. Finally the old lady was placed so that the light wavered over her, as though she were a fish in a net. Susan poured out tea, and was just remarking that they were having hot weather in Wiltshire too, when Mr. Venning asked whether he might join them.

"It's so nice to find a young man who doesn't despise tea," said Mrs. Paley, regaining her good humour. "One of my nephews the other day asked for a glass of sherry—at five o'clock! I told him he could get it at the public-house round the corner, but not in my drawing-room."

"I'd rather go without lunch than tea," said Mr. Venning. "That's not strictly true. I want both."

Mr. Venning was a dark young man, about thirty-two years of age, very slapdash and confident in his manner, although at this moment obviously a little excited. His friend Mr. Perrott was a barrister, and as Mr. Perrott refused to go anywhere without Mr. Venning it was necessary, when Mr. Perrott came to Santa Marina about a Company, for Mr. Venning to come too. He was a barrister also, but he loathed a profession which kept him indoors over books, and directly his widowed mother died he was going, so he confided to Susan, to take up flying seriously, and become partner in a large business for making aeroplanes. The talk rambled on. It dealt, of course, with the beauties and singularities of the place, the streets, the people, and the quantities of unowned yellow dogs.

"Don't you think it dreadfully cruel the way they treat dogs in this country?" asked Mrs. Paley.

"I'd have 'em all shot," said Mr. Venning.

"Oh, but the darling puppies," said Susan.

"Jolly little chaps," said Mr. Venning. "Look here, you've got nothing to eat." A great wedge of cake was handed Susan on the point of a trembling knife. Her hand trembled too as she took it.

"I have such a dear dog at home," said Mrs. Elliot.

"My parrot can't bear dogs," said Mrs. Paley, with the air of one making a confidence. "I always suspect that he (or she) was teased by a dog when I was abroad."

"You didn't get far this morning, Miss Warrington," said Mr. Venning.

"It was hot," she answered. Their conversation became private, owing to Mrs. Paley's deafness and the long sad history which Mrs. Elliot had embarked upon of a wire-haired terrier, white with just one black spot, belonging to an uncle of hers, which had committed suicide. "Animals do commit suicide," she sighed, as if she asserted a painful fact.

"Couldn't we explore the town this evening?" Mr. Venning suggested.

"My aunt——" Susan began.

"You deserve a holiday," he said. "You're always doing things for other people."

"But that's my life," she said, under cover of refilling the teapot.

"That's no one's life," he returned, "no young person's. You'll come?"

"I should like to come," she murmured.

At this moment Mrs. Elliot looked up and exclaimed, "Oh, Hugh! He's bringing some one," she added.

"He would like some tea," said Mrs. Paley. "Susan, run and get some cups—there are the two young men."

"We're thirsting for tea," said Mr. Elliot. "You know Mr. Ambrose, Hilda? We met on the hill."

"He dragged me in," said Ridley, "or I should have been ashamed. I'm dusty and dirty and disagreeable." He pointed to his boots which were white with dust, while a dejected flower drooping in his buttonhole, like an exhausted animal over a gate, added to the effect of length and untidiness. He was introduced to the others. Mr. Hewet and Mr. Hirst brought chairs, and tea began again, Susan pouring cascades of water from pot to pot, always cheerfully, and with the competence of long use.

"My wife's brother," Ridley explained to Hilda, whom he failed to remember, "has a house here, which he has lent us. I was sitting on a rock thinking of nothing at all when Elliot started up like a fairy in a pantomime."

"Our chicken got into the salt," Hewet said dolefully to Susan. "Nor is it true that bananas include moisture as well as sustenance."

Hirst was already drinking.

"We've been cursing you," said Ridley in answer to Mrs. Elliot's kind enquiries about his wife. "You tourists eat up all the eggs, Helen tells me. That's an eyesore too"—he nodded his head at the hotel. "Disgusting luxury, I call it. We live with pigs in the drawing-room."

"The food is not at all what it ought to be, considering the price," said Mrs. Paley seriously. "But unless one goes to a hotel where is one to go to?"

"Stay at home," said Ridley. "I often wish I had! Every one ought to stay at home. But, of course, they won't."

Mrs. Paley conceived a certain grudge against Ridley, who seemed to be criticising her habits after an acquaintance of five minutes.

"I believe in foreign travel myself," she stated, "if one knows one's native land, which I think I can honestly say I do. I should not allow any one to travel until they had visited Kent and Dorsetshire—Kent for the hops, and Dorsetshire for its old stone cottages. There is nothing to compare with them here."

"Yes—I always think that some people like the flat and other people like the downs," said Mrs. Elliot rather vaguely.

Hirst, who had been eating and drinking without interruption, now lit a cigarette, and observed, "Oh, but we're all agreed by this time that nature's a mistake. She's either very ugly, appallingly uncomfortable, or absolutely terrifying. I don't know which alarms me most—a cow or a tree. I once met a cow in a field by night. The creature looked at me. I assure you it turned my hair grey. It's a disgrace that the animals should be allowed to go at large."

"And what did the cow think of *him?*" Venning mumbled to Susan, who immediately decided in her own mind that Mr. Hirst was a dreadful young man, and that although he had such an air of being clever he probably wasn't as clever as Arthur, in the ways that really matter.

"Wasn't it Wilde who discovered the fact that nature makes no allowance for hip-bones?" enquired Hughling Elliot. He knew by this time exactly what scholarships and distinctions Hirst enjoyed, and had formed a very high opinion of his capacities.

But Hirst merely drew his lips together very tightly and made no reply.

Ridley conjectured that it was now permissible for him to take his leave. Politeness required him to thank Mrs. Elliot for his tea, and to add, with a wave of his hand, "You must come up and see us."

The wave included both Hirst and Hewet, and Hewet answered, "I should like it immensely."

The party broke up, and Susan, who had never felt as happy in her life, was just about to start for her walk in the town with Arthur, when Mrs. Paley beckoned her back. She could not understand from the book how Double Demon patience is played; and suggested that if they sat down and worked it out together it would fill up the time nicely before dinner.

CHAPTER X

Among the promises which Mrs. Ambrose had made her niece should she stay was a room cut off from the rest of the house, large, private—a room in which she could play, read, think, defy the world, a fortress as well as a sanctuary. Rooms, she knew, became more like worlds than rooms at the age of twenty-four. Her judgment was correct, and when she shut the door Rachel entered an enchanted place, where the poets sang and things fell into their right proportions. Some days after the vision of the hotel by night she was sitting alone, sunk in an arm-chair, reading a brightly-covered red volume lettered on the back *Works of Henrik Ibsen*.[1] Music was open on the piano, and books of music rose in two jagged pillars on the floor; but for the moment music was deserted.

Far from looking bored or absent-minded, her eyes were concentrated almost sternly upon the page, and from her breathing, which was slow but repressed, it could be seen that her whole body was constrained by the working of her mind. At last she shut the book sharply, lay back, and drew a deep breath, expressive of the wonder which always marks the transition from the imaginary world to the real world.

"What I want to know," she said aloud, "is this: What is the truth?

What's the truth of it all?" She was speaking partly as herself, and partly as the heroine of the play she had just read. The landscape outside, because she had seen nothing but print for the space of two hours, now appeared amazingly solid and clear, but although there were men on the hill washing the trunks of olive trees with a white liquid, for the moment she herself was the most vivid thing in it—an heroic statue in the middle of the foreground, dominating the view. Ibsen's plays always left her in that condition. She acted them for days at a time, greatly to Helen's amusement; and then it would be Meredith's turn and she became Diana of the Crossways.[2] But Helen was aware that it was not all acting, and that some sort of change was taking place in the human being. When Rachel became tired of the rigidity of her pose on the back of the chair, she turned round, slid comfortably down into it, and gazed out over the furniture through the window opposite which opened on the garden. (Her mind wandered away from Nora;[3] but she went on thinking of other things that the book suggested to her; of women and life.)

During the three months she had been here she had made up considerably, as Helen meant she should, for time spent in interminable walks round sheltered gardens, and the household gossip of her aunts. But Mrs. Ambrose would have been the first to disclaim any influence, or indeed any belief that to influence was within her power. She saw her less shy, and less serious, which was all to the good, and the violent leaps and the interminable mazes which had led to that result were usually not even guessed at by her. Talk was the medicine she trusted to, talk about everything, talk that was free, unguarded, and as candid as a habit of talking with men made natural in her own case. Nor did she encourage those habits of unselfishness and amiability founded upon insincerity which are put at so high a value in mixed households of men and women. She desired that Rachel should think, and for this reason offered books and discouraged too entire a dependence upon Bach and Beethoven and Wagner. But when Mrs. Ambrose would have suggested Defoe, Maupassant,[4] or some spacious chronicle of family life, Rachel chose modern books, books in shiny yellow covers, books with a great deal of gilding on the back, which were tokens in her aunts' eyes of harsh wrangling and disputes about facts which had no such importance as the moderns claimed for them. But she did not interfere. Rachel read what she chose, reading with the curious literalness of one to whom written sentences are unfamiliar, and handling words as though they were made of wood, separately of great importance, and possessed of shapes like tables or chairs. In this way she came to conclusions, which had to be remodelled according to the adventures of the day, and were indeed recast as liberally as any one could desire, leaving always a small grain of belief behind them.

Ibsen was succeeded by a novel such as Mrs. Ambrose detested, whose purpose was to distribute the guilt of a woman's downfall upon the right shoulders; a purpose which was achieved, if the reader's discomfort were any proof of it. She threw the book down, looked out of the window, turned away from the window, and relapsed into an arm-chair.

The morning was hot, and the exercise of reading left her mind contracting and expanding like the mainspring of a clock. The sounds in the garden outside joined with the clock, and the small noises of midday, which one can ascribe to no definite cause, in a regular rhythm. It was all very real, very big, very impersonal, and after a moment or two she began to raise her first finger and to let it fall on the arm of her chair so as to bring back to herself some consciousness of her own existence. She was next overcome by the unspeakable queerness of the fact that she should be sitting in an arm-chair, in the morning, in the middle of the world. Who were the people moving in the house—moving things from one place to another? And life, what was that? It was only a light passing over the surface and vanishing, as in time she would vanish, though the furniture in the room would remain. Her dissolution became so complete that she could not raise her finger any more, and sat perfectly still, listening and looking always at the same spot. It became stranger and stranger. She was overcome with awe that things should exist at all.... She forgot that she had any fingers to raise.... The things that existed were so immense and so desolate.... She continued to be conscious of these vast masses of substance for a long stretch of time, the clock still ticking in the midst of the universal silence.

"Come in," she said mechanically, for a string in her brain seemed to be pulled by a persistent knocking at the door. With great slowness the door opened and a tall human being came towards her, holding out her arm and saying:

"What am I to say to this?"

The utter absurdity of a woman coming into a room with a piece of paper in her hand amazed Rachel.

"I don't know what to answer, or who Terence Hewet is," Helen continued, in the toneless voice of a ghost. She put a paper before Rachel on which were written the incredible words:

Dear Mrs. Ambrose—

I am getting up a picnic for next Friday, when we propose to start at eleven-thirty if the weather is fine, and to make the ascent of Monte Rosa. It will take some time, but the view should be magnificent. It would give me great pleasure if you and Miss Vinrace would consent to be of the party.—Yours sincerely,

Terence Hewet.

Rachel read the words aloud to make herself believe in them. For the same reason she put her hand on Helen's shoulder.

"Books—books—books," said Helen, in her absent-minded way. "More new books—I wonder what you find in them...."

For the second time Rachel read the letter, but to herself. This time, instead of seeming vague as ghosts, each word was astonishingly prominent; they came out as the tops of mountains come through a mist. *Friday—eleven-thirty—Miss Vinrace.* The blood began to run in her veins; she felt her eyes brighten.

"We must go," she said, rather surprising Helen by her decision. "We must certainly go"—such was the relief of finding that things still happened, and indeed they appeared the brighter for the mist surrounding them.

"Monte Rosa—that's the mountain over there, isn't it?" said Helen; "but Hewet—who's he? One of the young men Ridley met, I suppose. Shall I say yes, then? It may be dreadfully dull."

She took the letter back and went, for the messenger was waiting for her answer.

The party which had been suggested a few nights ago in Mr. Hirst's bedroom had taken shape and was the source of great satisfaction to Mr. Hewet, who had seldom used his practical abilities, and was pleased to find them equal to the strain. His invitations had been universally accepted, which was the more encouraging as they had been issued against Hirst's advice to people who were very dull, not at all suited to each other, and sure not to come.

"Undoubtedly," he said, as he twirled and untwirled a note signed Helen Ambrose, "the gifts needed to make a great commander have been absurdly overrated. About half the intellectual effort which is needed to review a book of modern poetry has enabled me to get together seven or eight people, of opposite sexes, at the same spot at the same hour on the same day. What else is generalship, Hirst? What more did Wellington do on the field of Waterloo? It's like counting the number of pebbles of a path, tedious but not difficult."

He was sitting in his bedroom, one leg over the arm of the chair, and Hirst was writing a letter opposite. Hirst was quick to point out that all the difficulties remained.

"For instance, here are two women you've never seen. Suppose one of them suffers from mountain-sickness, as my sister does, and the other——"

"Oh, the women are for you," Hewet interrupted. "I asked them solely for your benefit. What you want, Hirst, you know, is the society of young women of your own age. You don't know how to get on with women, which is a great defect, considering that half the world consists of women."

Hirst groaned that he was quite aware of that.

But Hewet's complacency was a little chilled as he walked with Hirst to the place where a general meeting had been appointed. He wondered why on earth he had asked these people, and what one really expected to get from bunching human beings together in a crowd.

"Cows," he reflected, "draw together in a field; ships in a calm; and we're just the same when we've nothing else to do. But why do we do it?—is it to prevent ourselves from seeing to the bottom of things" (he stopped by a stream and began stirring it with his walking-stick and clouding the water with mud), "making cities and mountains and whole universes out of nothing, or do we really love each other, or do we, on the other hand, live in a state of perpetual uncertainty, knowing nothing, leaping from moment to moment as from world to world?—which is, on the whole, the view *I* incline to."

He jumped over the stream; Hirst went round and joined him, remarking that he had long ceased to look for the reason of any human action.

Half a mile further, they came to a group of plane trees and the salmon-pink farmhouse standing by the stream which had been chosen as meeting-place. It was a shady spot, lying conveniently just where the hill sprung out from the flat. Between the thin stems of the plane trees the young men could see little knots of donkeys pasturing, and a tall woman rubbing the nose of one of them, while another woman was kneeling by the stream lapping water out of her palms.

As they entered the shady place, Helen looked up and then held out her hand.

"I must introduce myself," she said. "I am Mrs. Ambrose."

Having shaken hands, she said, "That's my niece."

Rachel approached awkwardly. She held out her hand, but withdrew it. "It's all wet," she said.

Scarcely had they spoken, when the first carriage drew up.

The donkeys were quickly jerked into attention, and the second carriage arrived. By degrees the grove filled with people—the Elliots, the Thornburys, Mr. Venning and Susan, Miss Allan, Evelyn Murgatroyd, and Mr. Perrott. Mr. Hirst acted the part of hoarse energetic sheep-dog. By means of a few words of caustic Latin he had the animals marshalled, and by inclining a sharp shoulder he lifted the ladies. "What Hewet fails to understand," he remarked, "is that we must break the back of the ascent before midday." He was assisting a young lady, by name Evelyn Murgatroyd, as he spoke. She rose light as a bubble to her seat. With a feather drooping from a broad-brimmed hat, in white from top to toe, she looked like a gallant lady of the time of Charles the First leading royalist troops into action.

"Ride with me," she commanded; and, as soon as Hirst had swung himself across a mule, the two started, leading the cavalcade.

"You're not to call me Miss Murgatroyd. I hate it," she said. "My name's Evelyn. What's yours?"

"St. John," he said.

"I like that," said Evelyn. "And what's your friend's name?"

"His initials being R. S. T., we call him Monk," said Hirst.

"Oh, you're all too clever," she said. "Which way? Pick me a branch. Let's canter."

She gave her donkey a sharp cut with a switch and started forward. The full and romantic career of Evelyn Murgatroyd is best hit off by her own words, "Call me Evelyn and I'll call you St. John." She said that on very slight provocation—her surname was enough—but although a great many young men had answered her already with considerable spirit she went on saying it and making choice of none. But her donkey stumbled to a jog-trot, and she had to ride in advance alone, for the path when it began to ascend one of the spines of the hill became narrow and scattered with stones. The calvacade wound on like a jointed caterpillar, tufted with the white parasols of the ladies, and the panama hats of the gentlemen. At one point where the ground rose sharply, Evelyn M. jumped off, threw her reins to the native boy, and adjured St. John Hirst to dismount too. Their example was followed by those who felt the need of stretching.

"I don't see any need to get off," said Miss Allan to Mrs. Elliot just behind her, "considering the difficulty I had in getting on."

"These little donkeys stand anything, *n'est-ce pas?*" Mrs. Elliot addressed the guide, who obligingly bowed his head.

"Flowers," said Helen, stooping to pick the lovely little bright flowers which grew separately here and there. "You pinch their leaves and then they smell," she said, laying one on Miss Allan's knee.

"Haven't we met before?" asked Miss Allan, looking at her.

"I was taking it for granted," Helen laughed, for in the confusion of meeting they had not been introduced.

"How sensible!" chirped Mrs. Elliot. "That's just what one would always like—only unfortunately it's not possible."

"Not possible?" said Helen. "Everything's possible. Who knows what mayn't happen before nightfall?" she continued, mocking the poor lady's timidity, who depended so implicitly upon one thing following another that the mere glimpse of a world where dinner could be disregarded, or the table moved one inch from its accustomed place, filled her with fears for her own stability.

Higher and higher they went, becoming separated from the world. The world, when they turned to look back, flattened itself out, and was marked with squares of thin green and grey.

"Towns are very small," Rachel remarked, obscuring the whole of Santa Marina and its suburbs with one hand. The sea filled in all the angles of the coast smoothly, breaking in a white frill, and here and there ships were set firmly in the blue. The sea was stained with purple and green blots, and there was a glittering line upon the rim where it met the sky. The air was very clear and silent save for the sharp noise of grasshoppers and the hum of bees, which sounded loud in the ear as they shot past and vanished. The party halted and sat for a time in a quarry on the hillside.

"Amazingly clear," exclaimed St. John, identifying one cleft in the land after another.

Evelyn M. sat beside him, propping her chin on her hand. She surveyed the view with a certain look of triumph.

"D'you think Garibaldi[5] was ever up here?" she asked Mr. Hirst. Oh, if she had been his bride! If, instead of a picnic party, this was a party of patriots, and she, red-shirted like the rest, had lain among grim men, flat on the turf, aiming her gun at the white turrets beneath them, screening her eyes to pierce through the smoke! So thinking, her foot stirred restlessly, and she exclaimed:

"I don't call this *life*, do you?"

"What do you call life?" said St. John.

"Fighting—revolution," she said, still gazing at the doomed city. "You only care for books, I know."

"You're quite wrong," said St. John.

"Explain," she urged, for there were no guns to be aimed at bodies, and she turned to another kind of warfare.

"What do I care for? People," he said.

"Well, I *am* surprised!" she exclaimed. "You look so awfully serious. Do let's be friends and tell each other what we're like. I hate being cautious, don't you?"

But St. John was decidedly cautious, as she could see by the sudden constriction of his lips, and had no intention of revealing his soul to a young lady.

"The ass is eating my hat," he remarked, and stretched out for it instead of answering her. Evelyn blushed very slightly and then turned with some impetuosity upon Mr. Perrott, and when they mounted again it was Mr. Perrott who lifted her to her seat.

"When one has laid the eggs one eats the omelette," said Hughling Elliot, exquisitely in French, a hint to the rest of them that it was time to ride on again.

The midday sun which Hirst had foretold was beginning to beat down hotly. The higher they got the more of the sky appeared, until the mountain was only a small tent of earth against an enormous blue background. The English fell silent; the natives who walked beside the donkeys broke into queer wavering songs and tossed jokes from one to the other. The way grew very steep, and each rider kept his eyes fixed on the hobbling curved form of the rider and donkey directly in front of him. Rather more strain was being put upon their bodies than is quite legitimate in a party of pleasure, and Hewet overheard one or two slightly grumbling remarks.

"Expeditions in such heat are perhaps a little unwise," Mrs. Elliot murmured to Miss Allan.

But Miss Allan returned, "I always like to get to the top"; and it was true, although she was a big woman, stiff in the joints, and unused to donkey-riding, but as her holidays were few she made the most of them.

The vivacious white figure rode well in front; she had somehow possessed herself of a leafy branch and wore it round her hat like a garland. They went on for a few minutes in silence.

"The view will be wonderful," Hewet assured them, turning round in his saddle and smiling encouragement. Rachel caught his eye and smiled too. They struggled on for some time longer, nothing being heard but the clatter of hooves striving on the loose stones. Then they saw that Evelyn was off her ass, and that Mr. Perrott was standing in the attitude of a statesman in Parliament Square, stretching an arm of stone towards the view. A little to the left of them was a low ruined wall, the stump of an Elizabethan watch-tower.

"I couldn't have stood it much longer," Mrs. Elliot confided to Mrs. Thornbury, but the excitement of being at the top in another moment and seeing the view prevented any one from answering her. One after another they came out on the flat space on the top and stood overcome with wonder. Before them they beheld an immense space—grey sands running into forest, and forest merging in mountains, and mountains washed by air,—the infinite distances of South America. A river ran across the plain, as flat as the land, and appearing quite as stationary. The effect of so much space was at first rather chilling. They felt themselves very small, and for some time no one said anything. Then Evelyn exclaimed, "Splendid!" She took hold of the hand that was next her; it chanced to be Miss Allan's hand.

"North—South—East—West," said Miss Allan, jerking her head slightly towards the points of the compass.

Hewet, who had gone a little in front, looked up at his guests as if to justify himself for having brought them. He observed how strangely the people standing in a row with their figures bent slightly forward and their clothes plastered by the wind to the shape of their bodies resembled naked statues. On their pedestal of earth they looked unfamiliar and noble, but in another moment they had broken their rank, and he had to see to the laying out of food. Hirst came to his help, and they handed packets of chicken and bread from one to another.

As St. John gave Helen her packet she looked him full in the face and said:

"Do you remember—two women?"

He looked at her sharply.

"I do," he answered.

"So you're the two women!" Hewet exclaimed, looking from Helen to Rachel.

"Your lights tempted us," said Helen. "We watched you playing cards, but we never knew that we were being watched."

"It was like a thing in a play," Rachel added.

"And Hirst couldn't describe you," said Hewet.

It was certainly odd to have seen Helen and to find nothing to say about her.

Hughling Elliot put up his eyeglass and grasped the situation.

"I don't know anything more dreadful," he said, pulling at the joint of a chicken's leg, "than being seen when one isn't conscious of it. One feels sure one has been caught doing something ridiculous—looking at one's tongue in a hansom, for instance."

Now the others ceased to look at the view, and drawing together sat down in a circle round the baskets.

"And yet those little looking-glasses in hansoms have a fascination of their own," said Mrs. Thornbury. "One's features look so different when one can only see a bit of them."

"There will soon be very few hansom cabs left," said Mrs. Elliot. "And four-wheeled cabs—I assure you even at Oxford it's almost impossible to get a four-wheeled cab."

"I wonder what happens to the horses," said Susan.

"Veal pie," said Arthur.

"It's high time that horses should become extinct anyhow," said Hirst. "They're distressingly ugly, besides being vicious."

But Susan, who had been brought up to understand that the horse is the noblest of God's creatures, could not agree, and Venning thought Hirst an unspeakable ass, but was too polite not to continue the conversation.

"When they see us falling out of aeroplanes they get some of their own back, I expect," he remarked.

"You fly?" said old Mr. Thornbury, putting on his spectacles to look at him.

"I hope to, some day," said Arthur.

Here flying was discussed at length, and Mrs. Thornbury delivered an opinion which was almost a speech to the effect that it would be quite necessary in time of war, and in England we were terribly behindhand. "If I were a young fellow," she concluded, "I should certainly qualify." It was odd to look at the little elderly lady, in her grey coat and skirt, with a sandwich in her hand, her eyes lighting up with zeal as she imagined herself a young man in an aeroplane. For some reason, however, the talk did not run easily after this, and all they said was about drink and salt and the view. Suddenly Miss Allan, who was seated with her back to the ruined wall, put down her sandwich, picked something off her neck, and remarked, "I'm covered with little creatures." It was true, and the discovery was very welcome. The ants were pouring down a glacier of loose earth heaped between the stones of the ruin—large brown ants with polished bodies. She held out one on the back of her hand for Helen to look at.

"Suppose they sting?" said Helen.

"They will not sting, but they may infest the victuals," said Miss Allan, and measures were taken at once to divert the ants from their course. At Hewet's suggestion it was decided to adopt the methods of modern warfare against an invading army. The table-cloth represented the invaded country, and round it they built barricades of baskets, set up the wine bottles in a rampart, made fortifications of bread and dug fosses of salt. When an ant got through it was exposed to a fire of bread-crumbs, until Susan pronounced that that was cruel, and rewarded those brave spirits with spoil in the shape of tongue. Playing this game they lost their stiffness, and even became unusually daring, for Mr. Perrott, who was very shy, said, "Permit me," and removed an ant from Evelyn's neck.

"It would be no laughing matter really," said Mrs. Elliot confidentially to Mrs. Thornbury, "if an ant did get between the vest and the skin."

The noise grew suddenly more clamorous, for it was discovered that a long line of ants had found their way on to the table-cloth by a back entrance, and if success could be gauged by noise, Hewet had every reason to think his party a success. Nevertheless he became, for no reason at all, profoundly depressed.

"They are not satisfactory; they are ignoble," he thought, surveying his guests from a little distance, where he was gathering together the plates. He glanced at them all, stooping and swaying and gesticulating round the table-cloth. Amiable and modest, respectable in many ways, lovable even in their contentment and desire to be kind, how mediocre they all were, and capable of what insipid cruelty to one another! There was Mrs. Thornbury, sweet but trivial in her maternal egoism; Mrs. Elliot, perpetually complaining of her lot; her husband a mere pea in a pod; and Susan—she had no self, and counted neither one way nor the other; Venning was as honest and as brutal as a schoolboy; poor old Thornbury merely trod his round like a horse in a mill; and the less one examined into Evelyn's character the better, he suspected. Yet these were the people with money, and to them rather than to others was given the management of the world. Put among them some one more vital, who cared for life or for beauty, and what an agony, what a waste would they inflict on him if he tried to share with them and not to scourge!

"There's Hirst," he concluded, coming to the figure of his friend; with his usual little frown of concentration upon his forehead he was peeling the skin off a banana. "And he's as ugly as sin." For the ugliness of St. John Hirst, and the limitations that went with it, he made the rest in some way responsible. It was their fault that he had to live alone. Then he came to Helen, attracted to her by the sound of her laugh. She was laughing at Miss Allan. "You wear combinations in this heat?" she said in a voice which was meant to be private. He liked the look of her immensely, not so much her beauty, but her largeness and simplicity, which made her stand out from the rest like a great stone woman, and he passed on in a gentler mood. His eye fell upon Rachel. She was lying back rather behind the others resting on one elbow; she might have been thinking precisely the same thoughts as Hewet himself. Her eyes were fixed rather sadly but not intently upon the row of people opposite her. Hewet crawled up to her on his knees, with a piece of bread in his hand.

"What are you looking at?" he asked.

She was a little startled, but answered directly, "Human beings."

Chapter XI

One after another they rose and stretched themselves, and in a few minutes divided more or less into two separate parties. One of these parties was dominated by Hughling Elliot and Mrs. Thornbury, who, having both read the same books and considered the same questions, were now anxious to name the places beneath them and to hang upon them stores of information about navies and armies, political parties, natives and mineral products—all of which combined, they said, to prove that South America was the country of the future.

Evelyn M. listened with her bright blue eyes fixed upon the oracles.

"How it makes one long to be a man!" she exclaimed.

Mr. Perrott answered, surveying the plain, that a country with a future was a very fine thing.

"If I were you," said Evelyn, turning to him and drawing her glove vehemently through her fingers, "I'd raise a troop and conquer some great territory and make it splendid. You'd want women for that. I'd love to start life from the very beginning as it ought to be—nothing squalid—but great halls and gardens and splendid men and women. But you—you only like Law Courts!"

"And would you really be content without pretty frocks and sweets and all the things young ladies like?" asked Mr. Perrott, concealing a certain amount of pain beneath his ironical manner.

"I'm not a young lady," Evelyn flashed; she bit her underlip. "Just because I like splendid things you laugh at me. Why are there no men like Garibaldi now?" she demanded.

"Look here," said Mr. Perrott, "you don't give me a chance. You think we ought to begin things fresh. Good. But I don't see precisely—conquer a territory? They're all conquered already, aren't they?"

"It's not any territory in particular," Evelyn explained. "It's the idea, don't you see? We lead such tame lives. And I feel sure you've got splendid things in you."

Hewet saw the scars and hollows in Mr. Perrott's sagacious face relax pathetically. He could imagine the calculations which even then went on within his mind, as to whether he would be justified in asking a woman to marry him, considering that he made no more than five hundred a year at the Bar, owned no private means, and had an invalid sister to support. Mr. Perrott again knew that he was not "quite," as Susan stated in her diary; not quite a gentleman she meant, for he was the son of a grocer in Leeds, had started life with a basket on his back, and now, though practically indistinguishable from a born gentleman, showed his origin to keen eyes in an impeccable neatness of dress, lack of freedom in manner, extreme cleanliness of person, and a certain indescribable timidity and precision with his knife and fork which might be the relic of days when meat was rare, and the way of handling it by no means gingerly.

The two parties who were strolling about and losing their unity now came together, and joined each other in a long stare over the yellow and green patches of the heated landscape below. The hot air danced across it, making it impossible to see the roofs of a village on the plain distinctly. Even on the top of the mountain where a breeze played lightly, it was very hot, and the heat, the food, the immense space, and perhaps some less well-defined cause produced a comfortable drowsiness and a sense of happy relaxation in them. They did not say much, but felt no constraint in being silent.

"Suppose we go and see what's to be seen over there?" said Arthur to Susan, and the pair walked off together, their departure certainly sending some thrill of emotion through the rest.

"An odd lot, aren't they?" said Arthur. "I thought we should never get 'em all to the top. But I'm glad we came, by Jove! I wouldn't have missed this for something."

"I don't *like* Mr. Hirst," said Susan inconsequently. "I suppose he's very clever, but why should clever people be so—I expect he's awfully nice, really," she added, instinctively qualifying what might have seemed an unkind remark.

"Hirst? Oh, he's one of these learned chaps," said Arthur indifferently. "He don't look as if he enjoyed it. You should hear him talking to Elliot. It's as much as I can do to follow 'em at all.... I was never good at my books."

With these sentences and the pauses that came between them they reached a little hillock, on the top of which grew several slim trees.

"D'you mind if we sit down here?" said Arthur, looking about him. "It's jolly in the shade—and the view—" They sat down, and looked straight ahead of them in silence for some time.

"But I do envy those clever chaps sometimes," Arthur remarked. "I don't suppose they ever . . ." He did not finish his sentence.

"I can't see why you should envy them," said Susan, with great sincerity.

"Odd things happen to one," said Arthur. "One goes along smoothly enough, one thing following another, and it's all very jolly and plain sailing, and you think you know all about it, and suddenly one doesn't know where one is a bit, and everything seems different from what it used to seem. Now to-day, coming up that path, riding behind you, I seemed to see everything as if—" he paused and plucked a piece of grass up by the roots. He scattered the little lumps of earth which were sticking to the roots—"As if it had a kind of meaning. You've made the difference to me," he jerked out, "I don't see why I shouldn't tell you. I've felt it ever since I knew you.... It's because I love you."

Even while they had been saying commonplace things Susan

had been conscious of the excitement of intimacy, which seemed not only to lay bare something in her, but in the trees and the sky, and the progress of his speech which seemed inevitable was positively painful to her, for no human being had ever come so close to her before.

She was struck motionless as his speech went on, and her heart gave great separate leaps at the last words. She sat with her fingers curled round a stone, looking straight in front of her down the mountain over the plain. So then, it had actually happened to her, a proposal of marriage.

Arthur looked round at her; his face was oddly twisted. She was drawing her breath with such difficulty that she could hardly answer.

"You might have known." He seized her in his arms; again and again and again they clasped each other, murmuring inarticulately.

"Well," sighed Arthur, sinking back on the ground, "that's the most wonderful thing that's ever happened to me." He looked as if he were trying to put things seen in a dream beside real things.

There was a long silence.

"It's the most perfect thing in the world," Susan stated, very gently and with great conviction. It was no longer merely a proposal of marriage, but of marriage with Arthur, with whom she was in love.

In the silence that followed, holding his hand tightly in hers, she prayed to God that she might make him a good wife.

"And what will Mr. Perrott say?" she asked at the end of it.

"Dear old fellow," said Arthur who, now that the first shock was over, was relaxing into an enormous sense of pleasure and contentment. "We must be very nice to him, Susan."

He told her how hard Perrott's life had been, and how absurdly devoted he was to Arthur himself. He went on to tell her about his mother, a widow lady, of strong character. In return Susan sketched the portraits of her own family—Edith in particular, her youngest sister, whom she loved better than any one else, "except you, Arthur.... Arthur," she continued, "what was it that you first liked me for?"

"It was a buckle you wore one night at sea," said Arthur, after due consideration. "I remember noticing—it's an absurd thing to notice!—that you didn't take peas, because I don't either."

From this they went on to compare their more serious tastes, or rather Susan ascertained what Arthur cared about, and professed herself very fond of the same thing. They would live in London, perhaps have a cottage in the country near Susan's family, for they would find it strange without her at first. Her mind, stunned to begin with, now flew to the various changes that her engagement would make—how delightful it would be to join the ranks of the married women—no longer to hang on to groups of girls much younger than herself—to escape the long solitude of an old maid's life. Now and then her amazing good fortune overcame her, and she turned to Arthur with an exclamation of love.

They lay in each other's arms and had no notion that they were observed. Yet two figures suddenly appeared among the trees above them.

"Here's shade," began Hewet, when Rachel suddenly stopped dead. They saw a man and woman lying on the ground beneath them, rolling slightly this way and that as the embrace tightened and slackened. The man then sat upright and the woman, who now appeared to be Susan Warrington, lay back upon the ground, with her eyes shut and an absorbed look upon her face, as though she were not altogether conscious. Nor could you tell from her expression whether she was happy, or had suffered something. When Arthur again turned to her, butting her as a lamb butts a ewe, Hewet and Rachel retreated without a word. Hewet felt uncomfortably shy.

"I don't like that," said Rachel after a moment.

"I can remember not liking it either," said Hewet. "I can remember—" but he changed his mind and continued in an ordinary tone of voice, "Well, we may take it for granted that they're engaged. D'you think he'll ever fly, or will she put a stop to that?"

But Rachel was still agitated; she could not get away from the sight they had just seen. Instead of answering Hewet she persisted: "Love's an odd thing, isn't it, making one's heart beat."

"It's so enormously important, you see," Hewet replied. "Their lives are now changed for ever."

"And it makes one sorry for them too," Rachel continued, as though she were tracing the course of her feelings. "I don't know either of them, but I could almost burst into tears. That's silly, isn't it?"

"Just because they're in love," said Hewet. "Yes," he added after a moment's consideration, "there's something horribly pathetic about it, I agree."

And now, as they had walked some way from the grove of trees, and had come to a rounded hollow very tempting to the back, they proceeded to sit down, and the impression of the lovers lost some of its force, though a certain intensity of vision, which was probably the result of the sight, remained with them. As a day upon which any emotion has been repressed is different from other days, so this day was now different, merely because they had seen other people at a crisis of their lives.

"A great encampment of tents they might be," said Hewet, looking in front of him at the mountains. "Isn't it like a water-colour too—you know the way water-colours dry in ridges all across the paper—I've been wondering what they looked like."

His eyes became dreamy, as though he were matching things, and reminded Rachel in their colour of the green flesh of a snail. She sat beside him looking at the mountains too. When it became painful to look any longer, the great size of the view seeming to enlarge her eyes beyond their natural limit, she looked at the ground; it pleased her to scrutinise this inch of the soil of South America so minutely that she noticed every grain of earth and made it into a world where she was endowed with the supreme power. She bent a blade of grass, and set an insect on the utmost tassel of it, and wondered if the insect realised his strange adventure, and thought how strange it was that she should have bent that tassel rather than any other of the million tassels.

"You've never told me your name," said Hewet suddenly. "Miss Somebody Vinrace.... I like to know people's Christian names."

"Rachel," she replied.

"Rachel," he repeated. "I have an aunt called Rachel, who put the life of Father Damien into verse. She is a religious fanatic—the result of the way she was brought up, down in Northamptonshire, never seeing a soul. Have you any aunts?"

"I live with them," said Rachel.

"And I wonder what they're doing now?" Hewet enquired.

"They are probably buying wool," Rachel determined. She tried to describe them. "They are small, rather pale women," she began, "very clean. We live in Richmond. They have an old dog, too, who will only eat the marrow out of bones.... They are always going to church. They tidy their drawers a good deal." But here she was overcome by the difficulty of describing people.

"It's impossible to believe that it's all going on still!" she exclaimed.

The sun was behind them and two long shadows suddenly lay upon the ground in front of them, one waving because it was made by a skirt, and the other stationary, because thrown by a pair of legs in trousers.

"You look very comfortable!" said Helen's voice above them.

"Hirst," said Hewet, pointing at the scissor-like shadow; he then rolled round to look up at them.

"There's room for us all here," he said.

When Hirst had seated himself comfortably, he said:

"Did you congratulate the young couple?"

It appeared that, coming to the same spot a few minutes after Hewet and Rachel, Helen and Hirst had seen precisely the same thing.

"No, we didn't congratulate them," said Hewet. "They seemed very happy."

"Well," said Hirst, pursing up his lips, "so long as I needn't marry either of them——"

"We were very much moved," said Hewet.

"I thought you would be," said Hirst. "Which was it, Monk? The thought of the immortal passions, or the thought of new-born males to keep the Roman Catholics out? I assure you," he said to Helen, "he's capable of being moved by either."

Rachel was a good deal stung by his banter, which she felt to be directed equally against them both, but she could think of no repartee.

"Nothing moves Hirst," Hewet laughed; he did not seem to be stung at all. "Unless it were a transfinite number falling in love with a finite one—I suppose such things do happen, even in mathematics."

"On the contrary," said Hirst with a touch of annoyance, "I consider myself a person of very strong passions." It was clear from the way he spoke that he meant it seriously; he spoke of course for the benefit of the ladies.

"By the way, Hirst," said Hewet, after a pause, "I have a terrible confession to make. Your book—the poems of Wordsworth, which if you remember I took off your table just as we were starting, and certainly put in my pocket here——"

"Is lost," Hirst finished for him.

"I consider that there is still a chance," Hewet urged, slapping himself to right and left, "that I never did take it after all."

"No," said Hirst. "It is here." He pointed to his breast.

"Thank God," Hewet exclaimed. "I need no longer feel as though I'd murdered a child!"

"I should think you were always losing things," Helen remarked, looking at him meditatively.

"I don't lose things," said Hewet. "I mislay them. That was the reason why Hirst refused to share a cabin with me on the voyage out."

"You came out together?" Helen enquired.

"I propose that each member of this party now gives a short biographical sketch of himself or herself," said Hirst, sitting upright. "Miss Vinrace, you come first; begin."

Rachel stated that she was twenty-four years of age, the daughter of a ship-owner, that she had never been properly educated; played the piano, had no brothers or sisters, and lived at Richmond with aunts, her mother being dead.

"Next," said Hirst, having taken in these facts; he pointed at Hewet.

"I am the son of an English gentleman. I am twenty-seven," Hewet began. "My father was a fox-hunting squire. He died when I was ten in the hunting field. I can remember his body coming home, on a shutter I suppose, just as I was going down to tea, and noticing that there was jam for tea, and wondering whether I should be allowed——"

"Yes; but keep to the facts," Hirst put in.

"I was educated at Winchester and Cambridge, which I had to leave after a time. I have done a good many things since——"

"Profession?"

"None—at least——"

"Tastes?"

"Literary. I'm writing a novel."

"Brothers and sisters?"

"Three sisters, no brother, and a mother."

"Is that all we're to hear about you?" said Helen. She stated that she was very old—forty last October, and her father had been a solicitor in the city who had gone bankrupt, for which reason she had never had much education—they lived in one place after another—but an elder brother used to lend her books.

"If I were to tell you everything——" she stopped and smiled. "It would take too long," she concluded. "I married when I was thirty, and I have two children. My husband is a scholar. And now—it's your turn," she nodded at Hirst.

"You've left out a great deal," he reproved her. "My name is St. John Alaric Hirst," he began in a jaunty tone of voice. "I'm twenty-four years old. I'm the son of the Reverend Sidney Hirst, vicar of Great Wappyng in Norfolk. Oh, I got scholarships everywhere—Westminster—King's. I'm now a fellow of King's. Don't it sound dreary? Parents both alive (alas). Two brothers and one sister. I'm a very distinguished young man," he added.

"One of the three, or is it five, most distinguished men in England," Hewet remarked.

"Quite correct," said Hirst.

"That's all very interesting," said Helen after a pause. "But of course we've left out the only questions that matter. For instance, are we Christians?"

"I am not," "I am not," both the young men replied.

"I am," Rachel stated.

"You believe in a personal God?" Hirst demanded, turning round and fixing her with his eyeglasses.

"I believe—I believe," Rachel stammered, "I believe there are things we don't know about, and the world might change in a minute and anything appear."

At this Helen laughed outright. "Nonsense," she said. "You're not a Christian. You've never thought what you are.—And there are lots of other questions," she continued, "though perhaps we can't ask them yet." Although they had talked so freely they were all uncomfortably conscious that they really knew nothing about each other.

"The important questions," Hewet pondered, "the really interesting ones. I doubt that one ever does ask them."

Rachel, who was slow to accept the fact that only a very few things can be said even by people who know each other well, insisted on knowing what he meant.

"Whether we've ever been in love?" she enquired. "Is that the kind of question you mean?"

Again Helen laughed at her, benignantly strewing her with handfuls of the long tasselled grass, for she was so brave and so foolish.

"Oh, Rachel," she cried. "It's like having a puppy in the house having you with one—a puppy that brings one's underclothes down into the hall."

But again the sunny earth in front of them was crossed by fantastic wavering figures, the shadows of men and women.

"There they are!" exclaimed Mrs. Elliot. There was a touch of peevishness in her voice. "And we've had *such* a hunt to find you. Do you know what the time is?"

Mrs. Elliot and Mr. and Mrs. Thornbury now confronted them; Mrs. Elliot was holding out her watch, and playfully tapping it upon the face. Hewet was recalled to the fact that this was a party for which he was responsible, and he immediately led them back to the watch-tower, where they were to have tea before starting home again. A bright crimson scarf fluttered from the top of the wall, which Mr. Perrott and Evelyn were tying to a stone as the others came up. The heat had changed just so far that instead of sitting in the shadow they sat in the sun, which was still hot enough to paint their faces red and yellow, and to colour great sections of the earth beneath them.

"There's nothing half so nice as tea!" said Mrs. Thornbury, taking her cup.

"Nothing," said Helen. "Can't you remember as a child chopping up hay—" she spoke much more quickly than usual, and kept her eye fixed upon Mrs. Thornbury, "and pretending it was tea, and getting scolded by the nurses—why I can't imagine, except that nurses are such brutes, won't allow pepper instead of salt though there's no earthly harm in it. Weren't your nurses just the same?"

During this speech Susan came into the group, and sat down by Helen's side. A few minutes later Mr. Venning strolled up from the opposite direction. He was a little flushed, and in the mood to answer hilariously whatever was said to him.

"What have you been doing to that old chap's grave?" he asked, pointing to the red flag which floated from the top of the stones.

"We have tried to make him forget his misfortune in having died three hundred years ago," said Mr. Perrott.

"It would be awful—to be dead!" ejaculated Evelyn M.

"To be dead?" said Hewet. "I don't think it would be awful. It's quite easy to imagine. When you go to bed tonight fold your hands so—breathe slower and slower—" He lay back with his hands clasped upon his breast, and his eyes shut, "Now," he murmured in an even, monotonous voice, "I shall never, never, never move again." His body, lying flat among them, did for a moment suggest death.

"This is a horrible exhibition, Mr. Hewet!" cried Mrs. Thornbury.

"More cake for us!" said Arthur.

"I assure you there's nothing horrible about it," said Hewet, sitting up and laying hands upon the cake.

"It's so natural," he repeated. "People with children should make them do that exercise every night.... Not that I look forward to being dead."

"And when you allude to a grave," said Mr. Thornbury, who spoke almost for the first time, "have you any authority for calling that ruin a grave? I am quite with you in refusing to accept the common interpretation which declares it to be the remains of an Elizabethan watch-tower—any more than I believe that the circular mounds or barrows which we find on the top of our English downs were camps. The antiquaries call everything a camp. I am always asking them, Well then, where do you think our ancestors kept their cattle? Half the camps in England are merely the ancient pound or barton as we call it in my part of the world. The argument that no one would keep his cattle in such exposed and inaccessible spots has no weight at all, if you reflect that in those days a man's cattle were his capital, his stock-in-trade, his daughter's dowries. Without cattle he was a serf, another man's man...." His eyes slowly lost their intensity, and he muttered a few concluding words under his breath, looking curiously old and forlorn.

Hughling Elliot, who might have been expected to engage the old gentleman in argument, was absent at the moment. He now came up holding out a large square of cotton upon which a fine design was printed in pleasant bright colours that made his hand look pale.

"A bargain," he announced, laying it down on the cloth. "I've just bought it from the big man with the ear-rings. Fine, isn't it? It wouldn't suit every one, of course, but it's just the thing—isn't it, Hilda?—for Mrs. Raymond Parry."

"Mrs. Raymond Parry!" cried Helen and Mrs. Thornbury at the same moment.

They looked at each other as though a mist hitherto obscuring their faces had been blown away.

"Ah—you have been to those wonderful parties too?" Mrs. Elliot asked with interest.

Mrs. Parry's drawing-room, though thousands of miles away, behind a vast curve of water on a tiny piece of earth, came before their eyes. They who had had no solidity or anchorage before seemed to be attached to it somehow, and at once grown more substantial. Perhaps they had been in the drawing-room at the same moment; perhaps they had passed each other on the stairs; at any rate they knew some of the same people. They looked one another up and down with new interest. But they could do no more than look at each other, for there was no time to enjoy the fruits of the discovery. The donkeys were advancing, and it was advisable to begin the descent immediately, for the night fell so quickly that it would be dark before they were home again.

Accordingly, remounting in order, they filed off down the hillside. Scraps of talk came floating back from one to another. There were jokes to begin with, and laughter; some walked part of the way, and picked flowers, and sent stones bounding before them.

"Who writes the best Latin verse in your college, Hirst?" Mr. Elliot called back incongruously, and Mr. Hirst returned that he had no idea.

The dusk fell as suddenly as the natives had warned them, the hollows of the mountain on either side filling up with darkness and the path becoming so dim that it was surprising to hear the donkeys' hooves still striking on hard rock. Silence fell upon one, and then upon another, until they were all silent, their minds spilling out into the deep blue air. The way seemed shorter in the dark than in the day; and soon the lights of the town were seen on the flat far beneath them.

Suddenly some one cried, "Ah!"

In a moment the slow yellow drop rose again from the plain below; it rose, paused, opened like a flower, and fell in a shower of drops.

"Fireworks," they cried.

Another went up more quickly; and then another; they could almost hear it twist and roar.

"Some Saint's day, I suppose," said a voice.

The rush and embrace of the rockets as they soared up into the air seemed like the fiery way in which lovers suddenly rose and united, leaving the crowd gazing up at them with strained white faces. But Susan and Arthur, riding down the hill, never said a word to each other, and kept accurately apart.

Then the fireworks became erratic, and soon they ceased altogether, and the rest of the journey was made almost in darkness, the mountain being a great shadow behind them, and bushes and trees little shadows which threw darkness across the road. Among the plane-trees they separated, bundling into carriages and driving off, without saying goodnight, or saying it only in a half-muffled way.

It was so late that there was no time for normal conversation between their arrival at the hotel and their retirement to bed. But Hirst wandered into Hewet's room, with a collar in his hand.

"Well, Hewet," he remarked, on the crest of a gigantic yawn, "that was a great success, I consider." He yawned. "But take care you're not landed with that young woman.... I don't really like young women...."

Hewet was too much drugged by hours in the open air to make any reply. In fact every one of the party was sound asleep within ten minutes or so of each other, with the exception of Susan Warrington. She lay for a considerable time looking blankly at the wall opposite, her hands clasped above her heart, and her light burning by her side. All articulate thought had long ago deserted her; her heart seemed to have grown to the size of a sun, and to illuminate her entire body, shedding like the sun a steady tide of warmth.

"I'm happy, I'm happy, I'm happy," she repeated. "I love every one. I'm happy."

Chapter XII

When Susan's engagement had been approved at home, and made public to any one who took an interest in it at the hotel—and by this time the society at the hotel was divided so as to point to invisible chalk-marks such as Mr. Hirst had described, the news was felt to justify some celebration—an expedition? That had been done already. A dance then. The advantage of a dance was that it abolished one of those long evenings which were apt to become tedious and lead to absurdly early hours in spite of bridge.

Two or three people standing under the erect body of the stuffed leopard in the hall very soon had the matter decided. Evelyn slid a pace or two this way and that, and pronounced that the floor was excellent. Signor Rodriguez informed them of an old Spaniard who fiddled at weddings—fiddled so as to make a tortoise waltz; and his daughter, although endowed with eyes as black as coal-scuttles, had the same power over the piano. If there were any so sick or so surly as to prefer sedentary occupations on the night in question to spinning and watching others spin, the drawing-room and billiard-room were theirs. Hewet made it his business to conciliate the outsiders as much as possible. To Hirst's theory of the invisible chalk-marks he would pay no attention whatever. He was treated to a snub or two, but, in reward, found obscure lonely gentlemen delighted to have this opportunity of talking to their kind, and the lady of doubtful character showed every symptom of confiding her case to him in the near future. Indeed it was made quite obvious to him that the two or three hours between dinner and bed contained an amount of unhappiness, which was really pitiable, since so many people had not succeeded in making friends.

It was settled that the dance was to be on Friday, one week after the engagement, and at dinner Hewet declared himself satisfied.

"They're all coming!" he told Hirst. "Pepper!" he called, seeing William Pepper slip past in the wake of the soup with a pamphlet beneath his arm, "We're counting on you to open the ball."

"You will certainly put sleep out of the question," Pepper returned.

"You are to take the floor with Miss Allan," Hewet continued, consulting a sheet of pencilled notes.

Pepper stopped and began a discourse upon round dances, country dances, morris dances, and quadrilles, all of which are entirely superior to the bastard waltz and spurious polka which have ousted them most unjustly in contemporary popularity—when the waiters gently pushed him on to his table in the corner.

The dining-room at this moment had a certain fantastic resemblance to a farmyard scattered with grain on which bright pigeons kept descending. Almost all the ladies wore dresses which they had not yet displayed, and their hair rose in waves and scrolls so as to appear like carved wood in Gothic churches rather than hair. The dinner was shorter and less formal than usual, even the waiters seeming to be affected by the general excitement. Ten minutes before the clock struck nine the committee made a tour through the ballroom. The hall, when emptied of its furniture, brilliantly lit, adorned with flowers whose scent tinged the air, presented a wonderful appearance of ethereal gaiety.

"It's like a starlit sky on an absolutely cloudless night," Hewet murmured, looking about him, at the airy empty room.

"A heavenly floor, anyhow," Evelyn added, taking a run and sliding two or three feet along it.

"What about those curtains?" asked Hirst. The crimson curtains were drawn across the long windows. "It's a perfect night outside."

"Yes, but curtains inspire confidence," Miss Allan decided. "When the ball is in full swing it will be time to draw them. We might even open the windows a little.... If we do it now elderly people will imagine there are draughts."

Her wisdom had come to be recognised, and held in respect. Meanwhile as they stood talking, the musicians were unwrapping their instruments, and the violin was repeating again and again a note struck upon the piano. Everything was ready to begin.

After a few minutes' pause, the father, the daughter, and the son-in-law who played the horn flourished with one accord. Like the rats who followed the piper, heads instantly appeared in the doorway. There was another flourish; and then the trio dashed spontaneously into the triumphant swing of the waltz. It was as though the room were instantly flooded with water. After a moment's hesitation first one couple, then another, leapt into midstream, and went round and round in the eddies. The rhythmic swish of the dancers sounded like a swirling pool. By degrees the room grew perceptibly hotter. The smell of kid gloves mingled with the strong scent of flowers. The eddies seemed to circle faster and faster, until the music wrought itself into a crash, ceased, and the circles were smashed into little separate bits. The couples struck off in different directions, leaving a thin row of elderly people stuck fast to the walls, and here and there a piece of trimming or a handkerchief or a flower lay upon the floor. There was a pause, and then the music started again, the eddies whirled, the couples circled round in them, until there was a crash, and the circles were broken up into separate bits.

When this had happened about five times, Hirst, who leant against a window-frame, like some singular gargoyle, perceived that Helen Ambrose and Rachel stood in the doorway. The crowd was such that they could not move, but he recognised them by a piece of Helen's shoulder and a glimpse of Rachel's head turning round. He made his way to them; they greeted him with relief.

"We are suffering the tortures of the damned," said Helen.

"This is my idea of hell," said Rachel.

Her eyes were bright and she looked bewildered.

Hewet and Miss Allan, who had been waltzing somewhat laboriously, paused and greeted the new-comers.

"This *is* nice," said Hewet. "But where is Mr. Ambrose?"

"Pindar," said Helen. "May a married woman who was forty in October dance? I can't stand still." She seemed to fade into Hewet, and they both dissolved in the crowd.

"We must follow suit," said Hirst to Rachel, and he took her resolutely by the elbow. Rachel, without being expert, danced well, because of a good ear for rhythm, but Hirst had no taste for music, and a few dancing lessons at Cambridge had only put him into possession of the anatomy of a waltz, without imparting any of its spirit. A single turn proved to them that their methods were incompatible; instead of fitting into each other their bones seemed to jut out in angles making smooth turning an impossibility, and cutting, moreover, into the circular progress of the other dancers.

"Shall we stop?" said Hirst. Rachel gathered from his expression that he was annoyed.

They staggered to seats in the corner, from which they had a view of the room. It was still surging, in waves of blue and yellow, striped by the black evening-clothes of the gentlemen.

"An amazing spectacle," Hirst remarked. "Do you dance much in London?" They were both breathing fast, and both a little excited, though each was determined not to show any excitement at all.

"Scarcely ever. Do you?"

"My people give a dance every Christmas."

"This isn't half a bad floor," Rachel said. Hirst did not attempt to answer her platitude. He sat quite silent, staring at the dancers. After three minutes the silence became so intolerable to Rachel that she was goaded to advance another commonplace about the beauty of the night. Hirst interrupted her ruthlessly.

"Was that all nonsense what you said the other day about being a Christian and having no education?" he asked.

"It was practically true," she replied. "But I also play the piano very well," she said, "better, I expect, than any one in this room. You are the most distinguished man in England, aren't you?" she asked shyly.

"One of the three," he corrected.

Helen, whirling past here, tossed a fan into Rachel's lap.

"She is very beautiful," Hirst remarked.

They were again silent. Rachel was wondering whether he thought her also nice-looking; St. John was considering the immense difficulty of talking to girls who had no experience of life. Rachel had obviously never thought or felt or seen anything, and she might be intelligent or she might be just like all the rest. But Hewet's taunt rankled in his mind—"you don't know how to get on with women," and he was determined to profit by this opportunity. Her evening-clothes bestowed on her just that degree of unreality and distinction which made it romantic to speak to her, and stirred a desire to talk, which irritated him because he did not know how to begin. He glanced at her, and she seemed to him very remote and inexplicable, very young and chaste. He drew a sigh, and began.

"About books now. What have you read? Just Shakespeare and the Bible?"

"I haven't read many classics," Rachel stated. She was slightly annoyed by his jaunty and rather unnatural manner, while his masculine acquirements induced her to take a very modest view of her own powers.

"D'you mean to tell me you've reached the age of twenty-four without reading Gibbon?" he demanded.

"Yes, I have," she answered.

"Mon Dieu!" he exclaimed, throwing out his hands. "You must begin to-morrow. I shall send you my copy. What I want to know is——" he looked at her critically. "You see, the problem is, can one really talk to you? Have you got a mind, or are you like the rest of your sex? You seem to me absurdly young compared with men of your age."

Rachel looked at him but said nothing.

"About Gibbon," he continued. "D'you think you'll be able to appreciate him? He's the test, of course. It's awfully difficult to tell about women," he continued, "how much, I mean, is due to lack of training, and how much is native incapacity. I don't see myself why you shouldn't understand—only I suppose you've led an absurd life until now—you've just walked in a crocodile, I suppose, with your hair down your back."

The music was again beginning. Hirst's eye wandered about the room in search of Mrs. Ambrose. With the best will in the world he was conscious that they were not getting on well together.

"I'd like awfully to lend you books," he said, buttoning his gloves, and rising from his seat. "We shall meet again. I'm going to leave you now."

He got up and left her.

Rachel looked round. She felt herself surrounded, like a child at a party, by the faces of strangers all hostile to her, with hooked noses and sneering, indifferent eyes. She was by a window, she pushed it open with a jerk, and stepped out into the garden. Her eyes swam with tears of rage.

"Damn that man!" she exclaimed, having acquired some of Helen's words. "Damn his insolence!"

She stood in the middle of the pale square of light which the window she had opened threw upon the grass. The forms of great black trees rose massively in front of her. She stood still, looking at them, shivering slightly with anger and excitement. She heard the trampling and swinging of the dancers behind her, and the rhythmic sway of the waltz music.

"There are trees," she said aloud. Would the trees make up for St. John Hirst? She would be a Persian princess far from civilisation, riding her horse upon the mountains alone, and making her women sing to her in the evening, far from all this, from the strife and men and women—A form came out of the shadow; a little red light burnt high up in its blackness.

"Miss Vinrace, is it?" said Hewet, peering at her. "You were dancing with Hirst?"

"He's made me furious!" she cried vehemently. "No one's any right to be insolent!"

"Insolent?" Hewet repeated, taking his cigar from his mouth in surprise. "Hirst—insolent?"

"It's insolent to——" said Rachel, and stopped. She did not know exactly why she had been made so angry. With a great effort she pulled herself together.

"Oh, well," she added, the vision of Helen and her mockery before her, "I dare say I'm a fool." She made as though she were going back into the ballroom, but Hewet stopped her.

"Please explain to me," he said. "I feel sure Hirst didn't mean to hurt you."

When Rachel tried to explain, she found it very difficult. She could not say that she found the vision of herself walking in a crocodile with her hair down her back peculiarly unjust and horrible, nor could she explain why Hirst's assumption of the superiority of his nature and experience had seemed to her not only galling but terrible—as if a gate had clanged in her face. Pacing up and down the terrace beside Hewet she said bitterly:

"It's no good; we should live separate; we cannot understand each other; we only bring out what's worst."

Hewet brushed aside her generalisations as to the natures of the two sexes, for such generalisations bored him and seemed to him generally untrue. But, knowing Hirst, he guessed fairly accurately what had happened, and, though secretly much amused, was determined that Rachel should not store the incident away in her mind to take its place in the view she had of life.

"Now you'll hate him," he said, "which is wrong. Poor old Hirst—he can't help his method. And really, Miss Vinrace, he was doing his best; he was paying you a compliment—he was trying—he was trying——" he could not finish for the laughter that overcame him.

Rachel veered round suddenly and laughed out too. She saw that there was something ridiculous about Hirst, and perhaps about herself.

"It's his way of making friends, I suppose," she laughed. "Well— I shall do my part. I shall begin—'Ugly in body, repulsive in mind as you are, Mr. Hirst——' "

"Hear, hear!" cried Hewet. "That's the way to treat him. You see, Miss Vinrace, you must make allowances for Hirst. He's lived all his life in front of a looking-glass, in a beautiful panelled room, hung with Japanese prints and lovely old chairs and tables, just one splash of colour, you know, in the right place,—between the windows I think it is,—and there he sits hour after hour with his toes on the fender, talking about philosophy and God and his liver and his heart and the hearts of his friends. They're all broken. You can't expect him to be at his best in a ballroom. He wants a cosy, smoky, masculine place, where he can stretch his legs out, and only speak when he's got something to say. For myself, I find it rather dreary. But I do respect it. They're all so much in earnest. They do take the serious things very seriously."

The description of Hirst's way of life interested Rachel so much that she almost forgot her private grudge against him, and her respect revived.

"They are really very clever then?" she asked.

"Of course they are. So far as brains go I think it's true what he said the other day; they're the cleverest people in England. But—you ought to take him in hand," he added. "There's a great deal more in him than's ever been got at. He wants some one to laugh at him. The idea of Hirst telling you that you've had no experiences! Poor old Hirst!"

They had been pacing up and down the terrace while they talked, and now one by one the dark windows were uncurtained by an invisible hand, and panes of light fell regularly at equal intervals upon the grass. They stopped to look in at the drawing-room, and perceived Mr. Pepper writing alone at a table.

"There's Pepper writing to his aunt," said Hewet. "She must be a very remarkable old lady, eighty-five, he tells me, and he takes her for walking tours in the New Forest.... Pepper!" he cried, rapping on the window. "Go and do your duty. Miss Allan expects you."

When they came to the windows of the ballroom, the swing of the dancers and the lilt of the music were irresistible.

"Shall we?" said Hewet, and they clasped hands and swept off magnificently into the great swirling pool. Although this was only the second time they had met, the first time they had seen a man and woman kissing each other, and the second time Mr. Hewet had found that a young woman angry is very like a child. So that when they joined hands in the dance they felt more at their ease than is usual.

It was midnight and the dance was now at its height. Servants were peeping in at the windows; the garden was sprinkled with the white shapes of couples sitting out. Mrs. Thornbury and Mrs. Elliot sat side by side under a palm tree, holding fans, handkerchiefs, and brooches deposited in their laps by flushed maidens. Occasionally they exchanged comments.

"Miss Warrington *does* look happy," said Mrs. Elliot; they both smiled; they both sighed.

"He has a great deal of character," said Mrs. Thornbury, alluding to Arthur.

"And character is what one wants," said Mrs. Elliot. "Now that young man is *clever* enough," she added, nodding at Hirst, who came past with Miss Allan on his arm.

"He does not look strong," said Mrs. Thornbury. "His complexion is not good.—Shall I tear it off?" she asked, for Rachel had stopped, conscious of a long strip trailing behind her.

"I hope you are enjoying yourselves?" Hewet asked the ladies.

"This is a very familiar position for me!" smiled Mrs. Thornbury. "I have brought out five daughters—and they all loved dancing! You love it too, Miss Vinrace?" she asked, looking at Rachel with maternal eyes. "I know I did when I was your age. How I used to beg my mother to let me stay—and now I sympathise with the poor mothers—but I sympathise with the daughters too!"

She smiled sympathetically, and at the same time looked rather keenly at Rachel.

"They seem to find a great deal to say to each other," said Mrs. Elliot, looking significantly at the backs of the couple as they turned away. "Did you notice at the picnic? He was the only person who could make her utter."

"Her father is a very interesting man," said Mrs. Thornbury. "He has one of the largest shipping businesses in Hull. He made a very able reply, you remember, to Mr. Asquith at the last election. It is so interesting to find that a man of his experience is a strong Protectionist."[1]

She would have liked to discuss politics, which interested her more than personalities, but Mrs. Elliot would only talk about the Empire in a less abstract form.

"I hear there are dreadful accounts from England about the rats," she said. "A sister-in law, who lives at Norwich, tells me it has been quite unsafe to order poultry. The plague—you see. It attacks the rats, and through them other creatures."

"And the local authorities are not taking proper steps?" asked Mrs. Thornbury.

"That she does not say. But she describes the attitude of the educated people—who should know better—as callous in the extreme. Of course, my sister-in-law is one of those active modern women, who always takes things up, you know—the kind of woman one admires, though one does not feel, at least I do not feel—but then she has a constitution of iron."

Mrs. Elliot, brought back to the consideration of her own delicacy, here sighed.

"A very animated face," said Mrs. Thornbury, looking at Evelyn M. who had stopped near them to pin tight a scarlet flower at her breast. It would not stay, and, with a spirited gesture of impatience, she thrust it into her partner's buttonhole. He was a tall melancholy youth, who received the gift as a knight might receive his lady's token.

"Very trying to the eyes," was Mrs. Elliot's next remark, after watching the yellow whirl in which so few of the whirlers had either name or character for her, for a few minutes. Bursting out of the crowd, Helen approached them, and took a vacant chair.

"May I sit by you?" she said, smiling and breathing fast. "I suppose I ought to be ashamed of myself," she went on, sitting down, "at my age."

Her beauty, now that she was flushed and animated, was more expansive than usual, and both the ladies felt the same desire to touch her.

"I *am* enjoying myself," she panted. "Movement—isn't it amazing?"

"I have always heard that nothing comes up to dancing if one is a good dancer," said Mrs. Thornbury, looking at her with a smile.

Helen swayed slightly as if she sat on wires.

"I could dance for ever!" she said. "They ought to let themselves go more!" she exclaimed. "They ought to leap and swing. Look! How they mince!"

"Have you seen those wonderful Russian dancers?" began Mrs. Elliot. But Helen saw her partner coming and rose as the moon rises. She was half round the room before they took their eyes off her, for they could not help admiring her, although they thought it a little odd that a woman of her age should enjoy dancing.

Directly Helen was left alone for a minute she was joined by St. John Hirst, who had been watching for an opportunity.

"Should you mind sitting out with me?" he asked. "I'm quite incapable of dancing." He piloted Helen to a corner which was supplied with two arm-chairs, and thus enjoyed the advantage of semi-privacy. They sat down, and for a few minutes Helen was too much under the influence of dancing to speak.

"Astonishing!" she exclaimed at last. "What sort of shape can she think her body is?" This remark was called forth by a lady who came past them, waddling rather than walking, and leaning on the arm of a stout man with globular green eyes set in a fat white face. Some support was necessary, for she was very stout, and so compressed that the upper part of her body hung considerably in advance of her feet, which could only trip in tiny steps, owing to the tightness of the skirt round her ankles. The dress itself consisted of a small piece of shiny yellow satin, adorned here and there indiscriminately with round shields of blue and green beads made to imitate the hues of a peacock's breast. On the summit of a frothy castle of hair a purple plume stood erect, while her short neck was encircled by a black velvet ribbon knobbed with gems, and golden bracelets were tightly wedged into the flesh of her fat gloved arms. She had the face of an impertinent but jolly little pig, mottled red under a dusting of powder.

St. John could not join in Helen's laughter.

"It makes me sick," he declared. "The whole thing makes me sick.... Consider the minds of those people—their feelings. Don't you agree?"

"I always make a vow never to go to another party of any description," Helen replied, "and I always break it."

She leant back in her chair and looked laughingly at the young man. She could see that he was genuinely cross, if at the same time slightly excited.

"However," he said, resuming his jaunty tone, "I suppose one must just make up one's mind to it."

"To what?"

"There never will be more than five people in the world worth talking to."

Slowly the flush and sparkle in Helen's face died away, and she looked as quiet and as observant as usual.

"Five people?" she remarked. "I should say there were more than five."

"You've been very fortunate, then," said Hirst. "Or perhaps I've been very unfortunate." He became silent.

"Should you say I was a difficult kind of person to get on with?" he asked abruptly.

"Most clever people are when they're young," Helen replied.

"And of course I am—immensely clever," said Hirst. "I'm infinitely cleverer than Hewet. It's quite possible," he continued in his curiously impersonal manner, "that I'm going to be one of the people who really matter. That's utterly different from being clever, though one can't expect one's family to see it," he added bitterly.

Helen thought herself justified in asking, "Do you find your family difficult to get on with?"

"Intolerable.... They want me to be a peer and a privy councillor. I've come out here partly in order to settle the matter. It's got to be settled. Either I must go to the bar, or I must stay on in Cambridge. Of course, there are obvious drawbacks to each, but the arguments certainly do seem to me in favour of Cambridge. This kind of thing!" he waved his hand at the crowded ballroom. "Repul-

sive. I'm conscious of great powers of affection too. I'm not susceptible, of course, in the way Hewet is. I'm very fond of a few people.
I think, for example, that there's something to be said for my
mother, though she is in many ways so deplorable.... At Cambridge, of course, I should inevitably become the most important man in the place, but there are other reasons why I dread
Cambridge——" he ceased.

"Are you finding me a dreadful bore?" he asked. He changed curiously from a friend confiding in a friend to a conventional young
man at a party.

"Not in the least," said Helen. "I like it very much."

"You can't think," he exclaimed, speaking almost with emotion,
"what a difference it makes finding some one to talk to! Directly I
saw you I felt you might possibly understand me. I'm very fond of
Hewet, but he hasn't the remotest idea what I'm like. You're the
only woman I've ever met who seems to have the faintest conception of what I mean when I say a thing."

The next dance was beginning; it was the Barcarolle out of Hoff-
man, which made Helen beat her toe in time to it; but she felt that
after such a compliment it was impossible to get up and go, and, besides being amused, she was really flattered, and the honesty of his
conceit attracted her. She suspected that he was not happy, and was
sufficiently feminine to wish to receive confidences.

"I'm very old," she sighed.

"The odd thing is that I don't find you old at all," he replied. "I
feel as though we were exactly the same age. Moreover—" here he
hesitated, but took courage from a glance at her face, "I feel as if I
could talk quite plainly to you as one does to a man—about the relations between the sexes, about ... and ..."

In spite of his certainty a slight redness came into his face as he
spoke the last two words.

She reassured him at once by the laugh with which she exclaimed, "I should hope so!"

He looked at her with real cordiality, and the lines which were
drawn about his nose and lips slackened for the first time.

"Thank God!" he exclaimed. "Now we can behave like civilised human beings."

Certainly a barrier which usually stands fast had fallen, and it was possible to speak of matters which are generally only alluded to between men and women when doctors are present, or the shadow of death. In five minutes he was telling her the history of his life. It was long, for it was full of extremely elaborate incidents, which led on to a discussion of the principles on which morality is founded, and thus to several very interesting matters, which even in this ballroom had to be discussed in a whisper, lest one of the pouter pigeon ladies or resplendent merchants should overhear them, and proceed to demand that they should leave the place. When they had come to an end, or, to speak more accurately, when Helen intimated by a slight slackening of her attention that they had sat there long enough, Hirst rose, exclaiming, "So there's no reason whatever for all this mystery!"

"None, except that we are English people," she answered. She took his arm and they crossed the ballroom, making their way with difficulty between the spinning couples, who were now perceptibly dishevelled, and certainly to a critical eye by no means lovely in their shapes. The excitement of undertaking a friendship and the length of their talk had made them hungry, and they went in search of food to the dining-room, which was now full of people eating at little separate tables. In the doorway they met Rachel, going up to dance again with Arthur Venning. She was flushed and looked very happy, and Helen was struck by the fact that in this mood she was certainly more attractive than the generality of young women. She had never noticed it so clearly before.

"Enjoying yourself?" she asked, as they stopped for a second.

"Miss Vinrace," Arthur answered for her, "has just made a confession; she'd no idea that dances could be so delightful."

"Yes!" Rachel exclaimed. "I've changed my view of life completely!"

"You don't say so!" Helen mocked. They passed on.

"That's typical of Rachel," she said. "She changes her view of life about every other day. D'you know, I believe you're just the person I want," she said, as they sat down, "to help me to complete her education? She's been brought up practically in a nunnery. Her father's too absurd. I've been doing what I can—but I'm too old, and I'm a woman. Why shouldn't you talk to her—explain things to her—talk to her, I mean, as you talk to me?"

"I have made one attempt already this evening," said St. John. "I rather doubt that it was successful. She seems to me so very young and inexperienced. I have promised to lend her Gibbon."

"It's not Gibbon exactly," Helen pondered. "It's the facts of life, I think—d'you see what I mean? What really goes on, what people feel, although they generally try to hide it? There's nothing to be frightened at. It's so much more beautiful than the pretences— always more interesting—always better, I should say, than *that* kind of thing."

She nodded her head at a table near them, where two girls and two young men were chaffing each other very loudly, and carrying on an arch insinuating dialogue, sprinkled with endearments, about, it seemed, a pair of stockings or a pair of legs. One of the girls was flirting a fan and pretending to be shocked, and the sight was very unpleasant, partly because it was obvious that the girls were secretly hostile to each other.

"In my old age, however," Helen sighed, "I'm coming to think that it doesn't much matter in the long run what one does: people always go their own way—nothing will ever influence them." She nodded her head at the supper party.

But St. John did not agree. He said that he thought one could really make a great deal of difference by one's point of view, books and so on, and added that few things at the present time mattered more than the enlightenment of women. He sometimes thought that almost everything was due to education.

In the ballroom, meanwhile, the dancers were being formed into squares for the lancers. Arthur and Rachel, Susan and Hewet, Miss Allan and Hughling Elliot found themselves together.

Miss Allan looked at her watch.

"Half-past one," she stated. "And I have to despatch Alexander Pope[2] to-morrow."

"Pope!" snorted Mr. Elliot. "Who reads Pope, I should like to know? And as for reading about him—— No, no, Miss Allan; be persuaded you will benefit the world much more by dancing than by writing." It was one of Mr. Elliot's affectations that nothing in the world could compare with the delights of dancing—nothing in the world was so tedious as literature. Thus he sought pathetically enough to ingratiate himself with the young, and to prove to them beyond a doubt that though married to a ninny of a wife, and rather pale and bent and careworn by his weight of learning, he was as much alive as the youngest of them all.

"It's a question of bread and butter," said Miss Allan calmly. "However, they seem to expect me." She took up her position and pointed a square black toe.

"Mr. Hewet, you bow to me." It was evident at once that Miss Allan was the only one of them who had a thoroughly sound knowledge of the figures of the dance.

After the lancers there was a waltz; after the waltz a polka; and then a terrible thing happened; the music, which had been sounding regularly with five-minute pauses, stopped suddenly. The lady with the great dark eyes began to swathe her violin in silk, and the gentleman placed his horn carefully in its case. They were surrounded by couples imploring them in English, in French, in Spanish, for one more dance, one only; it was still early. But the old man at the piano merely exhibited his watch and shook his head. He turned up the collar of his coat and produced a red silk muffler, which completely dashed his festive appearance. Strange as it seemed, the musicians were pale and heavy-eyed; they looked bored and prosaic, as if the summit of their desire was cold meat and beer, succeeded immediately by bed.

Rachel was one of those who had begged them to continue. When they refused she began turning over the sheets of dance music which lay upon the piano. The pieces were generally bound in coloured covers, with pictures on them of romantic scenes—

gondoliers astride the crescent of the moon, nuns peering through the bars of a convent window, or young women with their hair down pointing a gun at the stars. She remembered that the general effect of the music to which they had danced so gaily was one of passionate regret for dead love and the innocent years of youth; dreadful sorrows had always separated the dancers from their past happiness.

"No wonder they get sick of playing stuff like this," she remarked, reading a bar or two; "they're really hymn tunes, played very fast, with bits out of Wagner and Beethoven."

"Do you play? Would you play? Anything, so long as we can dance to it!" From all sides her gift for playing the piano was insisted upon, and she had to consent. As very soon she had played the only pieces of dance music she could remember, she went on to play an air from a sonata by Mozart.

"But that's not a dance," said some one pausing by the piano.

"It is," she replied, emphatically nodding her head. "Invent the steps." Sure of her melody she marked the rhythm boldly so as to simplify the way. Helen caught the idea; seized Miss Allan by the arm, and whirled round the room, now curtseying, now spinning round, now tripping this way and that like a child skipping through a meadow.

"This is the dance for people who don't know how to dance!" she cried. The tune changed to a minuet; St. John hopped with incredible swiftness first on his left leg, then on his right; the tune flowed melodiously; Hewet, swaying his arms and holding out the tails of his coat, swam down the room in imitation of the voluptuous dreamy dance of an Indian maiden dancing before her Rajah. The tune marched; and Miss Allan advanced with skirts extended and bowed profoundly to the engaged pair. Once their feet fell in with the rhythm they showed a complete lack of self-consciousness. From Mozart Rachel passed without stopping to old English hunting songs, carols, and hymn tunes, for, as she had observed, any good tune, with a little management, became a tune one could dance to. By degrees every person in the room was tripping and turning in pairs or alone. Mr. Pepper executed an ingenious pointed step derived from figure-skating, for which he once held some local championship; while Mrs. Thornbury tried to recall an old country dance which she had seen danced by her father's tenants in Dorsetshire in the old days. As for Mr. and Mrs. Elliot, they gallopaded round and round the room with such impetuosity that the other dancers shivered at their approach. Some people were heard to criticise the performance as a romp; to others it was the most enjoyable part of the evening.

"Now for the great round dance!" Hewet shouted. Instantly a gigantic circle was formed, the dancers holding hands and shouting out, "D'you ken John Peel," as they swung faster and faster and faster, until the strain was too great, and one link of the chain—Mrs. Thornbury—gave way, and the rest went flying across the room in all directions, to land upon the floor or the chairs or in each other's arms as seemed most convenient.

Rising from these positions, breathless and unkempt, it struck them for the first time that the electric lights pricked the air very vainly, and instinctively a great many eyes turned to the windows. Yes—there was the dawn. While they had been dancing the night had passed, and it had come. Outside, the mountains showed very pure and remote; the dew was sparkling on the grass, and the sky was flushed with blue, save for the pale yellows and pinks in the East. The dancers came crowding to the windows, pushed them open, and here and there ventured a foot upon the grass.

"How silly the poor old lights look!" said Evelyn M. in a curiously subdued tone of voice. "And ourselves; it isn't becoming." It was true; the untidy hair, and the green and yellow gems, which had seemed so festive half an hour ago, now looked cheap and slovenly. The complexions of the elder ladies suffered terribly, and, as if conscious that a cold eye had been turned upon them, they began to say good-night and to make their way up to bed.

Rachel, though robbed of her audience, had gone on playing to herself. From John Peel she passed to Bach, who was at this time the subject of her intense enthusiasm, and one by one some of the younger dancers came in from the garden and sat upon the deserted gilt chairs round the piano, the room being now so clear that they turned out the lights. As they sat and listened, their nerves were quieted; the heat and soreness of their lips, the result of incessant talking and laughing, was smoothed away. They sat very still as if they saw a building with spaces and columns succeeding each other rising in the empty space. Then they began to see themselves and their lives, and the whole of human life advancing very nobly under the direction of the music. They felt themselves ennobled, and when Rachel stopped playing they desired nothing but sleep.

Susan rose. "I think this has been the happiest night of my life!" she exclaimed. "I do adore music," she said, as she thanked Rachel. "It just seems to say all the things one can't say oneself." She gave a nervous little laugh and looked from one to another with great benignity, as though she would like to say something but could not find the words in which to express it. "Every one's been so kind—so very kind," she said. Then she too went to bed.

The party having ended in the very abrupt way in which parties do end, Helen and Rachel stood by the door with their cloaks on, looking for a carriage.

"I suppose you realise that there are no carriages left?" said St. John, who had been out to look. "You must sleep here."

"Oh, no," said Helen; "we shall walk."

"May we come too?" Hewet asked. "We can't go to bed. Imagine lying among bolsters and looking at one's washstand on a morning like this— Is that where you live?"

They had begun to walk down the avenue, and he turned and pointed at the white and green villa on the hillside, which seemed to have its eyes shut.

"That's not a light burning, is it?" Helen asked anxiously.

"It's the sun," said St. John. The upper windows had each a spot of gold on them.

"I was afraid it was my husband, still reading Greek," she said. "All this time he's been editing *Pindar*."

They passed through the town and turned up the steep road, which was perfectly clear, though still unbordered by shadows. Partly because they were tired, and partly because the early light subdued them, they scarcely spoke, but breathed in the delicious fresh air, which seemed to belong to a different state of life from the air at midday. When they came to the high yellow wall, where the lane turned off from the road, Helen was for dismissing the two young men.

"You've come far enough," she said. "Go back to bed."

But they seemed unwilling to move.

"Let's sit down a moment," said Hewet. He spread his coat on the ground. "Let's sit down and consider." They sat down and looked out over the bay; it was very still, the sea was rippling faintly, and lines of green and blue were beginning to stripe it. There were no sailing boats as yet, but a steamer was anchored in the bay, looking very ghostly in the mist; it gave one unearthly cry, and then all was silent.

Rachel occupied herself in collecting one grey stone after another and building them into a little cairn; she did it very quietly and carefully.

"And so you've changed your view of life, Rachel?" said Helen.

Rachel added another stone and yawned. "I don't remember," she said, "I feel like a fish at the bottom of the sea." She yawned again. None of these people possessed any power to frighten her out here in the dawn, and she felt perfectly familiar even with Mr. Hirst.

"My brain, on the contrary," said Hirst, "is in a condition of abnormal activity." He sat in his favourite position with his arms binding his legs together and his chin resting on the top of his knees. "I see through everything—absolutely everything. Life has no more mysteries for me." He spoke with conviction, but did not appear to wish for an answer. Near though they sat, and familiar though they felt, they seemed mere shadows to each other.

"And all those people down there going to sleep," Hewet began dreamily, "thinking such different things,—Miss Warrington, I suppose, is now on her knees; the Elliots are a little startled, it's not often *they* get out of breath, and they want to get to sleep as quickly as possible; then there's the poor lean young man who danced all night with Evelyn, he's putting his flower in water and asking him-

172 · *Virginia Woolf*

self, 'Is this love?'—and poor old Perrott, I daresay, can't get to sleep at all, and is reading his favourite Greek book to console himself— and the others—no, Hirst," he wound up, "I don't find it simple at all."

"I have a key," said Hirst cryptically. His chin was still upon his knees and his eyes fixed in front of him.

A silence followed. Then Helen rose and bade them good-night. "But," she said, "remember that you've got to come and see us."

They waved good-night and parted, but the two young men did not go back to the hotel; they went for a walk, during which they scarcely spoke, and never mentioned the names of the two women, who were, to a considerable extent, the subject of their thoughts. They did not wish to share their impressions. They returned to the hotel in time for breakfast.

CHAPTER XIII

There were many rooms in the villa, but one room which possessed a character of its own because the door was always shut, and no sound of music or laughter issued from it. Every one in the house was vaguely conscious that something went on behind that door, and without in the least knowing what it was, were influenced in their own thoughts by the knowledge that if they passed it the door would be shut, and if they made a noise Mr. Ambrose inside would be disturbed. Certain acts therefore possessed merit, and others were bad, so that life became more harmonious and less disconnected than it would have been had Mr. Ambrose given up editing *Pindar*, and taken to a nomad existence, in and out of every room in the house. As it was, every one was conscious that by observing certain rules, such as punctuality and quiet, by cooking well, and performing other small duties, one ode after another was satisfactorily restored, and they themselves shared the continuity of the scholar's life. Unfortunately, as age puts one barrier between human beings, and learning another, and sex a third, Mr. Ambrose in his study was some thousand miles distant from the nearest human being, who in this household was inevitably a woman. He sat hour after hour among white-leaved books, alone like an idol in an empty church, still except for the passage of his hand from one side of the sheet to another, silent save for an occasional choke, which drove him to extend his pipe a moment in the air. As he worked his way further and further into the heart of the poet, his chair became more and more deeply encircled by books, which lay open on the floor, and could only be crossed by a careful process of stepping, so delicate that his visitors generally stopped and addressed him from the outskirts.

On the morning after the dance, however, Rachel came into her uncle's room and hailed him twice, "Uncle Ridley," before he paid her any attention.

At length he looked over his spectacles.

"Well?" he asked.

"I want a book," she replied. "Gibbon's *History of the Roman Empire*. May I have it?"

She watched the lines on her uncle's face gradually rearrange themselves at her question. It had been smooth as a mask before she spoke.

"Please say that again," said her uncle, either because he had not heard or because he had not understood.

She repeated the same words and reddened slightly as she did so.

"Gibbon! What on earth d'you want him for?" he inquired.

"Somebody advised me to read it," Rachel stammered.

"But I don't travel about with a miscellaneous collection of eighteenth-century historians!" her uncle exclaimed. "Gibbon! Ten big volumes at least."

Rachel said that she was sorry to interrupt, and was turning to go.

"Stop!" cried her uncle. He put down his pipe, placed his book on one side, and rose and led her slowly round the room, holding her by the arm. "Plato," he said, laying one finger on the first of a row of small dark books, "and Jorrocks next door, which is wrong. Sophocles, Swift. You don't care for German commentators, I presume. French, then. You read French? You should read Balzac. Then we come to Wordsworth and Coleridge. Pope, Johnson, Addison, Wordsworth, Shelley, Keats. One thing leads to another. Why is Marlowe[1] here? Mrs. Chailey, I presume. But what's the use of reading if you don't read Greek? After all, if you read Greek, you need never read anything else, pure waste of time—pure waste of time," thus speaking half to himself, with quick movements of his hands; they had come round again to the circle of books on the floor, and their progress was stopped.

"Well," he demanded, "which shall it be?"

"Balzac," said Rachel, "or have you the *Speech on the American Revolution,* Uncle Ridley?"

"The Speech on the American Revolution?" he asked. He looked at her very keenly again. "Another young man at the dance?"

"No. That was Mr. Dalloway," she confessed.

"Good Lord!" he flung back his head in recollection of Mr. Dalloway.

She chose for herself a volume at random, submitted it to her uncle, who, seeing that it was *La Cousine Bette,*[2] bade her throw it away if she found it too horrible, and was about to leave him when he demanded whether she had enjoyed her dance?

He then wanted to know what people did at dances, seeing that he had only been to one thirty-five years ago, when nothing had seemed to him more meaningless and idiotic. Did they enjoy turning round and round to the screech of a fiddle? Did they talk, and say pretty things, and if so, why didn't they do it under reasonable conditions? As for himself—he sighed, and pointed at the signs of industry lying all about him, which, in spite of his sigh, filled his face with such satisfaction that his niece thought good to leave. On bestowing a kiss she was allowed to go, but not until she had bound herself to learn at any rate the Greek alphabet, and to return her French novel when done with, upon which something more suitable would be found for her.

As the rooms in which people live are apt to give off something of the same shock as their faces when seen for the first time, Rachel walked very slowly downstairs, lost in wonder at her uncle, and his books, and his neglect of dances, and his queer, utterly inexplicable, but apparently satisfactory view of life, when her eye was caught by a note with her name on it lying in the hall. The address was written in a small strong hand unknown to her, and the note which had no beginning, ran:—

> I send the first volume of Gibbon as I promised. Personally I find little to be said for the moderns, but I'm going to send you Wedekind when I've done him. Donne? Have you read Webster[3] and all that set? I envy you reading them for the first time. Completely exhausted after last night. And you?

The flourish of initials which she took to be St. J. A. H. wound up the letter. She was very much flattered that Mr. Hirst should have remembered her, and fulfilled his promise so quickly.

There was still an hour to luncheon, and with Gibbon in one hand, and Balzac in the other she strolled out of the gate and down the little path of beaten mud between the olive trees on the slope of the hill. It was too hot for climbing hills, but along the valley there were trees and a grass path running by the river bed. In this land where the population was centred in the towns it was possible to lose sight of civilisation in a very short time, passing only an occasional farmhouse, where the women were handling red roots in the courtyard; or a little boy lying on his elbows on the hillside surrounded by a flock of black strong-smelling goats. Save for a thread of water at the bottom, the river was merely a deep channel of dry yellow stones. On the bank grew those trees which Helen had said it was worth the voyage out merely to see. April had burst their buds, and they bore large blossoms among their glossy green leaves with petals of a thick wax-like substance coloured an exquisite cream or pink or deep crimson. But filled with one of those unreasonable exultations which start generally from an unknown cause, and sweep whole countries and skies into their embrace, she walked without seeing. The night was encroaching upon the day. Her ears hummed with the tunes she had played the night before; she sang, and the singing made her walk faster and faster. She did not see distinctly where she was going, the trees and the landscape appearing only as masses of green and blue, with an occasional space of differently coloured sky. Faces of people she had seen last night came before her; she heard their voices; she stopped singing, and began saying things over again or saying things differently, or inventing things that might have been said. The constraint of being among strangers in a long silk dress made it unusually exciting to stride thus alone. Hewet, Hirst, Mr. Venning, Miss Allan, the music, the light, the dark trees in the garden, the dawn,—as she walked they went surging round in her head, a tumultuous background from which the present moment, with its opportunity for doing exactly as she liked, sprung more wonderfully vivid even than the night before.

So she might have walked until she had lost all knowledge of her way, had it not been for the interruption of a tree, which, although it did not grow across her path, stopped her as effectively as if the branches had struck her in the face. It was an ordinary tree, but to her it appeared so strange that it might have been the only tree in the world. Dark was the trunk in the middle, and the branches sprang here and there, leaving jagged intervals of light between them as distinctly as if it had but that second risen from the ground. Having seen a sight that would last her for a lifetime, and for a lifetime would preserve that second, the tree once more sank into the ordinary ranks of trees, and she was able to seat herself in its shade and to pick the red flowers with the thin green leaves which were growing beneath it. She laid them side by side, flower to flower and stalk to stalk, caressing them for, walking alone, flowers and even pebbles in the earth had their own life and disposition, and brought back the feelings of a child to whom they were companions. Looking up, her eye was caught by the line of the mountains flying out energetically across the sky like the lash of a curling whip. She looked at the pale distant sky, and the high bare places on the mountain-tops lying exposed to the sun. When she sat down she had dropped her books on to the earth at her feet, and now she looked down on them lying there, so square in the grass, a tall stem bending over and tickling the smooth brown cover of Gibbon, while the mottled blue Balzac lay naked in the sun. With a feeling that to open and read would certainly be a surprising experience, she turned the historian's page and read that—

> His generals, in the early part of his reign, attempted the reduction of Aethiopia and Arabia Felix. They marched near a thousand miles to the south of the tropic; but the heat of the climate soon repelled the invaders and protected the unwarlike natives of those sequestered regions.... The northern countries of Europe scarcely deserved the expense and labour of conquest. The forests and morasses of Germany were filled with a hardy race of barbarians, who despised life when it was separated from freedom.

Never had any words been so vivid and so beautiful—Arabia Felix—Aethiopia. But those were not more noble than the others, hardy barbarians, forests, and morasses. They seemed to drive roads back to the very beginning of the world, on either side of which the populations of all times and countries stood in avenues, and by passing down them all knowledge would be hers, and the book of the world turned back to the very first page. Such was her excitement at the possibilities of knowledge now opening before her that she ceased to read, and a breeze turning the page, the covers of Gibbon gently ruffled and closed together. She then rose again and walked on. Slowly her mind became less confused and sought the origins of her exaltation, which were twofold and could be limited by an effort to the persons of Mr. Hirst and Mr. Hewet. Any clear analysis of them was impossible owing to the haze of wonder in which they were enveloped. She could not reason about them as about people whose feelings went by the same rule as her own did, and her mind dwelt on them with a kind of physical pleasure such as is caused by the contemplation of bright things hanging in the sun. From them all life seemed to radiate; the very words of books were steeped in radiance. She then became haunted by a suspicion which she was so reluctant to face that she welcomed a trip and stumble over the grass because thus her attention was dispersed, but in a second it had collected itself again. Unconsciously she had been walking faster and faster, her body trying to outrun her mind; but she was now on the summit of a little hillock of earth which rose above the river and displayed the valley. She was no longer able to juggle with several ideas, but must deal with the most persistent, and a kind of melancholy replaced her excitement. She sank down on to the earth, clasping her knees together, and looking blankly in front of her. For some time she observed a great yellow butterfly, which was opening and closing its wings very slowly on a little flat stone.

"What is it to be in love?" she demanded, after a long silence; each word as it came into being seemed to shove itself out into an unknown sea. Hypnotised by the wings of the butterfly, and awed by the discovery of a terrible possibility in life, she sat for some time longer. When the butterfly flew away, she rose, and with her two books beneath her arm returned home again, much as a soldier prepared for battle.

CHAPTER XIV

The sun of that same day going down, dusk was saluted as usual at the hotel by an instantaneous sparkle of electric lights. The hours between dinner and bedtime were always difficult enough to kill, and the night after the dance they were further tarnished by the peevishness of dissipation. Certainly, in the opinion of Hirst and Hewet, who lay back in long armchairs in the middle of the hall, with their coffee-cups beside them, and their cigarettes in their hands, the evening was unusually dull, the women unusually badly dressed, the men unusually fatuous. Moreover, when the mail had been distributed half an hour ago there were no letters for either of the two young men. As every other person, practically, had received two or three plump letters from England, which they were now engaged in reading, this seemed hard, and prompted Hirst to make the caustic remark that the animals had been fed. Their silence, he said, reminded him of the silence in the lion-house when each beast holds a lump of raw meat in its paws. He went on, stimulated by this comparison, to liken some to hippopotamuses, some to canary birds, some to swine, some to parrots, and some to loathsome reptiles curled round the half-decayed bodies of sheep. The intermittent sounds—now a cough, now a horrible wheezing or throat-clearing, now a little patter of conversation—were just, he declared, what you hear if you stand in the lion-house when the bones are being mauled. But these comparisons did not rouse Hewet, who, after a careless glance round the room, fixed his eyes upon a thicket of native spears which were so ingeniously arranged as to run their points at you whichever way you approached them. He was clearly oblivious of his surroundings; whereupon Hirst, perceiving that Hewet's mind was a complete blank, fixed his attention more closely upon his fellow-creatures. He was too far from them, however, to hear what they were saying, but it pleased him to construct little theories about them from their gestures and appearance.

Mrs. Thornbury had received a great many letters. She was completely engrossed in them. When she had finished a page she handed it to her husband, or gave him the sense of what she was reading in a series of short quotations linked together by a sound at the back of her throat. "Evie writes that George has gone to Glasgow. 'He finds Mr. Chadbourne so nice to work with, and we hope to spend Christmas together, but I should not like to move Betty and Alfred any great distance (no, quite right), though it is difficult to imagine cold weather in this heat.... Eleanor and Roger drove over in the new trap.... Eleanor certainly looked more like herself than I've seen her since the winter. She has put Baby on three bottles now, which I'm sure is wise (I'm sure it is too), and so gets better nights.... My hair still falls out. I find it on the pillow! But I am cheered by hearing from Tottie Hall Green.... Muriel is in Torquay enjoying herself greatly at dances. She *is* going to show her black pug after all.' ... A line from Herbert—so busy, poor fellow! Ah! Margaret says, 'Poor old Mrs. Fairbank died on the eighth, quite suddenly in the conservatory, only a maid in the house, who hadn't the presence of mind to lift her up, which they think might have saved her, but the doctor says it might have come at any moment, and one can only feel thankful that it was in her house and not in the street (I should think so!). The pigeons have increased terribly, just as the rabbits did five years ago....'" While she read her husband kept nodding his head very slightly, but very steadily in sign of approval.

Near by, Miss Allan was reading her letters too. They were not altogether pleasant, as could be seen from the slight rigidity which came over her large fine face as she finished reading them and replaced them neatly in their envelopes. The lines of care and responsibility on her face made her resemble an elderly man rather than a woman. The letters brought her news of the failure of last year's fruit crop in New Zealand, which was a serious matter, for Hubert, her only brother, made his living on a fruit farm, and if it failed again, of course he would throw up his place, come back to England, and what were they to do with him this time? The journey out here, which meant the loss of a term's work, became an extravagance and not the just and wonderful holiday due to her after fifteen years of punctual lecturing and correcting essays upon English literature. Emily, her sister, who was a teacher also, wrote: "We ought to be prepared, though I have no doubt Hubert will be more reasonable this time." And then went on in her sensible way to say that she was enjoying a very jolly time in the Lakes. "They are looking exceedingly pretty just now. I have seldom seen the trees so forward at this time of year. We have taken our lunch out several days. Old Alice is as young as ever, and asks after every one affectionately. The days pass very quickly, and term will soon be here. Political prospects *not* good, I think privately, but do not like to damp Ellen's enthusiasm. Lloyd George has taken the Bill up, but so have many before now, and we are where we are; but trust to find myself mistaken. Anyhow, we have our work cut out for us.... Surely Meredith lacks the *human* note one likes in W. W.?" she concluded, and went on to discuss some questions of English literature which Miss Allan had raised in her last letter.

At a little distance from Miss Allan, on a seat shaded and made semi-private by a thick clump of palm trees, Arthur and Susan were reading each other's letters. The big slashing manuscripts of hockey-playing young women in Wiltshire lay on Arthur's knee, while Susan deciphered tight little legal hands which rarely filled more than a page, and always conveyed the same impression of jocular and breezy goodwill.

"I do hope Mr. Hutchinson will like me, Arthur," she said, looking up.

"Who's your loving Flo?" asked Arthur.

"Flo Graves—the girl I told you about, who was engaged to that dreadful Mr. Vincent," said Susan. "Is Mr. Hutchinson married?" she asked.

Already her mind was busy with benevolent plans for her friends, or rather with one magnificent plan—which was simple too—they were all to get married—at once—directly she got back. Marriage, marriage, that was the right thing, the only thing, the solution required by every one she knew, and a great part of her meditations was spent in tracing every instance of discomfort, loneliness, ill-health, unsatisfied ambition, restlessness, eccentricity, taking things up and dropping them again, public speaking, and philanthropic activity on the part of men and particularly on the part of women to the fact that they wanted to marry, were trying to marry, and had not succeeded in getting married. If, as she was bound to own, these symptoms sometimes persisted after marriage, she could only ascribe them to the unhappy law of nature which decreed that there was only one Arthur Venning, and only one Susan who could marry him. Her theory, of course, had the merit of being fully supported by her own case. She had been vaguely uncomfortable at home for two or three years now, and a voyage like this with her selfish old aunt, who paid her fare but treated her as servant and companion in one, was typical of the kind of thing people expected of her. Directly she became engaged, Mrs. Paley behaved with instinctive respect, positively protested when Susan as usual knelt down to lace her shoes, and appeared really grateful for an hour of Susan's company where she had been used to exact two or three as her right. She therefore foresaw a life of far greater comfort than she had been used to, and the change had already produced a great increase of warmth in her feelings towards other people.

It was close on twenty years now since Mrs. Paley had been able to lace her own shoes or even to see them, the disappearance of her feet having coincided more or less accurately with the death of her husband, a man of business, soon after which event Mrs. Paley began to grow stout. She was a selfish, independent old woman, possessed of a considerable income, which she spent upon the up-keep of a house that needed seven servants and a charwoman in Lancaster Gate, and another with a garden and carriage-horses in Surrey. Susan's engagement relieved her of the one great anxiety of her life—that her son Christopher should "entangle himself" with his cousin. Now that this familiar source of interest was removed, she felt a little low and inclined to see more in Susan than she used to. She had decided to give her a very handsome wedding present, a cheque for two hundred, two hundred and fifty, or possi-bly, conceivably—it depended upon the under-gardener and Huths' bill for doing up the drawing-room—three hundred pounds sterling.

She was thinking of this very question, revolving the figures, as she sat in her wheeled chair with a table spread with cards by her side. The Patience had somehow got into a muddle, and she did not like to call for Susan to help her, as Susan seemed to be busy with Arthur.

"She's every right to expect a handsome present from me, of course," she thought, looking vaguely at the leopard on its hind legs, "and I've no doubt she does! Money goes a long way with every one. The young are very selfish. If I were to die, nobody would miss me but Dakyns, and she'll be consoled by the will! However, I've got no reason to complain.... I can still enjoy myself. I'm not a burden to any one.... I like a great many things a good deal, in spite of my legs."

Being slightly depressed, however, she went on to think of the only people she had known who had not seemed to her at all selfish or fond of money, who had seemed to her somehow rather finer than the general run; people, she willingly acknowledged, who were finer than she was. There were only two of them. One was her brother, who had been drowned before her eyes, the other was a girl, her greatest friend, who had died in giving birth to her first child. These things had happened some fifty years ago.

"They ought not to have died," she thought. "However, they did—and we selfish old creatures go on." The tears came to her eyes; she felt a genuine regret for them, a kind of respect for their youth and beauty, and a kind of shame for herself; but the tears did not fall; and she opened one of those innumerable novels which she used to pronounce good, bad, pretty middling, or really wonderful. "I can't think how people come to imagine such things," she would say, taking off her spectacles and looking up with the old faded eyes, that were becoming ringed with white.

Just behind the stuffed leopard Mr. Elliot was playing chess with Mr. Pepper. He was being defeated, naturally, for Mr. Pepper scarcely took his eyes off the board, and Mr. Elliot kept leaning back in his chair and throwing out remarks to a gentleman who had only arrived the night before, a tall handsome man, with a head resembling the head of an intellectual ram. After a few remarks of a general nature had passed, they were discovering that they knew some of the same people, as indeed had been obvious from their appearance directly they saw each other.

"Ah yes, old Truefit," said Mr. Elliot. "He has a son at Oxford. I've often stayed with them. It's a lovely old Jacobean house. Some exquisite Greuzes—one or two Dutch pictures which the old boy kept in the cellars. Then there were stacks upon stacks of prints. Oh, the dirt in that house! He was a miser, you know. The boy married a daughter of Lord Pinwell's. I know them too. The collecting mania tends to run in families. This chap collects buckles—men's shoe-buckles they must be, in use between the years 1580 and 1660; the dates mayn't be right, but the fact's as I say. Your true collector always has some unaccountable fad of that kind. On other points he's as level-headed as a breeder of shorthorns, which is what he happens to be. Then the Pinwells, as you probably know, have their share of eccentricity too. Lady Maud, for instance———" he was interrupted here by the necessity of considering his move,— "Lady Maud has a horror of cats and clergymen, and people with big front teeth. I've heard her shout across a table, 'Keep your mouth shut, Miss Smith; they're as yellow as carrots!' across a table, mind you. To me she's always been civility itself. She dabbles in literature, likes to collect a few of us in her drawing-room, but mention a clergyman, a bishop even, nay, the Archbishop himself, and she gobbles like a turkey-cock. I've been told it's a family feud—something to do with an ancestor in the reign of Charles the First. Yes," he continued, suffering check after check, "I always like to know something of the grandmothers of our fashionable young men. In my opinion they preserve all that we admire in the eighteenth century, with the advantage, in the majority of cases, that they are personally clean. Not that one would insult old Lady Barborough by calling her clean. How often d'you think, Hilda," he called out to his wife, "her ladyship takes a bath?"

"I should hardly like to say, Hugh," Mrs. Elliot tittered, "but wearing puce velvet, as she does even on the hottest August day, it somehow doesn't show."

"Pepper, you have me," said Mr. Elliot. "My chess is even worse than I remember." He accepted his defeat with great equanimity, because he really wished to talk.

He drew his chair beside Mr. Wilfred Flushing, the newcomer.

"Are these at all in your line?" he asked, pointing at a case in front of them, where highly polished crosses, jewels, and bits of embroidery, the work of the natives, were displayed to tempt visitors.

"Shams, all of them," said Mr. Flushing briefly. "This rug, now, isn't at all bad." He stooped and picked up a piece of the rug at their feet. "Not old, of course, but the design is quite in the right tradition. Alice, lend me your brooch. See the difference between the old work and the new."

A lady, who was reading with great concentration, unfastened her brooch and gave it to her husband without looking at him or acknowledging the tentative bow which Mr. Elliot was desirous of giving her. If she had listened, she might have been amused by the reference to old Lady Barborough, her great-aunt, but, oblivious of her surroundings, she went on reading.

The clock, which had been wheezing for some minutes like an old man preparing to cough, now struck nine. The sound slightly disturbed certain somnolent merchants, government officials, and men of independent means who were lying back in their chairs, chatting, smoking, ruminating about their affairs, with their eyes half shut; they raised their lids for an instant at the sound and then closed them again. They had the appearance of crocodiles so fully gorged by their last meal that the future of the world gives them no anxiety whatever. The only disturbance in the placid bright room was caused by a large moth which shot from light to light, whizzing over elaborate heads of hair, and causing several young women to raise their hands nervously and exclaim, "Some one ought to kill it!"

Absorbed in their own thoughts, Hewet and Hirst had not spoken for a long time.

When the clock struck, Hirst said:

"Ah, the creatures begin to stir...." He watched them raise themselves, look about them, and settle down again. "What I abhor most of all," he concluded, "is the female breast. Imagine being Venning and having to get into bed with Susan! But the really repulsive thing is that they feel nothing at all—about what I do when I have a hot bath. They're gross, they're absurd, they're utterly intolerable!"

So saying, and drawing no reply from Hewet, he proceeded to think about himself, about science, about Cambridge, about the Bar, about Helen and what she thought of him, until, being very tired, he was nodding off to sleep.

Suddenly Hewet woke him up.

"How d'you know what you feel, Hirst?"

"Are you in love?" asked Hirst. He put in his eyeglass.

"Don't be a fool," said Hewet.

"Well, I'll sit down and think about it," said Hirst. "One really ought to. If these people would only think about things, the world would be a far better place for us all to live in. Are you trying to think?"

That was exactly what Hewet had been doing for the last half-hour, but he did not find Hirst sympathetic at the moment.

"I shall go for a walk," he said.

"Remember we weren't in bed last night," said Hirst with a prodigious yawn.

Hewet rose and stretched himself.

"I want to go and get a breath of air," he said.

An unusual feeling had been bothering him all the evening and forbidding him to settle into any one train of thought. It was precisely as if he had been in the middle of a talk which interested him profoundly when some one came up and interrupted him. He could not finish the talk, and the longer he sat there the more he wanted to finish it. As the talk that had been interrupted was a talk with Rachel, he had to ask himself why he felt this, and why he wanted to go on talking to her. Hirst would merely say that he was in love with her. But he was not in love with her. Did love begin in that way, with the wish to go on talking? No. It always began in his case with definite physical sensations, and these were now absent; he did not even find her physically attractive. There was something, of course, unusual about her—she was young, inexperienced, and inquisitive; they had been more open with each other than was usually possible. He always found girls interesting to talk to, and surely these were good reasons why he should wish to go on talking to her; and last night, what with the crowd and the confusion, he had only been able to begin to talk to her. What was she doing now? Lying on a sofa and looking at the ceiling, perhaps. He could imagine her doing that, and Helen in an armchair, with her hands on the arm of it, so—looking ahead of her, with her great big eyes—oh no, they'd be talking, of course, about the dance. But suppose Rachel was going away in a day or two, suppose this was the end of her visit, and her father had arrived in one of the steamers anchored in the bay,—it was intolerable to know so little. Therefore he exclaimed, "How d'you know what you feel, Hirst?" to stop himself from thinking.

But Hirst did not help him, and the other people with their aimless movements and their unknown lives were disturbing, so that he longed for the empty darkness. The first thing he looked for when he stepped out of the hall door was the light of the Ambroses' villa.

When he had definitely decided that a certain light apart from the others higher up the hill was their light, he was considerably reassured. There seemed to be at once a little stability in all this incoherence. Without any definite plan in his head, he took the turning to the right and walked through the town and came to the wall by the meeting of the roads, where he stopped. The booming of the sea was audible. The dark-blue mass of the mountains rose against the paler blue of the sky. There was no moon, but myriads of stars, and lights were anchored up and down in the dark waves of earth all round him. He had meant to go back, but the single light of the Ambroses' villa had now become three separate lights, and he was tempted to go on. He might as well make sure that Rachel was still there. Walking fast, he soon stood by the iron gate of their garden, and pushed it open; the outline of the house suddenly appeared sharply before his eyes, and the thin column of the verandah cutting across the palely lit gravel of the terrace. He hesitated. At the back of the house some one was rattling cans. He approached the front; the light on the terrace showed him that the sitting-rooms were on that side. He stood as near the light as he could by the corner of the house, the leaves of a creeper brushing his face. After a moment he could hear a voice. The voice went on steadily; it was not talking, but from the continuity of the sound it was a voice reading aloud. He crept a little closer; he crumpled the leaves together so as to stop their rustling about his ears. It might be Rachel's voice. He left the shadow and stepped into the radius of the light, and then heard a sentence spoken quite distinctly.

"And there we lived from the year 1860 to 1895, the happiest years of my parents' lives, and there in 1862 my brother Maurice was born, to the delight of his parents, as he was destined to be the delight of all who knew him."

The voice quickened, and the tone became conclusive, rising slightly in pitch, as if these words were at the end of the chapter. Hewet drew back again into the shadow. There was a long silence. He could just hear chairs being moved inside. He had almost decided to go back, when suddenly two figures appeared at the window, not six feet from him.

"It was Maurice Fielding, of course, that your mother was engaged to," said Helen's voice. She spoke reflectively, looking out into the dark garden, and thinking evidently as much of the look of the night as of what she was saying.

"Mother?" said Rachel. Hewet's heart leapt, and he noticed the fact. Her voice, though low, was full of surprise.

"You didn't know that?" said Helen.

"I never knew there'd been any one else," said Rachel. She was clearly surprised, but all they said was said low and inexpressively, because they were speaking out into the cool dark night.

"More people were in love with her than with any one I've ever known," Helen stated. "She had that power—she enjoyed things. She wasn't beautiful, but—I was thinking of her last night at the dance. She got on with every kind of person, and then she made it all so amazingly—funny."

It appeared that Helen was going back into the past, choosing her words deliberately, comparing Theresa with the people she had known since Theresa died.

"I don't know how she did it," she continued, and ceased, and there was a long pause, in which a little owl called first here, then there, as it moved from tree to tree in the garden.

"That's so like Aunt Lucy and Aunt Katie," said Rachel at last. "They always make out that she was very sad and very good."

"Then why, for goodness' sake, did they do nothing but criticize her when she was alive?" said Helen. Very gentle their voices sounded, as if they fell through the waves of the sea.

"If I were to die to-morrow . . ." she began.

The broken sentences had an extraordinary beauty and detachment in Hewet's ears, and a kind of mystery too, as though they were spoken by people in their sleep.

"No, Rachel," Helen's voice continued, "I'm not going to walk in the garden; it's damp—it's sure to be damp; besides, I see at least a dozen toads."

"Toads? Those are stones, Helen. Come out. It's nicer out. The flowers smell," Rachel replied.

Hewet drew still farther back. His heart was beating very quickly.

Apparently Rachel tried to pull Helen out on to the terrace, and Helen resisted. There was a certain amount of scuffling, entreating, resisting, and laughter from both of them. Then a man's form appeared. Hewet could not hear what they were all saying. In a minute they had gone in; he could hear bolts grating then; there was dead silence, and all the lights went out.

He turned away, still crumpling and uncrumpling a handful of leaves which he had torn from the wall. An exquisite sense of pleasure and relief possessed him; it was all so solid and peaceful after the ball at the hotel, whether he was in love with them or not, and he was not in love with them; no, but it was good that they should be alive.

After standing still for a minute or two he turned and began to walk towards the gate. With the movement of his body, the excitement, the romance and the richness of life crowded into his brain. He shouted out a line of poetry, but the words escaped him, and he stumbled among lines and fragments of lines which had no meaning at all except for the beauty of the words. He shut the gate, and ran swinging from side to side down the hill, shouting any nonsense that came into his head. "Here am I," he cried rhythmically, as his feet pounded to the left and to the right, "plunging along, like an elephant in the jungle, stripping the branches as I go (he snatched at the twigs of a bush at the roadside), roaring innumerable words, lovely words about innumerable things, running downhill and talking nonsense aloud to myself about roads and leaves and lights and women coming out into the darkness—about women—about Rachel, about Rachel." He stopped and drew a deep breath. The night seemed immense and hospitable, and although it was so dark there seemed to be things moving down there in the harbour and movement out at sea. He gazed until the darkness numbed him, and then he walked on quickly, still murmuring to himself. "And I ought to be in bed, snoring and dreaming, dreaming, dreaming. Dreams and realities, dreams and realities, dreams and realities," he repeated all the way up the avenue, scarcely knowing what he said, until he reached the front door. Here he paused for a second, and collected himself before he opened the door.

His eyes were dazed, his hands very cold, and his brain excited and yet half asleep. Inside the door everything was as he had left it except that the hall was now empty. There were the chairs turning in towards each other where people had sat talking, and the empty glasses on little tables, and the newspapers scattered on the floor. As he shut the door he felt as if he were enclosed in a square box, and instantly shrivelled up. It was all very bright and very small. He stopped for a minute by the long table to find a paper which he had meant to read, but he was still too much under the influence of the dark and the fresh air to consider carefully which paper it was or where he had seen it.

As he fumbled vaguely among the papers he saw a figure cross the tail of his eye, coming downstairs. He heard the swishing sound of skirts, and to his great surprise, Evelyn M. came up to him, laid her hand on the table as if to prevent him from taking up a paper, and said:

"You're just the person I wanted to talk to." Her voice was a little unpleasant and metallic, her eyes were very bright, and she kept them fixed upon him.

"To talk to me?" he repeated. "But I'm half asleep."

"But I think you understand better than most people," she answered, and sat down on a little chair placed beside a big leather chair so that Hewet had to sit down beside her.

"Well?" he said. He yawned openly, and lit a cigarette. He could not believe that this was really happening to him. "What is it?"

"Are you really sympathetic, or is it just a pose?" she demanded.

"It's for you to say," he replied. "I'm interested, I think." He still felt numb all over and as if she was much too close to him.

"Any one can be interested!" she cried impatiently. "Your friend Mr. Hirst's interested, I daresay. However, I do believe in you. You look as if you'd got a nice sister, somehow." She paused, picking at some sequins on her knees, and then, as if she had made up her mind, she started off, "Anyhow, I'm going to ask your advice. D'you ever get into a state where you don't know your own mind? That's the state I'm in now. You see, last night at the dance Raymond Oliver,—he's the tall dark boy who looks as if he had Indian blood in him, but he says he's not really,—well, we were sitting out to-gether, and he told me all about himself, how unhappy he is at home, and how he hates being out here. They've put him into some beastly mining business. He says it's beastly—I should like it, I know, but that's neither here nor there. And I felt awfully sorry for him, one couldn't help being sorry for him, and when he asked me to let him kiss me, I did. I don't see any harm in that, do you? And then this morning he said he'd thought I meant something more, and I wasn't the sort to let any one kiss me. And we talked and talked. I daresay I was very silly, but one can't help liking people when one's sorry for them. I do like him most awfully——" She paused. "So I gave him half a promise, and then, you see, there's Al-fred Perrott."

"Oh, Perrott," said Hewet.

"We got to know each other on that picnic the other day," she continued. "He seemed so lonely, especially as Arthur had gone off with Susan, and one couldn't help guessing what was in his mind. So we had quite a long talk when you were looking at the ruins, and he told me all about his life, and his struggles, and how fearfully hard it had been. D'you know, he was a boy in a grocer's shop and took parcels to people's houses in a basket? That interested me aw-fully, because I always say it doesn't matter how you're born if you've got the right stuff in you. And he told me about his sister who's paralysed, poor girl, and one can see she's a great trial, though he's evidently very devoted to her. I must say I do admire people like that! I don't expect you do because you're so clever. Well, last night we sat out in the garden together, and I couldn't help seeing what he wanted to say, and comforting him a little, and telling him I did care—I really do—only, then, there's Raymond Oliver. What I want you to tell me is, can one be in love with two people at once, or can't one?"

She became silent, and sat with her chin on her hands, looking very intent, as if she were facing a real problem which had to be discussed between them.

"I think it depends what sort of person you are," said Hewet. He looked at her. She was small and pretty, aged perhaps twenty-eight or twenty-nine, but though dashing and sharply cut, her features expressed nothing very clearly, except a great deal of spirit and good health.

"Who are you, what are you; you see, I know nothing about you," he continued.

"Well, I was coming to that," said Evelyn M. She continued to rest her chin on her hands and to look intently ahead of her. "I'm the daughter of a mother and no father, if that interests you," she said. "It's not a very nice thing to be. It's what often happens in the country. She was a farmer's daughter, and he was rather a swell—the young man up at the great house. He never made things straight—never married her—though he allowed us quite a lot of money. His people wouldn't let him. Poor father! I can't help liking him. Mother wasn't the sort of woman who could keep him straight, anyhow. He was killed in the war. I believe his men worshipped him. They say great big troopers broke down and cried over his body on the battlefield. I wish I'd known him. Mother had all the life crushed out of her. The world—" She clenched her fist. "Oh, people can be horrid to a woman like that!" She turned upon Hewet.

"Well," she said, "d'you want to know any more about me?"

"But you?" he asked. "Who looked after you?"

"I've looked after myself mostly," she laughed. "I've had splendid friends. I do like people! That's the trouble. What would you do if you liked two people, both of them tremendously, and you couldn't tell which most?"

"I should go on liking them—I should wait and see. Why not?"

"But one has to make up one's mind," said Evelyn. "Or are you one of the people who doesn't believe in marriage and all that? Look here—this isn't fair, I do all the telling, and you tell nothing. Perhaps you're the same as your friend"—she looked at him suspiciously; "perhaps you don't like me?"

"I don't know you," said Hewet.

"I know when I like a person directly I see them! I knew I liked you the very first night at dinner. Oh dear," she continued impatiently, "what a lot of bother would be saved if only people would say the things they think straight out! I'm made like that. I can't help it."

"But don't you find it leads to difficulties?" Hewet asked.

"That's men's fault," she answered. "They always drag it in— love, I mean."

"And so you've gone on having one proposal after another," said Hewet.

"I don't suppose I've had more proposals than most women," said Evelyn, but she spoke without conviction.

"Five, six, ten?" Hewet ventured.

Evelyn seemed to intimate that perhaps ten was the right figure, but that really it was not a high one.

"I believe you're thinking me a heartless flirt," she protested. "But I don't care if you are. I don't care what any one thinks of me. Just because one's interested and likes to be friends with men, and talk to them as one talks to women, one's called a flirt."

"But Miss Murgatroyd——"

"I wish you'd call me Evelyn," she interrupted.

"After ten proposals do you honestly think that men are the same as women?"

"Honestly, honestly,—how I hate that word! It's always used by prigs," cried Evelyn. "Honestly I think they ought to be. That's what's so disappointing. Every time one thinks it's not going to happen, and every time it does."

"The pursuit of Friendship," said Hewet. "The title of a comedy."

"You're horrid," she cried. "You don't care a bit really. You might be Mr. Hirst."

"Well," said Hewet, "let's consider. Let us consider—" He paused, because for the moment he could not remember what it was that they had to consider. He was far more interested in her than in her story, for as she went on speaking his numbness had disappeared, and he was conscious of a mixture of liking, pity, and distrust. "You've promised to marry both Oliver and Perrott?" he concluded.

"Not exactly promised," said Evelyn. "I can't make up my mind

which I really like best. Oh how I detest modern life!" she flung off.
"It must have been so much easier for the Elizabethans! I thought
the other day on that mountain how I'd have liked to be one of
those colonists, to cut down trees and make laws and all that, instead of fooling about with all these people who think one's just a
pretty young lady. Though I'm not. I really might *do* something."
She reflected in silence for a minute. Then she said:

"I'm afraid right down in my heart that Alfred Perrott *won't* do.
He's not strong, is he?"

"Perhaps he couldn't cut down a tree," said Hewet. "Have you
never cared for anybody?" he asked.

"I've cared for heaps of people, but not to marry them," she said.
"I suppose I'm too fastidious. All my life I've wanted somebody I
could look up to, somebody great and big and splendid. Most men
are so small."

"What d'you mean by splendid?" Hewet asked. "People are—
nothing more."

Evelyn was puzzled.

"We don't care for people because of their qualities," he tried to
explain. "It's just them that we care for,"—he struck a match—"just
that," he said, pointing to the flames.

"I see what you mean," she said, "but I don't agree. I do know
why I care for people, and I think I'm hardly ever wrong. I see at
once what they've got in them. Now I think you must be rather
splendid; but not Mr. Hirst."

Hewet shook his head.

"He's not nearly so unselfish, or so sympathetic, or so big, or so
understanding," Evelyn continued.

Hewet sat silent, smoking his cigarette.

"I should hate cutting down trees," he remarked.

"I'm not trying to flirt with you, though I suppose you think I
am!" Evelyn shot out. "I'd never have come to you if I'd thought
you'd merely think odious things of me!" The tears came into her
eyes.

"Do you never flirt?" he asked.

"Of course I don't," she protested. "Haven't I told you? I want friendship; I want to care for some one greater and nobler than I am, and if they fall in love with me it isn't my fault; I don't want it; I positively hate it."

Hewet could see that there was very little use in going on with the conversation, for it was obvious that Evelyn did not wish to say anything in particular, but to impress upon him an image of herself, being, for some reason which she would not reveal, unhappy, or insecure. He was very tired, and a pale waiter kept walking ostentatiously into the middle of the room and looking at them meaningly.

"They want to shut up," he said. "My advice is that you should tell Oliver and Perrott to-morrow that you've made up your mind that you don't mean to marry either of them. I'm certain you don't. If you change your mind you can always tell them so. They're both sensible men; they'll understand. And then all this bother will be over." He got up.

But Evelyn did not move. She sat looking up at him with her bright eager eyes, in the depths of which he thought he detected some disappointment, or dissatisfaction.

"Good-night," he said.

"There are heaps of things I want to say to you still," she said. "And I'm going to, some time. I suppose you must go to bed now?"

"Yes," said Hewet. "I'm half asleep." He left her still sitting by herself in the empty hall.

"Why is it that they *won't* be honest?" he muttered to himself as he went upstairs. Why was it that relations between different people were so unsatisfactory, so fragmentary, so hazardous, and words so dangerous that the instinct to sympathise with another human being was an instinct to be examined carefully and probably crushed? What had Evelyn really wished to say to him? What was she feeling left alone in the empty hall? The mystery of life and the unreality even of one's own sensations overcame him as he walked down the corridor which led to his room. It was dimly lighted, but sufficiently for him to see a figure in a bright dressing-gown pass swiftly in front of him, the figure of a woman crossing from one room to another.

Chapter XV

Whether too slight or too vague the ties that bind people casually meeting in a hotel at midnight, they possess one advantage at least over the bonds which unite the elderly, who have lived together once and so must live for ever. Slight they may be, but vivid and genuine, merely because the power to break them is within the grasp of each, and there is no reason for continuance except a true desire that continue they shall. When two people have been married for years they seem to become unconscious of each other's bodily presence so that they move as if alone, speak aloud things which they do not expect to be answered, and in general seem to experience all the comfort of solitude without its loneliness. The joint lives of Ridley and Helen had arrived at this stage of community, and it was often necessary for one or the other to recall with an effort whether a thing had been said or only thought, shared or dreamt in private. At four o'clock in the afternoon two or three days later Mrs. Ambrose was standing brushing her hair, while her husband was in the dressing-room which opened out of her room, and occasionally, through the cascade of water—he was washing his face—she caught exclamations, "So it goes on year after year; I wish, I wish, I wish I could make an end of it," to which she paid no attention.

"It's white? Or only brown?" Thus she herself murmured, examining a hair which gleamed suspiciously among the brown. She pulled it out and laid it on the dressing-table. She was criticising her own appearance, or rather approving of it, standing a little way back from the glass and looking at her own face with superb pride and melancholy, when her husband appeared in the doorway in his shirt sleeves, his face half obscured by a towel.

"You often tell me I don't notice things," he remarked.

"Tell me if this is a white hair, then?" she replied. She laid the hair on his hand.

"There's not a white hair on your head," he exclaimed.

"Ah, Ridley, I begin to doubt," she sighed; and bowed her head under his eyes so that he might judge, but the inspection produced only a kiss where the line of parting ran, and husband and wife then proceeded to move about the room, casually murmuring.

"What was that you were saying?" Helen remarked, after an interval of conversation which no third person could have understood.

"Rachel—you ought to keep an eye upon Rachel," he observed significantly, and Helen, though she went on brushing her hair, looked at him. His observations were apt to be true.

"Young gentlemen don't interest themselves in young women's education without a motive," he remarked.

"Oh, Hirst," said Helen.

"Hirst and Hewet, they're all the same to me—all covered with spots," he replied. "He advises her to read Gibbon. Did you know that?"

Helen did not know that, but she would not allow herself inferior to her husband in powers of observation. She merely said:

"Nothing would surprise me. Even that dreadful flying man we met at the dance—even Mr. Dalloway—even——"

"I advise you to be circumspect," said Ridley. "There's Willoughby, remember—Willoughby"; he pointed at a letter.

Helen looked with a sigh at an envelope which lay upon her dressing-table. Yes, there lay Willoughby, curt, inexpressive, perpetually jocular, robbing a whole continent of mystery, enquiring after his daughter's manners and morals—hoping she wasn't a bore, and bidding them pack her off to him on board the very next ship if she were—and then grateful and affectionate with suppressed emotion, and then half a page about his own triumphs over wretched little natives who went on strike and refused to load his ships, until he roared English oaths at them, "popping my head out of the window just as I was, in my shirt sleeves. The beggars had the sense to scatter."

"If Theresa married Willoughby," she remarked, turning the page with a hairpin, "one doesn't see what's to prevent Rachel———"

But Ridley was now off on grievances of his own connected with the washing of his shirts, which somehow led to the frequent visits of Hughling Elliot, who was a bore, a pedant, a dry stick of a man, and yet Ridley couldn't simply point at the door and tell him to go. The truth of it was, they saw too many people. And so on and so on, more conjugal talk pattering softly and unintelligibly, until they were both ready to go down to tea.

The first thing that caught Helen's eye as she came downstairs was a carriage at the door, filled with skirts and feathers nodding on the tops of hats. She had only time to gain the drawing-room before two names were oddly mispronounced by the Spanish maid, and Mrs. Thornbury came in slightly in advance of Mrs. Wilfrid Flushing.

"Mrs. Wilfrid Flushing," said Mrs. Thornbury, with a wave of her hand. "A friend of our common friend Mrs. Raymond Parry."

Mrs. Flushing shook hands energetically. She was a woman of forty perhaps, very well set up and erect, splendidly robust, though not as tall as the upright carriage of her body made her appear.

She looked Helen straight in the face and said, "You have a charmin' house."

She had a strongly marked face, her eyes looked straight at you, and though naturally she was imperious in her manner she was nervous at the same time. Mrs. Thornbury acted as interpreter, making things smooth all round by a series of charming commonplace remarks.

"I've taken it upon myself, Mr. Ambrose," she said, "to promise that you will be so kind as to give Mrs. Flushing the benefit of your experience. I'm sure no one here knows the country as well as you do. No one takes such wonderful long walks. No one, I'm sure, has your encyclopaedic knowledge upon every subject. Mr. Wilfrid Flushing is a collector. He had discovered really beautiful things already. I had no notion that the peasants were so artistic—though of course in the past———"

"Not old things—new things," interrupted Mrs. Flushing curtly. "That is, if he takes my advice."

The Ambroses had not lived for many years in London without knowing something of a good many people, by name at least, and Helen remembered hearing of the Flushings. Mr. Flushing was a man who kept an old furniture shop; he had always said he would not marry because most women have red cheeks, and would not take a house because most houses have narrow staircases, and would not eat meat because most animals bleed when they are killed; and then he had married an eccentric aristocratic lady, who certainly was not pale, who looked as if she ate meat, who had forced him to do all the things he most disliked—and here then was the lady. Helen looked at her with interest. They had moved out into the garden, where the tea was laid under a tree, and Mrs. Flushing was helping herself to cherry jam. She had a peculiar jerking movement of the body when she spoke, which caused the canary-coloured plume on her hat to jerk too. Her small but finely cut and vigorous features, together with the deep red of lips and cheeks, pointed to many generations of well-trained and well-nourished ancestors behind her.

"Nothin' that's more than twenty years old interests me," she continued. "Mouldy old pictures, dirty old books, they stick 'em in museums when they're only fit for burnin'."

"I quite agree," Helen laughed. "But my husband spends his life in digging up manuscripts which nobody wants." She was amused by Ridley's expression of startled disapproval.

"There's a clever man in London called John who paints ever so much better than the old masters," Mrs. Flushing continued. "His pictures excite me—nothin' that's old excites me."

"But even his pictures will become old," Mrs. Thornbury intervened.

"Then I'll have 'em burnt, or I'll put it in my will," said Mrs. Flushing.

"And Mrs. Flushing lived in one of the most beautiful old houses in England—Chillingley," Mrs. Thornbury explained to the rest of them.

"If I'd my way I'd burn that to-morrow," Mrs. Flushing laughed. She had a laugh like the cry of a jay, at once startling and joyless.

"What does any sane person want with those great big houses?" she demanded. "If you go downstairs after dark you're covered with black beetles, and the electric lights always goin' out. What would you do if spiders came out of the tap when you turned on the hot water?" she demanded, fixing her eye on Helen.

Mrs. Ambrose shrugged her shoulders with a smile.

"This is what I like," said Mrs. Flushing. She jerked her head at the villa. "A little house in a garden. I had one once in Ireland. One could lie in bed in the mornin' and pick the roses outside the window with one's toes."

"And the gardeners, weren't they surprised?" Mrs. Thornbury enquired.

"There were no gardeners," Mrs. Flushing chuckled. "Nobody but me and an old woman without any teeth. You know the poor in Ireland lose their teeth after they're twenty. But you wouldn't expect a politician to understand that—Arthur Balfour wouldn't understand that."

Ridley sighed that he never expected any one to understand anything, least of all politicians.

"However," he concluded, "there's one advantage I find in extreme old age—nothing matters a hang except one's food and one's digestion. All I ask is to be left alone to moulder away in solitude. It's obvious that the world's going as fast as it can to—the Nethermost Pit, and all I can do is to sit still and consume as much of my own smoke as possible." He groaned, and with a melancholy glance laid the jam on his bread, for he felt the atmosphere of this abrupt lady distinctly unsympathetic.

"I always contradict my husband when he says that," said Mrs. Thornbury sweetly. "You men! Where would you be if it weren't for the women!"

"Read the *Symposium*," said Ridley grimly.

"*Symposium?*" cried Mrs. Flushing. "That's Latin or Greek? Tell me, is there a good translation?"

"No," said Ridley. "You will have to learn Greek."

Mrs. Flushing cried, "Ah, ah, ah! I'd rather break stones in the road. I always envy the men who break stones and sit on those nice little heaps all day wearin' spectacles. I'd infinitely rather break stones than clean out poultry runs, or feed the cows, or——"

Here Rachel came up from the lower garden with a book in her hand.

"What's that book?" said Ridley, when she had shaken hands.

"It's Gibbon," said Rachel as she sat down.

"*The Decline and Fall of the Roman Empire?*" said Mrs. Thornbury. "A very wonderful book, I know. My dear father was always quoting it at us, with the result that we resolved never to read a line."

"Gibbon the historian?" enquired Mrs. Flushing. "I connect him with some of the happiest hours of my life. We used to lie in bed and read Gibbon—about the massacres of the Christians, I remember—when we were supposed to be asleep. It's no joke, I can tell you, readin' a great big book, in double columns, by a night-light, and the light that comes through a chink in the door. Then there were the moths—tiger moths, yellow moths, and horrid cockchafers. Louisa, my sister, would have the window open. I wanted it shut. We fought every night of our lives over that window. Have you ever seen a moth dyin' in a night-light?" she enquired.

Again there was an interruption. Hewet and Hirst appeared at the drawing-room window and came up to the tea-table.

Rachel's heart beat hard. She was conscious of an extraordinary intensity in everything, as though their presence stripped some cover off the surface of things; but the greetings were remarkably commonplace.

"Excuse me," said Hirst, rising from his chair directly he had sat down. He went into the drawing-room, and returned with a cushion which he placed carefully upon his seat.

"Rheumatism," he remarked, as he sat down for the second time.

"The result of the dance?" Helen enquired.

"Whenever I get at all run down I tend to be rheumatic," Hirst stated. He bent his wrist back sharply. "I hear little pieces of chalk grinding together!"

Rachel looked at him. She was amused, and yet she was respectful; if such a thing could be, the upper part of her face seemed to laugh, and the lower part to check its laughter.

Hewet picked up the book that lay on the ground.

"You like this?" he asked in an undertone.

"No, I don't like it," she replied. She had indeed been trying all the afternoon to read it, and for some reason the glory which she had perceived at first had faded, and, read as she would, she could not grasp the meaning with her mind.

"It goes round, round, round, like a roll of oil-cloth," she hazarded. Evidently she meant Hewet alone to hear her words, but Hirst demanded, "What d'you mean?"

She was instantly ashamed of her figure of speech, for she could not explain it in words of sober criticism.

"Surely it's the most perfect style, so far as style goes, that's ever been invented," he continued. "Every sentence is practically perfect, and the wit——"

"Ugly in body, repulsive in mind," she thought, instead of thinking about Gibbon's style. "Yes, but strong, searching, unyielding in mind," she was forced to add. She looked at his big head, a disproportionate part of which was occupied by the forehead, and at the direct, severe eyes.

"I give you up in despair," he said. He meant it lightly, but she took it seriously, and believed that her value as a human being was lessened because she did not happen to admire the style of Gibbon.

The others were talking now in a group about the native villages which Mrs. Flushing ought to visit.

"I despair too," she said impetuously. "How are you going to judge people merely by their minds?"

"You agree with my spinster Aunt, I expect," said St. John in his jaunty manner, which was always irritating because it made the person he talked to appear unduly clumsy and in earnest. "'Be good, sweet maid'—I thought Mr. Kingsley and my Aunt were now obsolete."

"One can be very nice without having read a book," she asserted. Very silly and simple her words sounded, and laid her open to derision.

"Did I ever deny it?" Hirst enquired, raising his eyebrows.

Most unexpectedly Mrs. Thornbury here intervened, either because it was her mission to keep things smooth or because she had long wished to speak to Mr. Hirst, feeling as she did that all young men were her sons.

"I have lived all my life with people like your Aunt, Mr. Hirst," she said, leaning forward in her chair. Her brown squirrel-like eyes became even brighter than usual. "They have never heard of Gibbon. They only care for their pheasants and their peasants. They are great big men who look so fine on horseback, as people must have done, I think, in the days of the great wars. Say what you like against them—they are animal, they are unintellectual; they don't read themselves, and they don't want others to read, but they are some of the finest and the kindest human beings on the face of the earth! You would be surprised at some of the stories I could tell. You have never guessed, perhaps, at all the romances that go on in the heart of the country. Those are the people, I feel, among whom Shakespeare will be born if he is ever born again. In those old houses, up among the Downs——"

"My Aunt," Hirst interrupted, "spends her life in East Lambeth among the degraded poor. I only quoted my Aunt because she is inclined to persecute people she calls 'intellectual,' which is what I suspect Miss Vinrace of doing. It's all the fashion now. If you're clever it's always taken for granted that you're completely without sympathy, understanding, affection—all the things that really matter. Oh, you Christians! You're the most conceited, patronising, hypocritical set of old humbugs in the kingdom! Of course," he continued, "I'm the first to allow your country gentlemen great merits. For one thing, they're probably quite frank about their passions, which we are not. My father, who is a clergyman in Norfolk, says that there is hardly a squire in the county who does not——"

"But about Gibbon?" Hewet interrupted. The look of nervous tension which had come over every face was relaxed by the interruption.

"You find him monotonous, I suppose. But you know——" He opened the book, and began searching for passages to read aloud, and in a little time he found a good one which he considered suitable. But there was nothing in the world that bored Ridley more than being read aloud to, and he was besides scrupulously fastidious as to the dress and behaviour of ladies. In the space of fifteen minutes he had decided against Mrs. Flushing on the ground that her orange plume did not suit her complexion, that she spoke too loud, that she crossed her legs, and finally, when he saw her accept a cigarette that Hewet offered her, he jumped up, exclaiming something about "bar parlours," and left them. Mrs. Flushing was evidently relieved by his departure. She puffed her cigarette, stuck her legs out, and examined Helen closely as to the character and reputation of their common friend, Mrs. Raymond Parry. By a series of little stratagems she drove her to define Mrs. Parry as somewhat elderly, by no means beautiful, very much made up—an insolent old harridan, in short, whose parties were amusing because one met odd people; but Helen herself always pitied poor Mr. Parry, who was understood to be shut up downstairs with cases full of gems, while his wife enjoyed herself in the drawing-room. "Not that I believe what people say against her—although she hints, of course—" Upon which Mrs. Flushing cried out with delight:

"She's my first cousin! Go on—go on!"

When Mrs. Flushing rose to go she was obviously delighted with her new acquaintances. She made three or four different plans for meeting or going on an expedition, or showing Helen the things they had bought, on her way to the carriage. She included them all in a vague but magnificent invitation.

As Helen returned to the garden again, Ridley's words of warning came into her head, and she hesitated a moment, and looked at Rachel sitting between Hirst and Hewet. But she could draw no conclusions, for Hewet was still reading Gibbon aloud, and Rachel, for all the expression she had, might have been a shell, and his words water rubbing against her ears, as water rubs a shell on the edge of a rock.

Hewet's voice was very pleasant. When he reached the end of the period Hewet stopped, and no one volunteered any criticism.

"I do adore the aristocracy!" Hirst exclaimed after a moment's pause. "They're so amazingly unscrupulous. None of us would dare to behave as that woman behaves."

"What I like about them," said Helen as she sat down, "is that they're so well put together. Naked, Mrs. Flushing would be superb. Dressed as she dresses, it's absurd, of course."

"Yes," said Hirst. A shade of depression crossed his face. "I've never weighed more than ten stone in my life," he said, "which is ridiculous, considering my height, and I've actually gone down in weight since we came here. I daresay that accounts for the rheumatism." Again he jerked his wrist back sharply, so that Helen might hear the grinding of the chalk stones. She could not help smiling.

"It's no laughing matter for me, I assure you," he protested. "My mother's a chronic invalid, and I'm always expecting to be told that I've got heart disease myself. Rheumatism always goes to the heart in the end."

"For goodness' sake, Hirst," Hewet protested; "one might think you were an old cripple of eighty. If it comes to that, I had an aunt who died of cancer myself, but I put a bold face on it—" He rose and began tilting his chair backwards and forwards on its hind legs. "Is any one here inclined for a walk?" he said. "There's a magnificent walk, up behind the house. You come out on to a cliff and look right down into the sea. The rocks are all red; you can see them through the water. The other day I saw a sight that fairly took my breath away—about twenty jelly-fish, semi-transparent, pink, with long streamers, floating on the top of the waves."

"Sure they weren't mermaids?" said Hirst. "It's much too hot to climb uphill." He looked at Helen, who showed no signs of moving.

"Yes, it's too hot," Helen decided.

There was a short silence.

"I'd like to come," said Rachel.

"But she might have said that anyhow," Helen thought to herself as Hewet and Rachel went away together, and Helen was left alone with St. John, to St. John's obvious satisfaction.

He may have been satisfied, but his usual difficulty in deciding that one subject was more deserving of notice than another prevented him from speaking for some time. He sat staring intently at the head of a dead match, while Helen considered—so it seemed from the expression of her eyes—something not closely connected with the present moment.

At last St. John exclaimed, "Damn! Damn everything! Damn everybody!" he added. "At Cambridge there are people to talk to."

"At Cambridge there are people to talk to," Helen echoed him, rhythmically and absent-mindedly. Then she woke up.

"By the way, have you settled what you're going to do—is it to be Cambridge or the Bar?"

He pursed his lips, but made no immediate answer, for Helen was still slightly inattentive. She had been thinking about Rachel and which of the two young men she was likely to fall in love with, and now sitting opposite to Hirst she thought, "He's ugly. It's a pity they're so ugly."

She did not include Hewet in this criticism; she was thinking of the clever, honest, interesting young men she knew, of whom Hirst was a good example, and wondering whether it was necessary that thought and scholarship should thus maltreat their bodies, and should thus elevate their minds to a very high tower from which the human race appeared to them like rats and mice squirming on the flat.

"And the future?" she reflected, vaguely envisaging a race of men becoming more and more like Hirst, and a race of women becoming more and more like Rachel. "Oh no," she concluded, glancing at him, "one wouldn't marry you. Well, then, the future of the race is in the hands of Susan and Arthur; no—that's dreadful. Of farm labourers; no—not of the English at all, but of Russians and Chinese." This train of thought did not satisfy her, and was interrupted by St. John, who began again:

"I wish you knew Bennett. He's the greatest man in the world."

"Bennett?" she enquired. Becoming more at his ease, St. John dropped the concentrated abruptness of his manner, and explained that Bennett was a man who lived in an old windmill six miles out of Cambridge. He lived the perfect life, according to St. John, very lonely, very simple, caring only for the truth of things, always ready to talk, and extraordinarily modest, though his mind was of the greatest.

"Don't you think," said St. John, when he had done describing him, "that kind of thing makes this kind of thing rather flimsy? Did you notice at tea how poor old Hewet had to change the conversation? How they were all ready to pounce upon me because they thought I was going to say something improper? It wasn't anything, really. If Bennett had been there he'd have said exactly what he meant to say, or he'd have got up and gone. But there's something rather bad for the character in that—I mean if one hasn't got Bennett's character. It's inclined to make one bitter. Should you say that I was bitter?"

Helen did not answer, and he continued:

"Of course I am, disgustingly bitter, and it's a beastly thing to be. But the worst of me is that I'm so envious. I envy every one. I can't endure people who do things better than I do—perfectly absurd things too—waiters balancing piles of plates—even Arthur, because Susan's in love with him. I want people to like me, and they don't. It's partly my appearance, I expect," he continued, "though it's an absolute lie to say I've Jewish blood in me—as a matter of fact we've been in Norfolk, Hirst of Hirstbourne Hall, for three centuries at least. It must be awfully soothing to be like you—every one liking one at once."

"I assure you they don't," Helen laughed.

"They do," said Hirst with conviction. "In the first place, you're the most beautiful woman I've ever seen; in the second, you have an exceptionally nice nature."

If Hirst had looked at her instead of looking intently at his teacup he would have seen Helen blush, partly with pleasure, partly with an impulse of affection towards the young man who had seemed, and would seem again, so ugly and so limited. She pitied him, for she suspected that he suffered, and she was interested in him, for many of the things he said seemed to her true; she admired the morality of youth, and yet she felt imprisoned. As if her instinct were to escape to something brightly coloured and impersonal, which she could hold in her hands, she went into the house and returned with her embroidery. But he was not interested in her embroidery; he did not even look at it.

"About Miss Vinrace," he began,—"oh, look here, do let's be St. John and Helen, and Rachel and Terence—what's she like? Does she reason, does she feel, or is she merely a kind of footstool?"

"Oh, no," said Helen, with great decision. From her observations at tea she was inclined to doubt whether Hirst was the person to educate Rachel. She had gradually come to be interested in her niece, and fond of her; she disliked some things about her very much, she was amused by others; but she felt her, on the whole, a live if unformed human being, experimental, and not always fortunate in her experiments, but with powers of some kind, and a capacity for feeling. Somewhere in the depths of her, too, she was bound to Rachel by the indestructible if inexplicable ties of sex. "She seems vague, but she's a will of her own," she said, as if in the interval she had run through her qualities.

The embroidery, which was a matter for thought, the design being difficult and the colours wanting consideration, brought lapses into the dialogue when she seemed to be engrossed in her skeins of silk, or, with head a little drawn back and eyes narrowed, considered the effect of the whole. Thus she merely said, "Um—m—m," to St. John's next remark, "I shall ask her to go for a walk with me."

Perhaps he resented this division of attention. He sat silent watching Helen closely.

"You're absolutely happy," he proclaimed at last.

"Yes?" Helen enquired, sticking in her needle.

"Marriage, I suppose," said St. John.

"Yes," said Helen, gently drawing her needle out.

"Children?" St. John enquired.

"Yes," said Helen, sticking her needle in again. "I don't know why I'm happy," she suddenly laughed, looking him full in the face. There was a considerable pause.

"There's an abyss between us," said St. John. His voice sounded as if it issued from the depths of a cavern in the rocks. "You're infinitely simpler than I am. Women always are, of course. That's the difficulty. One never knows how a woman gets there. Supposing all the time you're thinking, 'Oh, what a morbid young man!' "

Helen sat and looked at him with her needle in her hand. From her position she saw his head in front of the dark pyramid of a magnolia-tree. With one foot raised on the rung of a chair, and her elbow out in the attitude for sewing, her own figure possessed the sublimity of a woman's of the early world, spinning the thread of fate—the sublimity possessed by many women of the present day who fall into the attitude required by scrubbing or sewing. St. John looked at her.

"I suppose you've never paid any one a compliment in the course of your life," he said irrelevantly.

"I spoil Ridley rather," Helen considered.

"I'm going to ask you point blank—do you like me?"

After a certain pause, she replied, "Yes, certainly."

"Thank God!" he exclaimed. "That's one mercy. You see," he continued with emotion, "I'd rather you liked me than any one I've ever met."

"What about the five philosophers?" said Helen, with a laugh, stitching firmly and swiftly at her canvas. "I wish you'd describe them."

Hirst had no particular wish to describe them, but when he

began to consider them he found himself soothed and strength-
ened. Far away on the other side of the world as they were, in
smoky rooms, and grey medieval courts, they appeared remarkable
figures, free-spoken men with whom one could be at ease; incomparably more subtle in emotion than the people here. They gave
him, certainly, what no woman would give him, not Helen even.
Warming at the thought of them, he went on to lay his own case before Mrs. Ambrose. Should he stay on at Cambridge or should he
go to the Bar? One day he thought one thing, another day another.
Helen listened attentively. At last, without any preface, she pronounced her decision.

"Leave Cambridge and go to the Bar," she said. He pressed her
for her reasons.

"I think you'd enjoy London more," she said. It did not seem
a very subtle reason, but she appeared to think it sufficient. She
looked at him against the background of flowering magnolia. There
was something curious in the sight. Perhaps it was that the heavy
wax-like flowers were so smooth and inarticulate, and his face—he
had thrown his hat away, his hair was rumpled, he held his eyeglasses in his hand, so that a red mark appeared on either side of
his nose—was so worried and garrulous. It was a beautiful bush,
spreading very widely, and all the time she had sat there talking she
had been noticing the patches of shade and the shape of the leaves,
and the way the great white flowers sat in the midst of the green.
She had noticed it half-consciously, but nevertheless the pattern
had become part of their talk. She laid down her sewing, and began
to walk up and down the garden, and Hirst rose too and paced by
her side. He was rather disturbed, uncomfortable, and full of
thought. Neither of them spoke.

The sun was beginning to go down, and a change had come over
the mountains, as if they were robbed of their earthly substance,
and composed merely of intense blue mist. Long thin clouds of
flamingo red, with edges like the edges of curled ostrich feathers,
lay up and down the sky at different altitudes. The roofs of the
town seemed to have sunk lower than usual; the cypresses appeared
very black between the roofs, and the roofs themselves were brown

and white. As usual in the evening, single cries and single bells became audible rising from beneath.

St. John stopped suddenly.

"Well, you must take the responsibility," he said. "I've made up my mind; I shall go to the Bar."

His words were very serious, almost emotional; they recalled Helen after a second's hesitation from her dream.

"I'm sure you're right," she said warmly, and shook the hand he held out. "You'll be a great man, I'm certain."

Then, as if to make him look at the scene, she swept her hand round the immense circumference of the view. From the sea, over the roofs of the town, across the crests of the mountains, over the river and the plain, and again across the crests of the mountains it swept until it reached the villa, the garden, the magnolia-tree, and the figures of Hirst and herself standing together, when it dropped to her side.

CHAPTER XVI

Hewet and Rachel had long ago reached the particular place on the edge of the cliff where, looking down into the sea, you might chance on jelly-fish and dolphins. Looking the other way, the vast expanse of land gave them a sensation which is given by no view, however extended, in England; the villages and the hills there having names, and the farthest horizon of hills as often as not dipping and showing a line of mist which is the sea; here the view was one of infinite sun-dried earth, earth pointed in pinnacles, heaped in vast barriers, earth widening and spreading away and away like the immense floor of the sea, earth chequered by day and by night, and partitioned into different lands, where famous cities were founded, and the races of men changed from dark savages to white civilised men, and back to dark savages again. Perhaps their English blood made this prospect uncomfortably impersonal and hostile to them, for having once turned their faces that way they next turned them to the sea, and for the rest of the time sat looking at the sea. The sea, though it was a thin and sparkling water here, which seemed incapable of surge or anger, eventually narrowed itself, clouded its pure tint with grey, and swirled through narrow channels and dashed in a shiver of broken waters against massive granite rocks. It was this sea that flowed up to the mouth of the Thames; and the Thames washed the roots of the city of London.

Hewet's thoughts had followed some such course as this, for the first thing he said as they stood on the edge of the cliff was—

"I'd like to be in England!"

Rachel lay down on her elbow, and parted the tall grasses which grew on the edge, so that she might have a clear view. The water was very calm; rocking up and down at the base of the cliff, and so clear that one could see the red of the stones at the bottom of it. So it had been at the birth of the world, and so it had remained ever since. Probably no human being had ever broken that water with boat or with body. Obeying some impulse, she determined to mar that eternity of peace, and threw the largest pebble she could find. It struck the water, and the ripples spread out and out. Hewet looked down too.

"It's wonderful," he said, as they widened and ceased. The freshness and the newness seemed to him wonderful. He threw a pebble next. There was scarcely any sound.

"But England," Rachel murmured in the absorbed tone of one whose eyes are concentrated upon some sight. "What d'you want with England?"

"My friends chiefly," he said, "and all the things one does."

He could look at Rachel without her noticing it. She was still absorbed in the water and the exquisitely pleasant sensations which a little depth of the sea washing over rocks suggests. He noticed that she was wearing a dress of deep blue colour, made of a soft thin cotton stuff, which clung to the shape of her body. It was a body with the angles and hollows of a young woman's body not yet developed, but in no way distorted, and thus interesting and even lovable. Raising his eyes Hewet observed her head; she had taken her hat off, and the face rested on her hand. As she looked down into the sea, her lips were slightly parted. The expression was one of childlike intentness, as if she were watching for a fish to swim past over the clear red rocks. Nevertheless her twenty-four years of life had given her a look of reserve. Her hand, which lay on the ground, the fingers curling slightly in, was well shaped and competent; the square-tipped and nervous fingers were the fingers of a musician. With something like anguish Hewet realised that, far from being unattractive, her body was very attractive to him. She looked up suddenly. Her eyes were full of eagerness and interest.

"You write novels?" she asked.

For the moment he could not think what he was saying. He was overcome with the desire to hold her in his arms.

"Oh, yes," he said. "That is, I want to write them."

She would not take her large grey eyes off his face.

"Novels," she repeated. "Why do you write novels? You ought to write music. Music, you see"—she shifted her eyes, and became less desirable as her brain began to work, inflicting a certain change upon her face—"music goes straight for things. It says all there is to say at once. With writing it seems to me there's so much"—she paused for an expression, and rubbed her fingers in the earth—"scratching on the matchbox. Most of the time when I was read-ing Gibbon this afternoon I was horribly, oh infernally, damnably bored!" She gave a shake of laughter, looking at Hewet, who laughed too.

"*I* shan't lend you books," he remarked.

"Why is it," Rachel continued, "that I can laugh at Mr. Hirst to you, but not to his face? At tea I was completely overwhelmed, not by his ugliness—by his mind." She enclosed a circle in the air with her hands. She realised with a great sense of comfort how easily she could talk to Hewet, those thorns or ragged corners which tear the surface of some relationships being smoothed away.

"So I observed," said Hewet. "That's a thing that never ceases to amaze me." He had recovered his composure to such an extent that he could light and smoke a cigarette, and feeling her ease, became happy and easy himself.

"The respect that women, even well-educated, very able women, have for men" he went on. "I believe we must have the sort of power over you that we're said to have over horses. They see us three times as big as we are or they'd never obey us. For that very reason, I'm inclined to doubt that you'll ever do anything even when you have the vote." He looked at her reflectively. She appeared very smooth and sensitive and young. "It'll take at least six generations before you're sufficiently thick-skinned to go into law courts and business offices. Consider what a bully the ordinary man is," he continued, "the ordinary hard-working, rather ambitious solicitor or man of business with a family to bring up and a certain position to maintain. And then, of course, the daughters have to give way to the sons; the sons have to be educated; they have to bully and shove for their wives and families, and so it all comes over again. And meanwhile there are the women in the background.... Do you really think that the vote will do you any good?"

"The vote?" Rachel repeated. She had to visualise it as a little bit of paper which she dropped into a box before she understood his question, and looking at each other they smiled at something absurd in the question.

"Not to me," she said. "But I play the piano.... Are men really like that?" she asked, returning to the question that interested her. "I'm not afraid of you." She looked at him easily.

"Oh, I'm different," Hewet replied. "I've got between six and seven hundred a year of my own. And then no one takes a novelist seriously, thank heavens. There's no doubt it helps to make up for the drudgery of a profession if a man's taken very, very seriously by every one—if he gets appointments, and has offices and a title, and lots of letters after his name, and bits of ribbon and degrees. I don't grudge it 'em, though sometimes it comes over me—what an amazing concoction! What a miracle the masculine conception of life is—judges, civil servants, army, navy, Houses of Parliament, lord mayors—what a world we've made of it! Look at Hirst now. I assure you," he said, "not a day's passed since we came here without a discussion as to whether he's to stay on at Cambridge or to go to the Bar. It's his career—his sacred career. And if I've heard it twenty times, I'm sure his mother and sister have heard it five hundred times. Can't you imagine the family conclaves, and the sister told to run out and feed the rabbits because St. John must have the schoolroom to himself—'St. John's working,' 'St. John wants his tea brought to him.' Don't you know the kind of thing? No wonder that St. John thinks it a matter of considerable importance. It is too. He has to earn his living. But St. John's sister—" Hewet puffed in silence. "No one takes her seriously, poor dear. She feeds the rabbits."

"Yes," said Rachel. "I've fed rabbits for twenty-four years; it seems odd now." She looked meditative, and Hewet, who had been talking much at random and instinctively adopting the feminine point of view, saw that she would now talk about herself, which was what he wanted, for so they might come to know each other.

She looked back meditatively upon her past life.

"How do you spend your day?" he asked.

She meditated still. When she thought of their day it seemed to her that it was cut into four pieces by their meals. These divisions were absolutely rigid, the contents of the day having to accommodate themselves within the four rigid bars. Looking back at her life, that was what she saw.

"Breakfast nine; luncheon one; tea five; dinner eight," she said.

"Well," said Hewet, "what d'you do in the morning?"

"I used to play the piano for hours and hours."

"And after luncheon?"

"Then I went shopping with one of my aunts. Or we went to see some one, or we took a message; or we did something that had to be done—the taps might be leaking. They visit the poor a good deal—old charwomen with bad legs, women who want tickets for hospitals. Or I used to walk in the park by myself. And after tea people sometimes called; or in summer we sat in the garden or played croquet; in winter I read aloud, while they worked; after dinner I played the piano and they wrote letters. If father was at home we had friends of his to dinner, and about once a month we went up to the play. Every now and then we dined out; sometimes I went to a dance in London, but that was difficult because of getting back. The people we saw were old family friends, and relations, but we didn't see many people. There was the clergyman, Mr. Pepper, and the Hunts. Father generally wanted to be quiet when he came home, because he works very hard at Hull. Also my aunts aren't very strong. A house takes up a lot of time if you do it properly. Our servants were always bad, and so Aunt Lucy used to do a good deal in the kitchen, and Aunt Clara, I think, spent most of the morning dusting the drawing-room and going through the linen and silver. Then there were the dogs. They had to be exercised, besides being washed and brushed. Now Sandy's dead, but Aunt Clara has a very old cockatoo that came from India. Everything in our house," she exclaimed, "comes from somewhere! It's full of old furniture, not really old, Victorian, things mother's family had or father's family had, which they didn't like to get rid of, I suppose, though we've really no room for them. It's rather a nice house," she continued, "except that it's a little dingy—dull I should say." She called up before her eyes a vision of the drawing-room at home; it was a large oblong room, with a square window opening on the garden. Green plush chairs stood against the wall; there was a heavy carved book-case, with glass doors, and a general impression of faded sofa covers, large spaces of pale green, and baskets with pieces of wool-work dropping out of them. Photographs from old Italian masterpieces hung on the walls, and views of Venetian bridges and Swedish waterfalls which members of the family had seen years ago. There were also one or two portraits of fathers and grandmothers, and an engraving of John Stuart Mill,[1] after the picture by Watts. It was a room without definite character, being neither typically and openly hideous, nor strenuously artistic, nor really comfortable. Rachel roused herself from the contemplation of this familiar picture.

"But this isn't very interesting for you."

"Good Lord!" Hewet exclaimed, "I've never been so much interested in my life." She then realised that while she had been thinking of Richmond, his eyes had never left her face. The knowledge of this excited her.

"Go on, please go on," he urged. "Let's imagine it's a Wednesday. You're all at luncheon. You sit there, and Aunt Lucy there, and Aunt Clara here;" he arranged three pebbles on the grass between them.

"Aunt Clara carves the neck of lamb," Rachel continued. She fixed her gaze upon the pebbles. "There's a very ugly yellow china stand in front of me, called a dumb waiter, on which are three dishes, one for biscuits, one for butter, and one for cheese. There's a pot of ferns. Then there's Blanche the maid, who snuffles because of her nose. We talk—oh yes, it's Aunt Lucy's afternoon at Walworth, so we're rather quick over luncheon. She goes off. She has a purple bag, and a black notebook. Aunt Clara has what they call a G.F.S. meeting in the drawing-room on Wednesday, so I take the dogs out. I go up Richmond Hill, along the terrace, into the park. It's the 18th of April—the same day as it is here. It's spring in England. The ground is rather damp. However, I cross the road and get on to the grass and we walk along, and I sing as I always do when I'm alone, until we come to the open place where you can see the whole of London beneath you on a clear day. Hampstead Church spire there, Westminster Cathedral over there, and factory chimneys about here. There's generally a haze over the low parts of London; but it's often blue over the park when London's in a mist. It's the open place that the balloons cross going over to Hurlingham. They're pale yellow. Well, then, it smells very good, particularly if they happen to be burning wood in the keeper's lodge which is there. I could tell you now how to get from place to place, and exactly what trees you'd pass, and where you'd cross the roads. You see, I played there when I was small. Spring is good, but it's best in the autumn when the deer are barking; then it gets dusky, and I go back through the streets, and you can't see people properly; they come past very quick, you just see their faces and then they're gone—that's what I like—and no one knows in the least what you're doing——"

"But you have to be back for tea, I suppose?" Hewet checked her.

"Tea? Oh yes. Five o'clock. Then I say what I've done, and my aunts say what they've done, and perhaps some one comes in: Mrs. Hunt, let's suppose. She's an old lady with a lame leg. She has or she once had eight children; so we ask after them. They're all over the world; so we ask where they are, and sometimes they're ill, or they're stationed in a cholera district, or in some place where it only rains once in five months. Mrs. Hunt," she said with a smile, "had a son who was hugged to death by a bear."

Here she stopped and looked at Hewet to see whether he was amused by the same things that amused her. She was reassured. But she thought it necessary to apologise again; she had been talking too much.

"You can't conceive how it interests me," he said. Indeed, his cigarette had gone out, and he had to light another.

"Why does it interest you?" she asked.

"Partly because you're a woman," he replied. When he said this, Rachel, who had become oblivious of anything, and had reverted to a childlike state of interest and pleasure, lost her freedom and became self-conscious. She felt herself at once singular and under observation, as she felt with St. John Hirst. She was about to launch into an argument which would have made them both feel bitterly against each other, and to define sensations which had no such importance as words were bound to give them when Hewet led her thoughts in a different direction.

"I've often walked along the streets where people live all in a row, and one house is exactly like another house, and wondered what on earth the women were doing inside," he said. "Just consider: it's the beginning of the twentieth century, and until a few years ago no woman had ever come out by herself and said things at all. There it was going on in the background, for all those thousands of years, this curious silent unrepresented life. Of course we're always writing about women—abusing them, or jeering at them, or worshipping them; but it's never come from women themselves. I believe we still don't know in the least how they live, or what they feel, or what they do precisely. If one's a man, the only confidences one gets are from young women about their love affairs. But the lives of women of forty, of unmarried women, of working women, of women who keep shops and bring up children, of women like your aunts or Mrs. Thornbury or Miss Allan—one knows nothing whatever about them. They won't tell you. Either they're afraid, or they've got a way of treating men. It's the man's view that's represented, you see. Think of a railway train: fifteen carriages for men who want to smoke. Doesn't it make your blood boil? If I were a woman I'd blow some one's brains out. Don't you laugh at us a great deal? Don't you think it all a great humbug? You, I mean—how does it all strike you?"

His determination to know, while it gave meaning to their talk, hampered her; he seemed to press further and further, and made it appear so important. She took some time to answer, and during that time she went over and over the course of her twenty-four years, lighting now on one point, now on another—on her aunts, her mother, her father, and at last her mind fixed upon her aunts and her father, and she tried to describe them as at this distance they appeared to her.

They were very much afraid of her father. He was a great dim force in the house, by means of which they held on to the great world which is represented every morning in the *Times*. But the real life of the house was something quite different from this. It went on independently of Mr. Vinrace, and tended to hide itself from him. He was good-humoured towards them, but contemptuous. She had always taken it for granted that his point of view was just, and founded upon an ideal scale of things where the life of one person was absolutely more important than the life of another, and that in that scale they were of much less importance than he was. But did she really believe that? Hewet's words made her think. She always submitted to her father, just as they did, but it was her aunts who influenced her really; her aunts who built up the fine, closely woven substance of their life at home. They were less splendid but more natural than her father was. All her rages had been against them; it was their world with its four meals, its punctuality, and servants on the stairs at half-past ten, that she examined so closely and wanted so vehemently to smash to atoms. Following these thoughts she looked up and said:

"And there's a sort of beauty in it—there they are at Richmond at this very moment building things up. They're all wrong, perhaps, but there's a sort of beauty in it," she repeated. "It's so unconscious, so modest. And yet they feel things. They do mind if people die. Old spinsters are always doing things. I don't quite know what they do. Only that was what I felt when I lived with them. It was very real."

She reviewed their little journeys to and fro, to Walworth, to charwomen with bad legs, to meetings for this and that, their minute acts of charity and unselfishness which flowered punctually from a definite view of what they ought to do, their friendships, their tastes and habits; she saw all these things like grains of sand falling, falling through innumerable days, making an atmosphere and building up a solid mass, a background. Hewet observed her as she considered this.

"Were you happy?" he demanded.

Again she had become absorbed in something else, and he called her back to an unusually vivid consciousness of herself.

"I was both," she replied. "I was happy and I was miserable. You've no conception what it's like—to be a young woman." She looked straight at him. "There are terrors and agonies," she said, keeping her eye on him as if to detect the slightest hint of laughter.

"I can believe it," he said. He returned her look with perfect sincerity.

"Women one sees in the streets," she said.

"Prostitutes?"

"Men kissing one."

He nodded his head.

"Things one guesses at."

"You were never told?"

She shook her head.

"And then," she began and stopped. Here came in the great space of life into which no one had ever penetrated. All that she had been saying about her father and her aunts and walks in Richmond Park, and what they did from hour to hour, was merely on the surface. Hewet was watching her. Did he demand that she should describe that also? Why did he sit so near and keep his eye on her? Why did they not have done with this searching and agony? Why did they not kiss each other simply? She wished to kiss him. But all the time she went on spinning out words.

"A girl is more lonely than a boy. No one cares in the least what she does. Nothing's expected of her. Unless one's very pretty people don't listen to what you say . . . And that is what I like," she added energetically, as if the memory were very happy. "I like walking in Richmond Park and singing to myself and knowing it doesn't matter a damn to anybody. I like seeing things go on—as we saw you that night when you didn't see us—I love the freedom of it—it's like being the wind or the sea." She turned with a curious fling of her hands and looked at the sea. It was still very blue, dancing away as far as the eye could reach, but the light on it was yellower, and the clouds were turning flamingo red.

A feeling of intense depression crossed Hewet's mind. It seemed plain that she would never care for one person rather than another; she was evidently indifferent to him; they seemed to come very near, and then they were as far apart as ever again; and her gesture as she turned away had been oddly beautiful.

"Nonsense," he said abruptly. "You like people. You like admiration. Your real grudge against Hirst is that he doesn't admire you."

She made no answer for some time. Then she said:

"That's probably true. Of course I like people—I like almost every one I've ever met."

She turned her back on the sea and regarded Hewet with friendly if critical eyes. He was good-looking in the sense that he had always had a sufficiency of beef to eat and fresh air to breathe. His head was big; the eyes were also large; though generally vague they could be forcible; and the lips were sensitive. One might account him a man of considerable passion and fitful energy, likely to be at the mercy of moods which had little relation to facts; at once tolerant and fastidious. The breadth of his forehead showed capacity for thought. The interest with which Rachel looked at him was heard in her voice.

"What novels do you write?" she asked.

"I want to write a novel about Silence," he said; "the things people don't say. But the difficulty is immense." He sighed. "However, you don't care," he continued. He looked at her almost severely. "Nobody cares. All you read a novel for is to see what sort of person the writer is, and, if you know him, which of his friends he's put in. As for the novel itself, the whole conception, the way one's seen the thing, felt about it, made it stand in relation to other things, not one in a million cares for that. And yet I sometimes wonder whether there's anything else in the whole world worth doing. These other people," he indicated the hotel, "are always wanting something they can't get. But there's an extraordinary satisfaction in writing, even in the attempt to write. What you said just now is true: one doesn't want to be things; one wants merely to be allowed to see them."

Some of the satisfaction of which he spoke came into his face as he gazed out to sea.

It was Rachel's turn now to feel depressed. As he talked of writing he had become suddenly impersonal. He might never care for any one; all that desire to know her and get at her, which she had felt pressing on her almost painfully, had completely vanished.

"Are you a good writer?" she asked shyly.

"Yes," he said. "I'm not first-rate, of course; I'm good second-rate; about as good as Thackeray, I should say."

Rachel was amazed. For one thing it amazed her to hear Thackeray called second-rate; and then she could not widen her point of view to believe that there could be great writers in existence at the present day, or if there were, that any one she knew could be a great writer; and his self-confidence astounded her, and he became more and more remote.

"My other novel," Hewet continued, "is about a young man who is obsessed by an idea—the idea of being a gentleman. He manages to exist at Cambridge on a hundred pounds a year. He has a coat; it was once a very good coat. But the trousers—they're not so good. Well, he goes up to London, gets into good society, owing to an early-morning adventure on the banks of the Serpentine. He is led into telling lies—my idea, you see, is to show the gradual corruption of the soul—calls himself the son of some great landed proprietor in Devonshire. Meanwhile the coat becomes older and older, and he hardly dares to wear the trousers. Can't you imagine the wretched man, after some splendid evening of debauchery, contemplating these garments—hanging them over the end of the bed, arranging them now in full light, now in shade, and wondering whether they will survive him, or he will survive them? Thoughts of suicide cross his mind. He has a friend, too, a man who somehow subsists upon selling small birds, for which he sets traps in the fields near Uxbridge. They're scholars, both of them. I know one or two wretched starving creatures like that who quote Aristotle at you over a fried herring and a pint of porter. Fashionable life, too, I have to represent at some length, in order to show my hero under all circumstances. Lady Theo Bingham Bingley, whose bay mare he had the good fortune to stop, is the daughter of a very fine old Tory peer. I'm going to describe the kind of parties I once went to—the fashionable intellectuals, you know, who like to have the latest book on their tables. They give parties, river parties, parties where you play games. There's no difficulty in conceiving incidents; the difficulty is to put them into shape—not to get run away with, as Lady Theo was. It ended disastrously for her, poor woman, for the book, as I planned it, was going to end in profound and sordid respectability. Disowned by her father, she marries my hero, and they live in a snug little villa outside Croydon, in which town he is set up as a house agent. He never succeeds in becoming a real gentleman after all. That's the interesting part of it. Does that seem to you the kind of book you'd like to read?" he enquired; "or perhaps you'd like my Stuart tragedy better," he continued, without waiting for her to answer him. "My idea is that there's a certain quality of beauty in the past, which the ordinary historical novelist completely ruins by his absurd conventions. The moon becomes the Regent of the Skies. People clap spurs to their horses, and so on. I'm going to treat people as though they were exactly the same as we are. The advantage is that, detached from modern conditions, one can make them more intense and more abstract than people who live as we do."

Rachel had listened to all this with attention, but with a certain amount of bewilderment. They both sat thinking their own thoughts.

"I'm not like Hirst," said Hewet, after a pause; he spoke meditatively; "I don't see circles of chalk between people's feet. I sometimes wish I did. It seems to me so tremendously complicated and confused. One can't come to any decision at all; one's less and less capable of making judgments. D'you find that? And then one never knows what any one feels. We're all in the dark. We try to find out, but can you imagine anything more ludicrous than one person's opinion of another person? One goes along thinking one knows; but one really doesn't know."

As he said this he was leaning on his elbow arranging and rearranging in the grass the stones which had represented Rachel and her aunts at luncheon. He was speaking as much to himself as to Rachel. He was reasoning against the desire, which had returned with intensity, to take her in his arms; to have done with indirectness; to explain exactly what he felt. What he said was against his belief; all the things that were important about her he knew; he felt them in the air around them, but he said nothing; he went on arranging the stones.

"I like you; d'you like me?" Rachel suddenly observed.

"I like you immensely," Hewet replied, speaking with the relief of a person who is unexpectedly given an opportunity of saying what he wants to say. He stopped moving the pebbles.

"Mightn't we call each other Rachel and Terence?" he asked.

"Terence," Rachel repeated. "Terence——that's like the cry of an owl."

She looked up with a sudden rush of delight, and in looking at Terence with eyes widened by pleasure she was struck by the change that had come over the sky behind them. The substantial blue day had faded to a paler and more ethereal blue; the clouds were pink, far away and closely packed together; and the peace of evening had replaced the heat of the southern afternoon, in which they had started on their walk.

"It must be late!" she exclaimed.

It was nearly eight o'clock.

"But eight o'clock doesn't count here, does it?" Terence asked, as they got up and turned inland again. They began to walk rather quickly down the hill on a little path between the olive trees.

They felt more intimate because they shared the knowledge of what eight o'clock in Richmond meant. Terence walked in front, for there was not room for them side by side.

"What I want to do in writing novels is very much what you want to do when you play the piano, I expect," he began, turning and speaking over his shoulder. "We want to find out what's behind things, don't we?—Look at the lights down there," he continued, "scattered about anyhow. Things I feel come to me like lights... I want to combine them... Have you ever seen fireworks that make figures?... I want to make figures... Is that what you want to do?"

Now they were out on the road and could walk side by side.

"When I play the piano? Music is different... But I see what you mean." They tried to invent theories and to make their theories agree. As Hewet had no knowledge of music, Rachel took his stick and drew figures in the thin white dust to explain how Bach wrote his fugues.

"My musical gift was ruined," he explained, as they walked on after one of these demonstrations, "by the village organist at home, who had invented a system of notation which he tried to teach me, with the result that I never got to the tune-playing at all. My mother thought music wasn't manly for boys; she wanted me to kill rats and birds—that's the worst of living in the country. We live in Devonshire. It's the loveliest place in the world. Only—it's always difficult at home when one's grown up. I'd like you to know one of my sisters... Oh, here's your gate—" He pushed it open. They paused for a moment. She could not ask him to come in. She could not say that she hoped they would meet again; there was nothing to be said, and so without a word she went through the gate, and was soon invisible. Directly Hewet lost sight of her, he felt the old discomfort return, even more strongly than before. Their talk had been interrupted in the middle, just as he was beginning to say the things he wanted to say. After all, what had they been able to say? He ran his mind over the things they had said, the random, unnecessary things which had eddied round and round and used up all the time, and drawn them so close together and flung them so far apart, and left him in the end unsatisfied, ignorant still of what she felt and of what she was like. What was the use of talking, talking, merely talking?

Chapter XVII

It was now the height of the season, and every ship that came from England left a few people on the shores of Santa Marina who drove up to the hotel. The fact that the Ambroses had a house where one could escape momentarily from the slightly inhuman atmosphere of an hotel was a source of genuine pleasure not only to Hirst and Hewet, but to the Elliots, the Thornburys, the Flushings, Miss Allan, Evelyn M., together with other people whose identity was so little developed that the Ambroses did not discover that they possessed names. By degrees there was established a kind of correspondence between the two houses, the big and the small, so that at most hours of the day one house could guess what was going on in the other, and the words "the villa" and "the hotel" called up the idea of two separate systems of life. Acquaintances showed signs of developing into friends, for that one tie to Mrs. Parry's drawing-room had inevitably split into many other ties attached to different parts of England, and sometimes these alliances seemed cynically fragile, and sometimes painfully acute, lacking as they did the supporting background of organised English life. One night when the moon was round between the trees, Evelyn M. told Helen the story of her life, and claimed her everlasting friendship; on another occasion, merely because of a sigh, or a pause, or a word thoughtlessly dropped, poor Mrs. Elliot left the villa half in tears, vowing never again to meet the cold and scornful woman who had insulted her, and in truth, meet again they never did. It did not seem worth while to piece together so slight a friendship.

Hewet, indeed, might have found excellent material at this time up at the villa for some chapters in the novel which was to be called "Silence, or the Things People Don't Say." Helen and Rachel had become very silent. Having detected, as she thought, a secret, and judging that Rachel meant to keep it from her, Mrs. Ambrose respected it carefully, but from that cause, though unintentionally, a curious atmosphere of reserve grew up between them. Instead of sharing their views upon all subjects, and plunging after an idea wherever it might lead, they spoke chiefly in comment upon the people they saw, and the secret between them made itself felt in what they said even of Thornburys and Elliots. Always calm and unemotional in her judgments, Mrs. Ambrose was now inclined to be definitely pessimistic. She was not severe upon individuals so much as incredulous of the kindness of destiny, fate, what happens in the long run, and apt to insist that this was generally adverse to people in proportion as they deserved well. Even this theory she was ready to discard in favour of one which made chaos triumphant, things happening for no reason at all, and every one groping about in illusion and ignorance. With a certain pleasure she developed these views to her niece, taking a letter from home as her text: which gave good news, but might just as well have given bad. How did she know that at this very moment both her children were not lying dead, crushed by motor omnibuses? "It's happening to somebody: why shouldn't it happen to me?" she would argue, her face taking on the stoical expression of anticipated sorrow. However sincere these views may have been, they were undoubtedly called forth by the irrational state of her niece's mind. It was so fluctuating, and went so quickly from joy to despair, that it seemed necessary to confront it with some stable opinion which naturally became dark as well as stable. Perhaps Mrs. Ambrose had some idea that in leading the talk into these quarters she might discover what was in Rachel's mind, but it was difficult to judge, for sometimes she would agree with the gloomiest thing that was said, at other times she refused to listen, and rammed Helen's theories down her throat with laughter, chatter, ridicule of the wildest, and fierce bursts of anger even at what she called the "croaking of a raven in the mud."

"It's hard enough without that," she asserted.

"What's hard?" Helen demanded.

"Life," she replied, and then they both became silent.

Helen might draw her own conclusions as to why life was hard, as to why an hour later, perhaps, life was something so wonderful and vivid that the eyes of Rachel beholding it were positively exhilarating to a spectator. True to her creed, she did not attempt to interfere, although there were enough of those weak moments of depression to make it perfectly easy for a less scrupulous person to press through and know all, and perhaps Rachel was sorry that she did not choose. All these moods ran themselves into one general effect, which Helen compared to the sliding of a river, quick, quicker, quicker still, as it races to a waterfall. Her instinct was to cry out Stop! but even had there been any use in crying Stop! she would have refrained, thinking it best that things should take their way, the water racing because the earth was shaped to make it race.

It seemed that Rachel herself had no suspicion that she was watched, or that there was anything in her manner likely to draw attention to her. What had happened to her she did not know. Her mind was very much in the condition of the racing water to which Helen compared it. She wanted to see Terence; she was perpetually wishing to see him when he was not there; it was an agony to miss seeing him; agonies were strewn all about her day on account of him, but she never asked herself what this force driving through her life arose from. She thought of no result any more than a tree perpetually pressed downwards by the wind considers the result of being pressed downwards by the wind.

During the two or three weeks which had passed since their walk, half a dozen notes from him had accumulated in her drawer. She would read them, and spend the whole morning in a daze of happiness; the sunny land outside the window being no less capable of analysing its own colour and heat than she was of analysing hers. In these moods she found it impossible to read or play the piano, even to move being beyond her inclination. The time passed without her noticing it. When it was dark she was drawn to the window by the lights of the hotel. A light that went in and out was the light in Terence's window: there he sat, reading perhaps, or now he was walking up and down pulling out one book after another; and now he was seated in his chair again, and she tried to imagine what he was thinking about. The steady lights marked the rooms where Terence sat with people moving round him. Every one who stayed in the hotel had a peculiar romance and interest about them. They were not ordinary people. She would attribute wisdom to Mrs. Elliot, beauty to Susan Warrington, a splendid vitality to Evelyn M., because Terence spoke to them. As unreflecting and pervasive were the moods of depression. Her mind was as the landscape outside when dark beneath clouds and straitly lashed by wind and hail. Again she would sit passive in her chair exposed to pain, and Helen's fantastical or gloomy words were like so many darts goading her to cry out against the hardness of life. Best of all were the moods when for no reason again this stress of feeling slackened, and life went on as usual, only with a joy and colour in its events that was unknown before; they had a significance like that which she had seen in the tree: the nights were black bars separating her from the days; she would have liked to run both nights and days into one long continuity of sensation. Although these moods were directly or indirectly caused by the presence of Terence or the thought of him, she never said to herself that she was in love with him, or considered what was to happen if she continued to feel such things, so that Helen's image of the river sliding on to the waterfall had a great likeness to the facts, and the alarm which Helen sometimes felt was justified.

In her curious condition of unanalysed sensations she was incapable of making a plan which should have any effect upon her state of mind. She abandoned herself to the mercy of accidents, missing Terence one day, meeting him the next, receiving his letters always with a start of surprise. Any woman experienced in the progress of courtship would have come by certain opinions from all this which would have given her at least a theory to go upon; but no one had ever been in love with Rachel, and she had never been in love with anyone. Moreover, none of the books she read, from *Wuthering Heights* to *Man and Superman,* and the plays of Ibsen, suggested from their analysis of love that what their heroines felt was what she was feeling now. It seemed to her that her sensations had no name.

She met Terence frequently. When they did not meet, he was apt to send a note with a book or about a book, for he had not been able after all to neglect that approach to intimacy. But sometimes he did not come or did not write for several days at a time. Again when they met their meeting might be one of inspiriting joy or of harassing despair. Over all their partings hung the sense of interruption, leaving them both unsatisfied, though ignorant that the other shared the feeling.

If Rachel was ignorant of her own feelings, she was even more completely ignorant of his. At first he moved as a god; as she came to know him better he was still the centre of light, but combined with this beauty a wonderful power of making her daring and confident of herself. She was conscious of emotions and powers which she had never suspected in herself, and of a depth in the world hitherto unknown. When she thought of their relationship she saw rather than reasoned, representing her view of what Terence felt by a picture of him drawn across the room to stand by her side. This passage across the room amounted to a physical sensation, but what it meant she did not know.

Thus the time went on, wearing a calm, bright look upon its surface. Letters came from England, letters came from Willoughby, and the days accumulated their small events which shaped the year. Superficially, three odes of Pindar were mended, Helen covered about five inches of her embroidery, and St. John completed the first two acts of a play. He and Rachel being now very good friends, he read them aloud to her, and she was so genuinely impressed by the skill of his rhythms and the variety of his adjectives, as well as by the fact that he was Terence's friend, that he began to wonder whether he was not intended for literature rather than for law. It was a time of profound thought and sudden revelations for more than one couple, and for several single people.

A Sunday came, which no one in the villa with the exception of Rachel and the Spanish maid proposed to recognise. Rachel still went to church, because she had never, according to Helen, taken the trouble to think about it. Since they had celebrated the service at the hotel she went there expecting to get some pleasure from her passage across the garden and through the hall of the hotel, although it was very doubtful whether she would see Terence, or at any rate have the chance of speaking to him.

As the greater number of visitors at the hotel were English, there was almost as much difference between Sunday and Wednesday as there is in England, and Sunday appeared here as there, the mute black ghost or penitent spirit of the busy weekday. The English could not pale the sunshine, but they could in some miraculous way slow down the hours, dull the incidents, lengthen the meals, and make even the servants and page-boys wear a look of boredom and propriety. The best clothes which every one put on helped the general effect; it seemed that no lady could sit down without bending a clean starched petticoat, and no gentleman could breathe without a sudden crackle from a stiff shirt-front.

As the hands of the clock neared eleven, on this particular Sunday, various people tended to draw together in the hall, clasping little red-leaved books in their hands. The clock marked a few minutes to the hour when a stout black figure passed through the hall with a preoccupied expression, as though he would rather not recognise salutations, although aware of them, and disappeared down the corridor which led from it.

"Mr. Bax," Mrs. Thornbury whispered.

The little group of people then began to move off in the same direction as the stout black figure. Looked at in an odd way by people who made no effort to join them, they moved with one exception slowly and consciously towards the stairs. Mrs. Flushing was the exception. She came running downstairs, strode across the hall, joined the procession much out of breath, demanding of Mrs. Thornbury in an agitated whisper, "Where, where?"

"We are all going," said Mrs. Thornbury gently, and soon they were descending the stairs two by two. Rachel was among the first to descend. She did not see that Terence and Hirst came in at the rear possessed of no black volume, but of one thin book bound in light-blue cloth, which St. John carried under his arm.

The chapel was the old chapel of the monks. It was a profound cool place where they had said Mass for hundreds of years, and done penance in the cold moonlight, and worshipped old brown pictures and carved saints which stood with upraised hands of blessing in the hollows in the walls. The transition from Catholic to Protestant worship had been bridged by a time of disuse, when there were no services, and the place was used for storing jars of oil, liqueur, and deck-chairs; the hotel flourishing, some religious body had taken the place in hand, and it was now fitted out with a number of glazed yellow benches, and claret-coloured footstools; it had a small pulpit, and a brass eagle carrying the Bible on its back, while the piety of different women had supplied ugly squares of carpet, and long strips of embroidery heavily wrought with monograms in gold.

As the congregation entered they were met by mild sweet chords issuing from a harmonium, seated at which Miss Willett struck emphatic chords with uncertain fingers. The sound spread through the chapel as the rings of water spread from a fallen stone. The twenty or twenty-five people who composed the congregation first bowed their heads and then sat up and looked about them. It was very quiet, and the light down here seemed paler than the light above. The usual bows and smiles were dispensed with, but they recognised each other. The Lord's Prayer was read over them. As the childlike babble of voices rose, the congregation, many of whom had only met on the staircase, felt themselves pathetically united and well-disposed towards each other. As if the prayer were a torch applied to fuel, a smoke seemed to rise automatically and fill the place with the ghosts of innumerable services on innumerable

Sunday mornings at home. Susan Warrington in particular was conscious of the sweetest sense of sisterhood, as she covered her face with her hands and saw slips of bent backs through the chinks between her fingers. Her emotions rose calmly and evenly, approving of herself and of life at the same time. It was all so quiet and so good. But having created this peaceful atmosphere Mr. Bax suddenly turned the page and read a psalm. Though he read it with no change of voice the mood was broken.

"Be merciful unto me, O God," he read, "for man goeth about to devour me: he is daily fighting and troubling me.... They daily mistake my words: all that they imagine is to do me evil. They hold all together and keep themselves close.... Break their teeth, O God, in their mouths; smite the jaw-bones of the lions, O Lord: let them fall away like water that runneth apace; and when they shoot their arrows let them be rooted out."

Nothing in Susan's experience at all corresponded with this, and as she had no love of language she had long ceased to attend to such remarks, although she followed them with the same kind of mechanical respect with which she heard many of Lear's speeches read aloud. Her mind was still serene and really occupied with praise of her own nature and praise of God—that is of the solemn and satisfactory order of the world.

But it could be seen from a glance at their faces that most of the others, the men in particular, felt the inconvenience of the sudden intrusion of this old savage. They looked more secular and critical as they listened to the ravings of the old black man with a cloth round his loins cursing with vehement gesture by a camp-fire in the desert. After that there was a general sound of pages being turned as if they were in class, and then they read a little bit of the Old Testament about making a well, very much as school boys translate an easy passage from the *Anabasis* when they have shut up their French grammar. Then they returned to the New Testament and the sad and beautiful figure of Christ. While Christ spoke they made another effort to fit his interpretation of life upon the lives they lived, but as they were all very different, some practical, some ambitious, some stupid, some wild and experimental, some in love, and others long past any feeling except a feeling of comfort, they did very different things with the words of Christ.

From their faces it seemed that for the most part they made no effort at all, and, recumbent as it were, accepted the ideas that the words gave as representing goodness, in the same way, no doubt, as one of those industrious needlewomen had accepted the bright ugly pattern on her mat as representing beauty.

Whatever the reason might be, for the first time in her life, instead of slipping at once into some curious pleasant cloud of emotion, too familiar to be considered, Rachel listened critically to what was being said. By the time they had swung in an irregular way from prayer to psalm, from psalm to history, from history to poetry, and Mr. Bax was giving out his text, she was in a state of acute discomfort. Such was the discomfort she felt when forced to sit through an unsatisfactory piece of music badly played. Tantalised, enraged by the clumsy insensitiveness of the conductor, who put the stress on the wrong places, and annoyed by the vast flock of the audience tamely praising and acquiescing without knowing or caring, so she was now tantalised and enraged, only here, with eyes half-shut and lips pursed together, the atmosphere of forced solemnity increased her anger. All round her were people pretending to feel what they did not feel, while somewhere above her floated the idea which they could none of them grasp, which they pretended to grasp, always escaping out of reach, a beautiful idea, an idea like a butterfly. One after another, vast and hard and cold, appeared to her the churches all over the world where this blundering effort and misunderstanding were perpetually going on, great buildings, filled with innumerable men and women, not seeing clearly, who finally gave up the effort to see, and relapsed tamely into praise and acquiescence, half-shutting their eyes and pursing up their lips. The thought had the same sort of physical discomfort that is caused by a film of mist always coming between the eyes and the printed page. She did her best to brush away the film and to conceive something to be worshipped as the service went on, but failed, always misled by the voice of Mr. Bax saying things which misrepresented the idea, and by the patter of baaing inexpressive human voices falling round her like damp leaves. The effort was tiring and dispiriting. She ceased to listen, and fixed her eyes on the face of a woman near her, a hospital nurse, whose expression of devout attention seemed to prove that she was at any rate receiving satisfaction. But looking at her carefully she came to the conclusion that the hospital nurse was only slavishly acquiescent, and that the look of satisfaction was produced by no splendid conception of God within her. How, indeed, could she conceive anything far outside her own experience, a woman with a commonplace face like hers, a little round red face, upon which trivial duties and trivial spites had drawn lines, whose weak blue eyes saw without intensity or individuality, whose features were blurred, insensitive, and callous? She was adoring something shallow and smug, clinging to it, so the obstinate mouth witnessed, with the assiduity of a limpet; nothing would tear her from her demure belief in her own virtue and the virtues of her religion. She was a limpet, with the sensitive side of her stuck to a rock, for ever dead to the rush of fresh and beautiful things past her. The face of this single worshipper became printed on Rachel's mind with an impression of keen horror, and she had it suddenly revealed to her what Helen meant and St. John meant when they proclaimed their hatred of Christianity. With the violence that now marked her feelings, she rejected all that she had before implicitly believed.

Meanwhile Mr. Bax was half-way through the second lesson. She looked at him. He was a man of the world with supple lips and an agreeable manner, he was indeed a man of much kindliness and simplicity, though by no means clever, but she was not in the mood to give any one credit for such qualities, and examined him as though he were an epitome of all the vices of his service.

Right at the back of the chapel Mrs. Flushing, Hirst, and Hewet sat in a row in a very different frame of mind. Hewet was staring at the roof with his legs stuck out in front of him, for as he had never tried to make the service fit any feeling or idea of his, he was able to enjoy the beauty of the language without hindrance. His mind was occupied first with accidental things, such as the women's hair in front of him, and the light on the faces; then with the words which seemed to him magnificent, and then more vaguely with the characters of the other worshippers. But when he suddenly perceived Rachel, all these thoughts were driven out of his head, and he thought only of her. The psalms, the prayers, the Litany, and the sermon were all reduced to one chanting sound which paused, and then renewed itself, a little higher or a little lower. He stared alternately at Rachel and at the ceiling, but his expression was now produced not by what he saw but by something in his mind. He was almost as painfully disturbed by his thoughts as she was by hers.

Early in the service Mrs. Flushing had discovered that she had taken up a Bible instead of a prayer-book, and, as she was sitting next to Hirst, she stole a glance over his shoulder. He was reading steadily in the thin pale-blue volume. Unable to understand, she peered closer, upon which Hirst politely laid the book before her, pointing to the first line of a Greek poem and then to the translation opposite.

"What's that?" she whispered inquisitively.

"Sappho," he replied. "The one Swinburne did—the best thing that's ever been written."

Mrs. Flushing could not resist such an opportunity. She gulped down the Ode to Aphrodite during the Litany, keeping herself with difficulty from asking when Sappho lived, and what else she wrote worth reading, and contriving to come in punctually at the end with "the forgiveness of sins, the Resurrection of the body, and the life everlastin'. Amen."

Meanwhile Hirst took out an envelope and began scribbling on the back of it. When Mr. Bax mounted the pulpit he shut up Sappho with his envelope between the pages, settled his spectacles, and fixed his gaze intently upon the clergyman. Standing in the pulpit he looked very large and fat; the light coming through the greenish unstained window-glass made his face appear smooth and white like a very large egg.

He looked round at all the faces looking mildly up at him; although some of them were the faces of men and women old enough to be his grandparents, and gave out his text with weighty significance. The argument of the sermon was that visitors to this beautiful land, although they were on a holiday, owed a duty to the natives. It did not, in truth, differ very much from a leading article upon topics of general interest in the weekly newspapers. It rambled with a kind of amiable verbosity from one heading to another, suggesting that all human beings are very much the same under their skins, illustrating this by the resemblance of the games which little Spanish boys play to the games little boys in London streets play, observing that very small things do influence people, particularly natives; in fact, a very dear friend of Mr. Bax's had told him that the success of our rule in India, that vast country, largely depended upon the strict code of politeness which the English adopted towards the natives, which led to the remark that small things were not necessarily small, and that somehow to the virtue of sympathy, which was a virtue never more needed than to-day, when we lived in a time of experiment and upheaval—witness the aeroplane and wireless telegraph, and there were other problems which hardly presented themselves to our fathers, but which no man who called himself a man could leave unsettled. Here Mr. Bax became more definitely clerical, and seemed to speak with a certain innocent craftiness, as he pointed out that all this laid a special duty upon earnest Christians. What men were inclined to say now was, "Oh, that fellow—he's a parson." What we want them to say is, "He's a good fellow"—in other words, "He is my brother." He exhorted them to keep in touch with men of the modern type; they must sympathise with their multifarious interests in order to keep before their eyes that whatever discoveries were made there was one discovery which could not be superseded, which was indeed as much of a necessity to the most successful and most brilliant of them all as it had been to their fathers. The humblest could help; the least important things had an influence (here his manner became definitely priestly and his remarks seemed to be directed to women, for indeed Mr. Bax's congregations were mainly composed of women, and he was used to assigning them their duties in his innocent clerical campaigns). Leaving more definite instruction, he passed on, and his theme broadened into a peroration for which he drew a long breath and stood very upright,—"As a drop of water, detached, alone, separate from others, falling from the cloud and entering the great ocean, alters, so scientists tell us, not only the immediate spot in the ocean where it falls, but all the myriad drops which together compose the great universe of waters, and by this means alters the configuration of the globe and the lives of millions of sea creatures, and finally the lives of the men and women who seek their living upon the shores—as all this is within the compass of a single drop of water, such as any rain shower sends in millions to lose themselves in the earth, to lose themselves we say, but we know very well that the fruits of the earth could not flourish without them—so is a marvel comparable to this within the reach of each one of us, who dropping a little word or a little deed into the great universe alters it; yea, it is a solemn thought, *alters* it, for good or for evil, not for one instant, or in one vicinity, but throughout the entire race, and for all eternity." Whipping round as though to avoid applause, he continued with the same breath, but in a different tone of voice,—"And now to God the Father ..."

He gave his blessing, and then, while the solemn chords again issued from the harmonium behind the curtain, the different people began scraping and fumbling and moving very awkwardly and consciously towards the door. Halfway upstairs, at a point where the lights and sounds of the upper world conflicted with the dimness and the dying hymn-tune of the under, Rachel felt a hand drop upon her shoulder.

"Miss Vinrace," Mrs. Flushing whispered peremptorily, "stay to luncheon. It's such a dismal day. They don't even give one beef for luncheon. Please stay."

Here they came out into the hall, where once more the little band was greeted with curious respectful glances by the people who had not gone to church, although their clothing made it clear that they approved of Sunday to the very verge of going to church. Rachel felt unable to stand any more of this particular atmosphere, and was about to say she must go back, when Terence passed them, drawn along in talk with Evelyn M. Rachel thereupon contented herself with saying that the people looked very respectable, which negative remark Mrs. Flushing interpreted to mean that she would stay.

"English people abroad!" she returned with a vivid flash of malice. "Ain't they awful! But we won't stay here," she continued, plucking at Rachel's arm. "Come up to my room."

She bore her past Hewet and Evelyn and the Thornburys and the Elliots. Hewet stepped forward.

"Luncheon—" he began.

"Miss Vinrace has promised to lunch with me," said Mrs. Flushing, and began to pound energetically up the staircase, as though the middle classes of England were in pursuit. She did not stop until she had slammed her bedroom door behind them.

"Well, what did you think of it?" she demanded, panting slightly.

All the disgust and horror which Rachel had been accumulating burst forth beyond her control.

"I thought it the most loathsome exhibition I'd ever seen!" she broke out. "How can they—how dare they—what do they mean by it—Mr. Bax, hospital nurses, old men, prostitutes, disgusting—"

She hit off the points she remembered as fast as she could, but she was too indignant to stop to analyse her feelings. Mrs. Flushing watched her with keen gusto as she stood ejaculating with emphatic movements of her head and hands in the middle of the room.

"Go on, go on, do go on," she laughed, clapping her hands. "It's delightful to hear you!"

"But why do you go?" Rachel demanded.

"I've been every Sunday of my life ever since I can remember," Mrs. Flushing chuckled, as though that were a reason by itself.

Rachel turned abruptly to the window. She did not know now what it was that had put her into such a passion; the sight of Terence in the hall had confused her thoughts, leaving her merely indignant. She looked straight at their own villa, halfway up the side of the mountain. The most familiar view seen framed through glass has a certain unfamiliar distinction, and she grew calm as she gazed. Then she remembered that she was in the presence of some one she did not know well, and she turned and looked at Mrs. Flushing. Mrs. Flushing was still sitting on the edge of the bed, looking up, with her lips parted, so that her strong white teeth showed in two rows.

"Tell me," she said, "which d'you like best, Mr. Hewet or Mr. Hirst?"

"Mr. Hewet," Rachel replied, but her voice did not sound natural.

"Which is the one who reads Greek in church?" Mrs. Flushing demanded.

It might have been either of them, and while Mrs. Flushing proceeded to describe them both, and to say that both frightened her, but one frightened her more than the other, Rachel looked for a chair. The room, of course, was one of the largest and most luxurious in the hotel. There were a great many arm-chairs and settees covered in brown holland, but each of these was occupied by a large square piece of yellow cardboard, and all the pieces of cardboard were dotted or lined with spots or dashes of bright oil paint.

"But you're not to look at those," said Mrs. Flushing as she saw Rachel's eye wander. She jumped up, and turned as many as she could, face downwards, upon the floor. Rachel, however, managed to possess herself of one of them, and, with the vanity of an artist, Mrs. Flushing demanded anxiously, "Well, well?"

"It's a hill," Rachel replied. There could be no doubt that Mrs. Flushing had represented the vigorous and abrupt fling of the earth up into the air; you could almost see the clods flying as it whirled.

Rachel passed from one to another. They were all marked by something of the jerk and decision of their maker; they were all perfectly untrained onslaughts of the brush upon some half-realised idea suggested by hill or tree; and they were all in some way characteristic of Mrs. Flushing.

"I see things movin'," Mrs. Flushing explained. "So"—she swept her hand through a yard of the air. She then took up one of the cardboards which Rachel had laid aside, seated herself on a stool, and began to flourish a stump of charcoal. While she occupied herself in strokes which seemed to serve her as speech serves others, Rachel, who was very restless, looked about her.

"Open the wardrobe," said Mrs. Flushing after a pause, speaking indistinctly because of a paint-brush in her mouth, "and look at the things."

As Rachel hesitated, Mrs. Flushing came forward, still with a paint-brush in her mouth, flung open the wings of her wardrobe, and tossed a quantity of shawls, stuffs, cloaks, embroideries, on to the bed. Rachel began to finger them. Mrs. Flushing came up once more, and dropped a quantity of beads, brooches, earrings, bracelets, tassels, and combs among the draperies. Then she went back to her stool and began to paint in silence. The stuffs were coloured and dark and pale; they made a curious swarm of lines and colours upon the counterpane, with the reddish lumps of stone and peacocks' feathers and clear pale tortoise-shell combs lying among them.

"The women wore them hundreds of years ago, they wear 'em still," Mrs. Flushing remarked. "My husband rides about and finds 'em; they don't know what they're worth, so we get 'em cheap. And we shall sell 'em to smart women in London," she chuckled, as though the thought of these ladies and their absurd appearance amused her. After painting for some minutes, she suddenly laid down her brush and fixed her eyes upon Rachel.

"I tell you what I want to do," she said. "I want to go up there and see things for myself. It's silly stayin' here with a pack of old maids as though we were at the seaside in England. I want to go up the river and see the natives in their camps. It's only a matter of ten days under canvas. My husband's done it. One would lie out under the trees at night and be towed down the river by day, and if we saw anythin' nice we'd shout out and tell 'em to stop." She rose and began piercing the bed again and again with a long golden pin, as she watched to see what effect her suggestion had upon Rachel.

"We must make up a party," she went on. "Ten people could hire a launch. Now you'll come, and Mrs. Ambrose'll come, and will Mr. Hirst and t'other gentleman come? Where's a pencil?"

She became more and more determined and excited as she evolved her plan. She sat on the edge of the bed and wrote down a list of surnames, which she invariably spelt wrong. Rachel was enthusiastic, for indeed the idea was immeasurably delightful to her. She had always had a great desire to see the river, and the name of

Terence threw a lustre over the prospect, which made it almost too good to come true. She did what she could to help Mrs. Flushing by suggesting names, helping her to spell them, and counting up the days of the week upon her fingers. As Mrs. Flushing wanted to know all she could tell her about the birth and pursuits of every person she suggested, and threw in wild stories of her own as to the temperaments and habits of artists, and people of the same name who used to come to Chillingley in the old days, but were doubtless not the same, though they too were very clever men interested in Egyptology, the business took some time. At last Mrs. Flushing sought her diary for help, the method of reckoning dates on the fingers proving unsatisfactory. She opened and shut every drawer in her writing-table, and then cried furiously, "Yarmouth! Yarmouth! Drat the woman! She's always out of the way when she's wanted!"

At this moment the luncheon gong began to work itself into its midday frenzy. Mrs. Flushing rang her bell violently. The door was opened by a handsome maid who was almost as upright as her mistress.

"Oh, Yarmouth," said Mrs. Flushing, "just find my diary and see where ten days from now would bring us to, and ask the hall porter how many men 'ud be wanted to row eight people up the river for a week, and what it 'ud cost, and put it on a slip of paper and leave it on my dressing-table. Now—" she pointed at the door with a superb forefinger so that Rachel had to lead the way.

"Oh, and Yarmouth," Mrs. Flushing called back over her shoulder. "Put those things away and hang 'em in their right places, there's a good girl, or it fusses Mr. Flushin'."

To all of which Yarmouth merely replied, "Yes, ma'am."

As they entered the long dining-room it was obvious that the day was still Sunday, although the mood was slightly abating. The Flushings' table was set by the side in the window, so that Mrs. Flushing could scrutinise each figure as it entered, and her curiosity seemed to be intense.

"Old Mrs. Paley," she whispered as the wheeled chair slowly made its way through the door, Arthur pushing behind. "Thorn-

246 · *Virginia Woolf*

burys" came next. "That nice woman," she nudged Rachel to look at Miss Allan. "What's her name?" The painted lady who always came in late, tripping into the room with a prepared smile as though she came out upon a stage, might well have quailed before Mrs. Flushing's stare, which expressed her steely hostility to the whole tribe of painted ladies. Next came the two young men whom Mrs. Flushing called collectively the Hirsts. They sat down opposite, across the gangway.

Mr. Flushing treated his wife with a mixture of admiration and indulgence, making up by the suavity and fluency of his speech for the abruptness of hers. While she darted and ejaculated he gave Rachel a sketch of the history of South American art. He would deal with one of his wife's exclamations, and then return as smoothly as ever to his theme. He knew very well how to make a luncheon pass agreeably, without being dull or intimate. He had formed the opinion, so he told Rachel, that wonderful treasures lay hid in the depths of the land; the things Rachel had seen were merely trifles picked up in the course of one short journey. He thought there might be giant gods hewn out of stone in the mountainside; and colossal figures standing by themselves in the middle of vast green pasture lands, where none but natives had ever trod. Before the dawn of European art he believed that the primitive huntsmen and priests had built temples of massive stone slabs, had formed out of the dark rocks and the great cedar trees majestic figures of gods and of beasts, and symbols of the great forces, water, air, and forest among which they lived. There might be prehistoric towns, like those in Greece and Asia, standing in open places among the trees, filled with the works of this early race. Nobody had been there; scarcely anything was known. Thus talking and displaying the most picturesque of his theories, Rachel's attention was fixed upon him.

She did not see that Hewet kept looking at her across the gangway, between the figures of waiters hurrying past with plates. He was inattentive, and Hirst was finding him also very cross and disagreeable. They had touched upon all the usual topics—upon politics and literature, gossip and Christianity. They had quarrelled over the service, which was every bit as fine as Sappho, according to Hewet; so that Hirst's paganism was mere ostentation. Why go to church, he demanded, merely in order to read Sappho? Hirst observed that he had listened to every word of the sermon, as he could prove if Hewet would like a repetition of it; and he went to church in order to realise the nature of his Creator, which he had done very vividly that morning, thanks to Mr. Bax, who had inspired him to write three of the most superb lines in English literature, an invocation to the Deity.

"I wrote 'em on the back of the envelope of my aunt's last letter," he said, and pulled it from between the pages of Sappho.

"Well, let's hear them," said Hewet, slightly mollified by the prospect of a literary discussion.

"My dear Hewet, do you wish us both to be flung out of the hotel by an enraged mob of Thornburys and Elliots?" Hirst enquired. "The merest whisper would be sufficient to incriminate me for ever. God!" he broke out, "what's the use of attempting to write when the world's peopled by such damned fools? Seriously, Hewet, I advise you to give up literature. What's the good of it? There's your audience."

He nodded his head at the tables where a very miscellaneous collection of Europeans were now engaged in eating, in some cases in gnawing, the stringy foreign fowls. Hewet looked, and grew more out of temper than ever. Hirst looked too. His eyes fell upon Rachel, and he bowed to her.

"I rather think Rachel's in love with me," he remarked, as his eyes returned to his plate. "That's the worst of friendships with young women—they tend to fall in love with one."

To that Hewet made no answer whatever, and sat singularly still. Hirst did not seem to mind getting no answer, for he returned to Mr. Bax again, quoting the peroration about the drop of water; and when Hewet scarcely replied to these remarks either, he merely pursed his lips, chose a fig, and relapsed quite contentedly into his own thoughts, of which he always had a very large supply. When luncheon was over they separated, taking their cups of coffee to different parts of the hall.

From his chair beneath the palm-tree Hewet saw Rachel come out of the dining-room with the Flushings; he saw them look round for chairs, and choose three in a corner where they could go on talking in private. Mr. Flushing was now in the full tide of his discourse. He produced a sheet of paper upon which he made drawings as he went on with his talk. He saw Rachel lean over and look, pointing to this and that with her finger. Hewet unkindly compared Mr. Flushing, who was extremely well dressed for a hot climate, and rather elaborate in his manner, to a very persuasive shop-keeper. Meanwhile, as he sat looking at them, he was entangled in the Thornburys and Miss Allan, who, after hovering about for a minute or two, settled in chairs round him, holding their cups in their hands. They wanted to know whether he could tell them anything about Mr. Bax. Mr. Thornbury as usual sat saying nothing, looking vaguely ahead of him, occasionally raising his eyeglasses, as if to put them on, but always thinking better of it at the last moment, and letting them fall again. After some discussion, the ladies put it beyond a doubt that Mr. Bax was not the son of Mr. William Bax. There was a pause. Then Mrs. Thornbury remarked that she was still in the habit of saying Queen instead of King in the National Anthem. There was another pause. Then Miss Allan observed reflectively that going to church abroad always made her feel as if she had been to a sailor's funeral. There was then a very long pause, which threatened to be final, when, mercifully, a bird about the size of a magpie, but of a metallic blue colour, appeared on the section of the terrace that could be seen from where they sat. Mrs. Thornbury was led to enquire whether we should like it if all our rooks were blue—"What do *you* think, William?" she asked, touching her husband on the knee.

"If all our rooks were blue," he said,—he raised his glasses; he actually placed them on his nose,—"they would not live long in Wiltshire," he concluded; he dropped his glasses to his side again. The three elderly people now gazed meditatively at the bird, which was so obliging as to stay in the middle of the view for a considerable space of time, thus making it unnecessary for them to speak again. Hewet began to wonder whether he might not cross over to the Flushings' corner, when Hirst appeared from the background, slipped into a chair by Rachel's side, and began to talk to her with every appearance of familiarity. Hewet could stand it no longer. He rose, took his hat and dashed out of doors.

Chapter XVIII

Everything he saw was distasteful to him. He hated the blue and white, the intensity and definiteness, the hum and heat of the south; the landscape seemed to him as hard and as romantic as a cardboard background on the stage, and the mountain but a wooden screen against a sheet painted blue. He walked fast in spite of the heat of the sun.

Two roads led out of the town on the eastern side; one branched off towards the Ambroses' villa, the other struck into the country, eventually reaching a village on the plain, but many footpaths, which had been stamped in the earth when it was wet, led off from it, across great dry fields, to scattered farmhouses, and the villas of rich natives. Hewet stepped off the road on to one of these, in order to avoid the hardness and heat of the main road, the dust of which was always being raised in small clouds by carts and ramshackle flies which carried parties of festive peasants, or turkeys swelling unevenly like a bundle of air balls beneath a net, or the brass bedstead and black wooden boxes of some newly wedded pair.

The exercise indeed served to clear away the superficial irritations of the morning, but he remained miserable. It seemed proved beyond a doubt that Rachel was indifferent to him, for she had scarcely looked at him, and she had talked to Mr. Flushing with just the same interest with which she talked to him. Finally, Hirst's odious words flicked his mind like a whip, and he remembered that he had left her talking to Hirst. She was at this moment talking to him, and it might be true, as he said, that she was in love with him. He went over all the evidence for this supposition—her sudden interest in Hirst's writing, her way of quoting his opinions respectfully, or with only half a laugh; her very nickname for him, "the great Man," might have some serious meaning in it. Supposing that there were an understanding between them, what would it mean to him?

"Damn it all!" he demanded, "am I in love with her?" To that he could only return himself one answer. He certainly was in love with her, if he knew what love meant. Ever since he had first seen her he had been interested and attracted, more and more interested and attracted, until he was scarcely able to think of anything except Rachel. But just as he was sliding into one of the long feasts of meditation about them both, he checked himself by asking whether he wanted to marry her? That was the real problem, for these miseries and agonies could not be endured, and it was necessary that he should make up his mind. He instantly decided that he did not want to marry any one. Partly because he was irritated by Rachel the idea of marriage irritated him also. It immediately suggested the picture of two people sitting alone over the fire; the man was reading, the woman sewing. There was a second picture. He saw a man jump up, say good-night, leave the company and hasten away with the quiet secret look of one who is stealing to certain happiness. Both these pictures were very unpleasant, and even more so was a third picture, of husband and wife and friend; and the married people glancing at each other as though they were content to let something pass unquestioned, being themselves possessed of the deeper truth. Other pictures—he was walking very fast in his irritation, and they came before him without any conscious effort, like pictures on a sheet—succeeded these. Here were the worn husband and wife sitting with their children round them, very patient, tolerant, and wise. But that, too, was an unpleasant picture. He tried all sorts of pictures, taking them from the lives of friends of his, for he knew many different married couples; but he saw them always, walled up in a warm firelit room. When, on the other hand, he began to think of unmarried people, he saw them active in an unlimited world; above all, standing on the same ground as the rest, without shelter or advantage. All the most individual and humane of his friends were bachelors and spinsters; indeed he was surprised to find that the women he most admired and knew best were unmarried women. Marriage seemed to be worse for them than it was for men. Leaving these general pictures he considered the people whom he had been observing lately at the hotel. He had often revolved these questions in his mind, as he watched Susan and Arthur, or Mr. and Mrs. Thornbury, or Mr. and Mrs. Elliot. He had observed how the shy happiness and surprise of the engaged couple had gradually been replaced by a comfortable, tolerant state of mind, as if they had already done with the adventure of intimacy and were taking up their parts. Susan used to pursue Arthur about with a sweater, because he had one day let slip that a brother of his had died of pneumonia. The sight amused him, but was not pleasant if you substituted Terence and Rachel for Arthur and Susan; and Arthur was far less eager to get you in a corner and talk about flying and the mechanics of aeroplanes. They would settle down. He then looked at the couples who had been married for several years. It was true that Mrs. Thornbury had a husband, and that for the most part she was wonderfully successful in bringing him into the conversation, but one could not imagine what they said to each other when they were alone. There was the same difficulty with regard to the Elliots, except that they probably bickered openly in private. They sometimes bickered in public, though these disagreements were painfully covered over by little insincerities on the part of the wife, who was afraid of public opinion, because she was much stupider than her husband, and had to make efforts to keep hold of him. There could be no doubt, he decided, that it would have been far better for the world if these couples had separated. Even the Ambroses, whom he admired and respected profoundly—in spite of all the love between them, was not their marriage too a compromise? She gave way to him; she spoilt him; she arranged things for him; she who was all truth to others was not true to her husband, was not true to her friends if they came in conflict with her husband. It was a strange and piteous flaw in her nature. Perhaps Rachel had been right, then, when she said that night in the garden, "We bring out what's worst in each other—we should live separate."

No, Rachel had been utterly wrong! Every argument seemed to be against undertaking the burden of marriage until he came to Rachel's argument, which was manifestly absurd. From having been the pursued, he turned and became the pursuer. Allowing the case against marriage to lapse, he began to consider the peculiarities of character which had led to her saying that. Had she meant it? Surely one ought to know the character of the person with whom one might spend all one's life; being a novelist, let him try to discover what sort of person she was. When he was with her he could not analyse her qualities, because he seemed to know them instinctively, but when he was away from her it sometimes seemed to him that he did not know her at all. She was young, but she was also old; she had little self-confidence, and yet she was a good judge of people. She was happy; but what made her happy? If they were alone and the excitement had worn off, and they had to deal with the ordinary facts of the day, what would happen? Casting his eye upon his own character, two things appeared certain to him: that he was very unpunctual, and that he disliked answering notes. As far as he knew Rachel was inclined to be punctual, but he could not remember that he had ever seen her with a pen in her hand. Let him next imagine a dinner-party, say at the Crooms, and Wilson, who had taken her down, talking about the state of the Liberal party. She would say—of course she was absolutely ignorant of politics. Nevertheless she was intelligent certainly, and honest, too. Her temper was uncertain—that he had noticed—and she was not domestic, and she was not easy, and she was not quiet, or beautiful, except in some dresses in some lights. But the great gift she had was that she understood what was said to her; there had never been any one like her for talking to. You could say anything—you could say everything, and yet she was never servile. Here he pulled himself up, for it seemed to him suddenly that he knew less about her than about any one. All these thoughts had occurred to him many times already; often had he tried to argue and reason; and again he had reached the old state of doubt. He did not know her, and he did not know what she felt, or whether they could live together, or whether he wanted to marry her, and yet he was in love with her.

Supposing he went to her and said (he slackened his pace and began to speak aloud, as if he were speaking to Rachel):

"I worship you, but I loathe marriage, I hate its smugness, its safety, its compromise, and the thought of you interfering in my work, hindering me; what would you answer?"

He stopped, leant against the trunk of a tree, and gazed without seeing them at some stones scattered on the bank of the dry river-bed. He saw Rachel's face distinctly, the grey eyes, the hair, the mouth; the face that could look so many things—plain, vacant, almost insignificant, or wild, passionate, almost beautiful, yet in his eyes was always the same because of the extraordinary freedom with which she looked at him, and spoke as she felt. What would she answer? What did she feel? Did she love him, or did she feel nothing at all for him or for any other man, being, as she had said the other afternoon, free, like the wind or the sea?

"Oh, you're free!" he exclaimed, in exultation at the thought of her, "and I'd keep you free. We'd be free together. We'd share everything together. No happiness would be like ours. No lives would compare with ours." He opened his arms wide as if to hold her and the world in one embrace.

No longer able to consider marriage, or to weigh coolly what her nature was, or how it would be if they lived together, he dropped to the ground and sat absorbed in the thought of her, and soon tormented by the desire to be in her presence again.

Chapter XIX

But Hewet need not have increased his torments by imagining that Hirst was still talking to Rachel. The party very soon broke up, the Flushings going in one direction, Hirst in another, and Rachel remaining in the hall, pulling the illustrated papers about, turning from one to another, her movements expressing the unformed restless desire in her mind. She did not know whether to go or to stay, though Mrs. Flushing had commanded her to appear at tea. The hall was empty, save for Miss Willett who was playing scales with her fingers upon a sheet of sacred music, and the Carters, an opulent couple who disliked the girl, because her shoe laces were untied, and she did not look sufficiently cheery, which by some indirect process of thought led them to think that she would not like them. Rachel certainly would not have liked them, if she had seen them, for the excellent reason that Mr. Carter waxed his moustache, and Mrs. Carter wore bracelets, and they were evidently the kind of people who would not like her; but she was too much absorbed by her own restlessness to think or to look.

She was turning over the slippery pages of an American magazine, when the hall door swung, a wedge of light fell upon the floor, and a small white figure upon whom the light seemed focussed, made straight across the room to her.

"What! You here?" Evelyn exclaimed. "Just caught a glimpse of you at lunch; but you wouldn't condescend to look at *me.*"

It was part of Evelyn's character that in spite of many snubs which she received or imagined, she never gave up the pursuit of people she wanted to know, and in the long run generally succeeded in knowing them and even in making them like her.

She looked round her. "I hate this place. I hate these people," she said. "I wish you'd come up to my room with me. I do want to talk to you."

As Rachel had no wish to go or to stay, Evelyn took her by the wrist and drew her out of the hall and up the stairs. As they went upstairs two steps at a time, Evelyn, who still kept hold of Rachel's hand, ejaculated broken sentences about not caring a hang what people said. "Why should one, if one knows one's right? And let 'em all go to blazes! Them's my opinions!"

She was in a state of great excitement, and the muscles of her arms were twitching nervously. It was evident that she was only waiting for the door to shut to tell Rachel all about it. Indeed, directly they were inside her room, she sat on the end of the bed and said, "I suppose you think I'm mad?"

Rachel was not in the mood to think clearly about any one's state of mind. She was however in the mood to say straight out whatever occurred to her without fear of the consequences.

"Somebody's proposed to you," she remarked.

"How on earth did you guess that?" Evelyn exclaimed, some pleasure mingling with her surprise. "Do I look as if I'd just had a proposal?"

"You look as if you had them every day," Rachel replied.

"But I don't suppose I've had more than you've had," Evelyn laughed rather insincerely.

"I've never had one."

"But you will—lots—it's the easiest thing in the world—But that's not what's happened this afternoon exactly. It's—Oh, it's a muddle, a detestable, horrible, disgusting muddle!"

She went to the wash-stand and began sponging her cheeks with cold water; for they were burning hot. Still sponging them and trembling slightly she turned and explained in the high pitched voice of nervous excitement: "Alfred Perrott says I've promised to marry him, and I say I never did. Sinclair says he'll shoot himself if I don't marry him, and I say, 'Well, shoot yourself!' But of course he doesn't—they never do. And Sinclair got hold of me this afternoon and began bothering me to give an answer, and accusing me of flirting with Alfred Perrott, and told me I'd no heart, and was merely a Siren, oh, and quantities of pleasant things like that. So at last I said to him, 'Well, Sinclair, you've said enough now. You can just let me go.' And then he caught me and kissed me—the disgusting brute—I can still feel his nasty hairy face just there—as if he'd any right to, after what he'd said!"

She sponged a spot on her left cheek energetically.

"I've never met a man that was fit to compare with a woman!" she cried; "they've no dignity, they've no courage, they've nothing but their beastly passions and their brute strength! Would any woman have behaved like that—if a man had said he didn't want her? We've too much self-respect; we're infinitely finer than they are."

She walked about the room, dabbing her wet cheeks with a towel. Tears were now running down together with the drops of cold water.

"It makes me angry," she explained, drying her eyes.

Rachel sat watching her. She did not think of Evelyn's position; she only thought that the world was full of people in torment.

"There's only one man here I really like," Evelyn continued; "Terence Hewet. One feels as if one could trust him."

At these words Rachel suffered an indescribable chill; her heart seemed to be pressed together by cold hands.

"Why?" she asked. "Why can you trust him?"

"I don't know," said Evelyn. "Don't you have feelings about people? Feelings you're absolutely certain are right? I had a long talk with Terence the other night. I felt we really were friends after that. There's something of a woman in him—" She paused as though she were thinking of very intimate things that Terence had told her, or so at least Rachel interpreted her gaze.

She tried to force herself to say, "Has he proposed to you?" but the question was too tremendous, and in another moment Evelyn was saying that the finest men were like women, and women were nobler than men—for example, one couldn't imagine a woman like Lillah Harrison thinking a mean thing or having anything base about her.

"How I'd like you to know her!" she exclaimed.

She was becoming much calmer, and her cheeks were now quite dry. Her eyes had regained their usual expression of keen vitality, and she seemed to have forgotten Alfred and Sinclair and her emotion.

"Lillah runs a home for inebriate women in the Deptford Road," she continued. "She started it, managed it, did everything off her own bat, and it's now the biggest of its kind in England. You can't think what those women are like—and their homes. But she goes among them at all hours of the day and night. I've often been with her.... That's what's the matter with us.... We don't *do* things. What do you *do?*" she demanded, looking at Rachel with a slightly ironical smile. Rachel had scarcely listened to any of this, and her expression was vacant and unhappy. She had conceived an equal dislike for Lillah Harrison and her work in the Deptford Road, and for Evelyn M. and her profusion of love affairs.

"I play," she said with an affectation of stolid composure.

"That's about it!" Evelyn laughed. "We none of us do anything but play. And that's why women like Lillah Harrison, who's worth twenty of you and me, have to work themselves to the bone. But I'm tired of playing," she went on, lying flat on the bed, and raising her arms above her head. Thus stretched out, she looked more diminutive than ever.

"I'm going to do something. I've got a splendid idea. Look here, you must join. I'm sure you've got any amount of stuff in you, though you look—well, as if you'd lived all your life in a garden." She sat up, and began to explain with animation. "I belong to a club in London. It meets every Saturday, so it's called the Saturday Club. We're supposed to talk about art, but I'm sick of talking about art— what's the good of it? With all kinds of real things going on round one? It isn't as if they'd got anything to say about art, either. So what I'm going to tell 'em is that we've talked enough about art, and we'd better talk about life for a change. Questions that really matter to people's lives, the White Slave Traffic, Woman Suffrage, the Insurance Bill, and so on. And when we've made up our mind what we want to do we could form ourselves into a society for doing it.... I'm certain that if people like ourselves were to take things in hand instead of leaving it to policemen and magistrates, we could put a stop to—prostitution"—she lowered her voice at the ugly word— "in six months. My idea is that men and women ought to join in these matters. We ought to go into Piccadilly and stop one of these poor wretches and say: 'Now, look here, I'm no better than you are, and I don't pretend to be any better, but you're doing what you know to be beastly, and I won't have you doing beastly things, be- cause we're all the same under our skins, and if you do a beastly thing it does matter to me.' That's what Mr. Bax was saying this morning, and it's true, though you clever people—you're clever too, aren't you?—don't believe it."

When Evelyn began talking—it was a fact she often regretted— her thoughts came so quickly that she never had any time to listen to other people's thoughts. She continued without more pause than was needed for taking breath.

"I don't see why the Saturday Club people shouldn't do a really great work in that way," she went on. "Of course it would want or- ganisation, some one to give their life to it, but I'm ready to do that. My notion's to think of the human beings first and let the abstract ideas take care of themselves. What's wrong with Lillah—if there is anything wrong—is that she thinks of Temperance first and the women afterwards. Now there's one thing I'll say to my credit," she continued; "I'm not intellectual or artistic or anything of that sort, but I'm jolly human." She slipped off the bed and sat on the floor, looking up at Rachel. She searched up into her face as if she were trying to read what kind of character was concealed behind the face. She put her hand on Rachel's knee.

"It *is* being human that counts, isn't it?" she continued. "Being real, whatever Mr. Hirst may say. Are you real?"

Rachel felt much as Terence had felt that Evelyn was too close to her, and that there was something exciting in this closeness, although it was also disagreeable. She was spared the need of finding an answer to the question, for Evelyn proceeded, "Do you *believe* in anything?"

In order to put an end to the scrutiny of these bright blue eyes, and to relieve her own physical restlessness, Rachel pushed back her chair and exclaimed, "In everything!" and began to finger different objects, the books on the table, the photographs, the fleshly leaved plant with the stiff bristles, which stood in a large earthenware pot in the window.

"I believe in the bed, in the photographs, in the pot, in the balcony, in the sun, in Mrs. Flushing," she remarked, still speaking recklessly, with something at the back of her mind forcing her to say the things that one usually does not say, "But I don't believe in God, I don't believe in Mr. Bax, I don't believe in the hospital nurse. I don't believe—" She took up a photograph and, looking at it, did not finish her sentence.

"That's my mother," said Evelyn, who remained sitting on the floor binding her knees together with her arms, and watching Rachel curiously.

Rachel considered the portrait. "Well, I don't much believe in her," she remarked after a time in a low tone of voice.

Mrs. Murgatroyd looked indeed as if the life had been crushed out of her; she knelt on a chair, gazing piteously from behind the body of a Pomeranian dog which she clasped to her cheek, as if for protection.

"And that's my dad," said Evelyn, for there were two photographs in one frame. The second photograph represented a handsome soldier with high regular features and a heavy black moustache; his hand rested on the hilt of his sword; there was a decided likeness between him and Evelyn.

"And it's because of them," said Evelyn, "that I'm going to help the other women. You've heard about me, I suppose? They weren't married, you see; I'm not anybody in particular. I'm not a bit ashamed of it. They loved each other anyhow, and that's more than most people can say of their parents."

Rachel sat down on the bed, with the two pictures in her hands, and compared them—the man and the woman who had, so Evelyn said, loved each other. That fact interested her more than the campaign on behalf of unfortunate women which Evelyn was once more beginning to describe. She looked again from one to the other.

"What d'you think it's like," she asked, as Evelyn paused for a minute, "being in love?"

"Have you never been in love?" Evelyn asked. "Oh no—one's only got to look at you to see that," she added. She considered. "I really was in love once," she said. She fell into reflection, her eyes losing their bright vitality and approaching something like an expression of tenderness. "It was heavenly!—while it lasted. The worst of it is it don't last, not with me. That's the bother."

She went on to consider the difficulty with Alfred and Sinclair about which she had pretended to ask Rachel's advice. But she did not want advice; she wanted intimacy. When she looked at Rachel, who was still looking at the photographs on the bed, she could not help seeing that Rachel was not thinking about her. What was she thinking about, then? Evelyn was tormented by the little spark of life in her which was always trying to work through to other people, and was always being rebuffed. Falling silent she looked at her visitor, her shoes, her stockings, the combs in her hair, all the details of her dress in short, as though by seizing every detail she might get closer to the life within.

Rachel at last put down the photographs, walked to the window and remarked, "It's odd. People talk as much about love as they do about religion."

"I wish you'd sit down and talk," said Evelyn impatiently.

Instead Rachel opened the window, which was made in two long panes, and looked down into the garden below.

"That's where we got lost the first night," she said. "It must have been in those bushes."

"They kill hens down there," said Evelyn. "They cut their heads off with a knife—disgusting! But tell me—what———"

"I'd like to explore the hotel," Rachel interrupted. She drew her head in and looked at Evelyn, who still sat on the floor.

"It's just like other hotels," said Evelyn.

That might be, although every room and passage and chair in the place had a character of its own in Rachel's eyes; but she could not bring herself to stay in one place any longer. She moved slowly towards the door.

"What is it you want?" said Evelyn. "You make me feel as if you were always thinking of something you don't say.... Do say it!"

But Rachel made no response to this invitation either. She stopped with her fingers on the handle of the door, as if she remembered that some sort of pronouncement was due from her.

"I suppose you'll marry one of them," she said, and then turned the handle and shut the door behind her. She walked slowly down the passage, running her hand along the wall beside her. She did not think which way she was going, and therefore walked down a passage which only led to a window and a balcony. She looked down at the kitchen premises, the wrong side of hotel life, which was cut off from the right side by a maze of small bushes. The ground was bare, old tins were scattered about, and the bushes wore towels and aprons upon their heads to dry. Every now and then a waiter came out in a white apron and threw rubbish on to a heap. Two large women in cotton dresses were sitting on a bench with blood-smeared tin trays in front of them and yellow bodies across their knees. They were plucking the birds, and talking as they plucked. Suddenly a chicken came floundering, half flying, half running into the space, pursued by a third woman whose age could hardly be under eighty. Although wizened and unsteady on her legs she kept up the chase, egged on by the laughter of the others; her face was expressive of furious rage, and as she ran she swore in Spanish. Frightened by hand-clapping here, a napkin there, the bird ran this way and that in sharp angles, and finally fluttered straight at the old woman, who opened her scanty grey skirts to enclose it, dropped upon it in a bundle, and then, holding it out, cut its head off with an expression of vindictive energy and triumph combined. The blood and the ugly wriggling fascinated Rachel, so that although she knew that some one had come up behind and was standing beside her, she did not turn round until the old woman had settled down on the bench beside the others. Then she looked up sharply, because of the ugliness of what she had seen. It was Miss Allan who stood beside her.

"Not a pretty sight," said Miss Allan, "although I daresay it's really more humane than our method.... I don't believe you've ever been in my room," she added, and turned away as if she meant Rachel to follow her. Rachel followed, for it seemed possible that each new person might remove the mystery which burdened her.

The bedrooms at the hotel were all on the same pattern, save that some were larger and some smaller; each had a floor of dark red tile; each had a high bed, draped in mosquito curtains; each had a writing-table and a dressing-table, and a couple of arm-chairs. But directly a box was unpacked the rooms became very different, so that Miss Allan's room was very unlike Evelyn's room. There were no variously coloured hatpins on her dressing-table; no scent-bottles; no narrow curved pairs of scissors; no great variety of shoes and boots; no silk petticoats lying on the chairs. The room was extremely neat. There seemed to be two pairs of everything. The writing-table, however, was piled with manuscript, and a table was drawn out to stand by the arm-chair on which were two separate heaps of dark library books, in which there were many slips of paper sticking out at different degrees of thickness. Miss Allan had asked Rachel to come in out of kindness, thinking that she was waiting about with nothing to do. Moreover, she liked young women, for she had taught many of them, and having received so much hospitality from the Ambroses she was glad to be able to repay a minute part of it. She looked about accordingly for something to show her. The room did not provide much entertainment. She touched her manuscript. "Age of Chaucer; Age of Elizabeth; Age of Dryden," she reflected; "I'm glad there aren't many more ages. I'm still in the middle of the eighteenth century. Won't you sit down, Miss Vinrace? The chair, though small, is firm.... Euphues.[1] The germ of the English novel," she continued, glancing at another page. "Is that the kind of thing that interests you?"

She looked at Rachel with great kindness and simplicity, as though she would do her utmost to provide anything she wished to have. This expression had a remarkable charm in a face otherwise much lined with care and thought.

"Oh no, it's music with you, isn't it?" she continued, recollecting, "and I generally find that they don't go together. Sometimes of course we have prodigies—" She was looking about her for something and now saw a jar on the mantelpiece which she reached down and gave to Rachel. "If you put your finger into this jar you may be able to extract a piece of preserved ginger. Are you a prodigy?"

But the ginger was deep and could not be reached.

"Don't bother," she said, as Miss Allan looked about for some other implement. "I daresay I shouldn't like preserved ginger."

"You've never tried?" enquired Miss Allan. "Then I consider that it is your duty to try now. Why, you may add a new pleasure to life, and as you are still young—" She wondered whether a button-hook would do. "I make it a rule to try everything," she said. "Don't you think it would be very annoying if you tasted ginger for the first time on your deathbed, and found you never liked anything so much? I should be so exceedingly annoyed that I think I should get well on that account alone."

She was now successful, and a lump of ginger emerged on the end of the button-hook. While she went to wipe the button-hook, Rachel bit the ginger and at once cried, "I must spit it out!"

"Are you sure you have really tasted it?" Miss Allan demanded.

For answer Rachel threw it out of the window.

"An experience anyhow," said Miss Allan calmly. "Let me see— I have nothing else to offer you, unless you would like to taste this." A small cupboard hung above her bed, and she took out of it a slim elegant jar filled with a bright green fluid.

"Crême de Menthe," she said. "Liqueur, you know. It looks as if

I drank, doesn't it? As a matter of fact it goes to prove what an exceptionally abstemious person I am. I've had that jar for six-and-twenty years," she added, looking at it with pride, as she tipped it over, and from the height of the liquid it could be seen that the bottle was still untouched.

"Twenty-six years?" Rachel exclaimed.

Miss Allan was gratified, for she had meant Rachel to be surprised.

"When I went to Dresden six-and-twenty years ago," she said, "a certain friend of mine announced her intention of making me a present. She thought that in the event of shipwreck or accident a stimulant might be useful. However, as I had no occasion for it, I gave it back on my return. On the eve of any foreign journey the same bottle always makes its appearance, with the same note; on my return in safety it is always handed back. I consider it a kind of charm against accidents. Though I was once detained twenty-four hours by an accident to the train in front of me, I have never met with any accident myself. Yes," she continued, now addressing the bottle, "we have seen many climes and cupboards together, have we not? I intend one of these days to have a silver label made with an inscription. It is a gentleman, as you may observe, and his name is Oliver.... I do not think I could forgive you, Miss Vinrace, if you broke my Oliver," she said, firmly taking the bottle out of Rachel's hands and replacing it in the cupboard.

Rachel was swinging the bottle by the neck. She was interested by Miss Allan to the point of forgetting the bottle.

"Well," she exclaimed, "I do think that odd; to have had a friend for twenty-six years, and a bottle, and—to have made all those journeys."

"Not at all; I call it the reverse of odd," Miss Allan replied. "I always consider myself the most ordinary person I know. It's rather distinguished to be as ordinary as I am. I forget—are you a prodigy, or did you say you were not a prodigy?"

She smiled at Rachel very kindly. She seemed to have known and experienced so much, as she moved cumbrously about the room, that surely there must be balm for all anguish in her words, could one induce her to have recourse to them. But Miss Allan, who was now locking the cupboard door, showed no signs of breaking the reticence which had snowed her under for years. An uncomfortable sensation kept Rachel silent; on the one hand, she wished to whirl high and strike a spark out of the cool pink flesh; on the other she perceived there was nothing to be done but to drift past each other in silence.

"I'm not a prodigy. I find it very difficult to say what I mean—" she observed at length.

"It's a matter of temperament, I believe," Miss Allan helped her. "There are some people who have no difficulty; for myself I find there are a great many things I simply cannot say. But then I consider myself very slow. One of my colleagues, now, knows whether she likes you or not—let me see, how does she do it?—by the way you say good-morning at breakfast. It is sometimes a matter of years before I can make up my mind. But most young people seem to find it easy?"

"Oh no," said Rachel. "It's hard!"

Miss Allan looked at Rachel quietly, saying nothing; she suspected that there were difficulties of some kind. Then she put her hand to the back of her head, and discovered that one of the grey coils of hair had come loose.

"I must ask you to be so kind as to excuse me," she said, rising, "if I do my hair. I have never yet found a satisfactory type of hairpin. I must change my dress, too, for the matter of that; and I should be particularly glad of your assistance, because there is a tiresome set of hooks which I *can* fasten for myself, but it takes from ten to fifteen minutes; whereas with your help—"

She slipped off her coat and skirt and blouse, and stood doing her hair before the glass, a massive homely figure, her petticoat being so short that she stood on a pair of thick slate-grey legs.

"People say youth is pleasant; I myself find middle age far pleasanter," she remarked, removing hairpins and combs, and taking up her brush. When it fell loose her hair only came down to her neck.

"When one was young," she continued, "things could seem so very serious if one was made that way.... And now my dress."

In a wonderfully short space of time her hair had been reformed in its usual loops. The upper half of her body now became dark green with black stripes on it; the skirt, however, needed hooking at various angles, and Rachel had to kneel on the floor, fitting the eyes to the hooks.

"Our Miss Johnson used to find life very unsatisfactory, I remember," Miss Allan continued. She turned her back to the light. "And then she took to breeding guinea-pigs for their spots, and became absorbed in that. I have just heard that the yellow guinea-pig has had a black baby. We had a bet of sixpence on about it. She will be very triumphant."

The skirt was fastened. She looked at herself in the glass with the curious stiffening of her face generally caused by looking in the glass.

"Am I in a fit state to encounter my fellow-beings?" she asked. "I forget which way it is—but they find black animals very rarely have coloured babies—it may be the other way round. I have had it so often explained to me that it is very stupid of me to have forgotten again."

She moved about the room acquiring small objects with quiet force, and fixing them about her—a locket, a watch and chain, a heavy gold bracelet, and the parti-coloured button of a suffrage society. Finally, completely equipped for Sunday tea, she stood before Rachel, and smiled at her kindly. She was not an impulsive woman, and her life had schooled her to restrain her tongue. At the same time, she was possessed of an amount of good-will towards others, and in particular towards the young, which often made her regret that speech was so difficult.

"Shall we descend?" she said.

She put one hand upon Rachel's shoulder, and stooping, picked up a pair of walking-shoes with the other, and placed them neatly side by side outside her door. As they walked down the passage they passed many pairs of boots and shoes, some black and some brown, all side by side, and all different, even to the way in which they lay together.

"I always think that people are so like their boots," said Miss

Allan. "That is Mrs. Paley's—" but as she spoke the door opened, and Mrs. Paley rolled out in her chair, equipped also for tea.

She greeted Miss Allan and Rachel.

"I was just saying that people are so like their boots," said Miss Allan. Mrs. Paley did not hear. She repeated it more loudly still. Mrs. Paley did not hear. She repeated it a third time. Mrs. Paley heard, but she did not understand. She was apparently about to repeat it for the fourth time, when Rachel suddenly said something inarticulate, and disappeared down the corridor. This misunderstanding, which involved a complete block in the passage, seemed to her unbearable. She walked quickly and blindly in the opposite direction, and found herself at the end of a *cul de sac*. There was a window, and a table and a chair in the window, and upon the table stood a rusty inkstand, an ash-tray, an old copy of a French newspaper, and a pen with a broken nib. Rachel sat down, as if to study the French newspaper, but a tear fell on the blurred French print, raising a soft blot. She lifted her head sharply, exclaiming aloud, "It's intolerable!" Looking out of the window with eyes that would have seen nothing even had they not been dazed by tears, she indulged herself at last in violent abuse of the entire day. It had been miserable from start to finish; first, the service in the chapel; then luncheon; then Evelyn; then Miss Allan; then old Mrs. Paley blocking up the passage. All day long she had been tantalized and put off. She had now reached one of those eminences, the result of some crisis, from which the world is finally displayed in its true proportions. She disliked the look of it immensely—churches, politicians, misfits, and huge impostures—men like Mr. Dalloway, men like Mr. Bax, Evelyn and her chatter, Mrs. Paley blocking up the passage. Meanwhile the steady beat of her own pulse represented the hot current of feeling that ran down beneath; beating, struggling, fretting. For the time, her own body was the source of all the life in the world, which tried to burst forth here—there—and was repressed now by Mr. Bax, now by Evelyn, now by the imposition of ponderous stupidity—the weight of the entire world. Thus tormented, she would twist her hands together, for all things were wrong, all people stupid. Vaguely seeing that there were people down in the garden beneath she represented them as aimless masses of matter, floating hither and thither, without aim except to impede her. What were they doing, those other people in the world?

"Nobody knows," she said. The force of her rage was beginning to spend itself, and the vision of the world which had been so vivid became dim.

"It's a dream," she murmured. She considered the rusty ink-stand, the pen, the ash-tray, and the old French newspaper. These small and worthless objects seemed to her to represent human lives.

"We're asleep and dreaming," she repeated. But the possibility which now suggested itself that one of the shapes might be the shape of Terence roused her from her melancholy lethargy. She became as restless as she had been before she sat down. She was no longer able to see the world as a town laid out beneath her. It was covered instead by a haze of feverish red mist. She had returned to the state in which she had been all day. Thinking was no escape. Physical movement was the only refuge, in and out of rooms, in and out of peoples' minds, seeking she knew not what. Therefore she rose, pushed back the table, and went downstairs. She went out of the hall door, and, turning the corner of the hotel, found herself among the people whom she had seen from the window. But owing to the broad sunshine after shaded passages, and to the substance of living people after dreams, the group appeared with startling intensity, as though the dusty surface had been peeled off everything, leaving only the reality and the instant. It had the look of a vision printed on the dark at night. White and grey and purple figures were scattered on the green; round wicker tables; in the middle the flame of the tea-urn made the air waver like a faulty sheet of glass; a massive green tree stood over them as if it were a moving force held at rest. As she approached, she could hear Evelyn's voice repeating monotonously, "Here then—here—good doggie, come here;" for a moment nothing seemed to happen; it all stood still, and then she realised that one of the figures was Helen Ambrose; and the dust again began to settle.

The group indeed had come together in a miscellaneous way;

one tea-table joining to another tea-table, and deck-chairs serving to connect two groups. But even at a distance it could be seen that Mrs. Flushing, upright and imperious, dominated the party. She was talking vehemently to Helen across the table.

"Ten days under canvas," she was saying. "No comforts. If you want comforts, don't come. But I may tell you, if you don't come you'll regret it all your life. You say yes?"

At this moment Mrs. Flushing caught sight of Rachel.

"Ah, there's your niece. She's promised. You're coming, aren't you?" Having adopted the plan, she pursued it with the energy of a child.

Rachel took her part with eagerness.

"Of course I'm coming. So are you, Helen. And Mr. Pepper too." As she sat down she realised that she was surrounded by men and women she knew, but that Terence was not among them. From various angles people began saying what they thought of the proposed expedition. According to some it would be hot, but the nights would be cold; according to others, the difficulties would lie rather in getting a boat, and in speaking the language. Mrs. Flushing disposed of all objections, whether due to man or due to nature, by announcing that her husband would settle all that.

Meanwhile Mr. Flushing quietly explained to Helen that the expedition was really a simple matter; it took five days at the outside; and the place—a native village—was certainly well worth seeing before she returned to England. Helen murmured ambiguously, and did not commit herself to one answer rather than to another.

The tea-party, however, included too many different kinds of people for general conversation to flourish; and from Rachel's point of view possessed the great advantage that it was quite unnecessary for her to talk. Over there Susan and Arthur were explaining to Mrs. Paley that an expedition had been proposed; and Mrs. Paley having grasped the fact, gave the advice of an old traveller that they should take nice canned vegetables, fur cloaks, and insect powder. She leant over to Mrs. Flushing and whispered something which from the twinkle in her eyes probably had reference to bugs. Then Helen was reciting "Toll for the Brave" to St. John Hirst, in order apparently to win a sixpence which lay upon the table; while Mr. Hughling Elliot imposed silence upon his section of the audience by his fascinating anecdote of Lord Curzon[2] and the undergraduate's bicycle. Mrs. Thornbury was trying to remember the name of a man who might have been another Garibaldi, and had written a book which they ought to read; and Mr. Thornbury recollected that he had a pair of binoculars at anybody's service. Miss Allan meanwhile murmured with the curious intimacy which a spinster often achieves with dogs, to the fox-terrier which Evelyn had at last induced to come over to them. Little particles of dust or blossom fell on the plates now and then when the branches sighed above. Rachel seemed to see and hear a little of everything, much as a river feels the twigs that fall into it and sees the sky above, but her eyes were too vague for Evelyn's liking. She came across, and sat on the ground at Rachel's feet.

"Well," she asked suddenly, "what are you thinking about?"

"Miss Warrington," Rachel replied rashly, because she had to say something. She did indeed see Susan murmuring to Mrs. Elliot, while Arthur stared at her with complete confidence in his own love. Both Rachel and Evelyn then began to listen to what Susan was saying.

"There's the ordering and the dogs and the garden, and the children coming to be taught," her voice proceeded rhythmically as if checking the list, "and my tennis, and the village, and letters to write for father, and a thousand little things that don't sound much; but I never have a moment to myself, and when I go to bed, I'm so sleepy I'm off before my head touches the pillow. Besides I like to be a great deal with my Aunts—I'm a great bore, aren't I, Aunt Emma?" (she smiled at old Mrs. Paley, who with head slightly drooped was regarding the cake with speculative affection), "and father has to be very careful about chills in winter which means a great deal of running about, because he won't look after himself, any more than you will, Arthur! So it all mounts up!"

Her voice mounted too, in a mild ecstasy of satisfaction with her life and her own nature. Rachel suddenly took a violent dislike to Susan, ignoring all that was kindly, modest, and even pathetic about her. She appeared insincere and cruel; she saw her grown stout and prolific, the kind blue eyes now shallow and watery, the bloom of the cheeks congealed to a network of dry red canals.

Helen turned to her. "Did you go to church?" she asked. She had won her sixpence and seemed making ready to go.

"Yes," said Rachel. "For the last time," she added.

In preparing to put on her gloves, Helen dropped one.

"You're not going?" Evelyn asked, taking hold of one glove as if to keep them.

"It's high time we went," said Helen. "Don't you see how silent every one's getting————?"

A silence had fallen upon them all, caused partly by one of the accidents of talk, and partly because they saw some one approaching. Helen could not see who it was, but keeping her eyes fixed upon Rachel observed something which made her say to herself, "So it's Hewet." She drew on her gloves with a curious sense of the significance of the moment. Then she rose, for Mrs. Flushing had seen Hewet too, and was demanding information about rivers and boats which showed that the whole conversation would now come over again.

Rachel followed her, and they walked in silence down the avenue. In spite of what Helen had seen and understood, the feeling that was uppermost in her mind was now curiously perverse; if she went on this expedition, she would not be able to have a bath; the effort appeared to her to be great and disagreeable.

"It's so unpleasant, being cooped up with people one hardly knows," she remarked. "People who mind being seen naked."

"You don't mean to go?" Rachel asked.

The intensity with which this was spoken irritated Mrs. Ambrose.

"I don't mean to go, and I don't mean not to go," she replied. She became more and more casual and indifferent.

"After all, I daresay we've seen all there is to be seen; and there's the bother of getting there, and whatever they may say it's bound to be vilely uncomfortable."

For some time Rachel made no reply; but every sentence Helen spoke increased her bitterness. At last she broke out—

"Thank God, Helen, I'm not like you! I sometimes think you don't think or feel or care or do anything but exist! You're like Mr. Hirst. You see that things are bad, and you pride yourself on saying so. It's what you call being honest; as a matter of fact it's being lazy, being dull, being nothing. You don't help; you put an end to things."

Helen smiled as if she rather enjoyed the attack.

"Well?" she enquired.

"It seems to me bad—that's all," Rachel replied.

"Quite likely," said Helen.

At any other time Rachel would probably have been silenced by her Aunt's candour; but this afternoon she was not in the mood to be silenced by any one. A quarrel would be welcome.

"You're only half alive," she continued.

"Is that because I didn't accept Mr. Flushing's invitation?" Helen asked, "or do you always think that?"

At the moment it appeared to Rachel that she had always seen the same faults in Helen, from the very first night on board the *Euphrosyne,* in spite of her beauty, in spite of her magnanimity and their love.

"Oh, it's only what's the matter with every one!" she exclaimed. "No one feels—no one does anything but hurt. I tell you, Helen, the world's bad. It's an agony, living, wanting———"

Here she tore a handful of leaves from a bush and crushed them to control herself.

"The lives of these people," she tried to explain, "the aimlessness, the way they live. One goes from one to another, and it's all the same. One never gets what one wants out of any of them."

Her emotional state and her confusion would have made her an easy prey if Helen had wished to argue or had wished to draw confidences. But instead of talking she fell into a profound silence as they walked on. Aimless, trivial, meaningless, oh no—what she had seen at tea made it impossible for her to believe that. The little jokes, the chatter, the inanities of the afternoon had shrivelled up

before her eyes. Underneath the likings and spites, the comings together and partings, great things were happening—terrible things,
because they were so great. Her sense of safety was shaken, as if beneath twigs and dead leaves she had seen the movement of a snake.
It seemed to her that a moment's respite was allowed, a moment's
make-believe, and then again the profound and reasonless law asserted itself, moulding them all to its liking, making and destroying.

She looked at Rachel walking beside her, still crushing the leaves
in her fingers and absorbed in her own thoughts. She was in love,
and she pitied her profoundly. But she roused herself from these
thoughts and apologised. "I'm very sorry," she said, "but if I'm dull,
it's my nature, and it can't be helped." If it was a natural defect,
however, she found an easy remedy, for she went on to say that she
thought Mr. Flushing's scheme a very good one, only needing a little consideration, which it appeared she had given it by the time
they reached home. By that time they had settled that if anything
more was said, they would accept the invitation.

Chapter XX

When considered in detail by Mr. Flushing and Mrs. Ambrose the expedition proved neither dangerous nor difficult. They found also that it was not even unusual. Every year at this season English people made parties which steamed a short way up the river, landed, and looked at the native village, bought a certain number of things from the natives, and returned again without damage done to mind or body. When it was discovered that six people really wished the same thing the arrangements were soon carried out.

Since the time of Elizabeth very few people had seen the river, and nothing had been done to change its appearance from what it was to the eyes of the Elizabethan voyagers. The time of Elizabeth was only distant from the present time by a moment of space compared with the ages which had passed since the water had run between those banks, and the green thickets swarmed there, and the small trees grown to huge wrinkled trees in solitude. Changing only with the change of the sun and the clouds, the waving green mass had stood there for century after century, and the water had run between its banks ceaselessly, sometimes washing away earth and sometimes the branches of trees, while in other parts of the world one town had risen upon the ruins of another town, and the men in the towns had become more and more articulate and unlike each other. A few miles of this river were visible from the top of the mountain where some weeks before the party from the hotel had picnicked. Susan and Arthur had seen it as they kissed each other, and Terence and Rachel as they sat talking about Richmond, and Evelyn and Perrott as they strolled about, imagining that they were great captains sent to colonise the world. They had seen the broad blue mark across the sand where it flowed into the sea, and the green cloud of trees mass themselves about it farther up, and finally hide its waters altogether from sight. At intervals for the first twenty miles or so houses were scattered on the bank; by degrees the houses became huts, and, later still, there was neither hut nor house, but trees and grass, which were seen only by hunters, explorers, or merchants, marching or sailing, but making no settlement.

By leaving Santa Marina early in the morning, driving twenty miles and riding eight, the party, which was composed finally of six English people, reached the river-side as the night fell. They came cantering through the trees—Mr. and Mrs. Flushing, Helen Ambrose, Rachel, Terence, and St. John. The tired little horses then stopped automatically, and the English dismounted. Mrs. Flushing strode to the river-bank in high spirits. The day had been long and hot, but she had enjoyed the speed and the open air; she had left the hotel which she hated, and she found the company to her liking. The river was swirling past in the darkness; they could just distinguish the smooth moving surface of the water, and the air was full of the sound of it. They stood in an empty space in the midst of great tree-trunks, and out there a little green light moving slightly up and down showed them where the steamer lay in which they were to embark.

When they all stood upon its deck they found that it was a very small boat which throbbed gently beneath them for a few minutes, and then shoved smoothly through the water. They seemed to be driving into the heart of the night, for the trees closed in front of them, and they could hear all round them the rustling of leaves. The great darkness had the usual effect of taking away all desire for communication by making their words sound thin and small; and, after walking round the deck three or four times, they clustered together, yawning deeply, and looking at the same spot of deep gloom on the banks. Murmuring very low in the rhythmical tone of one oppressed by the air, Mrs. Flushing began to wonder where they were to sleep, for they could not sleep downstairs, they could not sleep in a doghole smelling of oil, they could not sleep on deck, they could not sleep— She yawned profoundly. It was as Helen had foreseen; the question of nakedness had risen already, although they were half asleep, and almost invisible to each other. With St. John's help she stretched an awning, and persuaded Mrs. Flushing that she could take off her clothes behind this, and that no one would notice if by chance some part of her which had been concealed for forty-five years was laid bare to the human eye. Mattresses were thrown down, rugs provided, and the three women lay near each other in the soft open air.

The gentlemen, having smoked a certain number of cigarettes, dropped the glowing ends into the river, and looked for a time at the ripples wrinkling the black water beneath them, undressed too, and lay down at the other end of the boat. They were very tired, and curtained from each other by the darkness. The light from one lantern fell upon a few ropes, a few planks of the deck, and the rail of the boat, but beyond that there was unbroken darkness, no light reached their faces, or the trees which were massed on the sides of the river.

Soon Wilfred Flushing slept, and Hirst slept. Hewet alone lay awake looking straight up into the sky. The gentle motion and the black shapes that were drawn ceaselessly across his eyes had the effect of making it impossible for him to think. Rachel's presence so near him lulled thought asleep. Being so near him, only a few paces off at the other end of the boat, she made it as impossible for him to think about her as it would have been impossible to see her if she had stood quite close to him, her forehead against his forehead. In some strange way the boat became identified with himself, and just as it would have been useless for him to get up and steer the boat, so was it useless for him to struggle any longer with the irresistible force of his own feelings. He was drawn on and on away from all he knew, slipping over barriers and past landmarks into unknown waters as the boat glided over the smooth surface of the river. In profound peace, enveloped in deeper unconsciousness than had been his for many nights, he lay on deck watching the tree-tops change their position slightly against the sky, and arch themselves, and sink and tower huge, until he passed from seeing them into dreams where he lay beneath the shadow of vast trees, looking up into the sky.

When they woke next morning they had gone a considerable way up the river; on the right was a high yellow bank of sand tufted with trees, on the left a swamp quivering with long reeds and tall bamboos on the top of which, swaying slightly, perched vivid green and yellow birds. The morning was hot and still. After breakfast they drew chairs together and sat in an irregular semi-circle in the bow. An awning above their heads protected them from the heat of the sun, and the breeze which the boat made aired them softly. Mrs. Flushing was already dotting and striping her canvas, her head jerking this way and that with the action of a bird nervously picking up grain; the others had books or pieces of paper or embroidery on their knees, at which they looked fitfully and again looked at the river ahead. At one point Hewet read part of a poem aloud, but the number of moving things entirely vanquished his words. He ceased to read, and no one spoke. They moved on under the shelter of the trees. There was now a covey of red birds feeding on one of the little islets to the left, or again a blue-green parrot flew shrieking from tree to tree. As they moved on the country grew wilder and wilder. The trees and the undergrowth seemed to be strangling each other near the ground in a multitudinous wrestle; while here and there a splendid tree towered high above the swarm, shaking its thin green umbrellas lightly in the upper air. Hewet looked at his book again. The morning was peaceful as the night had been, only it was very strange because it was light, and he could see Rachel and hear her voice and be near to her. He felt as if he were waiting, as if somehow he were stationary among things that passed over him and around him, voices, people's bodies, birds, only Rachel too was waiting with him. He looked at her sometimes as if she must know that they were waiting together, and being drawn on together, without being able to offer any resistance. Again he read from his book:

> Whoever you are holding me now in your hand,
> Without one thing all will be useless.[1]

A bird gave a wild laugh, a monkey chuckled a malicious question, and, as fire fades in the hot sunshine, his words flickered and went out.

By degrees as the river narrowed, and the high sandbanks fell to level ground thickly grown with trees, the sounds of the forest could be heard. It echoed like a hall. There were sudden cries; and then long spaces of silence, such as there are in a cathedral when a boy's voice has ceased and the echo of it still seems to haunt about the remote places of the roof. Once Mr. Flushing rose and spoke to a sailor, and even announced that some time after luncheon the steamer would stop, and they could walk a little way through the forest.

"There are tracks all through the trees there," he explained. "We're no distance from civilisation yet."

He scrutinised his wife's painting. Too polite to praise it openly, he contented himself with cutting off one half of the picture with one hand, and giving a flourish in the air with the other.

"God!" Hirst exclaimed, staring straight ahead. "Don't you think it's amazingly beautiful?"

"Beautiful?" Helen enquired. It seemed a strange little word, and Hirst and herself both so small that she forgot to answer him.

Hewet felt that he must speak.

"That's where the Elizabethans got their style," he mused, staring into the profusion of leaves and blossoms and prodigious fruits.

"Shakespeare? I hate Shakespeare!" Mrs. Flushing exclaimed; and Wilfred returned admiringly, "I believe you're the only person who dares to say that, Alice." But Mrs. Flushing went on painting.

She did not appear to attach much value to her husband's compliment, and painted steadily, sometimes muttering a half-audible word or groan.

The morning was now very hot.

"Look at Hirst!" Mr. Flushing whispered. His sheet of paper had slipped on to the deck, his head lay back, and he drew a long snoring breath.

Terence picked up the sheet of paper and spread it out before Rachel. It was a continuation of the poem on God which he had begun in the chapel, and it was so indecent that Rachel did not understand half of it although she saw that it was indecent. Hewet began to fill in words where Hirst had left spaces, but he soon ceased; his pencil rolled on deck. Gradually they approached nearer and nearer to the bank on the right-hand side, so that the light which covered them became definitely green, falling through a shade of green leaves, and Mrs. Flushing set aside her sketch and stared ahead of her in silence. Hirst woke up; they were then called to luncheon, and while they ate it, the steamer came to a standstill a little way out from the bank. The boat which was towed behind them was brought to the side, and the ladies were helped into it.

For protection against boredom, Helen put a book of memoirs beneath her arm, and Mrs. Flushing her paint-box, and, thus equipped, they allowed themselves to be set on shore on the verge of the forest.

They had not strolled more than a few hundred yards along the track which ran parallel with the river before Helen professed to find it unbearably hot. The river breeze had ceased, and a hot steamy atmosphere, thick with scents, came from the forest.

"I shall sit down here," she announced, pointing to the trunk of a tree which had fallen long ago and was now laced across and across by creepers and thong-like brambles. She seated herself, opened her parasol, and looked at the river which was barred by the stems of trees. She turned her back to the trees which disappeared in black shadow behind her.

"I quite agree," said Mrs. Flushing, and proceeded to undo her paint-box. Her husband strolled about to select an interesting point of view for her. Hirst cleared a space on the ground by Helen's side, and seated himself with great deliberation, as if he did not mean to move until he had talked to her for a long time. Terence and Rachel were left standing by themselves without occupation. Terence saw that the time had come as it was fated to come, but although he realised this he was completely calm and master of himself. He chose to stand for a few moments talking to Helen, and persuading her to leave her seat. Rachel joined him too in advising her to come with them.

"Of all the people I've ever met," he said, "you're the least adventurous. You might be sitting on green chairs in Hyde Park. Are you going to sit there the whole afternoon? Aren't you going to walk?"

"Oh, no," said Helen, "one's only got to use one's eye. There's everything here—everything," she repeated in a drowsy tone of voice. "What will you gain by walking?"

"You'll be hot and disagreeable by tea-time, we shall be cool and sweet," put in Hirst. Into his eyes as he looked up at them had come yellow and green reflections from the sky and the branches, robbing them of their intentness, and he seemed to think what he did not say. It was thus taken for granted by them both that Terence and Rachel proposed to walk into the woods together; with one look at each other they turned away.

"Good-bye!" cried Rachel.

"Good-bye. Beware of snakes," Hirst replied. He settled himself still more comfortably under the shade of the fallen tree and Helen's figure. As they went, Mr. Flushing called after them, "We must start in an hour. Hewet, please remember that. An hour."

Whether made by man, or for some reason preserved by nature, there was a wide pathway striking through the forest at right angles to the river. It resembled a drive in an English forest, save that tropical bushes with their sword-like leaves grew at the side, and the ground was covered with an unmarked springy moss instead of grass, starred with little yellow flowers. As they passed into the depths of the forest the light grew dimmer, and the noises of the ordinary world were replaced by those creaking and sighing sounds which suggest to the traveller in a forest that he is walking at the bottom of the sea. The path narrowed and turned; it was hedged in by dense creepers which knotted tree to tree, and burst here and there into star-shaped crimson blossoms. The sighing and creaking up above were broken every now and then by the jarring cry of some startled animal. The atmosphere was close and the air came at them in languid puffs of scent. The vast green light was broken here and there by a round of pure yellow sunlight which fell through some gap in the immense umbrella of green above, and in these yellow spaces crimson and black butterflies were circling and settling. Terence and Rachel hardly spoke.

Not only did the silence weigh upon them, but they were both unable to frame any thoughts. There was something between them which had to be spoken of. One of them had to begin, but which of them was it to be? Then Hewet picked up a red fruit and threw it as high as he could. When it dropped, he would speak. They heard the flapping of great wings; they heard the fruit go pattering through the leaves and eventually fall with a thud. The silence was again profound.

"Does this frighten you?" Terence asked when the sound of the fruit falling had completely died away.

"No," she answered. "I like it."

She repeated "I like it." She was walking fast, and holding herself more erect than usual. There was another pause.

"You like being with me?" Terence asked.

"Yes, with you," she replied.

He was silent for a moment. Silence seemed to have fallen upon the world.

"That is what I have felt ever since I knew you," he replied. "We are happy together." He did not seem to be speaking, or she to be hearing.

"Very happy," she answered.

They continued to walk for some time in silence. Their steps unconsciously quickened.

"We love each other," Terence said.

"We love each other," she repeated.

The silence was then broken by their voices which joined in tones of strange unfamiliar sound which formed no words. Faster and faster they walked; simultaneously they stopped, clasped each other in their arms, then, releasing themselves, dropped to the earth. They sat side by side. Sounds stood out from the background making a bridge across their silence; they heard the swish of the trees and some beast croaking in a remote world.

"We love each other," Terence repeated, searching into her face. Their faces were both very pale and quiet, and they said nothing. He was afraid to kiss her again. By degrees she drew close to him, and rested against him. In this position they sat for some time. She said "Terence" once; he answered "Rachel."

"Terrible—terrible," she murmured after another pause, but in saying this she was thinking as much of the persistent churning of the water as of her own feeling. On and on it went in the distance, the senseless and cruel churning of the water. She observed that the tears were running down Terence's cheeks.

The next movement was on his part. A very long time seemed to have passed. He took out his watch.

"Flushing said an hour. We've been gone more than half an hour."

"And it takes that to get back," said Rachel. She raised herself very slowly. When she was standing up she stretched her arms and drew a deep breath, half a sigh, half a yawn. She appeared to be very tired. Her cheeks were white. "Which way?" she asked.

"There," said Terence.

They began to walk back down the mossy path again. The sighing and creaking continued far overhead, and the jarring cries of animals. The butterflies were circling still in the patches of yellow sunlight. At first Terence was certain of his way, but as they walked he became doubtful. They had to stop to consider, and then to return and start once more, for although he was certain of the direction of the river he was not certain of striking the point where they had left the others. Rachel followed him, stopping where he stopped, turning where he turned, ignorant of the way, ignorant why he stopped or why he turned.

"I don't want to be late," he said, "because—" He put a flower into her hand and her fingers closed upon it quietly. "We're so late—so late—so horribly late," he repeated as if he were talking in his sleep. "Ah—this is right. We turn here."

They found themselves again in the broad path, like the drive in an English forest, where they had started when they left the others. They walked on in silence as people walking in their sleep, and were oddly conscious now and again of the mass of their bodies. Then Rachel exclaimed suddenly, "Helen!"

In the sunny space at the edge of the forest they saw Helen still sitting on the tree-trunk, her dress showing very white in the sun, with Hirst still propped on his elbow by her side. They stopped instinctively. At the sight of other people they could not go on. They stood hand in hand for a minute or two in silence. They could not bear to face other people.

"But we must go on," Rachel insisted at last, in the curious dull tone of voice in which they had both been speaking, and with a great effort they forced themselves to cover the short distance which lay between them and the pair sitting on the tree-trunk.

As they approached, Helen turned round and looked at them. She looked at them for some time without speaking, and when they were close to her she said quietly:

"Did you meet Mr. Flushing? He has gone to find you. He thought you must be lost, though I told him you weren't lost."

Hirst half turned round and threw his head back so that he looked at the branches crossing themselves in the air above him.

"Well, was it worth the effort?" he enquired dreamily.

Hewet sat down on the grass by his side and began to fan himself.

"Hot," he said.

Rachel had balanced herself near Helen on the end of the tree-trunk.

"Very hot," she said.

"You look exhausted anyhow," said Hirst.

"It's fearfully close in those trees," Helen remarked, picking up her book and shaking it free from the dried blades of grass which had fallen between the leaves. Then they were all silent, looking at the river swirling past in front of them between the trunks of the trees until Mr. Flushing interrupted them. He broke out of the trees a hundred yards to the left, exclaiming sharply:

"Ah, so you found the way after all. But it's late—much later than we arranged, Hewet."

He was slightly annoyed, and in his capacity as leader of the expedition, inclined to be dictatorial. He spoke quickly, using curiously sharp, meaningless words.

"Being late wouldn't matter normally, of course," he said, "but when it's a question of keeping the men up to time—"

He gathered them together and made them come down to the river-bank, where the boat was waiting to row them out to the steamer.

The heat of the day was going down, and over their cups of tea the Flushings tended to become communicative. It seemed to Terence as he listened to them talking, that existence now went on in two different layers. Here were the Flushings talking, talking somewhere high up in the air above him, and he and Rachel had dropped to the bottom of the world together. But with something of a child's directness, Mrs. Flushing had also the instinct which leads a child to suspect what its elders wish to keep hidden. She fixed Terence with her vivid blue eyes and addressed herself to him in particular. What would he do, she wanted to know, if the boat ran upon a rock and sank.

"Would you care for anythin' but savin' yourself? Should I? No, no," she laughed, "not one scrap—don't tell me. There's only two creatures the ordinary woman cares about," she continued, "her child and her dog; and I don't believe it's even two with men. One reads a lot about love—that's why poetry's so dull. But what happens in real life, eh? It ain't love!" she cried.

Terence murmured something unintelligible. Mr. Flushing, however, had recovered his urbanity. He was smoking a cigarette, and he now answered his wife.

"You must always remember, Alice," he said, "that your upbringing was very unnatural—unusual, I should say. They had no mother," he explained, dropping something of the formality of his tone; "and a father—he was a very delightful man, I've no doubt, but he cared only for racehorses and Greek statues. Tell them about the bath, Alice."

"In the stable-yard," said Mrs. Flushing. "Covered with ice in winter. We had to get in; if we didn't, we were whipped. The strong ones lived—the others died. What you call the survival of the fittest—a most excellent plan, I daresay, if you've thirteen children!"

"And all this going on in the heart of England, in the nineteenth century!" Mr. Flushing exclaimed, turning to Helen.

"I'd treat my children just the same if I had any," said Mrs. Flushing.

Every word sounded quite distinctly in Terence's ears; but what were they saying, and who were they talking to, and who were they, these fantastic people, detached somewhere high up in the air? Now that they had drunk their tea, they rose and leant over the bow of the boat. The sun was going down, and the water was dark and crimson. The river had widened again, and they were passing a little island set like a dark wedge in the middle of the stream. Two great white birds with red lights on them stood there on stilt-like legs, and the beach of the island was unmarked, save by the skeleton print of birds' feet. The branches of the trees on the bank looked more twisted and angular than ever, and the green of the leaves was lurid and splashed with gold. Then Hirst began to talk, leaning over the bow.

"It makes one awfully queer, don't you find?" he complained. "These trees get on one's nerves—it's all so crazy. God's undoubtedly mad. What sane person could have conceived a wilderness like this, and peopled it with apes and alligators? I should go mad if I lived here—raving mad."

Terence attempted to answer him, but Mrs. Ambrose replied instead. She bade him look at the way things massed themselves—look at the amazing colours, look at the shapes of the trees. She seemed to be protecting Terence from the approach of the others.

"Yes," said Mr. Flushing. "And in my opinion," he continued, "the absence of population to which Hirst objects is precisely the significant touch. You must admit, Hirst, that a little Italian town even would vulgarise the whole scene, would detract from the vastness—the sense of elemental grandeur." He swept his hand towards the forest, and paused for a moment, looking at the great green mass, which was now falling silent. "I own it makes us seem pretty small—us, but not them." He nodded his head at a sailor who leant over the side spitting into the river. "And that, I think, is what my wife feels, the essential superiority of the peasant—"

Under cover of Mr. Flushing's words, which continued now gently reasoning with St. John and persuading him, Terence drew Rachel to the side, pointing ostensibly to a great gnarled tree-trunk which had fallen and lay half in the water. He wished, at any rate, to be near her, but he found that he could say nothing. They could hear Mr. Flushing flowing on, now about his wife, now about art, now about the future of the country, little meaningless words floating high in air. As it was becoming cold he began to pace the deck with Hirst. Fragments of their talk came out distinctly as they passed—art, emotion, truth, reality.

"Is it true, or is it a dream?" Rachel murmured, when they had passed.

"It's true, it's true," he replied.

But the breeze freshened, and there was a general desire for movement. When the party rearranged themselves under cover of rugs and cloaks, Terence and Rachel were at opposite ends of the circle, and could not speak to each other. But as the dark descended, the words of the others seemed to curl up and vanish as the ashes of burnt paper, and left them sitting perfectly silent at the bottom of the world. Occasional starts of exquisite joy ran through them, and then they were peaceful again.

Chapter XXI

Thanks to Mr. Flushing's discipline, the right stages of the river were reached at the right hours, and when next morning after breakfast the chairs were again drawn out in a semicircle in the bow, the launch was within a few miles of the native camp which was the limit of the journey. Mr. Flushing, as he sat down, advised them to keep their eyes fixed on the left bank, where they would soon pass a clearing, and in that clearing was a hut where Mackenzie, the famous explorer, had died of fever some ten years ago, almost within reach of civilisation—Mackenzie, he repeated, the man who went farther inland than any one's been yet. Their eyes turned that way obediently. The eyes of Rachel saw nothing. Yellow and green shapes did, it is true, pass before them, but she only knew that one was large and another small; she did not know that they were trees. These directions to look here and there irritated her, as interruptions irritate a person absorbed in thought, although she was not thinking of anything. She was annoyed with all that was said, and with the aimless movements of people's bodies, because they seemed to interfere with her and to prevent her from speaking to Terence. Very soon Helen saw her staring moodily at a coil of rope, and making no effort to listen. Mr. Flushing and St. John were engaged in more or less continuous conversation about the future of the country from a political point of view, and the degree to which it had been explored; the others, with their legs stretched out, or chins poised on the hands, gazed in silence.

Mrs. Ambrose looked and listened obediently enough, but inwardly she was a prey to an uneasy mood not readily to be ascribed to any one cause. Looking on shore as Mr. Flushing bade her, she thought the country very beautiful, but also sultry and alarming. She did not like to feel herself the victim of unclassified emotions, and certainly as the launch slipped on and on, in the hot morning sun, she felt herself unreasonably moved. Whether the unfamiliarity of the forest was the cause of it, or something less definite, she could not determine. Her mind left the scene and occupied itself with anxieties for Ridley, for her children, for far-off things, such as old age and poverty and death. Hirst, too, was depressed. He had been looking forward to this expedition as to a holiday, for, once away from the hotel, surely wonderful things would happen, instead of which nothing happened, and here they were as uncomfortable, as restrained, as self-conscious as ever. That, of course, was what came of looking forward to anything; one was always disappointed. He blamed Wilfrid Flushing, who was so well dressed and so formal; he blamed Hewet and Rachel. Why didn't they talk? He looked at them sitting silent and self-absorbed, and the sight annoyed him. He supposed that they were engaged, or about to become engaged, but instead of being in the least romantic or exciting, that was as dull as everything else; it annoyed him, too, to think that they were in love. He drew close to Helen and began to tell her how uncomfortable his night had been, lying on the deck, sometimes too hot, sometimes too cold, and the stars so bright that he couldn't get to sleep. He had lain awake all night thinking, and when it was light enough to see, he had written twenty lines of his poem on God, and the awful thing was that he'd practically proved the fact that God did exist. He did not see that he was teasing her, and he went on to wonder what would happen if God did exist—

"an old gentleman in a beard and a long blue dressing-gown, extremely testy and disagreeable as he's bound to be? Can you suggest a rhyme? God, rod, sod—all used; any others?"

Although he spoke much as usual, Helen could have seen, had she looked, that he was also impatient and disturbed. But she was not called upon to answer, for Mr. Flushing now exclaimed "There!" They looked at the hut on the bank, a desolate place with a large rent in the roof, and the ground round it yellow, scarred with fires and scattered with rusty open tins.

"Did they find his dead body there?" Mrs. Flushing exclaimed, leaning forward in her eagerness to see the spot where the explorer had died.

"They found his body and his skins and a notebook," her husband replied. But the boat had soon carried them on and left the place behind.

It was so hot that they scarcely moved, except now to change a foot, or, again, to strike a match. Their eyes, concentrated upon the bank, were full of the same green reflections, and their lips were slightly pressed together as though the sights they were passing gave rise to thoughts, save that Hirst's lips moved intermittently as half consciously he sought rhymes for God. Whatever the thoughts of the others, no one said anything for a considerable space. They had grown so accustomed to the wall of trees on either side that they looked up with a start when the light suddenly widened out and the trees came to an end.

"It almost reminds one of an English park," said Mr. Flushing.

Indeed no change could have been greater. On both banks of the river lay an open lawn-like space, grass covered and planted, for the gentleness and order of the place suggested human care, with graceful trees on the top of little mounds. As far as they could gaze, this lawn rose and sank with the undulating motion of an old English park. The change of scene naturally suggested a change of position, grateful to most of them. They rose and leant over the rail.

"It might be Arundel or Windsor," Mr. Flushing continued, "if you cut down that bush with the yellow flowers; and, by Jove, look!"

Rows of brown backs paused for a moment and then leapt, with a motion as if they were springing over waves, out of sight.

For a moment no one of them could believe that they had really seen live animals in the open—a herd of wild deer, and the sight aroused a childlike excitement in them, dissipating their gloom.

"I've never in my life seen anything bigger than a hare!" Hirst exclaimed with genuine excitement. "What an ass I was not to bring my Kodak!"

Soon afterwards the launch came gradually to a standstill, and the captain explained to Mr. Flushing that it would be pleasant for the passengers if they now went for a stroll on shore; if they chose to return within an hour, he would take them on to the village; if they chose to walk—it was only a mile or two farther on—he would meet them at the landing-place.

The matter being settled, they were once more put on shore: the sailors, producing raisins and tobacco, leant upon the rail and watched the six English, whose coats and dresses looked so strange upon the green, wander off. A joke that was by no means proper set them all laughing, and then they turned round and lay at their ease upon the deck.

Directly they landed, Terence and Rachel drew together slightly in advance of the others.

"Thank God!" Terence exclaimed, drawing a long breath. "At last we're alone."

"And if we keep ahead we can talk," said Rachel.

Nevertheless, although their position some yards in advance of the others made it possible for them to say anything they chose, they were both silent.

"You love me?" Terence asked at length, breaking the silence painfully. To speak or to be silent was equally an effort, for when they were silent they were keenly conscious of each other's presence, and yet words were either too trivial or too large.

She murmured inarticulately, ending, "And you?"

"Yes, yes," he replied; but there were so many things to be said, and now that they were alone it seemed necessary to bring themselves still more near, and to surmount a barrier which had grown up since they had last spoken. It was difficult, frightening even, oddly embarrassing. At one moment he was clear-sighted, and, at the next, confused.

"Now I'm going to begin at the beginning," he said resolutely. "I'm going to tell you what I ought to have told you before. In the first place, I've never been in love with other women, but I've had other women. Then I've great faults. I'm very lazy, I'm moody—" He persisted, in spite of her exclamation, "You've got to know the worst of me. I'm lustful. I'm overcome by a sense of futility— incompetence. I ought never to have asked you to marry me, I expect. I'm a bit of a snob; I'm ambitious——"

"Oh, our faults!" she cried. "What do they matter?" Then she demanded, "Am I in love—is this being in love—are we to marry each other?"

Overcome by the charm of her voice and her presence, he exclaimed, "Oh, you're free, Rachel. To you, time will make no difference, or marriage or——"

The voices of the others behind them kept floating, now farther, now nearer, and Mrs. Flushing's laugh rose clearly by itself.

"Marriage?" Rachel repeated.

The shouts were renewed behind, warning them that they were bearing too far to the left. Improving their course, he continued, "Yes, marriage." The feeling that they could not be united until she knew all about him made him again endeavour to explain.

"All that's been bad in me, the things I've put up with—the second best——"

She murmured, considered her own life, but could not describe how it looked to her now.

"And the loneliness!" he continued. A vision of walking with her through the streets of London came before his eyes. "We will go for walks together," he said. The simplicity of the idea relieved them, and for the first time they laughed. They would have liked had they dared to take each other by the hand, but the consciousness of eyes fixed on them from behind had not yet deserted them.

"Books, people, sights—Mrs. Nutt, Greeley, Hutchinson," Hewet murmured.

With every word the mist which had enveloped them, making them seem unreal to each other, since the previous afternoon melted a little further, and their contact became more and more natural. Up through the sultry southern landscape they saw the world they knew appear clearer and more vividly than it had ever appeared before. As upon that occasion at the hotel when she had sat in the window, the world once more arranged itself beneath her gaze very vividly and in its true proportions. She glanced curiously at Terence from time to time, observing his grey coat and his purple tie; observing the man with whom she was to spend the rest of her life.

After one of these glances she murmured, "Yes, I'm in love. There's no doubt; I'm in love with you."

Nevertheless, they remained uncomfortably apart; drawn so close together, as she spoke, that there seemed no division between them, and the next moment separate and far away again. Feeling this painfully, she exclaimed, "It will be a fight."

But as she looked at him she perceived from the shape of his eyes, the lines about his mouth, and other peculiarities that he pleased her, and she added:

"Where I want to fight, you have compassion. You're finer than I am; you're much finer."

He returned her glance and smiled, perceiving, much as she had done, the very small individual things about her which made her delightful to him. She was his for ever. This barrier being surmounted, innumerable delights lay before them both.

"I'm not finer," he answered. "I'm only older, lazier; a man, not a woman."

"A man," she repeated, and a curious sense of possession coming over her, it struck her that she might now touch him; she put out her hand and lightly touched his cheek. His fingers followed where hers had been, and the touch of his hand upon his face brought back the overpowering sense of unreality. This body of his was unreal; the whole world was unreal.

"What's happened?" he began. "Why did I ask you to marry me? How did it happen?"

"Did you ask me to marry you?" she wondered. They faded far away from each other, and neither of them could remember what had been said.

"We sat upon the ground," he recollected.

"We sat upon the ground," she confirmed him. The recollection of sitting upon the ground, such as it was, seemed to unite them again, and they walked on in silence, their minds sometimes working with difficulty and sometimes ceasing to work, their eyes alone perceiving the things round them. Now he would attempt again to tell her his faults, and why he loved her; and she would describe what she had felt at this time or at that time, and together they would interpret her feeling. So beautiful was the sound of their voices that by degrees they scarcely listened to the words they framed. Long silences came between their words, which were no longer silences of struggle and confusion but refreshing silences, in which trivial thoughts moved easily. They began to speak naturally of ordinary things, of the flowers and the trees, how they grew there so red, like garden flowers at home, and there bent and crooked like the arm of a twisted old man.

Very gently and quietly, almost as if it were the blood singing in her veins, or the water of the stream running over stones, Rachel became conscious of a new feeling within her. She wondered for a moment what it was, and then said to herself, with a little surprise at recognising in her own person so famous a thing:

"This is happiness, I suppose." And aloud to Terence she spoke, "This is happiness."

On the heels of her words he answered, "This is happiness," upon which they guessed that the feeling had sprung in both of them at the same time. They began therefore to describe how this felt and that felt, how like it was and yet how different; for they were very different.

Voices crying behind them never reached through the waters in which they were now sunk. The repetition of Hewet's name in short, dissevered syllables was to them the crack of a dry branch or the laughter of a bird. The grasses and breezes sounding and murmuring all round them, they never noticed that the swishing of the grasses grew louder and louder, and did not cease with the lapse of the breeze. A hand dropped abrupt as iron on Rachel's shoulder; it might have been a bolt from heaven. She fell beneath it, and the grass whipped across her eyes and filled her mouth and ears. Through the waving stems she saw a figure, large and shapeless against the sky. Helen was upon her. Rolled this way and that, now seeing only forests of green, and now the high blue heaven, she was speechless and almost without sense. At last she lay still, all the grasses shaken round her and before her by her panting. Over her loomed two great heads, the heads of a man and woman, of Terence and Helen.

Both were flushed, both laughing, and the lips were moving; they came together and kissed in the air above her. Broken fragments of speech came down to her on the ground. She thought she heard them speak of love and then of marriage. Raising herself and sitting up, she too realised Helen's soft body, the strong and hospitable arms, and happiness swelling and breaking in one vast wave. When this fell away, and the grasses once more lay low, and the sky became horizontal, and the earth rolled out flat on each side, and the trees stood upright, she was the first to perceive a little row of human figures standing patiently in the distance. For the moment she could not remember who they were.

"Who are they?" she asked, and then recollected.

Falling into line behind Mr. Flushing, they were careful to leave at least three yards' distance between the toe of his boot and the rim of her skirt.

He led them across a stretch of green by the river-bank and then through a grove of trees, and bade them remark the signs of human habitation, the blackened grass, the charred tree-stumps, and there, through the trees, strange wooden nests, drawn together in an arch where the trees drew apart, the village which was the goal of their journey.

Stepping cautiously, they observed the women, who were squatting on the ground in triangular shapes, moving their hands, either plaiting straw or in kneading something in bowls. But when they had looked for a moment undiscovered, they were seen, and Mr.

Flushing, advancing into the centre of the clearing, was engaged in talk with a lean majestic man, whose bones and hollows at once made the shapes of the Englishman's body appear ugly and unnatural. The women took no notice of the strangers, except that their hands paused for a moment and their long narrow eyes slid round and fixed upon them with the motionless inexpressive gaze of those removed from each other far, far beyond the plunge of speech. Their hands moved again, but the stare continued. It followed them as they walked, as they peered into the huts where they could distinguish guns leaning in the corner, and bowls upon the floor, and stacks of rushes; in the dusk the solemn eyes of babies regarded them, and old women stared out too. As they sauntered about, the stare followed them, passing over their legs, their bodies, their heads, curiously, not without hostility, like the crawl of a winter fly. As she drew apart her shawl and uncovered her breast to the lips of her baby, the eyes of a woman never left their faces, although they moved uneasily under her stare, and finally turned away, rather than stand there looking at her any longer. When sweetmeats were offered them, they put out great red hands to take them, and felt themselves treading cumbrously like tight-coated soldiers among these soft instinctive people. But soon the life of the village took no notice of them; they had become absorbed into it. The women's hands became busy again with the straw; their eyes dropped. If they moved, it was to fetch something from the hut, or to catch a straying child, or to cross the space with a jar balanced on their heads; if they spoke, it was to cry some harsh unintelligible cry. Voices rose when a child was beaten, and fell again; voices rose in song, which slid up a little way and down a little way, and settled again upon the same low and melancholy note. Seeking each other, Terence and Rachel drew together under a tree. Peaceful, and even beautiful at first, the sight of the women, who had given up looking at them, made them now feel very cold and melancholy.

"Well," Terence sighed at length, "it makes us seem insignificant, doesn't it?"

Rachel agreed. So it would go on for ever and ever, she said, those women sitting under the trees, the trees and the river. They turned away and began to walk through the trees, leaning, without fear of discovery, upon each other's arms. They had not gone far before they began to assure each other once more that they were in love, were happy, were content; but why was it so painful being in love, why was there so much pain in happiness?

The sight of the village indeed affected them all curiously though all differently. St. John had left the others and was walking slowly down to the river, absorbed in his own thoughts, which were bitter and unhappy, for he felt himself alone; and Helen, standing by herself in the sunny space among the native women, was exposed to presentiments of disaster. The cries of the senseless beasts rang in her ears high and low in the air, as they ran from tree-trunk to tree-top. How small the little figures looked wandering through the trees! She became acutely conscious of the little limbs, the thin veins, the delicate flesh of men and women, which breaks so easily and lets the life escape compared with these great trees and deep waters. A falling branch, a foot that slips, and the earth has crushed them or the water drowned them. Thus thinking, she kept her eyes anxiously fixed upon the lovers, as if by doing so she could protect them from their fate. Turning, she found the Flushings by her side.

They were talking about the things they had bought and arguing whether they were really old, and whether there were not signs here and there of European influence. Helen was appealed to. She was made to look at a brooch, and then at a pair of ear-rings. But all the time she blamed them for having come on this expedition, for having ventured too far and exposed themselves. Then she roused herself and tried to talk, but in a few moments she caught herself seeing a picture of a boat upset on the river in England, at midday. It was morbid, she knew, to imagine such things; nevertheless she sought out the figures of the others between the trees, and whenever she saw them she kept her eyes fixed on them, so that she might be able to protect them from disaster.

But when the sun went down and the steamer turned and began to steam back towards civilisation, again her fears were calmed. In the semi-darkness the chairs on deck and the people sitting in them were angular shapes, the mouth being indicated by a tiny burning spot, and the arm by the same spot moving up or down as the cigar or cigarette was lifted to and from the lips. Words crossed the darkness, but, not knowing where they fell, seemed to lack energy and substance. Deep sighs proceeded regularly, although with some attempt at suppression, from the large white mound which represented the person of Mrs. Flushing. The day had been long and very hot, and now that all the colours were blotted out the cool night air seemed to press soft fingers upon the eyelids, sealing them down. Some philosophical remark directed, apparently, at St. John Hirst missed its aim, and hung so long suspended in the air until it was engulfed by a yawn, that it was considered dead, and this gave the signal for stirring of legs and murmurs about sleep. The white mound moved, finally lengthened itself and disappeared, and after a few turns and paces St. John and Mr. Flushing withdrew, leaving three chairs still occupied by three silent bodies. The light which came from a lamp high on the mast and a sky pale with stars left them with shapes but without features; but even in this darkness the withdrawal of the others made them feel each other very near, for they were all thinking of the same thing. For some time no one spoke, then Helen said with a sigh, "So you're both very happy?"

As if washed by the air her voice sounded more spiritual and softer than usual. Voices at a little distance answered her, "Yes."

Through the darkness she was looking at them both, and trying to distinguish him. What was there for her to say? Rachel had passed beyond her guardianship. A voice might reach her ears, but never again would it carry as far as it had carried twenty-four hours ago. Nevertheless, speech seemed to be due from her before she went to bed. She wished to speak, but she felt strangely old and depressed.

"D'you realise what you're doing?" she demanded. "She's young, you're both young; and marriage——" Here she ceased. They begged her, however, to continue, with such earnestness in their voices, as if they only craved advice, that she was led to add:

"Marriage! well, it's not easy."

"That's what we want to know," they answered, and she guessed that now they were looking at each other.

"It depends on both of you," she stated. Her face was turned towards Terence, and although he could hardly see her, he believed that her words really covered a genuine desire to know more about him. He raised himself from his semi-recumbent position and proceeded to tell her what she wanted to know. He spoke as lightly as he could in order to take away her depression.

"I'm twenty-seven, and I've about seven hundred a year," he began. "My temper is good on the whole, and health excellent, though Hirst detects a gouty tendency. Well, then, I think I'm very intelligent." He paused as if for confirmation.

Helen agreed.

"Though, unfortunately, rather lazy. I intend to allow Rachel to be a fool if she wants to, and— Do you find me on the whole satisfactory in other respects?" he asked shyly.

"Yes, I like what I know of you," Helen replied. "But then—one knows so little."

"We shall live in London," he continued, "and—" With one voice they suddenly enquired whether she did not think them the happiest people that she had ever known.

"Hush," she checked them, "Mrs. Flushing, remember. She's behind us."

Then they fell silent, and Terence and Rachel felt instinctively that their happiness had made her sad, and, while they were anxious to go on talking about themselves, they did not like to.

"We've talked too much about ourselves," Terence said. "Tell us——"

"Yes, tell us——" Rachel echoed. They were both in the mood to believe that every one was capable of saying something very profound.

"What can I tell you?" Helen reflected, speaking more to herself in a rambling style than as a prophetess delivering a message. She forced herself to speak.

"After all, though I scold Rachel, I'm not much wiser myself. I'm older, of course, I'm half-way through, and you're just beginning. It's puzzling—sometimes, I think, disappointing; the great things aren't as great, perhaps, as one expects—but it's interesting— Oh, yes you're certain to find it interesting—— And so it goes on," they became conscious here of the procession of dark trees into which, as far as they could see, Helen was now looking, "and there are pleasures where one doesn't expect them (you must write to your father), and you'll be very happy, I've no doubt. But I must go to bed, and if you are sensible you will follow in ten minutes, and so," she rose and stood before them, almost featureless and very large, "Good-night." She passed behind the curtain.

After sitting in silence for the greater part of the ten minutes she allowed them, they rose and hung over the rail. Beneath them the smooth black water slipped away very fast and silently. The spark of a cigarette vanished behind them. "A beautiful voice," Terence murmured.

Rachel assented. Helen had a beautiful voice.

After a silence she asked, looking up into the sky, "Are we on the deck of a steamer on a river in South America? Am I Rachel, are you Terence?"

The great black world lay round them. As they were drawn smoothly along it seemed possessed of immense thickness and endurance. They could discern pointed tree-tops and blunt rounded tree-tops. Raising their eyes above the trees, they fixed them on the stars and the pale border of sky above the trees. The little points of frosty light infinitely far away drew their eyes and held them fixed, so that it seemed as if they stayed a long time and fell a great distance when once more they realised their hands grasping the rail and their separate bodies standing side by side.

"You'd forgotten completely about me," Terence reproached her, taking her arm and beginning to pace the deck, "and I never forget you."

"Oh, no," she whispered, she had not forgotten, only the stars—the night—the dark——

"You're like a bird half asleep in its nest, Rachel. You're asleep. You're talking in your sleep."

Half asleep, and murmuring broken words, they stood in the angle made by the bow of the boat. It slipped on down the river. Now a bell struck on the bridge, and they heard the lapping of water as it rippled away on either side, and once a bird, startled in its sleep, creaked, flew on to the next tree, and was silent again. The darkness poured down profusely, and left them with scarcely any feeling of life, except that they were standing there together in the darkness.

CHAPTER XXII

The darkness fell, but rose again, and as each day spread widely over the earth and parted them from the strange day in the forest when they had been forced to tell each other what they wanted, this wish of theirs was revealed to other people, and in the process became slightly strange to themselves. Apparently it was not anything unusual that had happened; it was that they had become engaged to marry each other. The world, which consisted for the most part of the hotel and the villa, expressed itself glad on the whole that two people should marry, and allowed them to see that they were not expected to take part in the work which has to be done in order that the world shall go on, but might absent themselves for a time. They were accordingly left alone until they felt the silence as if, playing in a vast church, the door had been shut on them. They were driven to walk alone, and sit alone, to visit secret places where the flowers had never been picked and the trees were solitary. In solitude they could express those beautiful but too vast desires which were so oddly uncomfortable to the ears of other men and women—desires for a world, such as their own world which contained two people seemed to them to be, where people knew each other intimately and thus judged each other by what was good, and never quarrelled, because that was waste of time.

They would talk of such questions among books, or out in the sun, or sitting in the shade of a tree undisturbed. They were no longer embarrassed, or half-choked with meaning which could not express itself; they were not afraid of each other, or, like travellers down a twisting river, dazzled with sudden beauties when the corner is turned; the unexpected happened, but even the ordinary was lovable, and in many ways preferable to the ecstatic and mysterious, for it was refreshingly solid, and called out effort, and effort under such circumstances was not effort but delight.

While Rachel played the piano, Terence sat near her, engaged, as far as the occasional writing of a word in pencil testified, in shaping the world as it appeared to him now that he and Rachel were going to be married. It was different certainly. The book called *Silence* would not now be the same book that it would have been. He would then put down his pencil and stare in front of him, and wonder in what respects the world was different—it had, perhaps, more solidity, more coherence, more importance, greater depth. Why, even the earth sometimes seemed to him very deep; not carved into hills and cities and fields, but heaped in great masses. He would look out of the window for ten minutes at a time; but no, he did not care for the earth swept of human beings. He liked human beings—he liked them, he suspected, better than Rachel did. There she was, swaying enthusiastically over her music, quite forgetful of him,— but he liked that quality in her. He liked the impersonality which it produced in her. At last, having written down a series of little sentences, with notes of interrogation attached to them, he observed aloud, " 'Women—under the heading Women I've written:

" 'Not really vainer than men. Lack of self-confidence at the base of most serious faults. Dislike of own sex traditional, or founded on fact? Every woman not so much a rake at heart, as an optimist, because they don't think.' What do you say, Rachel?" He paused with his pencil in his hand and a sheet of paper on his knee.

Rachel said nothing. Up and up the steep spiral of a very late

Beethoven sonata she climbed, like a person ascending a ruined staircase, energetically at first, then more laboriously advancing her feet with effort until she could go no higher and returned with a run to begin at the very bottom again.

" 'Again, it's the fashion now to say that women are more practical and less idealistic than men, also that they have considerable organising ability but no sense of honour'—query, what is meant by masculine term, honour?—what corresponds to it in your sex? Eh?"

Attacking her staircase once more, Rachel again neglected this opportunity of revealing the secrets of her sex. She had, indeed, advanced so far in the pursuit of wisdom that she allowed these secrets to rest undisturbed; it seemed to be reserved for a later generation to discuss them philosophically.

Crashing down a final chord with her left hand, she exclaimed at last, swinging round upon him:

"No, Terence, it's no good; here am I, the best musician in South America, not to speak of Europe and Asia, and I can't play a note because of you in the room interrupting me every other second."

"You don't seem to realise that that's what I've been aiming at for the last half-hour," he remarked. "I've no objection to nice, simple tunes—indeed, I find them very helpful to literary composition, but that kind of thing is merely like an unfortunate old dog going round on its hind legs in the rain."

He began turning over the little sheets of note-paper which were scattered on the table, conveying the congratulations of their friends.

" '——all possible wishes for all possible happiness,' " he read; "correct, but not very vivid, are they?"

"They're sheer nonsense!" Rachel exclaimed. "Think of words compared with sounds!" she continued. "Think of novels and plays and histories——" Perched on the edge of the table, she stirred the red and yellow volumes contemptuously. She seemed to herself to be in a position where she could despise all human learning. Terence looked at them too.

"God, Rachel, you do read trash!" he exclaimed. "And you're behind the times too, my dear. No one dreams of reading this kind of thing now—antiquated problem plays, harrowing descriptions of life in the east end—oh, no, we've exploded all that. Read poetry, Rachel, poetry, poetry, poetry!"

Picking up one of the books, he began to read aloud, his intention being to satirise the short sharp bark of the writer's English; but she paid no attention, and after an interval of meditation exclaimed:

"Does it ever seem to you, Terence, that the world is composed entirely of vast blocks of matter, and that we're nothing but patches of light—" she looked at the soft spots of sun wavering over the carpet and up the wall—"like that?"

"No," said Terence, "I feel solid; immensely solid; the legs of my chair might be rooted in the bowels of the earth. But at Cambridge, I can remember, there were times when one fell into ridiculous states of semi-coma about five o'clock in the morning. Hirst does now, I expect—oh, no, Hirst wouldn't."

Rachel continued, "The day your note came, asking us to go on the picnic, I was sitting where you're sitting now, thinking that; I wonder if I could think that again? I wonder if the world's changed? and if so, when it'll stop changing, and which is the real world?"

"When I first saw you," he began, "I thought you were like a creature who'd lived all its life among pearls and old bones. Your hands were wet, d'you remember, and you never said a word until I gave you a bit of bread, and then you said, 'Human Beings!' "

"And I thought you—a prig," she recollected. "No; that's not quite it. There were the ants who stole the tongue, and I thought you and St. John were like those ants—very big, very ugly, very energetic, with all your virtues on your backs. However, when I talked to you I liked you——"

"You fell in love with me," he corrected her. "You were in love with me all the time, only you didn't know it."

"No, I never fell in love with you," she asserted.

"Rachel—what a lie—didn't you sit here looking at my window—didn't you wander about the hotel like an owl in the sun——?"

"No," she repeated, "I never fell in love, if falling in love is what people say it is, and it's the world that tells the lies and I tell the truth. Oh, what lies—what lies!"

She crumpled together a handful of letters from Evelyn M., from Mr. Pepper, from Mrs. Thornbury and Miss Allan, and Susan Warrington. It was strange, considering how very different these people were, that they used almost the same sentences when they wrote to congratulate her upon her engagement.

That any one of these people had ever felt what she felt, or could ever feel it, or had even the right to pretend for a single second that they were capable of feeling it, appalled her much as the church service had done, much as the face of the hospital nurse had done; and if they didn't feel a thing why did they go and pretend to? The simplicity and arrogance and hardness of her youth, now concentrated into a single spark as it was by her love of him, puzzled Terence; being engaged had not that effect on him; the world was different, but not in that way; he still wanted the things he had always wanted, and in particular he wanted the companionship of other people more than ever perhaps. He took the letters out of her hand, and protested:

"Of course they're absurd, Rachel; of course they say things just because other people say them, but even so, what a nice woman Miss Allan is; you can't deny that; and Mrs. Thornbury too; she's got too many children I grant you, but if half-a-dozen of them had gone to the bad instead of rising infallibly to the tops of their trees—hasn't she a kind of beauty—of elemental simplicity as Flushing would say? Isn't she rather like a large old tree murmuring in the moonlight, or a river going on and on and on? By the way, Ralph's been made governor of the Carroway Islands—the youngest governor in the service; very good, isn't it?"

But Rachel was at present unable to conceive that the vast majority of the affairs of the world went on unconnected by a single thread with her own destiny.

"I won't have eleven children," she asserted; "I won't have the eyes of an old woman. She looks at one up and down, up and down, as if one were a horse."

"We must have a son and we must have a daughter," said Terence, putting down the letters, "because, let alone the inestimable advantage of being our children, they'd be so well brought up." They went on to sketch an outline of the ideal education—how their daughter should be required from infancy to gaze at a large square of cardboard, painted blue, to suggest thoughts of infinity, for women were grown too practical; and their son—he should be taught to laugh at great men, that is, at distinguished successful men, at men who wore ribands and rose to the tops of their trees. He should in no way resemble (Rachel added) St. John Hirst.

At this Terence professed the greatest admiration for St. John Hirst. Dwelling upon his good qualities he became seriously convinced of them; he had a mind like a torpedo, he declared, aimed at falsehood. Where should we all be without him and his like? Choked in weeds; Christians, bigots,—why, Rachel herself, would be a slave with a fan to sing songs to men when they felt drowsy.

"But you'll never see it!" he exclaimed; "because with all your virtues you don't, and you never will, care with every fibre of your being for the pursuit of truth! You've no respect for facts, Rachel; you're essentially feminine."

She did not trouble to deny it, nor did she think good to produce the one unanswerable argument against the merits which Terence admired. St. John had said that she was in love with him; she would never forgive that; but the argument was not one to appeal to a man.

"But I like him," she said, and she thought to herself that she also pitied him, as one pities those unfortunate people who are outside the warm mysterious globe full of changes and miracles in which we ourselves move about; she thought that it must be very dull to be St. John Hirst.

She summed up what she felt about him by saying that she would not kiss him supposing he wished it, which was not likely.

As if some apology were due to Hirst for the kiss which she then bestowed upon himself, Terence protested:

"And compared with Hirst I'm a perfect Zany."

The clock here struck twelve instead of eleven.

"We're wasting the morning—I ought to be writing my book, and you ought to be answering these."

"We've only got twenty-one whole mornings left," said Rachel. "And my father'll be here in a day or two."

However, she drew a pen and paper towards her and began to write laboriously,

"My dear Evelyn——"

Terence, meanwhile, read a novel which some one else had written, a process which he found essential to the composition of his own. For a considerable time nothing was to be heard but the ticking of the clock and the fitful scratch of Rachel's pen, as she produced phrases which bore a considerable likeness to those which she had condemned. She was struck by it herself, for she stopped writing and looked up; looked at Terence deep in the arm-chair, looked at the different pieces of furniture, at her bed in the corner, at the window-pane which showed the branches of a tree filled in with sky, heard the clock ticking, and was amazed at the gulf which lay between all that and her sheet of paper. Would there ever be a time when the world was one and indivisible? Even with Terence himself—how far apart they could be, how little she knew what was passing in his brain now! She then finished her sentence, which was awkward and ugly, and stated that they were "both very happy, and are going to be married in the autumn probably and hope to live in London, where we hope you will come and see us when we get back." Choosing "affectionately," after some further speculation, rather than sincerely, she signed the letter and was doggedly beginning on another when Terence remarked, quoting from his book:

"Listen to this, Rachel. 'It is probable that Hugh' (he's the hero, a literary man), 'had not realised at the time of his marriage, any more than the young man of parts and imagination usually does realise, the nature of the gulf which separates the needs and desires of the male from the needs and desires of the female.... At first they had been very happy. The walking tour in Switzerland had been a time of jolly companionship and stimulating revelations for both of them. Betty had proved herself the ideal comrade.... They had shouted *Love in the Valley* to each other across the snowy slopes of the Riffelhorn' (and so on, and so on—I'll skip the descriptions)... 'But in London, after the boy's birth, all was changed. Betty was an admirable mother; but it did not take her long to find out that motherhood, as that function is understood by the mother of the upper middle classes, did not absorb the whole of her energics. She was young and strong, with healthy limbs and a body and brain that called urgently for exercise....' (In short she began to give tea-parties.)... 'Coming in late from this singular talk with old Bob Murphy in his smoky, book-lined room, where the two men had each unloosened his soul to the other, with the sound of the traffic humming in his ears, and the foggy London sky slung tragically across his mind ... he found women's hats dotted about among his papers. Women's wraps and absurd little feminine shoes and umbrellas were in the hall.... Then the bills began to come in.... He tried to speak frankly to her. He found her lying on the great polar-bear skin in their bedroom, half-undressed, for they were dining with the Greens in Wilton Crescent, the ruddy firelight making the diamonds wink and twinkle on her bare arms and in the delicious curve of her breast—a vision of adorable femininity. He forgave her all.' (Well, this goes from bad to worse, and finally, about fifty pages later, Hugh takes a week-end ticket to Swanage and 'has it out with himself on the downs above Corfe.'... Here there's fifteen pages or so which we'll skip. The conclusion is...) 'They were different. Perhaps, in the far future, when generations of men had struggled and failed as he must now struggle and fail, woman would be, indeed, what she now made a pretence of being— the friend and companion—not the enemy and parasite of man.'

"The end of it is, you see, Hugh went back to his wife, poor fellow. It was his duty, as a married man. Lord, Rachel," he concluded, "will it be like that when we're married?"

Instead of answering him she asked,

"Why don't people write about the things they do feel?"

"Ah, that's the difficulty!" he sighed, tossing the book away.

"Well, then, what will it be like when we're married? What are the things people do feel?"

She seemed doubtful.

"Sit on the floor and let me look at you," he commanded. Resting her chin on his knee, she looked straight at him.

He examined her curiously.

"You're not beautiful," he began, "but I like your face. I like the way your hair grows down in a point, and your eyes too—they never see anything. Your mouth's too big, and your cheeks would be better if they had more colour in them. But what I like about your face is that it makes one wonder what the devil you're thinking about—it makes me want to do that—" He clenched his fist and shook it so near her that she started back, "because now you look as if you'd blow my brains out. There are moments," he continued, "when, if we stood on a rock together, you'd throw me into the sea."

Hypnotised by the force of his eyes in hers, she repeated, "If we stood on a rock together——"

To be flung into the sea, to be washed hither and thither, and driven about the roots of the world—the idea was incoherently delightful. She sprang up, and began moving about the room, bending and thrusting aside the chairs and tables as if she were indeed striking through the waters. He watched her with pleasure; she seemed to be cleaving a passage for herself, and dealing triumphantly with the obstacles which would hinder their passage through life.

"It does seem possible!" he exclaimed, "though I've always thought it the most unlikely thing in the world—I shall be in love with you all my life, and our marriage will be the most exciting thing that's ever been done! We'll never have a moment's peace—" He caught her in his arms as she passed him, and they fought for mastery, imagining a rock, and the sea heaving beneath them. At last she was thrown to the floor, where she lay gasping, and crying for mercy.

"I'm a mermaid! I can swim," she cried, "so the game's up." Her dress was torn across, and peace being established, she fetched a needle and thread and began to mend the tear.

"And now," she said, "be quiet and tell me about the world; tell me about everything that's ever happened, and I'll tell you—let me see, what can I tell you?—I'll tell you about Miss Montgomerie and the river party. She was left, you see, with one foot in the boat, and the other on shore."

They had spent much time already in thus filling out for the other the course of their past lives, and the characters of their friends and relations, so that very soon Terence knew not only what Rachel's aunts might be expected to say upon every occasion, but also how their bedrooms were furnished, and what kind of bonnets they wore. He could sustain a conversation between Mrs. Hunt and Rachel, and carry on a tea-party including the Rev. William Johnson and Miss Macquoid, the Christian Scientists, with remarkable likeness to the truth. But he had known many more people, and was far more highly skilled in the art of narrative than Rachel was, whose experiences were, for the most part, of a curiously childlike and humorous kind, so that it generally fell to her lot to listen and ask questions.

He told her not only what had happened, but what he had thought and felt, and sketched for her portraits which fascinated her of what other men and women might be supposed to be thinking and feeling, so that she became very anxious to go back to England, which was full of people, where she could merely stand in the streets and look at them. According to him, too, there was an order, a pattern which made life reasonable, or, if that word was foolish, made it of deep interest anyhow, for sometimes it seemed possible to understand why things happened as they did. Nor were people so solitary and uncommunicative as she believed. She should look for vanity—for vanity was a common quality—first in herself, and then in Helen, in Ridley, in St. John, they all had their share of it—and she would find it in ten people out of every twelve she met; and once linked together by one such tie she would find them not separate and formidable, but practically indistinguishable, and she would come to love them when she found that they were like herself. If she denied this, she must defend her belief that human beings were as various as the beasts at the Zoo, which had stripes and manes, and horns and humps; and so, wrestling over the entire list of their acquaintances, and diverging into anecdote and theory and speculation, they came to know each other. The hours passed quickly, and seemed to them full to leaking-point. After a night's solitude they were always ready to begin again.

The virtues which Mrs. Ambrose had once believed to exist in free talk between men and women did in truth exist for both of them, although not quite in the measure she prescribed. Far more than upon the nature of sex they dwelt upon the nature of poetry, but it was true that talk which had no boundaries deepened and enlarged the strangely small bright view of a girl. In return for what he could tell her she brought him such curiosity and sensitiveness of perception, that he was led to doubt whether any gift bestowed by much reading and living was quite the equal of that for pleasure and pain. What would experience give her after all, except a kind of ridiculous formal balance, like that of a drilled dog in the street? He looked at her face and wondered how it would look in twenty years' time, when the eyes had dulled, and the forehead wore those little persistent wrinkles which seem to show that the middle-aged are facing something hard which the young do not see. What would the hard thing be for them, he wondered? Then his thoughts turned to their life in England.

The thought of England was delightful, for together they would see the old things freshly; it would be England in June, and there would be June nights in the country; and the nightingales singing in the lanes, into which they could steal when the room grew hot; and there would be English meadows gleaming with water and set with stolid cows, and clouds dipping low and trailing across the green hills. As he sat in the room with her, he wished very often to be back again in the thick of life, doing things with Rachel.

He crossed to the window and exclaimed, "Lord, how good it is to think of lanes, muddy lanes, with brambles and nettles, you know, and real grass fields, and farmyards with pigs and cows, and men walking beside carts with pitchforks—there's nothing to compare with that here—look at the stony red earth, and the bright blue sea, and the glaring white houses—how tired one gets of it! And the air, without a stain or a wrinkle. I'd give anything for a sea mist."

Rachel, too, had been thinking of the English country: the flat land rolling away to the sea, and the woods and the long straight roads, where one can walk for miles without seeing any one, and the great church towers and the curious houses clustered in the valleys, and the birds, and the dusk, and the rain beating against the windows.

"But London, London's the place," Terence continued. They looked together at the carpet, as though London itself were to be seen there lying on the floor, with all its spires and pinnacles pricking through the smoke.

"On the whole, what I should like best at this moment," Terence pondered, "would be to find myself walking down Kingsway, by those big placards, you know, and turning into the Strand. Perhaps I might go and look over Waterloo Bridge for a moment. Then I'd go along the Strand past the shops with all the new books in them, and through the little archway into the Temple. I always like the quiet after the uproar. You hear your own footsteps suddenly quite loud. The Temple's very pleasant. I think I should go and see if I could find dear old Hodgkin—the man who writes books about van Eyck, you know. When I left England he was very sad about his tame magpie. He suspected that a man had poisoned it. And then Russell lives on the next staircase. I think you'd like him. He's a passion for Handel. Well, Rachel," he concluded, dismissing the vision of London, "we shall be doing that together in six weeks' time, and it'll be the middle of June then,—and June in London—my God! how pleasant it all is!"

"And we're certain to have it too," she said. "It isn't as if we were expecting a great deal—only to walk about and look at things."

"Only a thousand a year and perfect freedom," he replied. "How many people in London d'you think have that?"

"And now you've spoilt it," she complained. "Now we've got to think of the horrors." She looked grudgingly at the novel which had once caused her perhaps an hour's discomfort, so that she had never opened it again, but kept it on her table, and looked at it occasionally, as some medieval monk kept a skull, or a crucifix to remind him of the frailty of the body.

314 · *Virginia Woolf*

"Is it true, Terence," she demanded, "that women die with bugs crawling across their faces?"

"I think it's very probable," he said. "But you must admit, Rachel, that we so seldom think of anything but ourselves that an occasional twinge is really rather pleasant."

Accusing him of an affectation of cynicism which was just as bad as sentimentality itself, she left her position by his side and knelt upon the window sill, twisting the curtain tassels between her fingers. A vague sense of dissatisfaction filled her.

"What's so detestable in this country," she exclaimed, "is the blue—always blue sky and blue sea. It's like a curtain—all the things one wants are on the other side of that. I want to know what's going on behind it. I hate these divisions, don't you, Terence? One person all in the dark about another person. Now I liked the Dalloways," she continued, "and they're gone. I shall never see them again. Just by going on a ship we cut ourselves off entirely from the rest of the world. I want to see England there—London there—all sorts of people—why shouldn't one? why should one be shut up all by oneself in a room?"

While she spoke thus half to herself and with increasing vagueness, because her eye was caught by a ship that had just come into the bay, she did not see that Terence had ceased to stare contentedly in front of him, and was looking at her keenly and with dissatisfaction. She seemed to be able to cut herself adrift from him, and to pass away to unknown places where she had no need of him. The thought roused his jealousy.

"I sometimes think you're not in love with me and never will be," he said energetically. She started and turned round at his words.

"I don't satisfy you in the way you satisfy me," he continued. "There's something I can't get hold of in you. You don't want me as I want you—you're always wanting something else."

He began pacing up and down the room.

"Perhaps I ask too much," he went on. "Perhaps it isn't really possible to have what I want. Men and women are too different. You can't understand—you don't understand———"

He came up to where she stood looking at him in silence.

It seemed to her now that what he was saying was perfectly true, and that she wanted many more things than the love of one human being—the sea, the sky. She turned again and looked at the distant blue, which was so smooth and serene where the sky met the sea; she could not possibly want only one human being.

"Or is it only this damnable engagement?" he continued. "Let's be married here, before we go back—or is it too great a risk? Are we sure we want to marry each other?"

They began pacing up and down the room, but although they came very near each other in their pacing, they took care not to touch each other. The hopelessness of their position overcame them both. They were impotent; they could never love each other sufficiently to overcome all these barriers, and they could never be satisfied with less. Realising this with intolerable keenness she stopped in front of him and exclaimed:

"Let's break it off, then."

The words did more to unite them than any amount of argument. As if they stood on the edge of a precipice they clung together. They knew that they could not separate; painful and terrible it might be, but they were joined for ever. They lapsed into silence, and after a time crept together in silence. Merely to be so close soothed them, and sitting side by side the divisions disappeared, and it seemed as if the world were once more solid and entire, and as if, in some strange way, they had grown larger and stronger.

It was long before they moved, and when they moved it was with great reluctance. They stood together in front of the looking-glass, and with a brush tried to make themselves look as if they had been feeling nothing all the morning, neither pain nor happiness. But it chilled them to see themselves in the glass, for instead of being vast and indivisible they were really very small and separate, the size of the glass leaving a large space for the reflection of other things.

CHAPTER XXIII

But no brush was able to efface completely the expression of happiness, so that Mrs. Ambrose could not treat them when they came downstairs as if they had spent the morning in a way that could be discussed naturally. This being so, she joined in the world's conspiracy to consider them for the time incapacitated from the business of life, struck by their intensity of feeling into enmity against life, and almost succeeded in dismissing them from her thoughts.

She reflected that she had done all that it was necessary to do in practical matters. She had written a great many letters, and had obtained Willoughby's consent. She had dwelt so often upon Mr. Hewet's prospects, his profession, his birth, appearance, and temperament, that she had almost forgotten what he was really like. When she refreshed herself by a look at him, she used to wonder again what he was like, and then, concluding that they were happy at any rate, thought no more about it.

She might more profitably consider what would happen in three years' time, or what might have happened if Rachel had been left to explore the world under her father's guidance. The result, she was honest enough to own, might have been better—who knows? She did not disguise from herself that Terence had faults. She was in-

clined to think him too easy and tolerant, just as he was inclined to
think her perhaps a trifle hard—no, it was rather that she was uncompromising. In some ways she found St. John preferable; but
then, of course, he would never have suited Rachel. Her friendship
with St. John was established, for although she fluctuated between
irritation and interest in a way that did credit to the candour of her
disposition, she liked his company on the whole. He took her outside this little world of love and emotion. He had a grasp of facts.
Supposing, for instance, that England made a sudden move towards
some unknown port on the coast of Morocco, St. John knew what
was at the back of it, and to hear him engaged with her husband in
argument about finance and the balance of power, gave her an odd
sense of stability. She respected their arguments without always listening to them, much as she respected a solid brick wall, or one of
those immense municipal buildings which, although they compose
the greater part of our cities, have been built day after day and year
after year by unknown hands. She liked to sit and listen, and even
felt a little elated when the engaged couple, after showing their
profound lack of interest, slipped from the room, and were seen
pulling flowers to pieces in the garden. It was not that she was jealous of them, but she did undoubtedly envy them their great unknown future that lay before them. Slipping from one such thought
to another, she was at the present moment wandering from drawing-
room to dining-room with fruit in her hands. Sometimes she
stopped to straighten a candle stooping with the heat, or disturbed
some too rigid arrangement of the chairs. She had reason to suspect
that Chailey had been balancing herself on the top of a ladder with
a wet duster during their absence, and the room had never been
quite like itself since. Returning from the dining-room for the third
time, she perceived that one of the arm-chairs was now occupied by
St. John. He lay back in it, with his eyes half shut, looking, as he always did, curiously buttoned up in a neat grey suit, and fenced
against the exuberance of a foreign climate which might at any moment proceed to take liberties with him. Her eyes rested on him
gently and then passed on over his head. Finally she took the chair
opposite.

"I didn't want to come here," he said at last, "but I was positively driven to it. ... Evelyn M.," he groaned.

He sat up, and began to explain with mock solemnity how the detestable woman was set upon marrying him.

"She pursues me about the place. This morning she appeared in the smoking-room. All I could do was to seize my hat and fly. I didn't want to come, but I couldn't stay and face another meal with her."

"Well, we must make the best of it," Helen replied philosophically. It was very hot, and they were indifferent to any amount of silence, so that they lay back in their chairs waiting for something to happen. The bell rang for luncheon, but there was no sound of movement in the house. Was there any news? Helen asked; anything in the papers? St. John shook his head. O yes, he had a letter from home, a letter from his mother, describing the suicide of the parlour-maid. She was called Susan Jane, and she came into the kitchen one afternoon, and said that she wanted cook to keep her money for her; she had twenty pounds in gold. Then she went out to buy herself a hat. She came in at half-past five and said that she had taken poison. They had only just time to get her into bed and call a doctor before she died.

"Well?" Helen enquired.

"There'll have to be an inquest," said St. John.

Why had she done it? He shrugged his shoulders. Why do people kill themselves? Why do the lower orders do any of the things they do do? Nobody knows. They sat in silence.

"The bell's rung fifteen minutes and they're not down," said Helen at length.

When they appeared, St. John explained why it had been necessary for him to come to luncheon. He imitated Evelyn's enthusiastic tone as she confronted him in the smoking-room. "She thinks there can be nothing *quite* so thrilling as mathematics, so I've lent her a large work in two volumes. It'll be interesting to see what she makes of it."

Rachel could now afford to laugh at him. She reminded him of Gibbon; she had the first volume somewhere still; if he were undertaking the education of Evelyn, that surely was the test; or she had heard that Burke, upon the American Rebellion—Evelyn ought to read them both simultaneously. When St. John had disposed of her argument and had satisfied his hunger, he proceeded to tell them that the hotel was seething with scandals, some of the most appalling kind, which had happened in their absence; he was indeed much given to the study of his kind.

"Evelyn M., for example—but that was told me in confidence."

"Nonsense," Terence interposed.

"You've heard about poor Sinclair, too?"

"Oh, yes, I've heard about Sinclair. He's retied to his mine with a revolver. He writes to Evelyn daily that he's thinking of committing suicide. I've assured her that he's never been so happy in his life, and, on the whole, she's inclined to agree with me."

"But then she's entangled herself with Perrott," St. John continued; "and I have reason to think, from something I saw in the passage, that everything isn't as it should be between Arthur and Susan. There's a young female lately arrived from Manchester. A very good thing if it were broken off, in my opinion. Their married life is something too horrible to contemplate. Oh, and I distinctly heard old Mrs. Paley rapping out the most fearful oaths as I passed her bedroom door. It's supposed that she tortures her maid in private—it's practically certain she does. One can tell it from the look in her eyes."

"When you're eighty and the gout tweezes you, you'll be swearing like a trooper," Terence remarked. "You'll be very fat, very testy, very disagreeable. Can't you imagine him—bald as a coot, with a pair of sponge-bag trousers, a little spotted tie, and a corporation?"

After a pause Hirst remarked that the worst infamy had still to be told. He addressed himself to Helen.

"They've hoofed out the prostitute. One night while we were away that old numskull Thornbury was doddering abut the passages very late. (Nobody seems to have asked him what *he* was up to.) He saw the Signora Lola Mendoza, as she calls herself, cross the passage in her nightgown. He communicated his suspicions next morning to Elliot, with the result that Rodriguez went to the woman and gave her twenty-four hours in which to clear out of the place. No one seems to have enquired into the truth of the story, or to have asked Thornbury and Elliot what business it was of theirs; they had it entirely their own way. I propose that we should all sign a Round Robin, go to Rodriguez in a body, and insist upon a full enquiry. Something's got to be done, don't you agree?"

Hewet remarked that there could be no doubt as to the lady's profession.

"Still," he added, "it's a great shame, poor woman; only I don't see what's to be done——"

"I quite agree with you, St. John," Helen burst out. "It's monstrous. The hypocritical smugness of the English makes my blood boil. A man who's made a fortune in trade as Mr. Thornbury has is bound to be twice as bad as any prostitute."

She respected St. John's morality, which she took far more seriously than any one else did, and now entered into a discussion with him as to the steps that were to be taken to enforce their peculiar view of what was right. The argument led to some profoundly gloomy statements of a general nature. Who were they, after all—what authority had they—what power against the mass of superstition and ignorance? It was the English, of course; there must be something wrong in the English blood. Directly you met an English person, of the middle classes, you were conscious of an indefinable sensation of loathing; directly you saw the brown crescent of houses above Dover, the same thing came over you. But unfortunately St. John added, you couldn't trust these foreigners——

They were interrupted by sounds of strife at the further end of the table. Rachel appealed to her aunt.

"Terence says we must go to tea with Mrs. Thornbury because she's been so kind, but I don't see it; in fact, I'd rather have my right hand sawn in pieces—just imagine! the eyes of all those women!"

"Fiddlesticks, Rachel," Terence replied. "Who wants to look at you? You're consumed with vanity! You're a monster of conceit! Surely, Helen, you ought to have taught her by this time that she's a person of no conceivable importance whatever—not beautiful, or

well dressed, or conspicuous for elegance or intellect, or deport-
ment. A more ordinary sight than you are," he concluded, "except
for the tear across your dress has never been seen. However, stay at
home if you want to. I'm going."

She appealed again to her aunt. It wasn't the being looked at, she
explained, but the things people were sure to say. The women in
particular. She liked women, but where emotion was concerned
they were as flies on a lump of sugar. They would be certain to ask
her questions. Evelyn M. would say: "Are you in love? Is it nice
being in love?" And Mrs. Thornbury—her eyes would go up and
down, up and down—she shuddered at the thought of it. Indeed,
the retirement of their life since their engagement had made her so
sensitive, that she was not exaggerating her case.

She found an ally in Helen, who proceeded to expound her
views of the human race, as she regarded with complacency the
pyramid of variegated fruits in the centre of the table. It wasn't that
they were cruel, or meant to hurt, or even stupid exactly; but she
had always found that the ordinary person had so little emotion in
his own life that the scent of it in the lives of others was like the
scent of blood in the nostrils of a bloodhound. Warming to the
theme, she continued:

"Directly anything happens—it may be a marriage, or a birth, or
a death—on the whole they prefer it to be death—every one wants
to see you. They insist upon seeing you. They've got nothing to say;
they don't care a rap for you; but you've got to go to lunch or to tea
or to dinner, and if you don't you're damned. It's the smell of
blood," she continued; "I don't blame 'em; only they shan't have
mine if I know it!"

She looked about her as if she had called up a legion of human
beings, all hostile and all disagreeable, who encircled the table,
with mouths gaping for blood, and made it appear a little island of
neutral country in the midst of the enemy's country.

Her words roused her husband, who had been muttering rhythmically to himself, surveying his guests and his food and his wife
with eyes that were now melancholy and now fierce, according to
the fortunes of the lady in his ballad. He cut Helen short with a

protest. He hated even the semblance of cynicism in women. "Nonsense, nonsense," he remarked abruptly.

Terence and Rachel glanced at each other across the table, which meant that when they were married they would not behave like that. The entrance of Ridley into the conversation had a strange effect. It became at once more formal and more polite. It would have been impossible to talk quite easily of anything that came into their heads, and to say the word prostitute as simply as any other word. The talk now turned upon literature and politics, and Ridley told stories of the distinguished people he had known in his youth. Such talk was of the nature of an art, and the personalities and informalities of the young were silenced. As they rose to go, Helen stopped for a moment, leaning her elbows on the table.

"You've all been sitting here," she said, "for almost an hour, and you haven't noticed my figs, or my flowers, or the way the light comes through, or anything. I haven't been listening, because I've been looking at you. You looked very beautiful; I wish you'd go on sitting for ever."

She led the way to the drawing-room, where she took up her embroidery, and began again to dissuade Terence from walking down to the hotel in this heat. But the more she dissuaded, the more he was determined to go. He became irritated and obstinate. There were moments when they almost disliked each other. He wanted other people; he wanted Rachel to see them with him. He suspected that Mrs. Ambrose would now try to dissuade her from going. He was annoyed by all this space and shade and beauty, and Hirst, recumbent, drooping a magazine from his wrist.

"I'm going," he repeated. "Rachel needn't come unless she wants to."

"If you go, Hewet, I wish you'd make enquiries about the prostitute," said Hirst. "Look here," he added, "I'll walk half the way with you."

Greatly to their surprise he raised himself, looked at his watch, and remarked that, as it was now half an hour since luncheon, the gastric juices had had sufficient time to secrete; he was trying a system, he explained, which involved short spells of exercise interspaced by longer intervals of rest.

"I shall be back at four," he remarked to Helen, "when I shall lie down on the sofa and relax all my muscles completely."

"So you're going, Rachel?" Helen asked. "You won't stay with me?"

She smiled, but she might have been sad.

Was she sad, or was she really laughing? Rachel could not tell, and she felt for the moment very uncomfortable between Helen and Terence. Then she turned away, saying merely that she would go with Terence, on condition that he did all the talking.

A narrow border of shadow ran along the road, which was broad enough for two, but not broad enough for three. St. John therefore dropped a little behind the pair, and the distance between them increased by degrees. Walking with a view to digestion, and with one eye upon his watch, he looked from time to time at the pair in front of him. They seemed to be so happy, so intimate, although they were walking side by side much as other people walk. They turned slightly toward each other now and then, and said something which he thought must be something very private. They were really disputing about Helen's character, and Terence was trying to explain why it was that she annoyed him so much sometimes. But St. John thought that they were saying things which they did not want him to hear, and was led to think of his own isolation. These people were happy, and in some ways he despised them for being made happy so simply, and in other ways he envied them. He was much more remarkable than they were, but he was not happy. People never liked him; he doubted sometimes whether even Helen liked him. To be simple, to be able to say simply what one felt, without the terrific self-consciousness which possessed him, and showed him his own face and words perpetually in a mirror, that would be worth almost any other gift, for it made one happy. Happiness, happiness, what was happiness? He was never happy. He saw too clearly the little vices and deceits and flaws of life and seeing them, it seemed to him honest to take notice of them. That was the reason, no doubt, why people generally disliked him, and complained that he was heartless and bitter. Certainly they never told him the things he wanted to be told, that he was nice and kind, and that they liked him. But it was true that half the sharp things that he said about them were said because he was unhappy or hurt himself. But he admitted that he had very seldom told any one that he cared for them, and when he had been demonstrative, he had generally regretted it afterwards. His feelings about Terence and Rachel were so complicated that he had never yet been able to bring himself to say that he was glad that they were going to be married. He saw their faults so clearly, and the inferior nature of a great deal of their feeling for each other, and he expected that their love would not last. He looked at them again, and very strangely, for he was so used to thinking that he very seldom saw anything, the look of them filled him with a simple emotion of affection in which there were some traces of pity also. What, after all, did people's faults matter in comparison with what was good in them? He resolved that he would now tell them what he felt. He quickened his pace and came up with them just as they reached the corner where the lane joined the main road. They stood still and began to laugh at him, and to ask him whether the gastric juices————but he stopped them and began to speak very quickly and stiffly.

"D'you remember the morning after the dance?" he demanded. "It was here we sat, and you talked nonsense, and Rachel made little heaps of stones. I, on the other hand, had the whole meaning of life revealed to me in a flash." He paused for a second, and drew his lips together in a tight little purse. "Love," he said. "It seems to me to explain everything. So, on the whole, I'm very glad that you two are going to be married." He then turned round abruptly, without looking at them, and walked back to the villa. He felt both exalted and ashamed of himself for having thus said what he felt. Probably they were laughing at him, probably they thought him a fool, and, after all, had he really said what he felt?

It was true that they laughed when he was gone; but the dispute about Helen which had become rather sharp, ceased, and they became peaceful and friendly.

CHAPTER XXIV

They reached the hotel rather early in the afternoon, so that most people were still lying down, or sitting speechless in their bedrooms, and Mrs. Thornbury, although she had asked them to tea, was nowhere to be seen. They sat down, therefore, in the shady hall, which was almost empty, and full of the light swishing sounds of air going to and fro in a large, empty space. Yes, this arm-chair was the same arm-chair in which Rachel had sat that afternoon when Evelyn came up, and this was the magazine she had been looking at, and this the very picture, a picture of New York by lamplight. How odd it seemed—nothing had changed.

By degrees a certain number of people began to come down the stairs and to pass through the hall, and in this dim light their figures possessed a sort of grace and beauty, although they were all unknown people. Sometimes they went straight through and out into the garden by the swing door, sometimes they stopped for a few minutes and bent over the tables and began turning over the newspapers. Terence and Rachel sat watching them through their half-closed eyelids—the Johnsons, the Parkers, the Baileys, the Simmons', the Lees, the Morleys, the Campbells, the Gardiners. Some were dressed in white flannels and were carrying racquets under their arms, some were short, some tall, some were only children, and some perhaps were servants, but they all had their standing, their reason for following each other through the hall, their money, their position, whatever it might be. Terence soon gave up looking at them, for he was tired; and, closing his eyes, he fell half asleep in his chair. Rachel watched the people for some time longer; she was fascinated by the certainty and the grace of their movements, and by the inevitable way in which they seemed to follow each other, and loiter and pass on and disappear. But after a time her thoughts wandered, and she began to think of the dance, which had been held in this room, only then the room itself looked quite different. Glancing round, she could hardly believe that it was the same room. It had looked so bare and so bright and formal on that night when they came into it out of the darkness; it had been filled, too, with little red, excited faces, always moving, and people so brightly dressed and so animated that they did not seem in the least like real people, nor did you feel that you could talk to them. And now the room was dim and quiet, and beautiful silent people passed through it, to whom you could go and say anything you liked. She felt herself amazingly secure as she sat in her arm-chair, and able to review not only the night of the dance, but the entire past, tenderly and humorously, as if she had been turning in a fog for a long time, and could now see exactly where she had turned. For the methods by which she had reached her present position, seemed to her very strange, and the strangest thing about them was that she had not known where they were leading her. That was the strange thing, that one did not know where one was going, or what one wanted, and followed blindly, suffering so much in secret, always unprepared and amazed and knowing nothing; but one thing led to another and by degrees something had formed itself out of nothing, and so one reached at last this calm, this quiet, this certainty, and it was this process that people called living. Perhaps, then, every one really knew as she knew now where they were going; and things formed themselves into a pattern not only for her, but for them, and in that pattern lay satisfaction and meaning. When she looked back she could see that a meaning of some kind was apparent in the lives of her aunts, and in the brief visit of the Dalloways whom she would never see again, and in the life of her father.

The sound of Terence, breathing deep in his slumber, confirmed her in her calm. She was not sleepy although she did not see anything very distinctly, but although the figures passing through the hall became vaguer and vaguer, she believed that they all knew exactly where they were going, and the sense of their certainty filled her with comfort. For the moment she was as detached and disinterested as if she had no longer any lot in life, and she thought that she could now accept anything that came to her without being perplexed by the form in which it appeared. What was there to frighten or to perplex in the prospect of life? Why should this insight ever again desert her? The world was in truth so large, so hospitable, and after all it was so simple. "Love," St. John had said, "that seems to explain it all." Yes, but it was not the love of man for woman, of Terence for Rachel. Although they sat so close together, they had ceased to be little separate bodies; they had ceased to struggle and desire one another. There seemed to be peace between them. It might be love, but it was not the love of man for woman.

Through her half-closed eyelids she watched Terence lying back in his chair, and she smiled as she saw how big his mouth was, and his chin so small, and his nose curved like a switch-back with a knob at the end. Naturally, looking like that he was lazy, and ambitious, and full of moods and faults. She remembered their quarrels, and in particular how they had been quarrelling about Helen that very afternoon, and she thought how often they would quarrel in the thirty, or forty, or fifty years in which they would be living in the same house together, catching trains together, and getting annoyed because they were so different. But all this was superficial, and had nothing to do with the life that went on beneath the eyes and the mouth and the chin, for that life was independent of her, and independent of everything else. So too, although she was going to marry him and to live with him for thirty, or forty, or fifty years, and to quarrel, and to be so close to him, she was independent of him; she was independent of everything else. Nevertheless, as St. John said, it was love that made her understand this, for she had never felt this independence, this calm, and this certainty until she fell in love with him, and perhaps this too was love. She wanted nothing else.

For perhaps two minutes Miss Allan had been standing at a little distance looking at the couple lying back so peacefully in their arm-chairs. She could not make up her mind whether to disturb them or not, and then, seeming to recollect something, she came across the hall. The sound of her approach woke Terence, who sat up and rubbed his eyes. He heard Miss Allan talking to Rachel.

"Well," she was saying, "this is very nice. It is very nice indeed. Getting engaged seems to be quite the fashion. It cannot often happen that two couples who have never seen each other before meet in the same hotel and decide to get married." Then she paused and smiled, and seemed to have nothing more to say, so that Terence rose and asked her whether it was true that she had finished her book. Some one had said that she had really finished it. Her face lit up; she turned to him with a livelier expression than usual.

"Yes, I think I can fairly say I have finished it," she said. "That is, omitting Swinburne—Beowulf to Browning—I rather like the two B's myself. Beowulf to Browning," she repeated, "I think that is the kind of title which might catch one's eye on a railway bookstall."

She was indeed very proud that she had finished her book, for no one knew what an amount of determination had gone to the making of it. Also she thought that it was a good piece of work, and, considering what anxiety she had been in about her brother while she wrote it, she could not resist telling them a little more about it.

"I must confess," she continued, "that if I had known how many classics there are in English literature, and how verbose the best of them contrive to be, I should never have undertaken the work. They only allow one seventy thousand words, you see."

"Only seventy thousand words!" Terence exclaimed.

"Yes, and one has to say something about everybody," Miss Allan added. "That is what I find so difficult, saying something different about everybody." Then she thought that she had said enough about herself, and she asked whether they had come down to join the tennis tournament. "The young people are very keen about it. It begins again in half an hour."

Her gaze rested benevolently upon them both, and, after a momentary pause, she remarked, looking at Rachel as if she had remembered something that would serve to keep her distinct from other people:

"You're the remarkable person who doesn't like ginger." But the kindness of the smile in her rather worn and courageous face made them feel that although she would scarcely remember them as individuals, she had laid upon them the burden of the new generation.

"And in that I quite agree with her," said a voice behind; Mrs. Thornbury had overheard the last few words about not liking ginger. "It's associated in my mind with a horrid old aunt of ours (poor thing, she suffered dreadfully, so it isn't fair to call her horrid) who used to give it us when we were small, and we never had the courage to tell her we didn't like it. We just had to put it out in the shrubbery—she had a big house near Bath."

They began moving slowly across the hall, when they were stopped by the impact of Evelyn, who dashed into them, as though in running downstairs to catch them her legs had got beyond her control.

"Well," she exclaimed, with her usual enthusiasm, seizing Rachel by the arm, "I call this splendid! I guessed it was going to happen from the very beginning! I saw you two were made for each other. Now you've just got to tell me all about it—when's it to be, where are you going to live—are you both tremendously happy?"

But the attention of the group was diverted to Mrs. Elliot, who was passing them with her eager but uncertain movement, carrying in her hands a plate and an empty hot-water bottle. She would have passed them, but Mrs. Thornbury went up and stopped her.

"Thank you, Hughling's better," she replied, in answer to Mrs. Thornbury's enquiry, "but he's not an easy patient. He wants to know what his temperature is, and if I tell him he gets anxious, and if I don't tell him he suspects. You know what men are when they're ill! And of course there are none of the proper appliances, and, though he seems very willing and anxious to help" (here she lowered her voice mysteriously), "one can't feel that Dr. Rodriguez is the same as a proper doctor. If you would come and see him, Mr. Hewet," she added, "I know it would cheer him up—lying there in bed all day—and the flies— But I must go and find Angelo—the food here—of course, with an invalid, one wants things particularly nice." And she hurried past them in search of the head waiter. The worry of nursing her husband had fixed a plaintive frown upon her forehead; she was pale and looked unhappy and more than usually inefficient, and her eyes wandered more vaguely than ever from point to point.

"Poor thing!" Mrs. Thornbury exclaimed. She told them that for some days Hughling Elliot had been ill, and the only doctor available was the brother of the proprietor, or so the proprietor said, whose right to the title of doctor was not above suspicion.

"I know how wretched it is to be ill in a hotel," Mrs. Thornbury remarked, once more leading the way with Rachel to the garden. "I spent six weeks on my honeymoon in having typhoid at Venice," she continued. "But even so, I look back upon them as some of the happiest weeks in my life. Ah, yes," she said, taking Rachel's arm, "you think yourself happy now, but it's nothing to the happiness that comes afterwards. And I assure you I could find it in my heart to envy you young people! You've a much better time than we had, I may tell you. When I look back upon it, I can hardly believe how things have changed. When we were engaged I wasn't allowed to go for walks with William alone—some one had always to be in the room with us—I really believe I had to show my parents all his letters!—though they were very fond of him too. Indeed, I may say they looked upon him as their own son. It amuses me," she continued, "to think how strict they were to us, when I see how they spoil their grandchildren!"

The table was laid under the tree again, and taking her place before the teacups, Mrs. Thornbury beckoned and nodded until she had collected quite a number of people, Susan and Arthur and Mr. Pepper, who were strolling about, waiting for the tournament to begin. A murmuring tree, a river brimming in the moonlight, Terence's words came back to Rachel as she sat drinking the tea and listening to the words which flowed on so lightly, so kindly, and with such silvery smoothness. This long life and all these children had left her very smooth; they seemed to have rubbed away the marks of individuality, and to have left only what was old and maternal.

"And the things you young people are going to see!" Mrs. Thornbury continued. She included them all in her forecast, she included them all in her maternity, although the party comprised William Pepper and Miss Allan, both of whom might have been supposed to have seen a fair share of the panorama. "When I see how the world has changed in my lifetime," she went on, "I can set no limit to what may happen in the next fifty years. Ah, no, Mr. Pepper, I don't agree with you in the least," she laughed, interrupting his gloomy remark about things going steadily from bad to worse. "I know I ought to feel that, but I don't, I'm afraid. They're going to be much better people than we were. Surely everything goes to prove that. All around me I see women, young women, women with household cares of every sort, going out and doing things that we should not have thought it possible to do."

Mr. Pepper thought her sentimental and irrational like all old women, but her manner of treating him as if he were a cross old baby baffled him and charmed him, and he could only reply to her with a curious grimace which was more a smile than a frown.

"And they remain women," Mrs. Thornbury added. "They give a great deal to their children."

As she said this she smiled slightly in the direction of Susan and Rachel. They did not like to be included in the same lot, but they both smiled a little self-consciously, and Arthur and Terence glanced at each other too. She made them feel that they were all in the same boat together, and they looked at the women they were going to marry and compared them. It was inexplicable how any one could wish to marry Rachel, incredible that any one should be ready to spend his life with Susan; but singular though the other's taste must be, they bore each other no ill-will on account of it; indeed, each liked the other rather the better for the eccentricity of his choice.

"I really must congratulate you," Susan remarked, as she leant across the table for the jam.

There seemed to be no foundation for St. John's gossip about Arthur and Susan. Sunburnt and vigorous they sat side by side, with their racquets across their knees, not saying much but smiling slightly all the time. Through the thin white clothes which they wore, it was possible to see the lines of their bodies and legs, the beautiful curves of their muscles, his leanness and her flesh, and it was natural to think of the firm-fleshed sturdy children that would be theirs. Their faces had too little shape in them to be beautiful, but they had clear eyes and an appearance of great health and power of endurance, for it seemed as if the blood would never cease to run in his veins, or to lie deeply and calmly in her cheeks. Their eyes at the present moment were brighter than usual, and wore the peculiar expression of pleasure and self-confidence which is seen in the eyes of athletes, for they had been playing tennis, and they were both first-rate at the game.

Evelyn had not spoken, but she had been looking from Susan to Rachel. Well—they had both made up their minds very easily, they had done in a very few weeks what it sometimes seemed to her that she would never be able to do. Although they were so different, she thought that she could see in each the same look of satisfaction and completion, the same calmness of manner, and the same slowness of movement. It was that slowness, that confidence, that content which she hated, she thought to herself. They moved so slowly because they were not single but double, and Susan was attached to Arthur, and Rachel to Terence, and for the sake of this one man they had renounced all other men, and movement, and the real things of life. Love was all very well, and those snug domestic houses, with the kitchen below and the nursery above, which were so secluded and self-contained, like little islands in the torrents of the world; but the real things were surely the things that happened, the causes, the wars, the ideals, which happened in the great world outside, and went on independently of these women, turning so quietly and beautifully towards the men. She looked at them sharply. Of course they were happy and content, but there must be better things than that. Surely one could get nearer to life, one could get more out of life, one could enjoy more and feel more than they would ever do. Rachel in particular looked so young— what could she know of life? She became restless, and getting up, crossed over to sit beside Rachel. She reminded her that she had promised to join her club.

"The bother is," she went on, "that I mayn't be able to start work seriously till October. I've just had a letter from a friend of mine whose brother is in business in Moscow. They want me to stay with them, and as they're in the thick of all the conspiracies and anar- chists, I've a good mind to stop on my way home. It sounds too thrilling." She wanted to make Rachel see how thrilling it was. "My friend knows a girl of fifteen who's been sent to Siberia for life merely because they caught her addressing a letter to an anarchist. And the letter wasn't from her, either. I'd give all I have in the world to help on a revolution against the Russian government, and it's bound to come."

She looked from Rachel to Terence. They were both a little touched by the sight of her remembering how lately they had been listening to evil words about her, and Terence asked her what her scheme was, and she explained that she was going to found a club— a club for doing things, really doing them. She became very ani- mated, as she talked on and on, for she professed herself certain that if once twenty people—no, ten would be enough if they were keen—set about doing things instead of talking about doing them, they could abolish almost every evil that exists. It was brains that were needed. If only people with brains—of course they would want a room, a nice room, in Bloomsbury preferably, where they could meet once a week....

As she talked Terence could see the traces of fading youth in her face, the lines that were being drawn by talk and excitement round her mouth and eyes, but he did not pity her; looking into those bright, rather hard, and very courageous eyes, he saw that she did not pity herself, or feel any desire to exchange her own life for the more refined and orderly lives of people like himself and St. John, although, as the years went by, the fight would become harder and harder. Perhaps, though, she would settle down; perhaps, after all, she would marry Perrott. While his mind was half occupied with what she was saying, he thought of her probable destiny, the light clouds of tobacco smoke serving to obscure his face from her eyes.

Terence smoked and Arthur smoked and Evelyn smoked, so that the air was full of the mist and fragrance of good tobacco. In the intervals when no one spoke, they heard far off the low murmur of the sea, as the waves quietly broke and spread the beach with a film of water, and withdrew to break again. The cool green light fell through the leaves of the tree, and there were soft crescents and diamonds of sunshine upon the plates and the table-cloth. Mrs. Thornbury, after watching them all for a time in silence, began to ask Rachel kindly questions—When did they all go back? Oh, they expected her father. She must want to see her father—there would be a great deal to tell him, and (she looked sympathetically at Terence) he would be so happy, she felt sure. Years ago, she continued, it might have been ten or even twenty years ago, she remembered meeting Mr. Vinrace at a party, and, being so much struck by his face, which was so unlike the ordinary face one sees at a party, that she had asked who he was, and she was told that it was Mr. Vinrace, and she had always remembered the name,—an uncommon name,—and he had a lady with him, a very sweet-looking woman, but it was one of those dreadful London crushes, where you don't talk,—you only look at each other,—and though she had shaken hands with Mr. Vinrace, she didn't think they had said anything. She sighed very slightly, remembering the past.

Then she turned to Mr. Pepper, who had become very dependent on her, so that he always chose a seat near her, and attended to what she was saying, although he did not often make any remark of his own.

"You who know everything, Mr. Pepper," she said, "tell us how did those wonderful French ladies manage their salons? Did we ever do anything of the same kind in England, or do you think that there is some reason why we cannot do it in England?"

Mr. Pepper was pleased to explain very accurately why there has never been an English salon. There were three reasons, and they were very good ones, he said. As for himself, when he went to go to a party, as one was sometimes obliged to, from a wish not to give offence—his niece, for example, had been married the other day— he walked into the middle of the room, said "Ha! ha!" as loud as ever he could, considered that he had done his duty, and walked away again. Mrs. Thornbury protested. She was going to give a party directly she got back, and they were all to be invited, and she should set people to watch Mr. Pepper, and if she heard that he had been caught saying "Ha! ha!" she would—she would do something very dreadful indeed to him. Arthur Venning suggested that what she must do was to rig up something in the nature of a surprise—a portrait, for example, of a nice old lady in a lace cap, concealing a bath of cold water, which at a signal could be sprung on Pepper's head; or they'd have a chair which shot him twenty feet high directly he sat on it.

Susan laughed. She had done her tea; she was feeling very well contented, partly because she had been playing tennis brilliantly, and then every one was so nice; she was beginning to find it so much easier to talk, and to hold her own even with quite clever people, for somehow clever people did not frighten her any more. Even Mr. Hirst, whom she had disliked when she first met him, really wasn't disagreeable; and, poor man, he always looked so ill; perhaps he was in love; perhaps he had been in love with Rachel—she really shouldn't wonder; or perhaps it was Evelyn—she was of course very attractive to men. Leaning forward, she went on with the conversation. She said that she thought that the reason why parties were so dull was mainly because gentlemen will not dress: even in London, she stated, it struck her very much how people don't think it necessary to dress in the evening, and of course if they don't dress in London they won't dress in the country. It was really quite a treat at Christmas-time when there were the Hunt balls, and the gentlemen wore nice red coats, but Arthur didn't care for dancing, so she supposed that they wouldn't go even to the ball in their little country town. She didn't think that people who were fond of one sport often cared for another, although her father was an exception. But then he was an exception in every way—such a gardener, and he knew all about birds and animals, and of course he was simply adored by all the old women in the village, and at the same time what he really liked best was a book. You always knew where to find him if he were wanted; he would be in his study with a book. Very likely it would be an old, old book, some fusty old thing that no one else would dream of reading. She used to tell him that he would have made a first-rate old bookworm if only he hadn't had a family of six to support, and six children, she added, charmingly confident of universal sympathy, didn't leave one much time for being a bookworm.

Still talking about her father, of whom she was very proud, she rose, for Arthur upon looking at his watch found that it was time they went back again to the tennis court. The others did not move.

"They're very happy!" said Mrs. Thornbury, looking benignantly after them. Rachel agreed; they seemed to be so certain of themselves; they seemed to know exactly what they wanted.

"D'you think they *are* happy?" Evelyn murmured to Terence in an undertone, and she hoped that he would say that he did not think them happy; but, instead, he said that they must go too—go home, for they were always being late for meals, and Mrs. Ambrose, who was very stern and particular, didn't like that. Evelyn laid hold of Rachel's skirt and protested. Why should they go? It was still early, and she had so many things to say to them.

"No," said Terence, "we must go, because we walk so slowly. We stop and look at things, and we talk."

"What d'you talk about?" Evelyn enquired, upon which he laughed and said that they talked about everything.

Mrs. Thornbury went with them to the gate, trailing very slowly and gracefully across the grass and the gravel, and talking all the time about flowers and birds. She told them that she had taken up the study of botany since her daughter married, and it was wonderful what a number of flowers there were which she had never seen, although she had lived in the country all her life and she was now seventy-two. It was a good thing to have some occupation which was quite independent of other people, she said, when one got old. But the odd thing was that one never felt old. She always felt that she was twenty-five, not a day more or a day less, but, of course, one couldn't expect other people to agree to that.

"It must be very wonderful to be twenty-five and not merely to imagine that you're twenty-five," she said, looking from one to the other with her smooth, bright glance. "It must be very wonderful, very wonderful indeed." She stood talking to them at the gate for a long time; she seemed reluctant that they should go.

Chapter XXV

The afternoon was very hot, so hot that the breaking of the waves on the shore sounded like the repeated sigh of some exhausted creature, and even on the terrace under an awning the bricks were hot, and the air danced perpetually over the short dry grass. The red flowers in the stone basins were drooping with the heat, and the white blossoms which had been so smooth and thick only a few weeks ago were now dry, and their edges were curled and yellow. Only the stiff and hostile plants of the south, whose fleshy leaves seemed to be grown upon spines, still remained standing upright and defied the determination of the sun to beat them down. It was too hot to talk, and it was not easy to find any book that would withstand the power of the sun. Many books had been tried and then let fall, and now Terence was reading Milton aloud, because he said the words of Milton[1] had substance and shape, so that it was not necessary to understand what he was saying; one could merely listen to his words; one could almost handle them.

There is a gentle nymph not far from hence,

he read,

> That with moist curb sways the smooth Severn stream.
> Sabrina is her name, a virgin pure;
> Whilom she was the daughter of Locrine,
> That had the sceptre from his father Brute.

The words, in spite of what Terence had said, seemed to be laden with meaning, and perhaps it was for this reason that it was painful to listen to them; they sounded strange; they meant different things from what they usually meant. Rachel at any rate could not keep her attention fixed upon them, but went off upon curious trains of thought suggested by words such as "curb" and "Locrine" and "Brute," which brought unpleasant sights before her eyes, independently of their meaning. Owing to the heat and the dancing air the garden too looked strange—the trees were either too near or too far, and her head almost certainly ached. She was not quite certain, and therefore she did not know, whether to tell Terence now, or to let him go on reading. She decided that she would wait until he came to the end of a stanza, and if by that time she had turned her head this way and that, and it ached in every position undoubtedly, she would say very calmly that her head ached.

> Sabrina fair,
>   Listen where thou art sitting
> Under the glassy, cool, translucent wave,
>   In twisted braids of lilies knitting
> The loose train of thy amber dropping hair,
> Listen for dear honour's sake,
> Goddess of the silver lake,
> Listen and save!

But her head ached; it ached whichever way she turned it.

She sat up and said as she had determined, "My head aches so that I shall go indoors."

He was half-way through the next verse, but he dropped the book instantly.

"Your head aches?" he repeated.

For a few moments they sat looking at one another in silence, holding each other's hands. During this time his sense of dismay and catastrophe were almost physically painful; all round him he seemed to hear the shiver of broken glass which, as it fell to earth, left him sitting in the open air. But at the end of two minutes, noticing that she was not sharing his dismay, but was only rather more languid and heavy-eyed than usual, he recovered, fetched Helen, and asked her to tell them what they had better do, for Rachel had a headache.

Mrs. Ambrose was not discomposed, but advised that she should go to bed, and added that she must expect her head to ache if she sat up to all hours and went out in the heat, but a few hours in bed would cure it completely. Terence was unreasonably reassured by her words, as he had been unreasonably depressed the moment before. Helen's sense seemed to have much in common with the ruthless good sense of nature, which avenged rashness by a headache, and, like nature's good sense, might be depended upon.

Rachel went to bed; she lay in the dark, it seemed to her, for a very long time, but at length, waking from a transparent kind of sleep, she saw the windows white in front of her, and recollected that some time before she had gone to bed with a headache, and that Helen had said it would be gone when she woke. She supposed, therefore, that she was now quite well again. At the same time the wall of her room was painfully white, and curved slightly, instead of being straight and flat. Turning her eyes to the window, she was not reassured by what she saw there. The movement of the blind as it filled with air and blew slowly out, drawing the cord with a little trailing sound along the floor, seemed to her terrifying, as if it were the movement of an animal in the room. She shut her eyes, and the pulse in her head beat so strongly that each thump seemed to tread upon a nerve, piercing her forehead with a little stab of pain. It might not be the same headache, but she certainly had a headache. She turned from side to side, in the hope that the coolness of the sheets would cure her, and that when she next opened her eyes to look the room would be as usual. After a considerable number of vain experiments, she resolved to put the matter beyond a doubt. She got out of bed and stood upright, holding on to the brass ball at the end of the bedstead. Ice-cold at first, it soon became as hot as the palm of her hand, and as the pains in her head and body and the instability of the floor proved that it would be far more intolerable to stand and walk than to lie in bed, she got into bed again; but though the change was refreshing at first, the discomfort of bed was soon as great as the discomfort of standing up. She accepted the idea that she would have to stay in bed all day long, and as she laid her head on the pillow, relinquished the happiness of the day.

When Helen came in an hour or two later, suddenly stopped her cheerful words, looked startled for a second and then unnaturally calm, the fact that she was ill was put beyond a doubt. It was confirmed when the whole household knew of it, when the song that some one was singing in the garden stopped suddenly, and when Maria, as she brought water, slipped past the bed with averted eyes. There was all the morning to get through, and then all the afternoon, and at intervals she made an effort to cross over into the ordinary world, but she found that her heat and discomfort had put a gulf between her world and the ordinary world which she could not bridge. At one point the door opened, and Helen came in with a little dark man who had—it was the chief thing she noticed about him—very hairy hands. She was drowsy and intolerably hot, and as he seemed shy and obsequious she scarcely troubled to answer him, although she understood that he was a doctor. At another point the door opened and Terence came in very gently, smiling too steadily, as she realised, for it to be natural. He sat down and talked to her, stroking her hands until it became irksome to her to lie any more in the same position and she turned round, and when she looked up again Helen was beside her and Terence had gone. It did not matter; she would see him to-morrow when things would be ordinary again. Her chief occupation during the day was to try to remember how the lines went:

> Under the glassy, cool, translucent wave,
>   In twisted braids of lilies knitting
> The loose train of thy amber dropping hair;

and the effort worried her because the adjectives persisted in getting into the wrong places.

The second day did not differ very much from the first day, except that her bed had become very important, and the world outside, when she tried to think of it, appeared distinctly further off. The glassy, cool, translucent wave was almost visible before her, curling up at the end of the bed, and as it was refreshingly cool she tried to keep her mind fixed upon it. Helen was here, and Helen was there all day long; sometimes she said that it was lunchtime, and sometimes that it was tea-time; but by the next day all landmarks were obliterated, and the outer world was so far away that the different sounds, such as the sounds of people passing on the stairs, and the sounds of people moving overhead, could only be ascribed to their cause by a great effort of memory. The recollection of what she had felt, or of what she had been doing and thinking three days before, had faded entirely. On the other hand, every object in the room, and the bed itself, and her own body with its various limbs and their different sensations were more and more important each day. She was completely cut off, and unable to communicate with the rest of the world, isolated alone with her body.

Hours and hours would pass thus, without getting any further through the morning, or again a few minutes would lead from broad daylight to the depths of the night. One evening when the room appeared very dim, either because it was evening or because the blinds were drawn, Helen said to her, "Some one is going to sit here to-night. You won't mind?"

Opening her eyes, Rachel saw not only Helen but a nurse in spectacles, whose face vaguely recalled something that she had once seen. She had seen her in the chapel.

"Nurse McInnis," said Helen, and the nurse smiled steadily as they all did, and said that she did not find many people who were frightened of her. After waiting for a moment they both disappeared, and having turned on her pillow Rachel woke to find herself in the midst of one of those interminable nights which do not end at twelve, but go on into the double figures—thirteen, fourteen, and so on until they reach the twenties, and then the thirties, and then the forties. She realised that there is nothing to prevent nights from doing this if they choose. At a great distance an elderly woman sat with her head bent down; Rachel raised herself slightly and saw with dismay that she was playing cards by the light of a candle which stood in the hollow of a newspaper. The sight had something inexplicably sinister about it, and she was terrified and cried out, upon which the woman laid down her cards and came across the room, shading the candle with her hands. Coming nearer and nearer across the great space of the room, she stood at last above Rachel's head and said, "Not asleep? Let me make you comfortable."

She put down the candle and began to arrange the bedclothes. It struck Rachel that a woman who sat playing cards in a cavern all night long would have very cold hands, and she shrunk from the touch of them.

"Why, there's a toe all the way down there!" the woman said, proceeding to tuck in the bedclothes. Rachel did not realise that the toe was hers.

"You must try and lie still," she proceeded, "because if you lie still you will be less hot, and if you toss about you will make yourself more hot, and we don't want you to be any hotter than you are." She stood looking down upon Rachel for an enormous length of time.

"And the quieter you lie the sooner you will be well," she repeated.

Rachel kept her eyes fixed upon the peaked shadow on the ceiling, and all her energy was concentrated upon the desire that this shadow should move. But the shadow and the woman seemed to be eternally fixed above her. She shut her eyes. When she opened them again several more hours had passed, but the night still lasted interminably. The woman was still playing cards, only she sat now in a tunnel under a river, and the light stood in a little archway in the wall above her. She cried "Terence!" and the peaked shadow again moved across the ceiling, as the woman with an enormous slow movement rose, and they both stood still above her.

"It's just as difficult to keep you in bed as it was to keep Mr. Forrest in bed," the woman said, "and he was such a tall gentleman."

In order to get rid of this terrible stationary sight Rachel again shut her eyes, and found herself walking through a tunnel under the Thames, where there were little deformed women sitting in archways playing cards, while the bricks of which the wall was made oozed with damp, which collected into drops and slid down the wall. But the little old women became Helen and Nurse McInnis after a time, standing in the window together whispering, whispering incessantly.

Meanwhile outside her room the sounds, the movements, and the lives of the other people in the house went on in the ordinary light of the sun, throughout the usual succession of hours. When, on the first day of her illness, it became clear that she would not be absolutely well, for her temperature was very high, until Friday, that day being Tuesday, Terence was filled with resentment, not against her, but against the force outside them which was separating them. He counted up the number of days that would almost certainly be spoilt for them. He realised, with an odd mixture of pleasure and annoyance, that, for the first time in his life, he was so dependent upon another person that his happiness was in her keeping. The days were completely wasted upon trifling, immaterial things, for after three weeks of such intimacy and intensity all the usual occupations were unbearably flat and beside the point. The least intolerable occupation was to talk to St. John about Rachel's illness, and to discuss every symptom and its meaning, and, when this subject was exhausted, to discuss illness of all kinds, and what caused them, and what cured them.

Twice every day he went in to sit with Rachel, and twice every day the same thing happened. On going into her room, which was not very dark, where the music was lying about as usual, and her books and letters, his spirits rose instantly. When he saw her he felt completely reassured. She did not look very ill. Sitting by her side he would tell her what he had been doing, using his natural voice to speak to her, only a few tones lower down than usual; but by the time he had sat there for five minutes he was plunged in the deepest gloom. She was not the same; he could not bring them back to their old relationship; but although he knew that it was foolish he could not prevent himself from endeavouring to bring her back, to make her remember, and when this failed he was in despair. He always concluded as he left her room that it was worse to see her than not to see her, but by degrees, as the day wore on, the desire to see her returned and became almost too great to be borne.

On Thursday morning when Terence went into her room he felt the usual increase of confidence. She turned round and made an effort to remember certain facts from the world that was so many millions of miles away.

"You have come up from the hotel?" she asked.

"No; I'm staying here for the present," he said. "We've just had luncheon," he continued, "and the mail has come in. There's a bundle of letters for you—letters from England."

Instead of saying, as he meant her to say, that she wished to see them, she said nothing for some time.

"You see, there they go, rolling off the edge of the hill," she said suddenly.

"Rolling, Rachel? What do you see rolling? There's nothing rolling."

"The old woman with the knife," she replied, not speaking to Terence in particular, and looking past him. As she appeared to be looking at a vase on the shelf opposite, he rose and took it down.

"Now they can't roll any more," he said cheerfully. Nevertheless she lay gazing at the same spot, and paid him no further attention although he spoke to her. He became so profoundly wretched that he could not endure to sit with her, but wandered about until he found St. John, who was reading *The Times* in the verandah. He laid it aside patiently, and heard all that Terence had to say about delirium. He was very patient with Terence. He treated him like a child.

By Friday it could not be denied that the illness was no longer an attack that would pass off in a day or two; it was a real illness that required a good deal of organisation, and engrossed the attention of at least five people, but there was no reason to be anxious. Instead of lasting five days it was going to last ten days. Rodriguez was understood to say that there were well-known varieties of this illness. Rodriguez appeared to think that they were treating the illness with undue anxiety. His visits were always marked by the same show of confidence, and in his interviews with Terence he always waved aside his anxious and minute questions with a kind of flourish which seemed to indicate that they were all taking it much too seriously. He seemed curiously unwilling to sit down.

"A high temperature," he said, looking furtively about the room, and appearing to be more interested in the furniture and in Helen's embroidery than in anything else. "In this climate you must expect a high temperature. You need not be alarmed by that. It is the pulse we go by" (he tapped his own hairy wrist), "and the pulse continues excellent."

Thereupon he bowed and slipped out. The interview was conducted laboriously upon both sides in French, and this, together with the fact that he was optimistic, and that Terence respected the medical profession from hearsay, made him less critical than he would have been had he encountered the doctor in any other capacity. Unconsciously he took Rodriguez' side against Helen, who seemed to have taken an unreasonable prejudice against him.

When Saturday came it was evident that the hours of the day must be more strictly organised than they had been. St. John offered his services; he said that he had nothing to do, and that he might as well spend the day at the villa if he could be of use. As if they were starting on a difficult expedition together, they parcelled out their duties between them, writing out an elaborate scheme of hours upon a large sheet of paper which was pinned to the drawing-room door. Their distance from the town, and the difficulty of procuring rare things with unknown names from the most unexpected places, made it necessary to think very carefully, and they found it unexpectedly difficult to do the simple but practical things that were required of them, as if they, being very tall, were asked to stoop down and arrange minute grains of sand in a pattern on the ground.

It was St. John's duty to fetch what was needed from the town, so that Terence would sit all through the long hot hours alone in the drawing-room, near the open door, listening for any movement upstairs, or call from Helen. He always forgot to pull down the blinds, so that he sat in bright sunshine, which worried him without his knowing what was the cause of it. The room was terribly stiff and uncomfortable. There were hats in the chairs, and medicine bottles among the books. He tried to read, but good books were too good, and bad books were too bad, and the only thing he could tolerate was the newspaper, which with its news of London, and the movements of real people who were giving dinner-parties and making speeches, seemed to give a little background of reality to what was otherwise mere nightmare. Then, just as his attention was fixed on the print, a soft call would come from Helen, or Mrs. Chailey would bring in something which was wanted upstairs, and he would run up very quietly in his socks, and put the jug on the little table which stood crowded with jugs and cups outside the bedroom door; or if he could catch Helen for a moment he would ask, "How is she?"

"Rather restless.... On the whole, quieter, I think."

The answer would be one or the other.

As usual she seemed to reserve something which she did not say, and Terence was conscious that they disagreed, and, without saying it aloud, were arguing against each other. But she was too hurried and preoccupied to talk.

The strain of listening, and the effort of making practical arrangements and seeing that things worked smoothly, absorbed all Terence's power. Involved in this long dreary nightmare, he did not attempt to think what it amounted to. Rachel was ill; that was all; he must see that there was medicine and milk, and that things were ready when they were wanted. Thought had ceased; life itself had come to a stand-still. Sunday was rather worse than Saturday had been, simply because the strain was a little greater every day, although nothing else had changed. The separate feelings of pleasure, interest, and pain, which combine to make up the ordinary day, were merged in one long-drawn sensation of sordid misery and profound boredom. He had never been so bored since he was shut up in the nursery alone as a child. The vision of Rachel as she was now, confused and heedless, had almost obliterated the vision of her as she had been once long ago; he could hardly believe that they had ever been happy, or engaged to be married, for what were feelings, what was there to be felt? Confusion covered every sight and person, and he seemed to see St. John, Ridley, and the stray people who came up now and then from the hotel to enquire, through a mist; the only people who were not hidden in this mist were Helen and Rodriguez, because they could tell him something definite about Rachel.

Nevertheless the day followed the usual forms. At certain hours they went into the dining-room, and when they sat round the table they talked about indifferent things. St. John generally made it his business to start the talk and to keep it from dying out.

"I've discovered the way to get Sancho past the white house," said St. John on Sunday at luncheon. "You crackle a piece of paper in his ear, then he bolts for about a hundred yards, but he goes on quite well after that."

"Yes, but he wants corn. You should see that he has corn."

"I don't think much of the stuff they give him; and Angelo seems a dirty little rascal."

There was then a long silence. Ridley murmured a few lines of poetry under his breath, and remarked, as if to conceal the fact that he had done so, "Very hot to-day."

"Two degrees higher than it was yesterday," said St. John. "I wonder where these nuts come from," he observed, taking a nut out of the plate, turning it over in his fingers, and looking at it curiously.

"London, I should think," said Terence, looking at the nut too.

"A competent man of business could make a fortune here in no time," St. John continued. "I suppose the heat does something funny to people's brains. Even the English go a little queer. Anyhow they're hopeless people to deal with. They kept me three-quarters of an hour waiting at the chemist's this morning, for no reason whatever."

There was another long pause. Then Ridley enquired, "Rodriguez seems satisfied?"

"Quite," said Terence with decision. "It's just got to run its course." Whereupon Ridley heaved a deep sigh. He was genuinely sorry for every one, but at the same time he missed Helen considerably, and was a little aggrieved by the constant presence of the two young men.

They moved back into the drawing-room.

"Look here, Hirst," said Terence, "there's nothing to be done for two hours." He consulted the sheet pinned to the door. "You go and lie down. I'll wait here. Chailey sits with Rachel while Helen has her luncheon."

It was asking a good deal of Hirst to tell him to go without waiting for a sight of Helen. These little glimpses of Helen were the only respites from strain and boredom, and very often they seemed to make up for the discomfort of the day, although she might not have anything to tell them. However, as they were on an expedition together, he had made up his mind to obey.

Helen was very late in coming down. She looked like a person who has been sitting for a long time in the dark. She was pale and thinner, and the expression of her eyes was harassed but determined. She ate her luncheon quickly, and seemed indifferent to what she was doing. She brushed aside Terence's enquiries, and at last, as if he had not spoken, she looked at him with a slight frown and said:

"We can't go on like this, Terence. Either you've got to find another doctor, or you must tell Rodriguez to stop coming, and I'll manage for myself. It's no use for him to say that Rachel's better; she's not better; she's worse."

Terence suffered a terrific shock, like that which he had suffered when Rachel said, "My head aches." He stilled it by reflecting that Helen was overwrought, and he was upheld in this opinion by his obstinate sense that she was opposed to him in the argument.

"Do you think she's in danger?" he asked.

"No one can go on being as ill as that day after day—" Helen replied. She looked at him, and spoke as if she felt some indignation with somebody.

"Very well, I'll talk to Rodriguez this afternoon," he replied.

Helen went upstairs at once.

Nothing now could assuage Terence's anxiety. He could not read, nor could he sit still, and his sense of security was shaken, in spite of the fact that he was determined that Helen was exaggerating, and that Rachel was not very ill. But he wanted a third person to confirm him in his belief.

Directly Rodriguez came down he demanded, "Well, how is she? Do you think her worse?"

"There is no reason for anxiety, I tell you—none," Rodriguez replied in his execrable French, smiling uneasily, and making little movements all the time as if to get away.

Hewet stood firmly between him and the door. He was determined to see for himself what kind of man he was. His confidence in the man vanished as he looked at him and saw his insignificance, his dirty appearance, his shiftiness, and his unintelligent, hairy face. It was strange that he had never seen this before.

"You won't object, of course, if we ask you to consult another doctor?" he continued.

At this the little man became openly incensed.

"Ah!" he cried. "You have not confidence in me? You object to my treatment? You wish me to give up the case?"

"Not at all," Terence replied, "but in serious illness of this kind—"

Rodriguez shrugged his shoulders.

"It is not serious, I assure you. You are over-anxious. The young lady is not seriously ill, and I am a doctor. The lady of course is frightened," he sneered. "I understand that perfectly."

"The name and address of the doctor is———?" Terence continued.

"There is no other doctor," Rodriguez replied sullenly. "Every one has confidence in me. Look! I will show you."

He took out a packet of old letters and began turning them over as if in search of one that would confute Terence's suspicions. As he searched, he began to tell a story about an English lord who had trusted him—a great English lord, whose name he had, unfortunately, forgotten.

"There is no other doctor in the place," he concluded, still turning over the letters.

"Never mind," said Terence shortly. "I will make enquiries for myself." Rodriguez put the letters back in his pocket.

"Very well," he remarked. "I have no objection."

He lifted his eyebrows, shrugged his shoulders, as if to repeat that they took the illness much too seriously and that there was no other doctor, and slipped out, leaving behind him an impression that he was conscious that he was distrusted, and that his malice was aroused.

After this Terence could no longer stay downstairs. He went up, knocked at Rachel's door, and asked Helen whether he might see her for a few minutes. He had not seen her yesterday. She made no objection, and went and sat at a table in the window.

Terence sat down by the bedside. Rachel's face was changed. She looked as though she were entirely concentrated upon the effort of keeping alive. Her lips were drawn, and her cheeks were sunken and flushed, though without colour. Her eyes were not entirely shut, the lower half of the white part showing, not as if she saw, but as if they remained open because she was too much exhausted to close them. She opened them completely when he kissed her. But she only saw an old woman slicing a man's head off with a knife.

"There it falls!" she murmured. She then turned to Terence and asked him anxiously some question about a man with mules, which he could not understand. "Why doesn't he come? Why doesn't he come?" she repeated. He was appalled to think of the dirty little man downstairs in connection with illness like this, and turned instinctively to Helen, but she was doing something at a table in the window, and did not seem to realise how great the shock to him must be. He rose to go, for he could not endure to listen any longer; his heart beat quickly and painfully with anger and misery. As he passed Helen she asked him in the same weary, unnatural, but determined voice to fetch her more ice, and to have the jug outside filled with fresh milk.

When he had done these errands he went to find Hirst. Exhausted and very hot, St. John had fallen asleep on a bed, but Terence woke him without scruple.

"Helen thinks she's worse," he said. "There's no doubt she's frightfully ill. Rodriguez is useless. We must get another doctor."

"But there is no other doctor," said Hirst drowsily, sitting up and rubbing his eyes.

"Don't be a damned fool!" Terence exclaimed. "Of course there's another doctor, and, if there isn't, you've got to find one. It ought to have been done days ago. I'm going down to saddle the horse." He could not stay still in one place.

In less than ten minutes St. John was riding to the town in the scorching heat in search of a doctor, his orders being to find one and bring him back if he had to be fetched in a special train.

"We ought to have done it days ago," Hewet repeated angrily.

When he went back into the drawing-room he found that Mrs. Flushing was there, standing very erect in the middle of the room, having arrived, as people did in these days, by the kitchen or through the garden unannounced.

"She's better?" Mrs. Flushing enquired abruptly; they did not attempt to shake hands.

"No," said Terence. "If anything, they think she's worse."

Mrs. Flushing seemed to consider for a moment or two, looking straight at Terence all the time.

"Let me tell you," she said, speaking in nervous jerks, "it's always about the seventh day one begins to get anxious. I daresay you've been sittin' here worryin' by yourself. You think she's bad, but any one comin' with a fresh eye would see she was better. Mr. Elliot's had fever; he's all right now," she threw out. "It wasn't anythin' she caught on the expedition. What's it matter—a few days' fever? My brother had fever for twenty-six days once. And in a week or two he was up and about. We gave him nothin' but milk and arrowroot————"

Here Mrs. Chailey came in with a message.

"I'm wanted upstairs," said Terence.

"You see—she'll be better," Mrs. Flushing jerked out as he left the room. Her anxiety to persuade Terence was very great, and when he left her without saying anything she felt dissatisfied and restless; she did not like to stay, but she could not bear to go. She wandered from room to room looking for some one to talk to, but all the rooms were empty.

Terence went upstairs, stood inside the door to take Helen's directions, looked over at Rachel, but did not attempt to speak to her. She appeared vaguely conscious of his presence, but it seemed to disturb her, and she turned, so that she lay with her back to him.

For six days indeed she had been oblivious of the world outside, because it needed all her attention to follow the hot, red, quick sights which passed incessantly before her eyes. She knew that it was of enormous importance that she should attend to these sights and grasp their meaning, but she was always being just too late to hear or see something which would explain it all. For this reason, the faces,—Helen's face, the nurse's, Terence's, the doctor's,— which occasionally forced themselves very close to her, were worrying because they distracted her attention and she might miss the clue. However, on the fourth afternoon she was suddenly unable to keep Helen's face distinct from the sights themselves; her lips widened as she bent down over the bed, and she began to gabble unintelligibly like the rest. The sights were all concerned in some plot, some adventure, some escape. The nature of what they were doing changed incessantly, although there was always a reason behind it, which she must endeavour to grasp. Now they were among trees and savages, now they were on the sea; now they were on the tops of high towers; now they jumped; now they flew. But just as the crisis was about to happen, something invariably slipped in her brain, so that the whole effort had to begin over again. The heat was suffocating. At last the faces went further away; she fell into a deep pool of sticky water, which eventually closed over her head. She saw nothing and heard nothing but a faint booming sound, which was the sound of the sea rolling over her head. While all her tormentors thought that she was dead, she was not dead, but curled up at the bottom of the sea. There she lay, sometimes seeing darkness, sometimes light, while every now and then some one turned her over at the bottom of the sea.

———

After St. John had spent some hours in the heat of the sun wrangling with evasive and very garrulous natives, he extracted the information that there was a doctor, a French doctor, who was at present away on a holiday in the hills. It was quite impossible, so they said, to find him. With his experience of the country, St. John thought it unlikely that a telegram would either be sent or received; but having reduced the distance of the hill town, in which he was staying, from a hundred miles to thirty miles, and having hired a carriage and horses, he started at once to fetch the doctor himself. He succeeded in finding him, and eventually forced the unwilling man to leave his young wife and return forthwith. They reached the villa at midday on Tuesday.

Terence came out to receive them, and St. John was struck by the fact that he had grown perceptibly thinner in the interval; he was white too; his eyes looked strange. But the curt speech and the sulky masterful manner of Dr. Lesage impressed them both favourably, although at the same time it was obvious that he was very much annoyed at the whole affair. Coming downstairs he gave his directions emphatically, but it never occurred to him to give an opinion either because of the presence of Rodriguez who was now obsequious as well as malicious, or because he took it for granted that they knew already what was to be known.

"Of course," he said with a shrug of his shoulders, when Terence asked him, "Is she very ill?"

They were both conscious of a certain sense of relief when Dr. Lesage was gone, leaving explicit directions, and promising another visit in a few hours' time; but, unfortunately, the rise of their spirits led them to talk more than usual, and in talking they quarrelled. They quarrelled about a road, the Portsmouth Road. St. John said that it is macadamised where it passes Hindhead, and Terence knew as well as he knew his own name that it is not macadamised at that point. In the course of the argument they said some very sharp things to each other, and the rest of the dinner was eaten in silence, save for an occasional half-stifled reflection from Ridley.

When it grew dark and the lamps were brought in, Terence felt unable to control his irritation any longer. St. John went to bed in a state of complete exhaustion, bidding Terence good-night with rather more affection than usual because of their quarrel, and Ridley retired to his books. Left alone, Terence walked up and down the room; he stood at the open window.

The lights were coming out one after another in the town beneath, and it was very peaceful and cool in the garden, so that he stepped out on to the terrace. As he stood there in the darkness, able only to see the shapes of trees through the fine grey light, he was overcome by a desire to escape, to have done with this suffering, to forget that Rachel was ill. He allowed himself to lapse into forgetfulness of everything. As if a wind that had been raging incessantly suddenly fell asleep, the fret and strain and anxiety which had been pressing on him passed away. He seemed to stand in an unvexed space of air, on a little island by himself; he was free and immune from pain. It did not matter whether Rachel was well or ill; it did not matter whether they were apart or together; nothing mattered—nothing mattered. The waves beat on the shore far away, and the soft wind passed through the branches of the trees, seeming to encircle him with peace and security, with dark and nothingness. Surely the world of strife and fret and anxiety was not the real world, but this was the real world, the world that lay beneath the superficial world, so that, whatever happened, one was secure. The quiet and peace seemed to lap his body in a fine cool sheet, soothing every nerve; his mind seemed once more to expand, and become natural.

But when he had stood thus for a time a noise in the house roused him; he turned instinctively and went into the drawing-room. The sight of the lamp-lit room brought back so abruptly all that he had forgotten that he stood for a moment unable to move. He remembered everything, the hour, the minute even, what point they had reached, and what was to come. He cursed himself for making believe for a minute that things were different from what they are. The night was now harder to face than ever.

Unable to stay in the empty drawing-room, he wandered out and sat on the stairs half-way up to Rachel's room. He longed for some one to talk to, but Hirst was asleep, and Ridley was asleep; there was no sound in Rachel's room. The only sound in the house was the sound of Chailey moving in the kitchen. At last there was a rustling on the stairs overhead, and Nurse McInnis came down fastening the links in her cuffs, in preparation for the night's watch. Terence rose and stopped her. He had scarcely spoken to her, but it was possible that she might confirm him in the belief which still persisted in his own mind that Rachel was not seriously ill. He told her in a whisper that Dr. Lesage had been and what he had said.

"Now, Nurse," he whispered, "please tell me your opinion. Do you consider that she is very seriously ill? Is she in any danger?"

"The doctor has said——" she began.

"Yes, but I want your opinion. You have had experience of many cases like this?"

"I could not tell you more than Dr. Lesage, Mr. Hewet," she replied cautiously, as though her words might be used against her. "The case is serious, but you may feel quite certain that we are doing all we can for Miss Vinrace." She spoke with some professional self-approbation. But she realised perhaps that she did not satisfy the young man, who still blocked her way, for she shifted her feet slightly upon the stair and looked out of the window where they could see the moon over the sea.

"If you ask me," she began in a curiously stealthy tone, "I never like May for my patients."

"May?" Terence repeated.

"It may be a fancy, but I don't like to see anybody fall ill in May," she continued. "Things seem to go wrong in May. Perhaps it's the moon. They say the moon affects the brain, don't they, Sir?"

He looked at her but he could not answer her; like all the others, when one looked at her she seemed to shrivel beneath one's eyes and become worthless, malicious, and untrustworthy.

She slipped past him and disappeared.

Though he went to his room he was unable even to take his clothes off. For a long time he paced up and down, and then leaning out of the window gazed at the earth which lay so dark against the paler blue of the sky. With a mixture of fear and loathing he looked at the slim black cypress trees which were still visible in the garden, and heard the unfamiliar creaking and grating sounds which show that the earth is still hot. All these sights and sounds appeared sinister and full of hostility and foreboding; together with the natives and the nurse and the doctor and the terrible force of the illness itself they seemed to be in conspiracy against him. They seemed to join together in their effort to extract the greatest possible amount of suffering from him. He could not get used to his pain, it was a revelation to him. He had never realised before that underneath every action, underneath the life of every day, pain lies, quiescent, but ready to devour; he seemed to be able to see suffering, as if it were a fire, curling up over the edges of all action, eating away the lives of men and women. He thought for the first time with understanding of words which had before seemed to him empty: the struggle of life; the hardness of life. Now he knew for himself that life is hard and full of suffering. He looked at the scattered lights in the town beneath, and thought of Arthur and Susan, or Evelyn and Perrott venturing out unwittingly, and by their happiness laying themselves open to suffering such as this. How did they dare to love each other, he wondered; how had he himself dared to live as he had lived, rapidly and carelessly, passing from one thing to another, loving Rachel as he had loved her? Never again would he feel secure; he would never believe in the stability of life, or forget what depths of pain lie beneath small happiness and feelings of content and safety. It seemed to him as he looked back that their happiness had never been so great as his pain was now. There had always been something imperfect in their happiness, something they had wanted and had not been able to get. It had been fragmentary and incomplete, because they were so young and had not known what they were doing.

The light of his candle flickered over the boughs of a tree outside the window, and as the branch swayed in the darkness there came before his mind a picture of all the world that lay outside his window; he thought of the immense river and the immense forest, the vast stretches of dry earth and the plains of the sea that encircled the earth; from the sea the sky rose steep and enormous, and the air washed profoundly between the sky and the sea. How vast and dark it must be to-night, lying exposed to the wind; and in all this great space it was curious to think how few the towns were, and how like little rings of light they were, scattered here and there among the swelling uncultivated folds of the world. And in those towns were little men and women, tiny men and women. Oh, it was absurd, when one thought of it, to sit here in a little room suffering and caring. What did anything matter? Rachel, a tiny creature, lay ill beneath him, and here in his little room he suffered on her account. The nearness of their bodies in this vast universe, and the minuteness of their bodies, seemed to him absurd and laughable. Nothing mattered, he repeated; they had no power, no hope. He leant on the window-sill, thinking, until he almost forgot the time and the place. Nevertheless, although he was convinced that it was absurd and laughable, and that they were small and hopeless, he never lost the sense that these thoughts somehow formed part of a life which he and Rachel would live together.

Owing perhaps to the change of doctor, Rachel appeared to be rather better next day. Terribly pale and worn though Helen looked, there was a slight lifting of the cloud which had hung all these days in her eyes.

"She talked to me," she said voluntarily. "She asked me what day of the week it was, like herself."

Then suddenly, without any warning or any apparent reason, the tears formed in her eyes and rolled steadily down her cheeks. She cried with scarcely any attempt at movement of her features, and without any attempt to stop herself, as if she did not know that she was crying. In spite of the relief which her words gave him, Terence was dismayed by the sight; had everything given way? Were there no limits to the power of this illness? Would everything go down before it? Helen had always seemed to him strong and determined, and now she was like a child. He took her in his arms, and she clung to him like a child, crying softly and quietly upon his shoulder. Then she roused herself and wiped her tears away; it was silly to behave like that, she said; very silly, she repeated, when there could be no doubt that Rachel was better. She asked Terence to forgive her for her folly. She stopped at the door and came back and kissed him without saying anything.

On this day indeed Rachel was conscious of what went on round her. She had come to the surface of the dark, sticky pool, and a wave seemed to bear her up and down with it; she had ceased to have any will of her own; she lay on the top of the wave conscious of some pain, but chiefly of weakness. The wave was replaced by the side of a mountain. Her body became a drift of melting snow, above which her knees rose in huge peaked mountains of bare bone. It was true that she saw Helen and saw her room, but everything had become very pale and semi-transparent. Sometimes she could see through the wall in front of her. Sometimes when Helen went away she seemed to go so far that Rachel's eyes could hardly follow her. The room also had an odd power of expanding, and though she pushed her voice out as far as possible until sometimes it became a bird and flew away, she thought it doubtful whether it ever reached the person she was talking to. There were immense intervals or chasms, for things still had the power to appear visibly before her, between one moment and the next; it sometimes took an hour for Helen to raise her arm, pausing long between each jerky movement, and pour out medicine. Helen's form stooping to raise her in bed appeared of gigantic size, and came down upon her like the ceiling falling. But for long spaces of time she would merely lie conscious of her body floating on the top of the bed and her mind driven to some remote corner of her body, or escaped and gone flitting round the room. All sights were something of an effort, but the sight of Terence was the greatest effort, because he forced her to join mind to body in the desire to remember something. She did not wish to remember; it troubled her when people tried to disturb her loneliness; she wished to be alone. She wished for nothing else in the world.

Although she had cried, Terence observed Helen's greater hopefulness with something like triumph; in the argument between them she had made the first sign of admitting herself in the wrong. He waited for Dr. Lesage to come down that afternoon with considerable anxiety, but with the same certainty at the back of his mind that he would in time force them all to admit that they were in the wrong.

As usual, Dr. Lesage was sulky in his manner and very short in his answers. To Terence's demand, "She seems to be better?" he replied, looking at him in an odd way, "She has a chance of life."

The door shut and Terence walked across to the window. He leant his forehead against the pane.

"Rachel," he repeated to himself. "She has a chance of life. Rachel."

How could they say these things of Rachel? Had any one yesterday seriously believed that Rachel was dying? They had been engaged for four weeks. A fortnight ago she had been perfectly well. What could fourteen days have done to bring her from that state to this? To realise what they meant by saying that she had a chance of life was beyond him, knowing as he did that they were engaged. He turned, still enveloped in the same dreary mist, and walked towards the door. Suddenly he saw it all. He saw the room and the garden, and the trees moving in the air, they could go on without her; she could die. For the first time since she fell ill he remembered exactly what she looked like and the way in which they cared for each other. The intense happiness of feeling her close to him mingled with a more intense anxiety than he had felt yet. He could not let her die; he could not live without her. But after a momentary struggle, the curtain fell again, and he saw nothing and felt nothing clearly. It was all going on—going on still, in the same way as before. Save for a physical pain when his heart beat, and the fact that his fingers were icy cold, he did not realise that he was anxious about anything. Within his mind he seemed to feel nothing about Rachel or about any one or anything in the world. He went on giving orders, arranging with Mrs. Chailey, writing out lists, and every now and then he went upstairs and put something quietly on the table outside Rachel's door. That night Dr. Lesage seemed to be less sulky than usual. He stayed voluntarily for a few moments, and, addressing St. John and Terence equally, as if he did not remember which of them was engaged to the young lady, said, "I consider that her condition to-night is very grave."

Neither of them went to bed or suggested that the other should go to bed. They sat in the drawing-room playing picquet with the door open. St. John made up a bed upon the sofa, and when it was ready insisted that Terence should lie upon it. They began to quarrel as to who should lie on the sofa and who should lie upon a couple of chairs covered with rugs. St. John forced Terence at last to lie down upon the sofa.

"Don't be a fool, Terence," he said. "You'll only get ill if you don't sleep."

"Old fellow," he began, as Terence still refused, and stopped abruptly, fearing sentimentality; he found that he was on the verge of tears.

He began to say what he had long been wanting to say, that he was sorry for Terence, that he cared for him, that he cared for Rachel. Did she know how much he cared for her—had she said anything, asked perhaps? He was very anxious to say this, but he refrained, thinking that it was a selfish question after all, and what was the use of bothering Terence to talk about such things? He was already half asleep. But St. John could not sleep at once. If only, he thought to himself, as he lay in the darkness, something would happen—if only this strain would come to an end. He did not mind what happened, so long as the succession of these hard and dreary days was broken; he did not mind if she died. He felt himself disloyal in not minding it, but it seemed to him that he had no feelings left.

All night long there was no call or movement, except the opening and shutting of the bedroom door once. By degrees the light returned into the untidy room. At six the servants began to move; at seven they crept downstairs into the kitchen; and half an hour later the day began again.

Nevertheless it was not the same as the days that had gone before, although it would have been hard to say in what the difference consisted. Perhaps it was that they seemed to be waiting for something. There were certainly fewer things to be done than usual. People drifted through the drawing-room—Mr. Flushing, Mr. and Mrs. Thornbury. They spoke very apologetically in low tones, refusing to sit down, but remaining for a considerable time standing up, although the only thing they had to say was, "Is there anything we can do?" and there was nothing they could do.

Feeling oddly detached from it all, Terence remembered how Helen had said that whenever anything happened to you this was how people behaved. Was she right, or was she wrong? He was too little interested to frame an opinion of his own. He put things away in his mind, as if one of these days he would think about them, but not now. The mist of unreality had deepened and deepened until it had produced a feeling of numbness all over his body. Was it his body? Were those really his own hands?

This morning also for the first time Ridley found it impossible to sit alone in his room. He was very uncomfortable downstairs, and, as he did not know what was going on, constantly in the way; but he would not leave the drawing-room. Too restless to read, and having nothing to do, he began to pace up and down reciting poetry in an undertone. Occupied in various ways—now in undoing parcels, now in uncorking bottles, now in writing directions, the sound of Ridley's song and the beat of his pacing worked into the minds of Terence and St. John all the morning as a half comprehended refrain.

> They wrestled up, they wrestled down,
>   They wrestled sore and still:
> The fiend who blinds the eyes of men,
>   That night he had his will.
> Like stags full spent, among the bent
>   They dropped awhile to rest[2]——

"Oh, it's intolerable!" Hirst exclaimed, and then checked himself, as if it were a breach of their agreement. Again and again Terence would creep half-way up the stairs in case he might be able to glean news of Rachel. But the only news now was of a very fragmentary kind; she had drunk something; she had slept a little; she seemed quieter. In the same way, Dr. Lesage confined himself to talking about details, save once when he volunteered the information that he had just been called in to ascertain, by severing a vein in the wrist, that an old lady of eighty-five was really dead. She had a horror of being buried alive.

"It is a horror," he remarked, "that we generally find in the very old, and seldom in the young." They both expressed their interest in what he told them; it seemed to them very strange. Another strange thing about the day was that the luncheon was forgotten by all of them until it was late in the afternoon, and then Mrs. Chailey waited on them, and looked strange too, because she wore a stiff print dress, and her sleeves were rolled up above her elbows. She seemed as oblivious of her appearance, however, as if she had been called out of her bed by a midnight alarm of fire, and she had forgotten, too, her reserve and her composure; she talked to them quite familiarly as if she had nursed them and held them naked on her knee. She assured them over and over again that it was their duty to eat.

The afternoon, being thus shortened, passed more quickly than they expected. Once Mrs. Flushing opened the door, but on seeing them shut it again quickly; once Helen came down to fetch something, but she stopped as she left the room to look at a letter addressed to her. She stood for a moment turning it over, and the extraordinary and mournful beauty of her attitude struck Terence in the way things struck him now—as something to be put away in his mind and to be thought about afterwards. They scarcely spoke, the argument between them seeming to be suspended or forgotten.

Now that the afternoon sun had left the front of the house, Ridley paced up and down the terrace repeating stanzas of a long poem, in a subdued but suddenly sonorous voice. Fragments of the poem were wafted in at the open window as he passed and repassed.

> Peor and Baalim
> Forsake their Temples dim,
>   With that twice batter'd God of Palestine
> And mooned Astaroth[3]—

The sounds of these words were strangely discomforting to both the young men, but they had to be borne. As the evening drew on and the red light of the sunset glittered far away on the sea, the same sense of desperation attacked both Terence and St. John at the thought that the day was nearly over, and that another night was at hand. The appearance of one light after another in the town beneath them produced in Hirst a repetition of his terrible and disgusting desire to break down and sob. Then the lamps were brought in by Chailey. She explained that Maria, in opening a bottle, had been so foolish as to cut her arm badly, but she had bound it up; it was unfortunate when there was so much work to be done. Chailey herself limped because of the rheumatism in her feet, but it appeared to her mere waste of time to take any notice of the unruly flesh of servants. The evening went on. Dr. Lesage arrived unexpectedly, and stayed upstairs a very long time. He came down once and drank a cup of coffee.

"She is very ill," he said in answer to Ridley's question. All the annoyance had by this time left his manner, he was grave and formal, but at the same time it was full of consideration, which had not marked it before. He went upstairs again. The three men sat together in the drawing-room. Ridley was quite quiet now, and his attention seemed to be thoroughly awakened. Save for little half-voluntary movements and exclamations that were stifled at once, they waited in complete silence. It seemed as if they were at last brought together face to face with something definite.

It was nearly eleven o'clock when Dr. Lesage again appeared in the room. He approached them very slowly, and did not speak at once. He looked first at St. John and then at Terence, and said to Terence, "Mr. Hewet, I think you should go upstairs now."

Terence rose immediately, leaving the others seated with Dr. Lesage standing motionless between them.

Chailey was in the passage outside, repeating over and over again, "It's wicked—it's wicked."

Terence paid her no attention; he heard what she was saying, but it conveyed no meaning to his mind. All the way upstairs he kept saying to himself, "This has not happened to me. It is not possible that this has happened to me."

He looked curiously at his own hand on the banisters. The stairs were very steep, and it seemed to take him a long time to surmount them. Instead of feeling keenly, as he knew that he ought to feel, he felt nothing at all. When he opened the door he saw Helen sitting by the bedside. There were shaded lights on the table, and the room, though it seemed to be full of a great many things, was very tidy. There was a faint and not unpleasant smell of disinfectants. Helen rose and gave up her chair to him in silence. As they passed each other their eyes met in a peculiar level glance, he wondered at the extraordinary clearness of her eyes, and at the deep calm and sadness that dwelt in them. He sat down by the bedside, and a moment afterwards heard the door shut gently behind her. He was alone with Rachel, and a faint reflection of the sense of relief that they used to feel when they were left alone possessed him. He looked at her. He expected to find some terrible change in her, but there was none. She looked indeed very thin, and, as far as he could see, very tired, but she was the same as she had always been. Moreover, she saw him and knew him. She smiled at him and said, "Hullo, Terence."

The curtain which had been drawn between them for so long vanished immediately.

"Well, Rachel," he replied in his usual voice, upon which she opened her eyes quite widely and smiled with her familiar smile. He kissed her and took her hand.

"It's been wretched without you," he said.

She still looked at him and smiled, but soon a slight look of fatigue or perplexity came into her eyes and she shut them again.

"But when we're together we're perfectly happy," he said. He continued to hold her hand.

The light being dim, it was impossible to see any change in her face. An immense feeling of peace came over Terence, so that he had no wish to move or to speak. The terrible torture and unreality of the last days were over, and he had come out now into perfect certainty and peace. His mind began to work naturally again and with great ease. The longer he sat there the more profoundly was he conscious of the peace invading every corner of his soul. Once he held his breath and listened acutely; she was still breathing; he went on thinking for some time; they seemed to be thinking together; he seemed to be Rachel as well as himself; and then he listened again; no, she had ceased to breathe. So much the better—this was death. It was nothing; it was to cease to breathe. It was happiness, it was perfect happiness. They had now what they had always wanted to have, the union which had been impossible while they lived. Unconscious whether he thought the words or spoke them aloud, he said, "No two people have ever been so happy as we have been. No one has ever loved as we have loved."

It seemed to him that their complete union and happiness filled the room with rings eddying more and more widely. He had no wish in the world left unfulfilled. They possessed what could never be taken from them.

He was not conscious that any one had come into the room, but later, moments later, or hours later perhaps, he felt an arm behind him. The arms were round him. He did not want to have arms round him, and the mysterious whispering voices annoyed him. He laid Rachel's hand, which was now cold, upon the counterpane, and rose from his chair, and walked across to the window. The windows were uncurtained, and showed the moon, and a long silver pathway upon the surface of the waves.

"Why," he said, in his ordinary tone of voice, "look at the moon. There's a halo round the moon. We shall have rain to-morrow."

The arms, whether they were the arms of man or of woman, were round him again; they were pushing him gently towards the door. He turned of his own accord and walked steadily in advance of the arms, conscious of a little amusement at the strange way in which people behaved merely because some one was dead. He would go if they wished it, but nothing they could do would disturb his happiness.

As he saw the passage outside the room, and the table with the cups and the plates, it suddenly came over him that here was a world in which he would never see Rachel again.

"Rachel! Rachel!" he shrieked, trying to rush back to her. But they prevented him, and pushed him down the passage and into a bedroom far from her room. Downstairs they could hear the thud of his feet on the floor, as he struggled to break free; and twice they heard him shout, "Rachel, Rachel!"

CHAPTER XXVI

For two or three hours longer the moon poured its light through the empty air. Unbroken by clouds it fell straightly, and lay almost like a chill white frost over the sea and the earth. During these hours the silence was not broken, and the only movement was caused by the movement of trees and branches which stirred slightly, and then the shadows that lay across the white spaces of the land moved too. In this profound silence one sound only was audible, the sound of a slight but continuous breathing which never ceased, although it never rose and never fell. It continued after the birds had begun to flutter from branch to branch, and could be heard behind the first thin notes of their voices. It continued all through the hours when the east whitened, and grew red, and a faint blue tinged the sky, but when the sun rose it ceased, and gave place to other sounds.

The first sounds that were heard were little inarticulate cries, the cries, it seemed, of children or of the very poor, of people who were very weak or in pain. But when the sun was above the horizon, the air which had been thin and pale grew every moment richer and warmer, and the sounds of life became bolder and more full of courage and authority. By degrees the smoke began to ascend in wavering breaths over the houses, and these slowly thickened, until they were as round and straight as columns, and instead of striking upon pale white blinds, the sun shone upon dark windows, beyond which there was depth and space.

The sun had been up for many hours, and the great dome of air was warmed through and glittering with thin gold threads of sunlight, before any one moved in the hotel. White and massive it stood in the early light, half asleep with its blinds down.

At about half-past nine Miss Allan came very slowly into the hall, and walked very slowly to the table where the morning papers were laid, but she did not put out her hand to take one; she stood still, thinking, with her head a little sunk upon her shoulders. She looked curiously old, and from the way in which she stood, a little hunched together and very massive, you could see what she would be like when she was really old, how she would sit day after day in her chair looking placidly in front of her. Other people began to come into the room, and to pass her, but she did not speak to any of them or even look at them, and as last, as if it were necessary to do something, she sat down in a chair, and looked quietly and fixedly in front of her. She felt very old this morning, and useless too, as if her life had been a failure, as if it had been hard and laborious to no purpose. She did not want to go on living, and yet she knew that she would. She was so strong that she would live to be a very old woman. She would probably live to be eighty, and as she was now fifty, that left thirty years more for her to live. She turned her hands over and over in her lap and looked at them curiously; her old hands, that had done so much work for her. There did not seem to be much point in it all; one went on, of course one went on.... She looked up to see Mrs. Thornbury standing beside her, with lines drawn upon her forehead, and her lips parted as if she were about to ask a question.

Miss Allan anticipated her.

"Yes," she said. "She died this morning, very early, about three o'clock."

Mrs. Thornbury made a little exclamation, drew her lips together, and the tears rose in her eyes. Through them she looked at the hall which was now laid with great breadths of sunlight, and at the careless, casual groups of people who were standing beside the solid arm-chairs and tables. They looked to her unreal, or as people look who remain unconscious that some great explosion is about to take place beside them. But there was no explosion, and they went on standing by the chairs and the tables. Mrs. Thornbury no longer saw them, but, penetrating through them as though they were without substance, she saw the house, the people in the house, the room, the bed in the room, and the figure of the dead lying still in the dark beneath the sheets. She could almost see the dead. She could almost hear the voices of the mourners.

"They expected it?" she asked at length.

Miss Allan could only shake her head.

"I know nothing," she replied, "except what Mrs. Flushing's maid told me. She died early this morning."

The two women looked at each other with a quiet significant gaze, and then, feeling oddly dazed, and seeking she did not know exactly what, Mrs. Thornbury went slowly upstairs and walked quietly along the passages, touching the wall with her fingers as if to guide herself. Housemaids were passing briskly from room to room, but Mrs. Thornbury avoided them; she hardly saw them; they seemed to her to be in another world. She did not even look up directly when Evelyn stopped her. It was evident that Evelyn had been lately in tears, and when she looked at Mrs. Thornbury she began to cry again. Together they drew into the hollow of a window, and stood there in silence. Broken words formed themselves at last among Evelyn's sobs. "It was wicked," she sobbed, "it was cruel—they were so happy."

Mrs. Thornbury patted her on the shoulder.

"It seems hard—very hard," she said. She paused and looked out over the slope of the hill at the Ambroses' villa; the windows were blazing in the sun, and she thought how the soul of the dead had passed from those windows. Something had passed from the world. It seemed to her strangely empty.

"And yet the older one grows," she continued, her eyes regaining more than their usual brightness, "the more certain one becomes that there is a reason. How could one go on if there were no reason?" she asked.

She asked the question of some one, but she did not ask it of Evelyn. Evelyn's sobs were becoming quieter. "There must be a reason," she said. "It can't only be an accident. For it was an accident—it need never have happened."

Mrs. Thornbury sighed deeply.

"But we must not let ourselves think of that," she added, "and let us hope that they don't either. Whatever they had done it might have been the same. These terrible illnesses———"

"There's no reason—I don't believe there's any reason at all!" Evelyn broke out, pulling the blind down and letting it fly back with a little snap.

"Why should these things happen? Why should people suffer? I honestly believe," she went on, lowering her voice slightly, "that Rachel's in Heaven, but Terence...."

"What's the good of it all?" she demanded.

Mrs. Thornbury shook her head slightly but made no reply, and pressing Evelyn's hand she went on down the passage. Impelled by a strong desire to hear something, although she did not know exactly what there was to hear, she was making her way to the Flushings' room. As she opened their door she felt that she had interrupted some argument between husband and wife. Mrs. Flushing was sitting with her back to the light, and Mr. Flushing was standing near her, arguing and trying to persuade her of something.

"Ah, here is Mrs. Thornbury," he began with some relief in his voice. "You have heard, of course. My wife feels that she was in some way responsible. She urged poor Miss Vinrace to come on the expedition. I'm sure you will agree with me that it is most unreasonable to feel that. We don't even know—in fact I think it most unlikely—that she caught her illness there. These diseases—Besides, she was set on going. She would have gone whether you asked her or not, Alice."

"Don't, Wilfrid," said Mrs. Flushing, neither moving nor taking her eyes off the spot on the floor upon which they rested. "What's the use of talking? What's the use———?" She ceased.

"I was coming to ask you," said Mrs. Thornbury, addressing Wilfrid, for it was useless to speak to his wife. "Is there anything you think that one could do? Has the father arrived? Could one go and see?"

The strongest wish in her being at this moment was to be able to do something for the unhappy people—to see them—to assure them—to help them. It was dreadful to be so far away from them. But Mr. Flushing shook his head; he did not think that now—later perhaps one might be able to help. Here Mrs. Flushing rose stiffly, turned her back to them, and walked to the dressing-room opposite. As she walked, they could see her breast slowly rise and slowly fall. But her grief was silent. She shut the door behind her.

When she was alone by herself she clenched her fists together, and began beating the back of a chair with them. She was like a wounded animal. She hated death; she was furious, outraged, indignant with death, as if it were a living creature. She refused to relinquish her friends to death. She would not submit to dark and nothingness. She began to pace up and down, clenching her hands, and making no attempt to stop the quick tears which raced down her cheeks. She sat still at last, but she did not submit. She looked stubborn and strong when she had ceased to cry.

———

In the next room, meanwhile, Wilfrid was talking to Mrs. Thornbury with greater freedom now that his wife was not sitting there.

"That's the worst of these places," he said. "People will behave as though they were in England, and they're not. I've no doubt myself that Miss Vinrace caught the infection up at the villa itself. She probably ran risks a dozen times a day that might have given her the illness. It's absurd to say she caught it with us."

If he had not been sincerely sorry for them he would have been annoyed. "Pepper tells me," he continued, "that he left the house because he thought them so careless. He says they never washed their vegetables properly. Poor people! It's a fearful price to pay. But it's only what I've seen over and over again—people seem to forget that these things happen, and then they do happen, and they're surprised."

Mrs. Thornbury agreed with him that they had been very care-less, and that there was no reason whatever to think that she had caught the fever on the expedition; and after talking about other things for a short time, she left him and went sadly along the passage to her own room. There must be some reason why such things happen, she thought to herself, as she shut the door. Only at first it was not easy to understand what it was. It seemed so strange—so unbelievable. Why, only three weeks ago—only a fortnight ago, she had seen Rachel; when she shut her eyes she could almost see her now, the quiet, shy girl who was going to be married. She thought of all that she would have missed had she died at Rachel's age, the children, the married life, the unimaginable depths and miracles that seemed to her, as she looked back, to have lain about her, day after day, and year after year. The stunned feeling, which had been making it difficult for her to think, gradually gave way to a feeling of the opposite nature; she thought very quickly and very clearly, and, looking back over all her experiences, tried to fit them into a kind of order. There was undoubtedly much suffering, much struggling, but, on the whole, surely there was a balance of happiness—surely order did prevail. Nor were the deaths of young people really the saddest things in life—they were saved so much; they kept so much. The dead—she called to mind those who had died early, accidentally—were beautiful; she often dreamt of the dead. And in time Terence himself would come to feel—— She got up and began to wander restlessly about the room.

For an old woman of her age she was very restless, and for one of her clear, quick mind she was unusually perplexed. She could not settle to anything, so that she was relieved when the door opened. She went up to her husband, took him in her arms, and kissed him with unusual intensity, and then as they sat down together she began to pat him and question him as if he were a baby, an old, tired, querulous baby. She did not tell him about Miss Vinrace's death, for that would only disturb him, and he was put out already. She tried to discover why he was uneasy. Politics again? What were those horrid people doing? She spent the whole morning in discussing politics with her husband, and by degrees she became deeply interested in what they were saying. But every now and then what she was saying seemed to her oddly empty of meaning.

At luncheon it was remarked by several people that the visitors at the hotel were beginning to leave; there were fewer every day. There were only forty people at luncheon, instead of the sixty that there had been. So old Mrs. Paley computed, gazing about her with her faded eyes, as she took her seat at her own table in the window. Her party generally consisted of Mr. Perrott as well as Arthur and Susan, and to-day Evelyn was lunching with them also.

She was unusually subdued. Having noticed that her eyes were red, and guessing the reason, the others took pains to keep up an elaborate conversation between themselves. She suffered it to go on for a few minutes, leaning both elbows on the table, and leaving her soup untouched, when she exclaimed suddenly, "I don't know how you feel, but I can simply think of nothing else!"

The gentlemen murmured sympathetically, and looked grave.

Susan replied, "Yes—isn't it perfectly awful? When you think what a nice girl she was—only just engaged, and this need never have happened—it seems too tragic." She looked at Arthur as though he might be able to help her with something more suitable.

"Hard lines," said Arthur briefly. "But it was a foolish thing to do—to go up that river." He shook his head. "They should have known better. You can't expect Englishwomen to stand roughing it as the natives do who've been acclimatised. I'd half a mind to warn them at tea that day when it was being discussed. But it's no good saying these sort of things—it only puts people's backs up—it never makes any difference."

Old Mrs. Paley, hitherto contented with her soup, here intimated, by raising one hand to her ear, that she wished to know what was being said.

"You heard, Aunt Emma, that poor Miss Vinrace has died of the fever," Susan informed her gently. She could not speak of death loudly or even in her usual voice, so that Mrs. Paley did not catch a word. Arthur came to the rescue.

"Miss Vinrace is dead," he said very distinctly.

Mrs. Paley merely bent a little towards him and asked, "Eh?"

"Miss Vinrace is dead," he repeated. It was only by stiffening all the muscles round his mouth that he could prevent himself from bursting into laughter, and force himself to repeat for the third time, "Miss Vinrace.... She's dead."

Let alone the difficulty of hearing the exact words, facts that were outside her daily experience took some time to reach Mrs. Paley's consciousness. A weight seemed to rest upon her brain, impeding, though not damaging, its action. She sat vague-eyed for at least a minute before she realised what Arthur meant.

"Dead?" she said vaguely. "Miss Vinrace dead? Dear me ... that's very sad. But I don't at the moment remember which she was. We seem to have made so many new acquaintances here." She looked at Susan for help. "A tall dark girl, who just missed being handsome, with a high colour?"

"No," Susan interposed. "She was——" then she gave it up in despair. There was no use in explaining that Mrs. Paley was thinking of the wrong person.

"She ought not to have died," Mrs. Paley continued. "She looked so strong. But people will drink the water. I can never make out why. It seems such a simple thing to tell them to put a bottle of Seltzer water in your bedroom. That's all the precaution I've ever taken, and I've been in every part of the world, I may say—Italy a dozen times over.... But young people always think they know better, and then they pay the penalty. Poor thing—I am very sorry for her." But the difficulty of peering into a dish of potatoes and helping herself engrossed her attention.

Arthur and Susan both secretly hoped that the subject was now disposed of, for there seemed to them something unpleasant in this discussion. But Evelyn was not ready to let it drop. Why would people never talk about the things that mattered?

"I don't believe you care a bit!" she said, turning savagely upon Mr. Perrott, who had sat all this time in silence.

"I? Oh, yes, I do," he answered awkwardly, but with obvious sincerity. Evelyn's questions made him too feel uncomfortable.

"It seems so inexplicable," Evelyn continued. "Death, I mean. Why should she be dead, and not you or I? It was only a fortnight ago that she was here with the rest of us. What d'you believe?" she demanded of Mr. Perrott. "D'you believe that things go on, that she's still somewhere—or d'you think it's simply a game—we crumble up to nothing when we die? I'm positive Rachel's not dead."

Mr. Perrott would have said almost anything that Evelyn wanted him to say, but to assert that he believed in the immortality of the soul was not in his power. He sat silent, more deeply wrinkled than usual, crumbling his bread.

Lest Evelyn should next ask him what he believed, Arthur, after making a pause equivalent to a full stop, started a completely different topic.

"Supposing," he said, "a man were to write and tell you that he wanted five pounds because he had known your grandfather, what would you do? It was this way. My grandfather——"

"Invented a stove," said Evelyn. "I know all about that. We had one in the conservatory to keep the plants warm."

"Didn't know I was so famous," said Arthur. "Well," he continued, determined at all costs to spin his story out at length, "the old chap, being about the second best inventor of his day, and a capable lawyer too, died, as they always do, without making a will. Now Fielding, his clerk, with how much justice I don't know, always claimed that he meant to do something for him. The poor old boy's come down in the world through trying inventions on his own account, lives in Penge over a tobacconist's shop. I've been to see him there. The question is—must I stump up or not? What does the abstract spirit of justice require, Perrott? Remember, I didn't benefit under my grandfather's will, and I've no way of testing the truth of the story."

"I don't know much about the abstract spirit of justice," said Susan, smiling complacently at the others, "but I'm certain of one thing—he'll get his five pounds!"

As Mr. Perrott proceeded to deliver an opinion, and Evelyn insisted that he was much too stingy, like all lawyers, thinking of the letter and not of the spirit, while Mrs. Paley required to be kept informed between the courses as to what they were all saying, the

luncheon passed with no interval of silence, and Arthur congratulated himself upon the tact with which the discussion had been
smoothed over.

As they left the room it happened that Mrs. Paley's wheeled
chair ran into the Elliots, who were coming through the door, as she
was going out. Brought thus to a standstill for a moment, Arthur
and Susan congratulated Hughling Elliot upon his convalescence,—
he was down, cadaverous enough, for the first time,—and Mr. Perrott took occasion to say a few words in private to Evelyn.

"Would there be any chance of seeing you this afternoon, about
three-thirty say? I shall be in the garden, by the fountain."

The block dissolved before Evelyn answered. But as she left them
in the hall, she looked at him brightly and said, "Half-past three, did
you say? That'll suit me."

She ran upstairs with the feeling of spiritual exaltation and
quickened life which the prospect of an emotional scene always
aroused in her. That Mr. Perrott was again about to propose to her,
she had no doubt, and she was aware that on this occasion she ought
to be prepared with a definite answer, for she was going away in
three days' time. But she could not bring her mind to bear upon the
question. To come to a decision was very difficult to her, because
she had a natural dislike of anything final and done with; she liked
to go on and on—always on and on. She was leaving, and, therefore,
she occupied herself in laying her clothes out side by side upon the
bed. She observed that some were very shabby. She took the photograph of her father and mother, and, before she laid it away in her
box, she held it for a minute in her hand. Rachel had looked at it.
Suddenly the keen feeling of some one's personality, which things
that they have owned or handled sometimes preserves, overcame
her; she felt Rachel in the room with her; it was as if she were on a
ship at sea, and the life of the day was as unreal as the land in the
distance. But by degrees the feeling of Rachel's presence passed
away, and she could no longer realise her, for she had scarcely
known her. But this momentary sensation left her depressed and fa-
tigued. What had she done with her life? What future was there before her? What was make-believe, and what was real? Were these

proposals and intimacies and adventures real, or was the contentment which she had seen on the faces of Susan and Rachel more real than anything she had ever felt?

She made herself ready to go downstairs, absentmindedly, but her fingers were so well trained that they did the work of preparing her almost of their own accord. When she was actually on the way downstairs, the blood began to circle through her body of its own accord too, for her mind felt very dull.

Mr. Perrott was waiting for her. Indeed, he had gone straight into the garden after luncheon, and had been walking up and down the path for more than half an hour, in a state of acute suspense.

"I'm late as usual!" she exclaimed, as she caught sight of him. "Well, you must forgive me; I had to pack up.... My word! It looks stormy! And that's a new steamer in the bay, isn't it?"

She looked at the bay, in which a steamer was just dropping anchor, the smoke still hanging about it, while a swift black shudder ran through the waves. "One's quite forgotten what rain looks like," she added.

But Mr. Perrott paid no attention to the steamer or to the weather.

"Miss Murgatroyd," he began with his usual formality, "I asked you to come here from a very selfish motive, I fear. I do not think you need to be assured once more of my feelings; but, as you are leaving so soon, I felt that I could not let you go without asking you to tell me—have I any reason to hope that you will ever come to care for me?"

He was very pale, and seemed unable to say any more.

The little gush of vitality which had come into Evelyn as she ran downstairs had left her, and she felt herself impotent. There was nothing for her to say; she felt nothing. Now that he was actually asking her, in his elderly gentle words, to marry him, she felt less for him than she had ever felt before.

"Let's sit down and talk it over," she said rather unsteadily.

Mr. Perrott followed her to a curved green seat under a tree. They looked at the fountain in front of them, which had long ceased to play. Evelyn kept looking at the fountain instead of thinking of what she was saying; the fountain without any water seemed to be the type of her own being.

"Of course I care for you," she began, rushing her words out in a hurry; "I should be a brute if I didn't. I think you're quite one of the nicest people I've ever known, and one of the finest too. But I wish ... I wish you didn't care for me in that way. Are you sure you do?" For the moment she honestly desired that he should say no.

"Quite sure," said Mr. Perrott.

"You see, I'm not as simple as most women," Evelyn continued. "I think I want more. I don't know exactly what I feel."

He sat by her, watching her and refraining from speech.

"I sometimes think I haven't got it in me to care very much for one person only. Some one else would make you a better wife. I can imagine you very happy with some one else."

"If you think that there is any chance that you will come to care for me, I am quite content to wait," said Mr. Perrott.

"Well—there's no hurry, is there?" said Evelyn. "Suppose I thought it over and wrote and told you when I get back? I'm going to Moscow; I'll write from Moscow."

But Mr. Perrott persisted.

"You cannot give me any kind of idea. I do not ask for a date ... that would be most unreasonable." He paused, looking down at the gravel path.

As she did not immediately answer, he went on.

"I know very well that I am not—that I have not much to offer you either in myself or in my circumstances. And I forget; it cannot seem the miracle to you that it does to me. Until I met you I had gone on in my own quiet way—we are both very quiet people, my sister and I—quite content with my lot. My friendship with Arthur was the most important thing in my life. Now that I know you, all that has changed. You seem to put such a spirit into everything. Life seems to hold so many possibilities that I had never dreamt of."

"That's splendid!" Evelyn exclaimed, grasping his hand. "Now you'll go back and start all kinds of things and make a great name in the world; and we'll go on being friends, whatever happens ... we'll be great friends, won't we?"

"Evelyn!" he moaned suddenly, and took her in his arms, and kissed her. She did not resent it, although it made little impression on her.

As she sat upright again, she said, "I never see why one shouldn't go on being friends—though some people do. And friendships do make a difference, don't they? They are the kind of things that matter in one's life?"

He looked at her with a bewildered expression as if he did not really understand what she was saying. With a considerable effort he collected himself, stood up, and said, "Now I think I have told you what I feel, and I will only add that I can wait as long as ever you wish."

Left alone, Evelyn walked up and down the path. What did matter then? What was the meaning of it all?

CHAPTER XXVII

All that evening the clouds gathered, until they closed entirely over the blue of the sky. They seemed to narrow the space between earth and heaven, so that there was no room for the air to move in freely; and the waves, too, lay flat, and yet rigid, as if they were restrained. The leaves on the bushes and trees in the garden hung closely together, and the feeling of pressure and restraint was increased by the short chirping sounds which came from birds and insects.

So strange were the lights and the silence that the busy hum of voices which usually filled the dining-room at meal times had distinct gaps in it, and during these silences the clatter of the knives upon plates became audible. The first roll of thunder and the first heavy drop striking the pane caused a little stir.

"It's coming!" was said simultaneously in many different languages.

There was then a profound silence, as if the thunder had withdrawn into itself. People had just begun to eat again, when a gust of cold air came through the open windows, lifting tablecloths and skirts, a light flashed, and was instantly followed by a clap of thunder right over the hotel. The rain swished with it, and immediately there were all those sounds of windows being shut and doors slamming violently which accompany a storm.

The room grew suddenly several degrees darker, for the wind seemed to be driving waves of darkness across the earth. No one attempted to eat for a time, but sat looking out at the garden, with their forks in the air. The flashes now came frequently, lighting up faces as if they were going to be photographed, surprising them in tense and unnatural expressions. The clap followed close and violently upon them. Several women half rose from their chairs and then sat down again, but dinner was continued uneasily with eyes upon the garden. The bushes outside were ruffled and whitened, and the wind pressed upon them so that they seemed to stoop to the ground. The waiters had to press dishes upon the diners' notice; and the diners had to draw the attention of waiters, for they were all absorbed in looking at the storm. As the thunder showed no signs of withdrawing, but seemed massed right overhead, while the lightning aimed straight at the garden every time, an uneasy gloom replaced the first excitement.

Finishing the meal very quickly, people congregated in the hall, where they felt more secure than in any other place because they could retreat far from the windows, and although they heard the thunder, they could not see anything. A little boy was carried away sobbing in the arms of his mother.

While the storm continued, no one seemed inclined to sit down, but they collected in little groups under the central skylight, where they stood in a yellow atmosphere, looking upwards. Now and again their faces became white, as the lightning flashed, and finally a terrific crash came, making the panes of the skylight lift at the joints.

"Ah!" several voices exclaimed at the same moment.

"Something struck," said a man's voice.

The rain rushed down. The rain seemed now to extinguish the lightning and the thunder, and the hall became almost dark.

After a minute or two, when nothing was heard but the rattle of water upon the glass, there was a perceptible slackening of the sound, and then the atmosphere became lighter.

"It's over," said another voice.

At a touch, all the electric lights were turned on, and revealed a crowd of people all standing, all looking with rather strained faces up at the skylight, but when they saw each other in the artificial light they turned at once and began to move away. For some minutes the rain continued to rattle upon the skylight, and the thunder gave another shake or two; but it was evident from the clearing of the darkness and the light drumming of the rain upon the roof, that the great confused ocean of air was travelling away from them, and passing high over head with its clouds and its rods of fire, out to sea. The building, which had seemed so small in the tumult of the storm, now became as square and spacious as usual.

As the storm drew away, the people in the hall of the hotel sat down; and with a comfortable sense of relief, began to tell each other stories about great storms, and produced in many cases their occupations for the evening. The chessboard was brought out, and Mr. Elliot, who wore a stock instead of a collar as a sign of convalescence, but was otherwise much as usual, challenged Mr. Pepper to a final contest. Round them gathered a group of ladies with pieces of needlework, or in default of needlework, with novels, to superintend the game, much as if they were in charge of two small boys playing marbles. Every now and then they looked at the board and made some encouraging remark to the gentlemen.

Mrs. Paley just round the corner had her cards arranged in long ladders before her, with Susan sitting near to sympathise but not to correct, and the merchants and the miscellaneous people who had never been discovered to possess names were stretched in their arm-chairs with their newspapers on their knees. The conversation in these circumstances was very gentle, fragmentary, and intermittent, but the room was full of the indescribable stir of life. Every now and then the moth, which was now grey of wing and shiny of thorax, whizzed over their heads, and hit the lamps with a thud.

A young woman put down her needlework and exclaimed, "Poor creature! it would be kinder to kill it." But nobody seemed disposed to rouse himself in order to kill the moth. They watched it dash from lamp to lamp, because they were comfortable, and had nothing to do.

On the sofa, beside the chess-players, Mrs. Elliot was imparting a new stitch in knitting to Mrs. Thornbury, so that their heads came very near together, and were only to be distinguished by the old lace cap which Mrs. Thornbury wore in the evening. Mrs. Elliot was an expert at knitting, and disclaimed a compliment to that effect with evident pride.

"I suppose we're all proud of something," she said, "and I'm proud of my knitting. I think things like that run in families. We all knit well. I had an uncle who knitted his own socks to the day of his death—and he did it better than any of his daughters, dear old gentleman. Now I wonder that you, Miss Allan, who use your eyes so much, don't take up knitting in the evenings. You'd find it such a relief, I should say—such a rest to the eyes—and the bazaars are so glad of things." Her voice dropped into the smooth half-conscious tone of the expert knitter; the words came gently one after another. "As much as I do I can always dispose of, which is a comfort, for then I feel that I am not wasting my time——"

Miss Allan, being thus addressed, shut her novel and observed the others placidly for a time. At last she said, "It is surely not natural to leave your wife because she happens to be in love with you. But that—as far as I can make out—is what the gentleman in my story does."

"Tut, tut, that doesn't sound good—no, that doesn't sound at all natural," murmured the knitters in their absorbed voices.

"Still, it's the kind of book people call very clever," Miss Allan added.

"*Maternity*—by Michael Jessop[1]—I presume," Mr. Elliot put in, for he could never resist the temptation of talking while he played chess.

"D'you know," said Mrs. Elliot, after a moment, "I don't think people *do* write good novels now—not as good as they used to, anyhow."

No one took the trouble to agree with her or to disagree with her. Arthur Venning, who was strolling about, sometimes looking at the game, sometimes reading a page of a magazine, looked at Miss

Allan, who was half asleep, and said, humorously, "A penny for your thoughts, Miss Allan."

The others looked up. They were glad that he had not spoken to them. But Miss Allan replied without any hesitation, "I was thinking of my imaginary uncle. Hasn't every one got an imaginary uncle?" she continued. "I have one—a most delightful old gentleman. He's always giving me things. Sometimes it's a gold watch; sometimes it's a carriage and pair; sometimes it's a beautiful little cottage in the New Forest; sometimes it's a ticket to the place I most want to see."

She set them all thinking vaguely of the things they wanted. Mrs. Elliot knew exactly what she wanted; she wanted a child; and the usual little pucker deepened on her brow.

"We're such lucky people," she said, looking at her husband. "We really have no wants." She was apt to say this, partly in order to convince herself, and partly in order to convince other people. But she was prevented from wondering how far she carried conviction by the entrance of Mr. and Mrs. Flushing, who came through the hall and stopped by the chess-board. Mrs. Flushing looked wilder than ever. A great strand of black hair looped down across her brow, her cheeks were whipped a dark blood red, and drops of rain made wet marks upon them.

Mr. Flushing explained that they had been on the roof watching the storm.

"It was a wonderful sight," he said. "The lightning went right out over the sea, and lit up the waves and the ships far away. You can't think how wonderful the mountains looked too, with the lights on them, and the great masses of shadow. It's all over now."

He slid down into a chair, becoming interested in the final struggle of the game.

"And you go back to-morrow?" said Mrs. Thornbury, looking at Mrs. Flushing.

"Yes," she replied.

"And indeed one is not sorry to go back," said Mrs. Elliot, assuming an air of mournful anxiety, "after all this illness."

"Are you afraid of dyin'?" Mrs. Flushing demanded scornfully.

"I think we are all afraid of that," said Mrs. Elliot with dignity.

"I suppose we're all cowards when it comes to the point," said Mrs. Flushing, rubbing her cheek against the back of the chair. "I'm sure I am."

"Not a bit of it!" said Mr. Flushing, turning round, for Mr. Pepper took a very long time to consider his move. "It's not cowardly to wish to live, Alice. It's the very reverse of cowardly. Personally, I'd like to go on for a hundred years—granted, of course, that I had the full use of my faculties. Think of all the things that are bound to happen!"

"That is what I feel," Mrs. Thornbury rejoined. "The changes, the improvements, the inventions—and beauty. D'you know, I feel sometimes that I couldn't bear to die and cease to see beautiful things about me?"

"It would certainly be very dull to die before they have discovered whether there is life in Mars," Miss Allan added.

"Do you really believe there's life in Mars?" asked Mrs. Flushing, turning to her for the first time with keen interest. "Who tells you that? Some one who knows? D'you know a man called——?"

Here Mrs. Thornbury laid down her knitting, and a look of extreme solicitude came into her eyes.

"There is Mr. Hirst," she said quietly.

St. John had just come through the swing door. He was rather blown about by the wind, and his cheeks looked terribly pale, unshorn, and cavernous. After taking off his coat he was going to pass straight through the hall and up to his room, but he could not ignore the presence of so many people he knew, especially as Mrs. Thornbury rose and went up to him, holding out her hand. But the shock of the warm lamplit room, together with the sight of so many cheerful human beings sitting together at their ease, after the dark walk in the rain, and the long days of strain and horror, overcame him completely. He looked at Mrs. Thornbury and could not speak.

Every one was silent. Mr. Pepper's hand stayed upon his Knight. Mrs. Thornbury somehow moved him to a chair, sat herself beside him, and with tears in her own eyes said gently, "You have done everything for your friend."

Her action set them all talking again as if they had never stopped, and Mr. Pepper finished the move with his Knight.

"There was nothing to be done," said St. John. He spoke very slowly. "It seems impossible——"

He drew his hand across his eyes as if some dream came between him and the others and prevented him from seeing where he was.

"And that poor fellow," said Mrs. Thornbury, the tears falling again down her cheeks.

"Impossible," St. John repeated.

"Did he have the consolation of knowing——?" Mrs. Thornbury began very tentatively.

But St. John made no reply. He lay back in his chair, half-seeing the others, half-hearing what they said. He was terribly tired, and the light and warmth, the movements of the hands, and the soft communicative voices soothed him; they gave him a strange sense of quiet and relief. As he sat there, motionless, this feeling of relief became a feeling of profound happiness. Without any sense of disloyalty to Terence and Rachel he ceased to think about either of them. The movements and the voices seemed to draw together from different parts of the room, and to combine themselves into a pattern before his eyes; he was content to sit silently watching the pattern build itself up, looking at what he hardly saw.

The game was really a good one, and Mr. Pepper and Mr. Elliot were becoming more and more set upon the struggle. Mrs. Thornbury, seeing that St. John did not wish to talk, resumed her knitting.

"Lightning again!" Mrs. Flushing suddenly exclaimed. A yellow light flashed across the blue window, and for a second they saw the green trees outside. She strode to the door, pushed it open, and stood half out in the open air.

But the light was only the reflection of the storm which was over. The rain had ceased, the heavy clouds were blown away, and the air was thin and clear, although vapourish mists were being driven swiftly across the moon. The sky was once more a deep and solemn blue, and the shape of the earth was visible at the bottom of the air, enormous, dark, and solid, rising into the tapering mass of the mountain, and pricked here and there on the slopes by the tiny lights of villas. The driving air, the drone of the trees, and the flashing light which now and again spread a broad illumination over the earth filled Mrs. Flushing with exultation. Her breasts rose and fell.

"Splendid! Splendid!" she muttered to herself. Then she turned back into the hall and exclaimed in a peremptory voice, "Come outside and see, Wilfrid; it's wonderful."

Some half-stirred; some rose; some dropped their balls of wool and began to stoop to look for them.

"To bed—to bed," said Miss Allan.

"It was the move with your Queen that gave it away, Pepper," exclaimed Mr. Elliot triumphantly, sweeping the pieces together and standing up. He had won the game.

"What? Pepper beaten at last? I congratulate you!" said Arthur Venning, who was wheeling old Mrs. Paley to bed.

All these voices sounded gratefully in St. John's ears as he lay half-asleep, and yet vividly conscious of everything around him. Across his eyes passed a procession of objects, black and indistinct, the figures of people picking up their books, their cards, their balls of wool, their workbaskets, and passing him one after another on their way to bed.

NOTES

CHAPTER I

1. *Bluebeard:* dark-bearded figure from popular mythology who murdered his wives and kept them in a locked chamber in his castle.
2. *Lars Porsena ... suffer wrong no more:* from *Lays of Ancient Rome* (1842) by Thomas Babbington Macaulay (1800–59), English essayist and historian.
3. *Nelson:* probably Viscount Horatio Nelson (1758–1805), captain in the English Royal Navy who suffered many injuries throughout his years in battle, including the blinding of his right eye and the amputation of his right arm.
4. *Rotherhithe:* area in Surrey that was once a garden but by Woolf's time was converted to commercial docks.
5. Euphrosyne: Greek goddess of grace and beauty.
6. *Peterhouse:* college in Cambridge, England.
7. *Bruce collection ... Pump in Neville's Row:* fictitious references.
8. *"The Coliseum" ... Queen Alexandra:* the first print is a depiction of the Colosseum in Rome and the second of the wife of Edward VII.

CHAPTER II

1. *Pindar:* (c. 522–438 B.C.) chief lyric poet of Greece; although he wrote numerous odes, only *Epinicia* (*Odes of Victory*), in four books, have survived entire.

2. *Petronius . . . Catullus . . . Etruscan vases:* Arbiter Petronius (d. A.D. 66), Roman author of *The Satyricon,* a satirical romance about the licentious life of the upper class in Italy. Gaius Valerius Catullus (c. 84–54 B.C.), Roman lyric poet. The Etruscans were the Romans' principal early rivals and were at the height of their civilization in 500 B.C.

3. *Coryphaeus:* fictitious author.

4. Tristan: from *Tristan and Isolde,* an opera by Richard Wagner (1813–83), German writer; the following lines are Isolde's.

5. Cowper's Letters: English poet William Cowper (1731–1800).

CHAPTER III

1. *Fielding's grave:* Henry Fielding (1707–54), English novelist and political journalist best known for his novel *Tom Jones;* he died in Lisbon, Portugal.

2. *Whistler:* James Abbott McNeill Whistler (1834–1903), American artist; some of his paintings, etchings, and lithographs depict the London riverside and other waterside scenery.

3. *Shelley . . . 'Adonais':* Percy Bysshe Shelley (1792–1822), English Romantic poet; his elegy on the death of John Keats, "Adonais," was published in 1821.

4. *Matthew Arnold, 'What a set! What a set!':* Victorian poet and prose writer, Matthew Arnold (1822–88); the quote comes from the essay "Shelley" in his *Essays in Criticism* (1865) and refers to Shelley's personal life and friends.

5. Antigone: Sophocles (c. 496–406 B.C.), Greek playwright, author of the tragedy of Antigone. Lines 332–37, translated by Gilbert Murray:

> Wonders are many, but none there be
> So strange, so fell, as the child of man.
> He rangeth over the whitening sea,
> Through wintery winds he pursues his plan:
> About his going the deeps unfold,
> The crests o'er hang, but he passeth clear.

6. *twenty Clytemnestras:* in Greek mythology, Clytemnestra was the unfaithful and treacherous wife of Agamemnon. She does not appear in Sophocles's play *Antigone.*

7. *a Reynolds or a Romney:* two English portrait painters, Sir Joshua Reynolds (1723–92) and George Romney (1734–1802).

8. *Bayreuth:* German town that is the site of the Wagner festival.
9. Parsifal: Wagner's last opera, first staged in 1882.
10. *Watts and Joachim:* George Frederic Watts (1817–1904), English painter, and Joseph Joachim (1831–1907), Hungarian violinist.
11. *Pitt:* William Pitt or Pitt the Younger (1759–1806), British statesman and prime minister (1783–1801, 1804–1906).
12. *the little white volume of Pascal:* Blaise Pascal (1623–62), French mathematician, physicist, theologian, and man-of-letters whose work on Christianity, *Pensées,* was published in 1670.

CHAPTER IV
1. *Full fathom five thy father lies: The Tempest,* I, ii.
2. *Huxley, Herbert Spencer, and Henry George . . . Emerson and Thomas Hardy:* T. H. Huxley (1825–95), English biologist and foremost expounder of Darwinism; Herbert Spencer (1820–1903), English evolutionary philosopher and leading advocate of "Social Darwinism" whose main work is the nine-volume *System of Synthetic Philosophy* (1862–93); Henry George (1839–97), American social reformer and economist who wrote *Progress and Poverty* (1879); Ralph Waldo Emerson (1803–82), American poet and essayist, a transcendentalist in philosophy, a rationalist in religion, and an advocate of spiritual individualism; Thomas Hardy (1840–1928), English novelist and poet whose famous novels were generally tragic and pessimistic.
3. *Samuel Johnson:* (1709–84), lexicographer, critic and poet, known for his *Dictionary of the English Language* and *The Lives of the Most Eminent English Poets*. Dalloway misquotes from a poem attributed to Johnson: "Here lies poor duck/That Samuel Johnson trod on."
4. Wuthering Heights: Emily Brontë (1818–48), English novelist and poet; her only novel, *Wuthering Heights,* was published in 1847. Her sister, Charlotte Brontë (1816–55), is best know for her novel *Jane Eyre* (1847).
5. *Shelley . . . world's slow stain:* lines from Shelley's "Adonais."

CHAPTER V
1. *'Good, then' . . . Professor Henry Sidgwick:* the quote is from *Principia Ethica* (1903) by Cambridge philosopher G. E. Moore (1873–1958); Henry Sidgwick (1838–1900), English utilitarian philosopher and professor at Cambridge whose best-known work is *Methods of Ethics* (1874).

2. *Burke . . .* American Rebellion: Edmund Burke (1729–97), British statesman and political philosopher; Dalloway probably refers to his published speech "On Conciliation with America" (1775) and his letter "Reflections on the Revolution in France" (1790).

3. *Bright and Disraeli:* John Bright (1811–89), radical British statesman and orator whose name was closely associated with the Reform Act of 1867 and free-trade laws; Benjamin Disraeli (1804–81), British statesman and twice prime minister (1868, 1874–80) who was also a novelist.

CHAPTER VIII

1. *Asquith . . . Austen Chamberlain:* H. H. Asquith, 1st Earl of Oxford and Asquith (1852–1928), was prime minister, 1908–16. Austen Chamberlain (1863–1937) was chancellor of the exchequer, 1903–1905.

CHAPTER IX

1. *Wordsworth . . . "Prelude":* William Wordsworth (1770–1850), English Romantic poet whose long autobiographical poem, "The Prelude," was published posthumously in 1850.

2. *Beowulf to Swinburne: Beowulf,* a late-tenth-century Old English epic poem; Algernon Charles Swinburne (1837–1909), English poet and critic associated with the Pre-Raphaelite movement.

3. Modern Love . . . John Donne: *Modern Love, and Poems of the English Roadside, with Poems and Ballads* (1862) is a series of fifty connected poems by George Meredith (1828–1909), English novelist and poet. John Donne (1572–1631), English poet known best for his Metaphysical love poetry.

4. *I speak as one . . . the Curtain:* last stanza of Thomas Hardy's poem "He Abjures Love" (see note 2, Chapter IV).

5. *Coptic:* language related to ancient Egyptian.

CHAPTER X

1. Henrik Ibsen: (1828–1906) Norwegian playwright and poet whose plays include *A Doll's House* (1879) and *Hedda Gabler* (1890).

2. *Diana of the Crossways:* the beautiful heroine, whose marriage is failing, in George Meredith's 1885 novel *Diana of the Crossways.*

3. *Nora:* heroine of Ibsen's *A Doll's House.*

4. *Defoe, Maupassant:* Daniel Defoe (1660–1731), English political journalist and novelist; his novels include *Robinson Crusoe* (1719) and *Moll*

Flanders (1722). Guy de Maupassant (1850–93), French novelist and short-story writer.

5. *Garibaldi:* Giuseppe Garibaldi (1807–82), Italian patriot who joined numerous revolutionary wars waged against the Italian government. In 1834 he escaped a death sentence by fleeing to South America.

CHAPTER XII

1. *Protectionist:* leading issue of the election of 1906—whether to support free trade or the protection of British industries against foreign competition.

2. *Alexander Pope:* (1688–1744) English poet whose writings were formed on classical models and are often satirical or political.

CHAPTER XIII

1. *"Plato" . . . "Jorrocks" . . . "Marlowe":* Plato (c. 427–348 B.C.), the Greek philosopher; John Jorrocks, the Cockney city grocer, a celebrated character in the humorous sporting novels of R. S. Surtees (1803–64) who first appears in *Jorrocks's Jaunts and Jollities* (1838). Sophocles (see note 5, Chapter III). Jonathan Swift (1667–1745), English satirist whose works include *Gulliver's Travels* (1726). Honoré de Balzac (1799–1850), French novelist who wrote a series of novels depicting French society, *La Comédie humaine.* Wordsworth (see note 1, Chapter IX). Samuel Taylor Coleridge (1772–1834), English Romantic poet and critic whose works include "The Rime of the Ancient Mariner" and "Christabel." Pope (see note 2, Chapter XII). Johnson (see note 3, Chapter IV). Joseph Addison (1672–1719), English essayist and politician. Shelley (see note 3, Chapter III). John Keats (1795–1821), English Romantic poet whose works include "Lamia" and "The Eve of St. Agnes." Christopher Marlowe (1564–93), English playwright who was the most important predecessor of Shakespeare.

2. La Cousine Bette: novel by Balzac, published in 1847, part of *La Comédie humaine.*

3. *Wedekind . . . Donne . . . Webster:* Frank Wedekind (1864–1918), German playwright best known for his unconventional tragedies. Donne (see note 3, Chapter IX). John Webster (c. 1580–1625), English playwright who is best known for his two tragedies, *The White Devil* (1612) and *The Duchess of Malfi* (1623).

CHAPTER XVI

1. *John Stuart Mill:* (1806–73) English empiricist philosopher and social reformer who was among the first to fight for women's suffrage; author of *Utilitarianism* (1863) and *The Subjection of Women* (1869).

CHAPTER XIX

1. Euphues: John Lyly (c. 1554–1606), English writer; *Euphues* is his two-part prose romance (1578, 1580).
2. *Lord Curzon:* George Nathaniel Curzon (1859–1925), English statesman who served as viceroy of India between 1898–1905; in 1907 he was named chancellor of Oxford.

CHAPTER XX

1. *Whoever you are ... all will be useless:* from *Leaves of Grass* (1855), the poem by the American writer Walt Whitman (1819–92).

CHAPTER XXV

1. *Milton:* John Milton (1608–74), English poet whose work includes *Paradise Lost* (1667) and "Lycidas" (1638). The following lines come from *Comus* (1637).
2. *They wrestled up ... dropped awhile to rest:* from "A New Forest Ballad" by Charles Kingsley (1819–75), English novelist and poet.
3. *Peor and Baalim ... mooned Astaroth:* from "On the Morning of Christ's Nativity" (1629), by Milton.

CHAPTER XXVII

1. Maternity—*by Michael Jessop:* a fictitious novel.

COMMENTARY

E. M. FORSTER

VIRGINIA WOOLF

KATHERINE ANNE PORTER

W. H. AUDEN

E. M. FORSTER

[Perhaps] the first comment to make on [Virginia Woolf's] *The Voyage Out* is that it is absolutely unafraid, and that its courage springs, not from naiveté, but from education. . . . Here at last is a book which attains unity as surely as *Wuthering Heights,* though by a different path, a book which, while written by a woman and presumably from a woman's point of view, soars straight out of local questionings into the intellectual day.

Mrs Woolf's success is more remarkable since there is one serious defect in her equipment: her chief characters are not vivid. There is nothing false in them, but when she ceases to touch them they cease, they do not stroll out of their sentences, and even develop a tendency to merge shadowlike.

[If] Mrs Woolf does not 'do' her four main characters very vividly, and is apt to let them all become clever together, and differ only by their opinions, then on what does her success depend? Some readers—those who demand the milk of human kindness, even in its tinned form—will say that she has not succeeded; but the bigness of her achievement should impress anyone weaned from baby food. She believes in adventure—here is the main point—believes in it passionately, and knows that it can only be undertaken alone. Human relations are no substitute for adventure, because when real they are uncomfortable, and when comfortable they must be unreal. It is for a voyage into solitude that man was created, and Rachel, Helen, Hewet, Hirst, all learn this lesson, which is exquisitely reinforced by the setting of tropical scenery—the soul, like the body, voyages at her own risk. . . . Mrs Woolf's vision may be inferior to Dostoieffsky's—but she sees as clearly as he where efficiency ends and creation begins, and even more clearly that our supreme choice lies not between body and soul, but between immobility and motion. In her pages, body v. soul—that dreary medieval tug-of-war—does not find any place. It is as if the rope has broken, leaving pagans sprawling on one side and clergymen on the other. . . .

The writer can sweep together masses of characters for our amusement, then sweep them away; her comedy does not counteract her tragedy and at the close enhances it, for we see that the Hotel and the Villa will soon be dancing and gossiping just as before, that existence will continue the same, exactly the same, for everyone, for everyone except the reader; he, more fortunate than the actors, is established in the possession of beauty.

From *Daily News and Leader,* April 8, 1915

VIRGINIA WOOLF

Admitting the vagueness which afflicts all criticism of novels, let us hazard the opinion that for us at this moment the form of fiction most in vogue more often misses than secures the thing we seek. Whether we call it life or spirit, truth or reality, this, the essential thing, has moved off, or on, and refuses to be contained any longer in such ill-fitting vestments as we provide. Nevertheless, we go on perseveringly, conscientiously, constructing our two and thirty chapters after a design which more and more ceases to resemble the vision in our minds. So much of the enormous labour of proving the solidity, the likeness to life, of the story is not merely labour thrown away but labour misplaced to the extent of obscuring and blotting out the light of the conception. The writer seems constrained, not by his own free will but by some powerful and unscrupulous tyrant who has him in thrall to provide a plot, to provide comedy, tragedy, love, interest, and an air of probability embalming the whole so impeccable that if all his figures were to come to life they would find themselves dressed down to the last button of their coats in the fashion of the hour. The tyrant is obeyed; the novel is done to a turn. But sometimes, more and more often as time goes by, we suspect a momentary doubt, a spasm of rebellion, as the pages fill themselves in the customary way. Is life like this? Must novels be like this?

Look within and life, it seems, is very far from being "like this." Examine for a moment an ordinary mind on an ordinary day. The mind receives a myriad impressions—trivial, fantastic, evanescent, or engraved with the sharpness of steel. From all sides they come, an incessant shower of innumerable atoms; and as they fall, as they shape themselves into the life of Monday or Tuesday, the accent falls differently from of old; the moment of importance came not here but there; so that if a writer were a free man and not a slave, if he could write what he chose, not what he must, if he could base his work upon his own feeling and not upon convention, there would be no plot, no comedy, no tragedy, no love interest or catastrophe in the accepted style, and perhaps not a single button sewn on as the Bond Street tailors would have it. Life is not a series of gig lamps symmetrically arranged; but a luminous halo, a semi-transparent envelope surrounding us from the beginning of consciousness to the end. Is it not the task of the novelist to convey this varying, this unknown and uncircumscribed spirit, whatever aberration or complexity it may display, with as little mixture of the alien and external as possible? We are not pleading merely for courage and sincerity; we are suggesting that the proper stuff of fiction is a little other than custom would have us believe it.

· · · ·

The problem before the novelist at present, as we suppose it to have been in the past, is to contrive means of being free to set down what he chooses. He has to have the courage to say that what interests him is no longer "this" but "that": out of "that" alone must he construct his work. For the moderns "that," the point of interest, lies very likely in the dark places of psychology. At once, therefore, the accent falls a little differently; the emphasis is upon something hitherto ignored; at once a different outline of form becomes necessary, difficult for us to grasp, incomprehensible to our predecessors.

· · · ·

"The proper stuff of fiction" does not exist; everything is the proper stuff of fiction, every feeling, every thought; every quality of brain and spirit is drawn upon; no perception comes amiss. And if we can imagine the art of fiction come alive and standing in our midst, she would undoubtedly bid us break her and bully her, as well as honour and love her, for so her youth is renewed and her sovereignty assured.

From "Modern Fiction," in *The Common Reader,* 1925

KATHERINE ANNE PORTER

Almost everything has been said, over and over, about Virginia Woolf's dazzling style, her brilliant humor, her extraordinary sensibility. She has been called neurotic, and hypersensitive. Her style has been compared to cobwebs with dew drops, rainbows, landscapes seen by moonlight, and other unsubstantial but showy stuff. She has been called a Phoenix, Muse, Sybil, a Prophetess, in praise, or a Feminist, in disprise. Her beauty and remarkable personality, her short way with fools and that glance of hers, which chilled many a young literary man with its expression of seeing casually through a millstone—all of this got in the way. It disturbed the judgment and drew the attention from the true point of interest.

· · ·

Virginia Woolf was a great artist, one of the glories of our time, and she never published a line that was not worth reading.

· · ·

The world of the arts was her native territory; she ranged freely under her own sky, speaking her mother tongue fearlessly.

From "Virginia Woolf," in *The Collected Essays and
Occasional Writings of Katherine Anne Porter,* 1970

W. H. AUDEN

I do not know how Virginia Woolf is thought of by the younger literary generation; I do know that by my own, even in the palmiest days of social consciousness, she was admired and loved much more than she realized. I do not know if she is going to exert an influence on the future development of the novel—I rather suspect that her style and her vision were so unique that influence would only result in tame imitation—but I cannot imagine a time, however bleak, or a writer, whatever his school, when and for whom her devotion to her art, her industry, her severity with herself— above all, her passionate love, not only or chiefly for the big moments of life but also for its daily humdrum "sausage-and-haddock" details—will not remain an example that is at once an inspiration and a judge.

From "A Consciousness of Reality," in *Forewords and Afterwords,* 1973

READING GROUP GUIDE

1. Do you consider Rachel Vinrace a sympathetic character? Why or why not? Discuss Michael Cunningham's reading of her as "an engine of perception."

2. Critics have compared *The Voyage Out* to Jane Austen's novels, since both involve marriage plots. In what ways are they similar? Different?

3. Both Susan Warrington and Rachel receive marriage proposals in Santa Marina. Compare the attitudes each has toward marriage. How is each woman's social predicament different?

4. In his Introduction, Michael Cunningham writes that it was Woolf's conviction that "what's important in a life, what remains at its end, is less likely to be its supposed climaxes than its unexpected moments of awareness, often arising out of unremarkable experience, so deeply personal they can rarely be explained." Consider this notion in light of Rachel's character. What moments of awareness does Rachel experience? Compare her moments of awareness with those of another character, for instance, Helen Ambrose. What similarities or differences can you draw from the comparison?

5. Discuss the significance of the novel's title. To which "voyage" do you think it refers?

6. In Chapter XVIII, Terence considers the sacrifices women must make in marriage. He then resolves that Rachel, if she will marry him, will be "free, like the wind or the sea." In what ways does his later behavior indicate this may not be the case?

7. Why, ultimately, do you think Rachel dies? What effect does her death have on the novel's structure?

8. In her essay "Modern Fiction," which she published a decade after the publication of *The Voyage Out*, Woolf writes, "Life is not a series of gig lamps symmetrically arranged; but a luminous halo, a semi-transparent envelope surrounding us from the beginning of consciousness to the end." To what extent do you think *The Voyage Out* adheres to this vision?

A Note on the Type

The principal text of this Modern Library edition was set in a digitized
version of Janson, a typeface that dates from about 1690 and was cut by
Nicholas Kis, a Hungarian working in Amsterdam. The original matrices
have survived and are held by the Stempel foundry in Germany.
Hermann Zapf redesigned some of the weights and sizes for
Stempel, basing his revisions on the original design.